THE PROPHECIES

SIMONE CONWARD

CONTENTS

THE BOOK OF JONAH

Jonah—The son of a black man named Amittai

Time period—862 B.C.

In the large urban city of Nineva, lives a mixture of people of culture and race, who says they are believers, but they do not always obey the LAW of GOD. So, because Jonah lives in the suburbs near Nineva, GOD tells him that HE would use him to tell them that they would be punished, if they do not repent, and stop their sinning.

Jonah 1

So, after waiting even longer for them to change, they still would not change. Now GOD has had enough with their ways, and HE tell Jonah, it is time for him to tell them that they are sinning too much, and HE is disappointed in them, and wants them to repent. Yet, instead of Jonah going to warn the people like GOD commanded him to do, he goes to Joppa to flee from the task, because he had been waiting for the day for them to get punished for their sins, and while he is in Joppa, he books a ticket on a ship to Tarshish, and goes to the bottom of the ship to hide from GOD. Then GOD sends a wind to stir up the sea to let him know he could not hide from HIM. Immediately, a storm begins to break the ship apart. In fear, each mariner cries out to their own gods, but receives no response, and in a panic, they throw the cargo from the ship into the sea. While that was happening, Jonah is at the bottom of the ship sleeping.

Since none of the gods responded to the mariners, the captain wonders if someone else is on the ship. Then the captain searches the ship, and finds Jonah in the bottom sleeping, and because Jonah is the only one that did not call on his GOD yet, the captains yell out to him, "Get up!". Meanwhile, as the captain is talking, the crew is casting lot to see who is causing the disaster to come upon them, and when the lot fall on Jonah, they go to him, and ask him why his GOD is punishing him, what is his work, where did he come from, and what tribe is he from. He answered, "I am a Hebrew who fear the GOD WHO created the heavens and earth." They ask, "Why did you come on our ship to run from your GOD?" And as they are trying to figure out what to do to him next, he said, "Throw me off the ship into the sea." But since they really do not want to kill him, they row even harder to reach safety. But the storm keeps getting worse, and worse. Then when it seems there is no more hope, except to do what Jonah said, they beg his GOD not to find them guilty when they throw him overboard, and they pick him up, and throw him off the ship into the raging sea. Since they feel guilty about it, they offer a sacrifice to his GOD to show that they are sorry, and YAH, his GOD, prepares a big fish to swallow him up, and the fish swallows him.

For three days, and three nights he is in the belly of the fish praying to his GOD for mercy.

The prayer:

(Paraphrased) I am being tormented, and that is why I am crying out to YOU, my GOD. I am in hell, but I know that YOU can hear me, because it was YOU that threw me into the middle of the sea and then stirred up the winds. Now I feel like I am dead without YOU, but I know if I survive this, I will want YOU to like me again, and I feel like I am being strangled by the darkness, and I am in hell. But now I realize what YOU want. So, YOU are my LORD and my GOD, because when I was in a bunch of trouble, I remembered that there is a GOD, and I went into the holy temple to pray to YOU, because I know that those who

worship idols would not get any mercy. Now I will live a good life, and I will go and warn the people of Nineveh about what hell is like, because salvation is from YOU.

After the three days, GOD speaks to the fish, and it vomits him out onto dry land.

Symbolisms:
Sea—is the world
Winds—is trouble
Nineveh— is a city of gentile and Israelite believers who are living like unbelievers
Darkness—is hell

Jonah 3

Again, GOD tells him to go and tell the people of Nineveh what HE said. This time, he is so eager to warn the people, the journey which would have taken him three days to get through the city, only takes him one, and as he walks through the city, he says, "Yet forty days, and Nineveh would be overthrown."

Once the people hear the report, they believe, and immediately put on sack clothes, and gather to fast and pray. Then when the word gets to the king, he jumps up from his seat, tears off his royal robe, put on sack clothes, and sits in ashes to fast and pray along with the others. Afterwards, he makes a decree to all the nations that all the people and animals should put on sack clothes and go outside to pray. Which everyone in the nations he rules over agrees to do, since they know that it is time for them to repent. So, without hesitation, they put on sack clothes, and pray to GOD for forgiveness, and they stopped sinning, in hope that GOD would change HIS mind about destroying them, and when GOD sees that they changed from sinning, HE relents from the disaster HE said HE would do to them.

Now Jonah is very angry, because he wanted them to be destroyed in forty days like he proclaimed, and he grumbles to GOD, saying, "LORD, I knew that YOU would save them! And that was why I ran away to Tarshish in the first place, because I knew YOU would warn them, and YOU would be nice enough to give them time to change, and then YOU would show them great love by changing YOUR mind. So, take my life, because I'm better off dead than alive!" GOD responds, "What right do you have to be angry with ME for showing mercy?", and he storms from the presence of GOD, and goes to the eastside of the city, where he makes a shelter to stay in while he sulks in his anger.

Yet with compassion for him, GOD makes a plant grow overnight to give him shade from the heat to make him a little more comfortable as he sulks. And he is glad to have the plant. But to teach him a lesson, early the next morning, GOD cause a worm to damage the plant, which caused it to wither. Then when the sun rises, GOD cause a dry wind to come from the East, which dehydrates him, and he faints, and while he is laying there in the hot sun, unable to move, he is wishing he is dead. And GOD asks him, "Is it right for him to be angry about what happened to the plant?" He said, "Yes! It is right for me to be angry. Just look at me." Then GOD said, 'Why do you have pity for the plant that you did not labor for, which is just a plant that grew overnight, and yet you do not want Met to have pity on Nineveh, which is a city with more than 120 thousand people, plus live stocks?"

With that question, he should realize that GOD does not want to kill anyone, and all GOD wants is for people to repent, and stop sinning, so that when they die they would not go to hell.

JOEL'S PROPHESY
Time period—800 B.C.

Though GOD is using the Negro people of Israel as an example to teach the world, every race, and nation, including Israel, loves to sin, and because Israel failed to be an example, GOD took HIS blessings, and protection from them. Then HE caused every nation, especially the white nations to overcome them, and instead of directly speaking to them, HE speaks to them through prophets for them to understand that they would be in captivity in white nations, since they do not obey HIM, because they love the ways of white men so much.

To start with, GOD calls Joel, the son of Pethuel to be a prophet to HIS Negro people of Israel, and GOD tells him to ask them, "If there were any time in their days, or in their forefather's days did they ever see such devastation on their people, or in their land? And HE said to tell them to tell their children about how they came to that point. So, their children could tell their children, and their children's children could tell their children for generations after generation, because what the palmerworm left, the locust ate, and what the locust left, the cankerworm ate, and what the cankerworm left, the caterpillar ate. Which is why they should wake up, and cry over their loses, and since they are ignorant Negroes, HE is ignoring them for their idols, and false ways of worship. Because their idol, and false ways of worship was the reason why HE caused numerous amounts of strong white people with teeth and jawbones as the strength of lions to come take them and strip the land, and it is also the reason why they are crying like a virgin cry over her dead fiancé.

Also, since there are no more meat offerings, or drink offering being offered to HIM by them, that is the reason why the priests are continuing to mourn with lack of understanding, and why the fields are wasted, and the land mourns, since the corn, and the wine is dried up, and the oil is languished. Therefore, they should be ashamed of the farmers, and the vinedressers, since everything is languished. Even the pomegranate, the palm, and the apple trees, and there is no more joy amongst the people, and all their priests, and ministers of the altar are crying in sack cloths, because there is no more meat, or drink offerings being offered. At this point, they should call a fast, and tell everyone to fast, and gather to The House of THE LORD, and pray, because The Day of THE LORD is close, and it would be a great destruction from HIM, THE ALMIGHTY. So, HE is wondering if they do not realize that HE is gone from HIS house (The House of THE LORD), and the whole place is broken down, and overlaid with weeds, because even the wild beasts are wondering what is happening to the place, and why they do not have any pasture to feed upon."

Since awful things already happened, Joel said, "O GOD, to YOU I cry, and only to YOU, because the white people came, and destroyed the lands of YOUR people, and it affected the belief of other nations in YOU. Even the wild animals in the field are crying out to YOU, since YOUR people were taken, and the land dried up, and withered." And GOD said, "Tell them, I said, hear ME loud and clear, because MY wrath, The Day of THE LORD is coming soon, and it is a time of darkness, and gloominess. The time when the Roman white people would come to Africa to destroy all the Negro people of Israel, and when they come, even though the place looks like The Garden of Eden, it will become desolate and look like a wilderness when they are done. Nothing, and no one would be able to escape the invasion of the white folks from The Roman Empire, because they would be in battle gears from head to foot, riding in on chariots, and on battle horses that are also protected in gears, rushing in like mighty men, climbing walls, marching without breaking ranks, and without running into each other. Men that would not be wounded if stabbed by the sword, because of their armor of mail. From city to city, they would go and put a lot of fear into the people by climbing on houses and going through windows like thieves.

Then after the white people punished them enough, I would be ready to correct the whole world. MY wrath on the world would start, and the earth would quake, and the heavens would tremble, and the sun, and the moon would be dark, and the stars would not have any light at all as I tell MY army to do those things, because I AM the only one that is great, and powerful. Which is why I wants them to turn their hearts to ME by fasting and crying, and by changing their ways, and turning to ME again, since I AM gracious, merciful, slow to anger, and very kind, that if they repent, I will turn the evil from them, and maybe even return to the earth and leave a blessing. Therefore, they need to tell everyone to stop whatever they are doing, and to fast, and go to The House of THE LORD to cry out to ME to spare them, and not to make them look like a reproach to the world by making the heathens rule over them, and say that they do not have a GOD, because I would be jealous for MY land, and I would have pity on them, and answer them, and restore them, and I would never allow such a thing to happen to them again.

The plan is, after I allow the white men to take many of them to their white lands, and also take control of the rest of them that are left in the land, I would get rid of the white men and their armies from amongst them and send them into a barren desolate place between two seas, and they would stink, and act abominable (as cavemen). Then people would see them as the wicked white people they really are, and so, I AM telling them not to be afraid, even though things look bad for them (during the rule of The Roman Empire), because I would do a great thing by getting rid of the white folks from their land. And the wild beasts should not worry either, because I would do as I said. Then the land would be replenished, and the pastures would be green, and the vines, the figs, and all the fruit trees would return. Therefore, they should be glad, and rejoice in ME, because I made them rich and glorious before, and I would make them even richer, and more glorious than they were. So, they would have in abundance, and be full of joy, because everything that the white folks took away would be returned, and everyone in the land would be full, and satisfied.

Then they would only praise ME, and they would know that I AM with them, and they would never be ashamed, and when this happened, it would be the time for ME to pour out MY spirit upon all types of people in the world that want to know ME. And during that time, those of Israel in the land, who believes, would prophesy, and dream dreams, and have visions, so they could minister to the people of the nations that wants to know of ME. And I would show wonders in heaven and on the earth by making it rain blood and fire, and I would shoot pillars of smoke from the sky, and it would happen before The Great Tribulation, which is the great and terrible day. And whoever call on ME would be delivered, because I AM making a promise, that after I make a way of deliverance for those of Israel, I would call people of other nations to deliverance.

First, I would bring all the captives of Israel from the white Babylonian lands back to Africa, their native land. Then I would be ready to punish every nation of the world for mistreating them, and I will tell everyone to get ready to fight, because they traded MY people to the white nations, and sold off pieces of their land to them, and they made them slaves, and traded their sons for whores, and their daughters for wine, even though they do not want anything to do with ME. Especially the white people of Tyre and Sidon, and the biracial people of Philistia, because they took the silver and gold from

The House of THE LORD, and took them to the temples of their gods, and they sold the most righteous Negro of the tribe of Judah to the wicked white Grecians, so they were really far from their home in Jerusalem, The Holy Land, and because of that, I AM going to take all MY Negro people from where ever they are enslaved. Then I will punish the nations, like how they punished them, and I will give their sons and daughters over to the tribe of Judah, so Judah could sell them to the wicked Sabeans. Just like how they sold the people of Judah to the Grecians. Therefore, I want MY people of Israel to tell everyone that are not from their people, that it is time for war, and they should turn whatever they have into weapons, and join together as heathen nations, because their GOD is ready to fight them, and they better listen and get together, and come to the valley of Jehoshaphat, where the temples of their false gods are, where I would judge them, and kill all of them for their wickedness. Since it is time for punishment. Because there is too much wickedness against MY Negro people, and it is time for The Wrath to begin, which is The Day of THE LORD, and it is near, and the sun, the moon, and the stars would diminish their brightness, while I make a big fuss and cause problems for every unbeliever while I protect believers, no matter their color, or nationality. At the same time strengthening MY people of Israel. Then the world would know that I punish people for sinning, because I would punish all the wicked, while I protect the righteous.

Another thing. I wants the people of Israel to know that their land would be restored, and I would be with them in the holy mountain of Zion, since Jerusalem would be holy, and no strangers would come there, because Judah would be clean again. And I also want the people of Israel to know that the brown skinned Negroes people of Egypt, and the red skinned Negroes people of Edom would be punished, and become desolate nations, because of their violence against the righteous people of the tribe Judah. And the tribe of Judah would abide forever, even though Jerusalem would abide only for some generations. And because of the injustice to the tribe of Judah, they would be forgiven for killing anyone, because they killed in self-defense, and I AM their GOD, WHO justifies them."

AMOS' PROPHESY

Time period—In the days of Uzziah, Jeroboam, and Joash (Negro kings of Israel from 786 B.C.)

GOD is sick of people sinning, and two years before HE starts the earthquake to start "The Wrath", HE tells Amos to tell the people HE would roar from Zion, and people would cry, and mountains would crumble as each nation gets their punishment. So, because the white people in Damascus, Syria, threshed Gilead, HE would send fire upon their king, Hazael's family, and his son Ben-Hadad would lose his palace, and the people of Damascus would go into captivity to Kir. As for the white people in Gaza, they would also be punished, and their walls, and palaces would be destroyed, because they carried HIS Negro people from Gaza as captives to Edom, and they used the Gaza Strip regions for their worship to their false gods, Ashkelon and Ashdod.

The colored people of the Philistines (or the Palestinians) would also be punished, because they are in the Gaza Strip region, which is "The Promised Land", and they are worshipping Ekron, a false god. Also, Tyrus would be punished, because they are against the red skinned Negroes of Edom, and they made them captives, and forgot that they are brothers of the people of Israel. Yet, the red skinned Negroes of Edom, the Edomites, would also be punished, and a fire would burn Teman, and burn down the palace of Bozrah, because they constantly fought against the people of Israel, their brothers, and had no pity on them, and were angry with them all the time.

The white people of Ammon would also be punished, because they ripped the children from the pregnant Negro women of Israel in Gilead to get more of their land, but a fire in the walls of Rabbah would devour the palaces they built there, and their white king, and his princes would be taken as captives. As for the mix cultured nation of Moab, fire shall devour the palaces in Kirioth, and the people of Moab would die in tumult, because they burned the bones of the king of Edom, the brothers of Israel. And to be fair, the dark skinned Negroes of Judah, the most righteous of the people of Israel would also be punished, and a fire would devour all the palaces in Jerusalem, because they transgressed the LAW by not keeping the commandments, and it caused them to be false worshippers like their forefathers were. And the rest of the tribes of the Negro people of Israel would also be punished, because they sold their righteous people for silver, and sold the poor people for a pair of shoes, and they tortured the poor, and turned away from those who were meek, and a man and his father would sleep with the same woman and profane HIS holy name. They also bought bedspreads that were pledged to false gods, and they drank bad wine that they knew not to drink, even though HE destroyed the Amorite white people, and took them from them (during the Babylonian captivity).

Though HE also delivered them from the bondage of the colored people of Egypt, and led them for forty years through the wilderness to possess The Promised Land, which is The Land of Caanan that belonged to the white Amorites, and though their sons were raised up to be prophets, and the young men were raised to be Nazarites men, who does not drink wine, or cut their hair, they gave the Nazarites wine to drink, and told the prophets to shut up. That is why HE, their GOD, would crush them, and none of them would be able to save themselves, that even the mightiest of them would run away in shame, and so, HE is wondering, if they heard what HE said HE would do to them, HIS own family, the people of Israel, for their sinning.

Can two people walk together without both wanting to?

Would a lion roar in the forest if he had no prey?

Would a young lion cry out in his den, if he had taken nothing?

Can a bird get snared where there was no trap?

Could someone get snared if they did not steal anything?

Can the trumpet be sounded for war in a city without the people getting afraid?

Can there be evil in a city, and GOD is not involved?

The answers are "No".

Yet everyone is saying that GOD would not do anything, but HE reveals HIS plans only to those who serves HIM, and when HE starts HIS punishment, everyone will be afraid.

So, that's it.

GOD has spoken, and HE is the prophet of all prophets, and HE wants HIS righteous people to tell the false worshippers in Ashdod, and in Egypt to gather themselves to fight against HIM in Samaria, because of all the oppression that is in the land, and because they did not do right while they ruled over HIS people. As the shepherd take pieces of the sheep from the lion's mouth, a leg here, or a piece of ear there, that is how the people of Israel would be taken out that are forced to live in Samaria where many sleep in one bed, or in Damascus where they only get to sleep on the couch.

GOD is Angry, and HE wants every ungodly nation to know that the white people who invaded the lands of the people of Israel would be punished, and the altars they built in Bethel would be torn down, and the horns cut off, and it would crumble. Even all the great buildings that Solomon and the others great Negro men of Israel built over the years would be torn down. So, the white people in Bashan, who lives in the mountains of Samaria, better listen, since they are full, and merry, even though they are oppressing the poor, and are crushing the needy, and for that, they would be taken away from the land with hooks, and their prosperity would be gone. But GOD knows that even after the white people are gone from amongst HIS Negro people of Israel in Samaria, HIS Negro people would continue to live an unrighteous life there, and they would go to Bethel and Gilead to sin, and still take their sacrifices every morning, and their tithes every three years to offer thanksgiving with unleavened bread, while proclaiming the free offerings, just like they always do. But they would still be hungry, and wanting, because they would refuse to be righteous, even though HE, their GOD held back the rain, and ruined the harvest, and caused it to rain on one place, and not on the other, so that two, or three cities wondered to the city with water, which was not enough for everyone in the first place.

Yet they still did not repent and turn back to righteousness, and HE smote them with mildew that devoured all the trees, and the vineyards, and HE sent pestilence that killed off the young men in war, which depleted the army. Then HE caused many of the people to be devoured. But they still refuse to repent and be righteous. So, as HIS people, they better prepare to meet their GOD, because HE created the mountains, and created the wind, and HE tell human beings about things, like why the early morning is dark, and HE walks about on the highest mountains of the earth, because HE IS YAH, THE ALMIGHTY GOD.

The people of Israel should be crying, since their pureness is gone, and they would never rise to that height again, because they forsook the land, and there is no one to rise her up, and their big cities would be depleted to small cities, and the small cities would be almost non-existing. Therefore, whoever wants to live, better seek YAH, their GOD, and they better not go to Bethel, Gilgal, or Beersheba, because YAH, their GOD said, the people there would go into captivity, and they should seek HIM, and not the stars, because HE is the one who made them, and HE made morning from night, and made a border for the sea, and strengthens the weak against the strong, so they could fight against the people that hates them, to prevent those who rob the poor, and built up big houses in the land by their wicked ways from ever getting to live in them.

That is why HE is telling them to be prudent during this time, and seek good, and not evil, so HE could be with them, and they may live, and why HE wants them to hate evil, love good, and judge uprightly, so HE would be gracious to some, because there would be a lot of crying out in the streets, and in the vineyards. So, woe to anyone that is looking forward to The Day of THE LORD, because The Day of THE LORD is a time of darkness, not light, and nothing that a person does could make them escape their share of punishment, because if they run from a lion, a bear would get them, and if they run, and hide in a house, as they lean on a wall, a snake would bite them.

Don't you think that "The Day of THE LORD" should be a day of darkness, instead of a day of light?

Yes. It should be very dark, and have no light in it, because GOD said, HE hates, and despises the feasts days, and HE does not want to be assembled with HIS Negro people anymore, and even though they offer up to HIM burnt offerings, and meat offerings, HE will not accept them, and HE will not pay attention to the peace offering that is offered either. So, they may as well stop all the noise of singing, since HE does not want to hear their voices, and they should start doing what is right, because they did not have to offer sacrifices to HIM the forty years they were in the wilderness, and yet, they are sitting at Moloch's, and Chiun's table, and before the stars, which are idols they give sacrifices to, and for that, they would be taken into captivity to white nations farther than Damascus.

Woe to the Negroes of Israel that are having a good life in Zion, because they trust in the white people that govern them from the mountains in Samaria.

Let the people of Israel go to Hamath to the great colored people of Egypt, and then let them go to Gath to the colored people of the Philistines, and see what they do.

Is the kingdom of Israel better than the kingdoms of Egypt, or Palestine?

Are the borders of Egypt, or Palestine larger than the borders of Israel?

"No".

Therefore, the people of Israel are more evil than the people of Egypt and Palestine, because the people of Israel lay in their ivory beds, or stretch out on their couches to eat their rich foods, while chanting to spirits, and playing instruments to them, and they sing idly to the sounds of stringed instruments, like drunks, instead of being concerned about the punishment to come.

Israel has puffed themselves up against their GOD, and HE hates their false gods, and their idol worshipping, and HE swears that "The Day of THE LORD" would happen, and it would come to pass that if there are only ten people in one family, they would all die. Even family members would burn the dead bodies and wait for more to die. Because it would be time to smite the large families with breaches, and the small families with clefts.

Shall horses run upon rocks?

Will someone plow on rocks with oxen?

The answer is "No. Yet, Israel turned justice into gall, and the fruit of righteousness into wormwood. As if righteous justice is a light thing. And they rejoice for nothing, when they boast that they have gained what they got by their own strength, and for that, they are going to get punished.

So, GOD forms some grasshoppers right in front of Amos' eyes, and after the grasshoppers were formed, they mature into their latter state and ate all the grass in the land. Which symbolizes that a wicked nation would destroy the people of Israel. Therefore, Amos beg GOD not to do it, because they are small compared to other nations, and GOD told him, HE was sorry HE even thought of doing that, and HE would not do it. Then GOD shows him a vision of a great fire that is so hot, it dries up the sea. Which symbolizes that Israel would be hated by everyone. Therefore, Amos beg HIM not to do that either, and HE said, HE was sorry that HE thought of it, and HE would not do it. Then GOD shows him a vision of HIMSELF, standing on a wall with a plumbline in HIS hand, and HE asks him what he sees, and he said, he sees a plumbline. Which symbolizes that HE would punish and correct the people of Israel by HIMSELF by setting a plumbline amid them, and HE would not pass by them again, and the places of false worship would be desolate, the sanctuaries would be destroyed, and the family of Jeroboam, their king, would all be killed.

That sounds good to Amos. So, he agrees with it. Then he goes to Amaziah, the priest, and tell him what GOD planned to do. In unbelief, Amaziah calls him an old seer, which is a prophet. Then he runs him away from him and tells him to go hide in the land of Judah to eat his bread, and prophesy there, and not to come back to him, and prophesy again, because he is on the king's private property. But he tells Amaziah that he is not a prophet, and he is not even the son of a prophet. Instead, he is a herdsman. Someone who gathers sycamore fruits that GOD called, while he was taking care of the flock, and GOD told him to prophesy to the people of Israel, and to tell the king that his wife would be a whore in the city, his sons and daughters would be killed by the sword, and the land would be divided, and he would die in a polluted land, and those in his government of Israel would surely be taken captive.

After saying such terrible things, Amos leaves, and immediately, Amaziah sends a message to Jeroboam, the king of the kingdom of Israel, that said, Amos is conspiring against him, because he said the people of the kingdom of Israel would be taken away as captives, and he would die, but he sent him away, since he knew that the people would not want to hear what he was saying. Then GOD shows Amos a vision of a basket filled with summer fruits, and GOD asks him what he see, and he said, he sees a basket with summer fruits. And GOD tells him that, "It is the end for HIS people, because HE would not be with them, and the people would be crying in the temples of their idols, because of all the dead bodied that would be around them, and they need to listen, because they tortured the needy by making them fail at everything, and they say, when will the new moon be gone, so they could start selling the corn, and when would the Sabbath be over, so they could cheat on the weight of wheat by fixing the scales and deceive the people, because by knowing those things, it tells them when to buy the poor people with silver, or the needy for a pair of shoes, and when to sell the refuse of wheat for more profit. Which is why HE would never forget when they did all those things, and why everyone should be trembling and crying, knowing that the sun would go down at noon, and it would be dark at mid-day, and everyone's feasts would be ruined, and they would become malnourished, and their heads would become bald, since they would be in a famine, not of thirst, but in hearing the WORD. Therefore, they would go from land to land, seeking the WORD, and they would not find it, and the young people would faint, because of what is going on, since they insist on worshipping their idol Dan, and insist on saying he lives. And the same thing would happen to the people in Beer-Sheba, because of their idol worshipping.

Right then, in a vision, Amos sees GOD standing on an altar, saying, "Smite the lintel of the door, so the posts may shake, because all the people of Israel would be cut in the heads. And even if they dig into hell to try to escape, they would be killed. And if they go up to heaven, they would be dragged down and be killed. And even if they hide on top of Mount Carmel, they would be found and be killed. And if they go to the bottom of the sea, the sea serpent would be sent to bite them and kill them there. And when they are taken to captivity, their enemies would kill them. Yet, I want them to know that I would help them. Just like I helped the Ethiopians. And I would deliver them. Just like how I delivered them from the Egyptians, the Philistinians of Caphtor, and the Syrians of Kir. And I wants them to know, that MY eyes are watching the sinful kingdoms, and I would completely destroy all wicked nations, but I would not completely destroy them, MY people of Israel. Even though I would spread them all over the world to save all of them. So, they may as well believe that they would be captives, and they would be sifted in other nations, and all the sinners would die off, but the righteous ones would live. In the meanwhile, I would raise up the tabernacle of David that is in ruins, and I would close the breaches, and fix the walls, so it could look as it originally did. Then I would bring them from captivity, and they would build up the waste cities into habitable cities to live in, and they would plant vineyards, and drink wine, and plant gardens, and eat from them, and they would never be taken from the land again. At that time, the red skinned Negroes of Edom, and anyone else from any heathen nation that believes in righteousness would be able to come to have communion with them."

HOSEA'S PROPHESY

Time period—In the days of Uzziah, Jotham, Ahaz, and Hezekiah from 765 B.C.

During this time, GOD is using Hosea to prophesy to HIS people, and GOD tells him to get a whore, and make her his wife, and have children with her, as an example of how the people are acting as whores to false gods, and idols. Then Hosea takes Gomer, the daughter of Diblaim to be his wife, and she had a son for him, and GOD tells Hosea to name his son **Jezreel**, which means "vengeance", because HE would avenge the blood of Jezreel upon the family of Jehu and end the kingdom which they called "Israel". Then Gomer conceived again, and she had a daughter, and GOD tell Hosea to call her **Lo-Ruhamah**, which means "not loved, or no mercy", because HE would no longer have mercy upon the people of "The Kingdom of Israel".

After Lo-Ruhamah was weaned, Gomer conceives again, and she had another son, and GOD tell Hosea to call him **Loammi,** which means "not my people", because the people in "The Kingdom of Israel" are not HIS people, and HE would not be their GOD, even though they would be as numerous as the sand of the shores. But after a while, even though HE said they are not HIS people, they would be called HIS people again in their own inherited land, and at that time, all the people of "The Kingdom of Judah", and all the rest of the people in "The Kingdom of Israel" would join back together and have only one leader, and one government, because they would have stopped their whoring around with idols, and with the leaders of other nations.

Then GOD tell him to tell his brethren, **Ammi**, which is "The kingdom of Judah", and his sister, **Ruhamah,** which is "The Kingdom of Israel", to plead for their mother, "The Nation of Israel", because she is no longer HIS wife, nor would HE continue to be her HUSBAND, until she stops whoring around, and stop committing adultery. Therefore, HE will stop giving her blessings, and make her poor, until she dies, and HE would not have any mercy on the children that she gets from whoring around. Because she is a whore, and when she conceived them, she said she would go after her lovers that provides for her, and for that, HE is leaving her.

So, let her go after her lovers, and when she sees that none of them really want her, she would return to HIM, after seeing that she was better off with HIM. Then after she gets back with HIM, she would realize that HE took from the people of false gods to give her all they had, and once she knows that she would wait patiently for the things HE would provide for them. But for now, she must know that she is a whore, and she would have to sell the things she boasted of that her lovers gave to her, so she would be stripped of everything. Then HE would speak to her to comfort them, and HE would start to bless her again for her to have some hope, and she would acknowledge HIM as **"ISHI"** (The provider), instead of acknowledging Baal, because they would have stopped whoring after false gods.

Then HE would make a covenant with her and keep her as HIS righteous wife forever, so that the faithful people in other nations would have a good example of what a righteous, just, loving, and merciful nation should be like, with HIM, THE LIVING GOD, as their provider. Then at that time, HE would start to feel sorry for every people in the world, because HE heard their cries, and HE would send them blessings from the earth, and from the heavens above, because HE saw how witchcraft, idol worship, and the worship of false gods negatively affected everyone's life. And HE would heal the world, and things would grow bountifully, and HE would invite people of other nations to be HIS children, and those who believe would be called HIS children, and they would call HIM their GOD.

Then GOD tells him to get another adulterous wife that loves to get drunk, and is liked by her friends, and to love her just like how HE loves Israel. So, he goes and buy a whore for fifteen pieces of silver, and one and a half homer of barley. Then he tells her she cannot be a whore anymore, and she must commit herself to him, and he would be committed to her, because it is an example that GOD would use to show the people of "The Kingdom of Israel", which would interpret to say, they would live without a king, or princes, and without sacrifices, or sacred images, or Ephods and Teraphims for a long time.

As he continues to explain to his wife, he said, "In The Latter Days, The Kingdom of Israel would seek GOD, and HIS government, which would be governed by the people of the tribe of Judah, who are from the lineage of David. That is the reason why GOD wants them to listen, because HE has a controversy with all the inhabitants of the land of Israel, since there is no truth, or mercy, nor knowledge of HIM amongst them. Instead, there is swearing, lying, killing, stealing, and adultery, and everywhere there is bloodshed, and the land is mourning. Which is why there would be no more prophets for a time, and the nation, and its people would be destroyed for lack of knowledge, because they rejected the knowledge of GOD, and GOD decided to reject them, and said, HE does not want them to be HIS priests any longer, because the more they increase in number, the more they forget about the LAW. So, for the time being, GOD said, HE would forget about them, and HE would punish them when they do wrong, and would only reward them when they are doing right. Just like how HE does with everyone else in the world. Then they would eat, and would not have enough, and they would whore around, and still would not get anything, because they stopped listening to HIM, their GOD, and they would be full of sorrow while they whore around, and drink, and they would ask their false gods what to do, but they would not get any solution for their problems. Therefore, since everyone would be whoring around on each other, there would be no need for YAH, their GOD to intervene to help any of them, because whoever prays for help are also whores themselves, and while they play the whore, GOD would be hoping that "Judah" does not do the same. So, HE is begging the people of "The Kingdom of Israel" that worship false gods, and idols, not to go near the people of "The Kingdom of "Judah" to influence them, because the people of "The Kingdom of Judah" had been staying committed, even though the people of "The Kingdom of Israel" had been backsliding heifers, and had influenced the tribe of Benjamin to leave "The Kingdom of Judah" and join them in worshiping idols to whore around continually with white people who are Pagans. For that, GOD said, HE would punish them to shame them.

Therefore, GOD wants them, and all their priests to hear the warning, because HE said HE is ready to judge them for worshipping false gods, and idols, and for murdering, since HE told them not to do any of those things. Which is the reason why the Benjamite's in Mount Ephraim are corrupt, and the people of The Kingdom of Israel are defiled, since they refuse to turn back to HIM, YAH, their GOD, because of the spirit of whoredom among them. Therefore, they would fall, and they would try to seek GOD, but they would not find HIM, because HE would be gone from them, since they dealt treacherously with HIM by raising their children to be devils, and idol worshippers, and by worshipping false gods. That is why GOD said, they better know that the trumpet was already blown for war to start, and they would become desolate, and the same thing would happen to the people of "Judah, who does the same things like them, because when the people of Benjamin, in Mount Ephraim, were getting impoverished, the people of Judah saw themselves getting the same way, and they went to Jareb, the white Assyrian king for help when they knew that he could not help them, or heal them of their wounds.

It is for this, why GOD said HE would be like a lion that tears the people of Ephraim and Judah apart. Just like how HE is tearing the rest of Israel apart, and no one would be able to rescue them. Then HE would go back to heaven, until they acknowledge that they sinned, and acknowledge that they should do as HE says. Yet, what GOD really wants is for them to say, "Come, let us return to GOD, because even though HE had torn us, HE would heal us, and even though HE had smitten us, HE would bind us, and when HE cleanse us, and make us prosperous, HE would be with us, and we know that as long as we obey HIM we would be prosperous, and would be even better than we were before". Instead, GOD is crying and saying, "O people of Ephraim, and people of Judah! What should be done to make you change? Your faithfulness is like a morning cloud that vaporizes after the sun comes out. Though you were warned by the prophets, and were given verbal correction, you show yourselves to be abominable, because you refuse to change, since you rather be against ME. And like a bunch of robbers, you wait to rob someone, and you are counseled by your priests on how to murder, because the priests are also murderers."

That is what GOD is saying about HIS people. And even though HE saw the horrible things they did, HE wants them to know that after they are punished, they must remember that there would be a revival of all the people of "The Nation of Israel", especially of Judah, after they return from their captivities from the lands of the white Babylonians. But all this has to happen, because when HE tried to heal The Kingdom of Israel from their whoredom, the people of the tribe of Benjamin, in Mount Ephraim, became even more of devil, and idol worshippers. Then HE had to send the white people to take them into captivity, so they would really know what it would be like not to have HIM on their side, and because the Benjamite's caused HIM to look shameful to the other nations in the world when they left Judah, and joined the people of "The Kingdom of Israel" in worshipping idols as adulterers, and since they had been wasting HIS time ever since they had Saul, their first king, HE wants them to know that they are all hot in their evil, because they killed all the people that would righteously judge them, and all their kings are evil, and none of them pray to HIM anymore. Even worst, the people of Ephraim went to live with the Pagan white people, and they are like an undone cake, and they are used, and abused by all sorts of wicked people, and yet they are too stupid to know it, since all of them are so proud, that they do not even know how dumb they look from the time they turned from their GOD, and refuse to seek HIM for help. You see, they are like chickens, because when they are frightened, they go to the white people of Assyria, or to the ungodly colored nation of Egypt, who usually rob them, and run them away from them.

That is why woes came to all the people of The Nation of Israel, since they turned from their GOD, and turned from following the LAW, and why destruction came to them, even though GOD redeemed them. Since they still tell lies on GOD, and at nights while in bed, they refuse to ask for forgiveness by turning their backs completely to HIM, that is why they all get together begging for food, and drinks. Yet they continue to rebel against GOD, even as HE tries to correct them, because they cannot stop thinking about the mischiefs they are planning against the LAW. Some of them are even acting like they returned to following the LAW, and maybe they did, but not to YAH, THE MOST HIGH GOD, and because they are deceitful, GOD said, they would die for the things they spoke. As for Egypt, the same thing would happen to them, because they are Negro people from the lineage of Ham, through the people of Noah, who also worship idols, and false gods.

GOD said it loud, and HE said it clear. HE is coming as an eagle against the nation of Israel, because they turned against HIS covenant, and against HIS

LAW, and when HE starts the punishment, they would cry to HIM, and say they know HIM, even though they have stopped doing good, and for that, HE said the enemies are going to pursue them. Plus, punishment would also come to them for choosing king and princes throughout the years that were not godly, who HE did not choose. And punishment is coming to them for turning their silver and gold into idols, and their GOD is cutting them off, because all their idol calf in Samaria has kindled HIS anger against them, and they are acting innocent in their error, even though they know that as idol makers they are not godly anymore. So, since they pissed GOD off by their idol worship, the idol calf in Samaria would be broken to pieces. And for sowing to their ungodliness, they would reap a whirlwind of problems and become desolate. Therefore, whatever they have, a stranger would take it from them, and they would be swallowed up, and become unattractive to the gentile nations, because they are worshipping idols like the white people of Assyria, which the tribe of Benjamin in Mount Ephraim follows.

Since all the tribes of the people of Israel joined themselves with other ungodly nations, GOD said, HE would make them suffer a little. Especially since the tribe of Benjamin made altars for idols in Mt. Ephraim, as if they do not know that they are sinning, and that they are acting like the written LAW means nothing at all. And because all the people in Israel still makes sacrifices of meat offerings, as if they are still godly, that is the reason why GOD stopped accepting their offerings. So, because HE remembers all the evil they did, HE will punish them by letting them go back into slavery, just like when they were in Egypt, because they forgot HIM, their maker, and they also built temples to false gods, which caused "Judah" to gain great strength to have many fenced cities. And because the tribe of Judah started to act just like the rest of the tribes, fire would destroy all their strong cities, and all the palaces in them. So, they may as well stop being happy, because they whored themselves after false gods like the other nations, and they are going to be punished for it so severely, that they would not be able to live in their inherited land, and they would be slaves to the white Assyrians who do not believe in their GOD or offer sacrifices to HIM. Then when they eat the white people's food, they are going to be polluted, and they would not be able to communicate with YAH, their GOD.

So, what are they going to do when it is time to offer their sacrifices to YAH, their GOD, on the appointed days of feasts? Never mind, because the city of Jerusalem, and The House of THE LORD would be destroyed anyway, and everything would be taken by other nations when the time of punishment comes, because it would be a time for them to pay for their sins, and they would know that it starts when they see that the prophets are fools, and their spiritual leaders are mad. And because the prophets greatly corrupted themselves, and caused all the people to follow false gods, they would get what they deserve, since they are not loved by GOD anymore, and no matter how they try to save themselves, they would not be able to do it. Then every nation in the world would wonder what happened.

GOD knows that Israel is an empty vine, because they took all they had to the altars of their false gods, and their hearts are divided between HIM, and their false gods, and they are guilty of false worship. That is why GOD said HE will tear down the altars of the false gods, and destroy the idols, because their evil kings allowed them to practice false worship, and when they see it happen, they would say that they have no god, because they do not fear HIM, their GOD, and they made covenants with false gods, which caused judgment to come upon them. Yet they are still crying for their false gods.

First, GOD would give them to the white Assyrians as a gift, so that HE could make the land of Israel desolate to cleanse it from all the corrupted things that the white Assyrians showed them to do, and HE wants them to know that, because they had been sinning from the days of Gibeah, that is the reason why they lost the battle when they were invaded by their enemies in Gibeah, and why they had been suffering all along. That is why HE wants them to start doing the right thing, so HE would give them some mercy while they set their hearts right in seeking HIM until HE comes, and reigns blessings upon them again. Therefore, since they did evil, evil would come upon them, and because they trust in all the lies from other nations, those nations would come and take everything they have, and tear their women to pieces, and throw them at their children, just like how Shalman destroyed the people of Betharbel.

Most of all, GOD wants them to remember that before they became The Nation of Israel, HE loved them, and HE delivered them out of slavery from the ungodly colored people of Egypt. But they start to call on Balaam (a false human god), and they burn incense to many other idols. Yet HE took them from false worship, and healed them, and gave them all the blessings they needed. But they did not know that they were healed, and they did not know that even though they would never return to slavery in Egypt, they would become slaves to the white Assyrians in their white lands, because they refuse to turn back to HIM, their GOD. Then while many of them are captives in the ungodly white land, those that are left in their own land would be poor with white people would ruling over them, and devouring them, because they insist on listing to foolish counsel, even though they call YAH, their GOD. So, it is because they are so stubborn why GOD must do all that to make them return to HIM, and it is only because HE loves them so much why HE said HE would not completely crush them, and HE would bring them out of exile, and place them back into their houses. Therefore, they better remember that GOD is GOD, and not man.

Hosea continues to explain to his wife, and he said, 'GOD knows that the people in The Kingdom of Israel believes in lies, and even the people in The Kingdom of Judah are starting to believe lies, ever since they made a covenant with the white Assyrians. Which is the reason why their oil was carried away to the ungodly nations of the world, even though they are strong, and have power over the angels, and can talk to GOD. It is also the reason why GOD did not let them know that the Assyrian merchants are deceitful people that loves to oppress people, since they think that their own power makes them prosperous. Then to help them understand, GOD use the prophets and increase visions to warn them. But they ignored the warnings and continued to worship their idols and false gods. So, even though they were powerful and alive, when they started to worship false gods, they started to die. Yet they make more and more idols and kiss them, and sacrifice to them, and therefore, GOD, THE ANCHIENT OF DAYS said, they would be sifted, and many of them would be destroyed, because HE is jealous, and HE does not want them to serve anyone else, but HIM, since HE was the one that delivered them from the ungodly people of Egypt, and HE was the one that took time to know them as they wondered in the wilderness. Yet when they got blessed, they forgot about HIM, and for that, HE would tear them apart, like a lion tears its victim, and HE would watch them as they go about, so HE could pounce upon them as a leopard. Then HE would meet them as a bear and rip their children from them to devour them. But for the time being, HE is mourning, while HE is crying out telling them that they had destroyed themselves, and they could still call HIM, and HE would be their KING, and save them, because HE only gave them their human kings when HE was angry with them for the false worship in the land, and HE got rid of them to stop the false worship. So, even though they would be punished, they would be ransomed from death, and be blessed again, because HE is their punisher, and HE would be waiting to hear them repent, even though for a while HE would ignore their plead no matter how much they change for the better.

Hosea concludes and tell his wife that GOD is begging HIS people to please return to HIM as a way of showing that they are sorry for turning from HIM, and HE wants them to plead with HIM, and ask HIM to forgive them, and to receive them graciously. Then it would be a sweet savoring sacrifice of their lips, if they tell HIM that HE is their GOD, and they trust in HIM, and not in their own strength, and they would no longer worship idols and false gods, because HE is so merciful and HE is all they need. If they do that, then GOD would give them a good life again, and HE would show them love, because HE would forgive them for what they did to HIM, and they would not want to trust in idols and false gods anymore, because whoever is wise, or say they are wise would understand that HIS ways are right. Therefore, those who are just would abide by HIS ways, and be blessed, but transgressors would be punished.

ISAIAH'S PROPHESY

Isaiah—The son of a Negro man named Amoz

Time frame—In the days of Uzziah, Jotham, Ahaz, and Hezekiah, the

kings of Judah (Negro kings of Israel)

By this time, GOD is using Isaiah to prophesy to the people, and Isaiah had visions concerning the judgment on Israel in "The Wrath of GOD", and he prophesied to warn the people about the wrath over the reign of several kings, starting from 700 B.C. Now, since GOD is disgusted by the rejection of HIS people, HE cries out, and said, "Listen heaven and earth! I nourished and brought up children, but they do not obey ME. The animals know their owners, but Israel does not know their owner, and they do not even consider ME, because they turned into sinful people, and they are full of iniquity, and are evil doers, because they are a bunch of people who corrupt others. Yea, that is who they are, because they forgot about ME, and provoked ME to anger, since they no longer think about ME, THE HOLY ONE of Israel."

Time, after time, after time, they were punished, and GOD is wondering why HE should punish them again, when the more they get punished, the more they become rebels. After so much punishment, the whole nation became sick in the minds. All of them are fearful, and there is nothing but hurt, and resentment in them, and they are still feeling pain from things of the past, because their land is desolate and burned with fire since strangers came into the land and took everything while they watched and were left as empty booths out in a vineyard. If GOD did not plan to save a few of them, the entire nation would have been like the white nations of Sodom and Gomorrah, which were destroyed completely.

GOD wants them to listen, since they are sinful Negros, who need to obey the LAW, because they are acting like the white people of Gomorrah, from the time they took over the land. So, GOD wants to know why they are wasting their time sacrificing to HIM, when HE is tired of their rituals, and have already told them to stop wasting their time coming into HIS courtyard bringing HIM sacrifices, because they became an abomination to HIM. Not only that, BUT HE also told them, HE does not even want them to celebrate together any longer, because they are celebrating in their sins, and HE told them that even though HE is their FATHER, HE would not answer their prayers when they pray anymore, since they are a bunch of murderers. Because what HE really wants is for them to stop sinning and start living a clean life, and for them to put away their evil doings from before HIM, and cease from evil, and learn to do good. He also wants them to seek justice, help the oppressed, defend the fatherless, and plead for the widows. And because HE is their heavenly FATHER, HE wants to reason with them, and HE said, though their sins are many, HE would forgive them of all of them, and if they repent, and do right, their sins would be forgiven, and they would be healed, and be blessed in abundance, but if they refuse to obey the LAW, they would die one by one.

GOD knows The Holy City, Jerusalem, is corrupt, even though it used to be a place full of justice, because it became a place where murders live, and everything about the city is corrupted. Even their silver is impure, and the wine is watered down, and the leaders are companions of thieves, and lovers of bribes, and they do not practice godly things, which cause the poor, the widows, and orphans to be afraid of them. All GOD want is for them to stop sinning and to live a clean life. HE wants them to put away all their evil doings from before HIM, and cease from evil, and learn to do good by seeking justice, helping the oppressed, defending the fatherless, and pleading for widows.

The heavenly FATHER wants to reason with them. HE said, though their sins are many, HE would forgive them of all of them, and if they repent, and do right, their sins would be forgiven, and they would be healed, and be blessed in abundance. But if they refuse to obey the LAW, they would die one by one, because The Holy City, Jerusalem, is corrupt, and HE knows it used to be a place full of justice, but it became a place where murders lives, and everything about the city is corrupted, and even the silver is impure, and the wine is watered down, and the leaders are companions of thieves, and lovers of bribes, and they do not practice godly things, which caused the poor, the widows, and orphans to be afraid of them. Which is why GOD said that HE is ready to rid HIMSELF of HIS own people, since they are no better than wicked people. But instead of destroying them, HE would chasten them, so they would turn back to HIM. Then after HE makes them weak and poor, HE would restore them to who they were at first, and they would be called people of the righteous, and Jerusalem would be The Holy City again. Therefore, GOD is making sure that they know that Zion, and their Negro people would be glorified again, but those of her who are sinners would be destroyed.

Isaiah 2

GOD said HE would destroy the people of the kingdom of Judah, like HE did the people of the kingdom of Israel. But HE also said, after being punished, the people of Judah would regain their belief in the TRUTH and would be reestablished. Then many nations would come to her to learn of YAH, their GOD, and because they would be a good example to the world by their righteous ways of life, the world would learn from them, and wars would eventually cease. That is why HE is begging Judah to please live right, and stop following behind other spirits, and to seek HIM, and HIS HOLY SPIRIT instead, because things gained by witchcraft, and magic are only temporary, and those who prospered by it would lose it all eventually.

Since the people of GOD are bowing down to objects, GOD is ready to punish them, and HE said everyone better run, and hide, because HE is very angry at their idol worship, and HE would not share HIS praise with anyone, because HE alone is GOD, and HE alone would be exalted above all things. Therefore, GOD wants them to know that The Day of THE LORD would come, and things would be terrible for those who are proud and lofty, and all idols, and all idol worshippers would be abolished, and people would run, and hide themselves from the troubles, and though some people would repent and change, some would not. That is why they are being warned to make sure that they keep away from pride, and from those who are proud.

Chapter 3

So, GOD pronounced that Jerusalem would lose its glory for a while, and ends up being ruled by children, or by people with no wisdom, and their Negro people would oppress each other, and their Negro children would become disrespectful to the adults, and they would even despise their people of honor, because the people would be like animals. Therefore, no one would care for the other, and Jerusalem would stumble, and Judah would fall, because they are not telling others about their GOD, and they are disobedient to HIS LAW. Now, all the people of Israel are looking guilty, since they no longer hide their sins, or feel shame. Which is why GOD feel sorry for them, and why HE wants the righteous ones to know that everything would be good with them, but woe to the wicked ones, because it would be bad for them, as a payment for their unrighteousness, which is the reason why they got so sickened in their minds that children are oppressing them, and women are ruling over them. Now they need to regain their strength, because those who are leading them are leading them astray, and even though GOD is pleading with them, at the same time, HE is ready to judge them. But before HE judges them, HE would punish the older ones, and the leaders first, because they should have been good examples for the others to follow.

Also, because the daughters of Israel are acting foolish, and are dressing like whores, GOD would strike them with scab on the head to prevent their hair from growing, and the young ladies would be bald, and they would have no jewelry, because everything that makes them beautiful would be taken away from them. Leaving them with no fine jewelry, no expensive perfumes, and no quality designed clothing, and instead of smelling good, they would stink, and for a belt, they would wear a piece of cloth, and their heads would be bald, and their clothes would be the value of rags. Then after all that happens to the women, their men would be killed off, leaving them alone crying, and the few men left would be their mental pimps, and a man would have seven women.

Chapter 4

Then all seven women would try to impress the one man. Even though they are the ones bringing the money home to him. And they would beg their pimp (husband, boyfriend, son, or father) to love them, and even pay for their own food and clothing, just to have that person's last name. But the Negro women who are righteous would not have to worry about those things, because they would always be beautiful, and have enough money, so they do not have to whore themselves out to a man to survive in the world. Still, the day would come when only the righteous ones would be left in Jerusalem, because GOD would make them clean again by using HIS HOLY SPIRIT to judge them, and purify them, and when they are pure again, HE would make them comfortable and provide their every need. The only way the wicked ones would be there is if they are dead and buried, and since the people of Israel are stubborn and reluctant to change, Isaiah made up a song to tell them how GOD really felt about them, and he went to them, and said, "Let me sing a song to my people whom I love so much!." Then he sings the song to them.

Chapter 5

The Song:

My GOD had some Negro people of a very powerful race, and HE chose them and got rid of the stumbling blocks for them. Then HE placed them in the best region of the earth, and placed a temple in the midst of them, and governed them by HIS LAW, and HE expected HIS people to be righteous, but instead, HE yielded a bunch of sinners, and now HE looks to the righteous ones of HIS people, and is asking them to Judge each other, and let HIM know whether the people are good, or is it HE alone who is good, because HE is wondering what more could HE have done for them that HE did not do, and why did they turned out so bad, when HE did so much for them to be good. Now, because HE is disappointed in them, HE will take away their extra protection, and HE will cause them to die off, and cause the Holy City to come to desolation. Yes, they will lose a lot of their blessings.

Some terms:
"The vineyard" - is the House of Israel (all 12 tribes of Israel)
"Pleasant plant" – are the righteous ones (only the tribe of Judah at the time)

GOD knows that the righteous ones are looking for justice, but all they find is injustice and oppression, and even though the righteous one are seeking others to be righteous like them, there are not many who will repent, and change, and it is causing the righteous person to weep.

Woe to the greedy:

People are buying up land and building too many houses. They have so many houses, there is no empty land left, and they isolate themselves based on status, and GOD said, "Truly many houses shall be empty, because the great, and beautiful ones would have no dwellers, and would be as if they were worth nothing."

Woe to the lazy drunk:

People are getting up early in the morning to drink, and they do not stop getting drunk, until they go back to bed again, and they sing and dance, while they are drunk, but they do not consider what GOD instructed them to do. Nor can they recognize HIS works, and they are captives, because they are ignorant, and their honorable people get old, and die out, and the rest of them die because of lack of knowledge. Therefore, GOD said, the gate of hell was enlarged, so the multitude of sinners may enter, and HE would humble the proud to exalt HIMSELF, because HE desires the fruits of the land to be given only to those who deserves good.

Woe to the jealous:

Those who are back stabbers and are quick to do wickedness would be humbled, because they do their evil, and they dare any of the righteous ones to say anything about it.

Woe to deceivers:

The deceiver goes about and call evil good, and good evil, and they make people think that the truth is a lie, and the lie is the truth, and they are perceived to be righteous, but they are deceivers, and they will do you no good.

Woe to the wise:

These people think they are wise, because they have high positions and they can handle their businesses, but what they do not know is that they are ignorant, because they do not seek wisdom by the LAW of GOD.

Woe to all those who are faking it through life:

They are praised and paid, and yet they take away the justice from the righteous ones, and since they are all lovers of bribes, they would always reject GOD, and HIS LAW.

These are the reasons why GOD punishes people, and for these things, GOD said, HE would call all the nations of the world against HIS people of Israel, and they would be quick to come plunder everything from them, and none of the enemies would ever get tired of taking from them, because they would come on horses, with weapons to carry all they can take with great force, and they would make a lot of noise as they take them from their native land, and there would be a lot of sorrow for the people of Israel when they lose their glory for a while, since this chastening is from their GOD.

The Angelic Beings:

"The Seraphim" are angels of bright (white) light that were created on the first day of the creation. They were placed in the third heaven with GOD, and (the Seraph) Michael is the archangel, the first angel created, who rules over them to control the physical light of the sun, which was created on the fourth day.

"The Cherubim" are angelic beings of a lesser (amber) light, and they were also created on the first day as the Seraphim, but they were placed in the Second Heaven with (the Cherub) Satan, as the archangel, who was the second angel created to lead over them to control the physical stars, and moon, which were also created on the fourth day.

Chapter 6

In that same year when Uzziah, the king of Judah died, Isaiah had a vision of GOD sitting on HIS throne in heaven, and above the throne were Seraphim (angels), each having six wings, saying, "Holy, Holy, Holy is the LORD of hosts, the whole earth is full of HIS glory!" And the posts of the door were shaken by the voices, and inside the place filled with smoke from the glory of GOD. When Isaiah saw that, he said, "Woe, I am not ready for this! I am a man who still curses, and I live amongst other people who curse. I cannot believe that I saw GOD, THE KING, THE LORD of all the angels."

Term:

"Host" - is a troop of angels

Then one of the Seraphim takes a coal from the altar with a tong, and flies over to Isaiah, and touches his mouth with the coal, and said, "Behold, this has touched your lips. Your iniquity is taken away, and your sin purged", and GOD said, "Whom should I send, and who would go for us?", and Isaiah volunteered to go, and GOD gave him the message to give to the people.

The Message:

You keep on hearing, but you don't understand, and you keep on looking without finding answers, because I Am your GOD and I made it like that so that your hearts would be dull and your ears heavy, and I shut your eyes, because I don't want you to see, because if you see and hear, then you would ask for forgiveness and would be well again. So, you would be punished for your behavior, and the Holy City will be destroyed, but a tenth of the people would be saved for MY sake, and I will use the remnant to take root again and multiply them to continue in the TRUTH."

ISRAEL UNDER ATTACK

Isaiah 7

Uzziah—is the past Negro king of Judah

Ahaz (son of Jotham)—is Uzziah's grandson, the present king of Judah

Remaliah—is a white man who was king of Syria, who ruled over the Negroes of Israel that were left in their native land

Pekah—is another white man, who is the son of Remaliah

At this point in time, the people of Israel are divided into two kingdoms, which are Israel and Judah. At the same time, the tribe of Benjamin turned against all the other tribes by joining forces with the white Syrians and are completely worshipping idols. So, "The Kingdom of Judah" continue to be righteous by worshipping only YAH, their GOD, while "The Kingdom of Israel" continue to be compromising by worshipping YAH, their GOD, as well as worshipping idols, and Benjamin is completely unrighteous by worshipping idols and false gods with the Syrians.

Then since the kingdom of Judah is small, and is standing alone, looking like a target, Remaliah (the white man that took over Israel) takes forces against Jerusalem, The Holy City, where the people of Judah live. Then he makes war against them, but he could not prevail, because their GOD protects them in their righteousness. Later, the news got to the people of Judah (the household of David) that the Syrian forces joined with the tribe of Benjamin (the people of Ephraim) to fight against them, and they became concerned that one of their own tribes turned against them to join white people to fight them. So, GOD tells Isaiah, the prophet, to tell Ahaz, the king of Judah, to take heed and be quiet, and not to be afraid of Ephraim (the tribe of Benjamin) who joined with the white man, Resin, and the white Syrians against them, because they are just puffing smoke. And Isaiah tells Ahaz what GOD said, and he tell him he could ask for a sign to help his unbelief. But Ahaz would not ask for a sign, because he believed, and he did not want to weary GOD.

A VIRGIN SHALL COVCEIVE

Though Ahaz did not want a sign, he noticed that The House of David (the tribe of Judah) wants one, and he tell them that he knows that it is easy for them to weary men, but they seem to want to weary GOD also, and GOD would give them a sign to help their unbelief.

The Sign:

*A virgin shall conceive and bear a son and call His name "**Immanuel**", which means "God is with us."*

Facts:

Jesus is not GOD. Jesus is the Son of GOD. He was called Immanuel, because He is godly all the time, and GOD is always with him.

As prophesied, Jesus would live a sin free life to know the difference between good, and evil. But before the child (Jesus) is big enough to discern, and choose good over evil, the land of Babylon that the Negroes dread so much would be forsaken by both her kings (Resin and Remaliah). Then GOD would cause the white Assyrians to come against Israel like never before, by calling every white Babylonian nation against them to bring them to desolation, and those who are righteous would be saved from it, but they would fear the Assyrians. Then GOD would take revenge on the Assyrians for their wickedness, and for being so quick to make the Negroes of Israel suffer, and HE would meet the Assyrians in that valley near the Euphrates River, and let them know that compared to HIM, they are just little boys.

Chapter 8
THE CHILD MAHER-SHALAL-HASH-BAZ

Then GOD tell Isaiah to take a large scroll and write the name Mahar-Shalal-Hash-Baz on it. Which literally means, "Speed the spoil and hasten the booty". In other words, "Let's get this done and over with!" And GOD tells him to take some faithful witnesses to watch him, while he had sexual intercourse with his wife to let them record the details of the event. With full obedience, he takes the witnesses to watch him have intercourse with his wife (the prophetess), and she conceived that day. Then after she had the child, GOD tells him to give the child the name that is written on the scroll. Which is Mahar-Shalal-Hash-Baz. And GOD said, before Mahar-Shalal-Hash-Baz, the child, is old enough to say mama and dada, the Assyrians would be defeated.

Then GOD tells him about the many ways the white Assyrians would come to invade their chosen people with great force. But GOD promised him that as they enter the land, they would have walked into a trap. Because even though HE is using the white people against the disobedient ones of Israel, HE would destroy them in the end, since they were too willing to destroy The House of GOD, though they are the most wicked people on the earth. And because HIS people rejected HIM so much, and would rather serve Remaliah's son, HE would over flood the Euphrates River, and send the Babylonian army from Europe against them, and the white people would pass through Judah with great force to take over the land. But all the nations that are not part of Israel better listen and be afraid, as they get themselves ready to be plundered personally by HIM, because though they may council with each other to take over The Nation of Israel, it would not happen, and they can say what they want, because HE is with HIS people.

DON'T DO AS THE WICKED

GOD strongly stated to HIS people that they should not live their lives as the wicked, and HE beg them not to worry about the conspiracy against them, nor to be afraid of the threats from other nations, because HE is the GOD WHO made the angel, and they must fear HIM, since HE is holy, and HE would be their security. But HE said, if they are sinning, then HE would be a stumbling block, and cause them to be defeated, because HE is THE LORD of Hosts (of angels), WHO they should hallow, and be afraid of. Therefore, if they believe that, then from that day, they should testify that they live for HIM, and they would wait on HIM, while they teach their children to also do the same, because the righteous are the signs, and wonders of the house of Israel.

When someone says to the righteous, "Seek those who are fortune tellers and wizards", they should say, "Should I not seek my own GOD?" Because the righteous should stick to their conviction, so they could live by the LAW. Then they must wait on THE LORD (GOD) for HIS promises. And they should know that if a person does not speak according to the WORD, it is because there is no good in that person. Didn't Israel know that there is no hope for the wicked? The wicked get hungry, and have hard times like everyone else, but they get enraged, because neither the king of their government, nor their god can save them, and they look about, and are in total confusion, because they do not know which way to turn for answers. Next thing, they just lose their minds.

Isaiah 9

Though the Babylonian white people will attack the Negroes of Israel, GOD said, the Negroes of Israel would not feel gloomy, because Jesus would be walking about and preaching the TRUTH to them, and all those who walk in the darkness of lies would understand the TRUTH and would see the light. Then many other kinds of people would know, and believe in the TRUTH, and rejoice, because Jesus would have broken the yoke of oppression by using the truth to destroy the effects of the lies from the Romans, and send them to hell, and use their bodies as fuel in the fire.

For unto us a child is born

Unto us a Son is given

And the government will be upon His shoulders

And His name will be called, Wonderful, Counselor, and Mighty God, Everlasting Father, Prince of Peace.

Of the increase of His government and peace, there will be no end upon the throne of David, or over His Kingdom of GOD to order it, and establish it with judgment, and justice from that time forward. Even forever, because the zeal of GOD will perform it.

So, even though the children of Israel would suffer loss during that time, Jesus would be there with them while the temple is being destroyed, and GOD would prevent them from trying to rebuild it, because HIS anger is not done with. But in due season, GOD would replace everything better than before. So, woe to those who uses people's troubles to swindle, and scam them, and woe to the white Assyrians, because though GOD used them to punish HIS Negro people, HE would punish them twice as much for enjoying the dirty job.

Chapter 10

Woe to them who make unjust laws to issue oppressive decrees, to deprive the poor of their rights, and withhold justice from the oppressed, making widows prey, and robbing the fatherless.

What would they do on that day GOD appointed to punish them?

Who would they run to for help?

Who are they going to give their riches to?

Woe to the Assyrian white people, though GOD used them to correct others with their anger, because of trying to correct people, they wanted to destroy them.

Shall the ax boast itself against the one who chops with it? "No".

The white men cannot boast against GOD, because GOD is the one who said HE would use them to be against the Negroes of Israel. At the same time, HE let Israel know that a remnant of them would return to the Holy Land, and they would not need to depend on their enemies any longer, because they would repent, and depend on HIM, their GOD.

Chapter 11

For there shall come forth a rod (a government) from the stem of Jesse (the tribe of Judah), and a branch (Jesus) shall grow out of his roots (the linage of Judah), and the spirit of the LORD shall rest upon Him (Jesus), and the spirit of wisdom and understanding, the spirit of counsel, and might, the spirit of knowledge, and of the fear of GOD. Then Judah (the lineage of David) would delight themselves in fearing GOD, and they would judge according to the LAW, and be the example that others would have to follow, and they would judge, so the righteous may live safely, even while the wicked are amongst them. At that time, Jesus, who is from the root of Jesse, would stand as a banner to the people, because the gentiles would seek Him, and His resting place shall be glorious. Then by the time the gentiles are believing the truth, the people of Israel would have already returned from Babylon back to Africa, and GOD would have dried up waters, lowered mountains, and made streets in the desert for them to come home, because HE wants the twelve tribes to work as one again.

Chapter 12
THE LORD IS MY STRENGTH

Once the Negroes of Israel are together again, they would act as "The Chosen Ones", and praise GOD, because though HE was angry at their sins, HE forgave them. Then they would say, "JAH, the LORD is my strength, my song, and my salvation, and they would praise HIM, and call on HIM for all their needs, and tell the world how wonderful, and merciful HE is.

SOME NAMES OF GOD:
YAHWEY
YHWY
THE ALMIGHTY
JAH
YAH
JEHOVAH
ALLAH
GOD
THE ANCIENT OF DAYS

LORD

THE LORD OF HOSTS

FATHER

THE HOLY SPIRIT

Facts:

YHWH is the name of the GOD of Israel. YHWH is pronounced as JEHOVAH, in their tongue, which sounds like YAH- O- WAY in our ears. YHWH is the only GOD, the one that created the heavens, the earth, and everything.

Isaiah 13

So, Israel had been warned that GOD would send many Babylonian nations to destroy them, and The Holy Land, as the punishment for their sins. Now everyone is crying, because their judgement is near.

Some Terms:

"Enter the gates of the nobles" - This is the gates of the city of Jerusalem in which the Babylonians will enter through

"My sanctified and MY mighty ones for MY anger" - These are the Babylonians that GOD will use to punish HIS people Israel

"The noise of the multitude" - This is the sound of Babylon's arm, charging into Africa

"From a far country" - This means far from outside the continent of Africa

Chapter 14-17

Therefore, by the fierce Roman army, charging in on their battle horses, GOD would punish The Nation of Israel for the sins they committed in The Holy Land. But HE would restore them with HIS love in the TRUTH and then punish the Babylonians for being quick to punish them, because they knew they were worst sinners than the people of Israel. So, Babylon would fall for what they did to Israel, because GOD loves HIS children (Israel), and would have mercy upon them. Then after they are chastened, they would praise HIM, and many nations, and races would come to them, just to be their servants, and they would be the head again with others as their servants, instead of being slaves or being in bondage to others.

These nations would be destroyed for mistreating the Negro people of GOD:

1) Assyria (ungodly white people in white lands)

2) Philistia (ungodly colored people in colored lands)

3) Moab (ungodly colored in their land with ungodly whites living

with them)

4) Damascus, the capital of Lebanon (a flourishing white land given

to Israel by GOD, but it was never taken over by them.

These nations and their people are the root of the works of the devil. Vipers and a bunch of flying serpents they are, because they would try to keep the Negros of Israel from their inherited Promised Land of the Gaza Strip for many, many years.

Though GOD is using the wicked white nations to punish HIS Negro people of Isreal, HE tells the other ungodly nations that hates them, that HE dares them to help the Romans to conquer them, and they better help them, if they run to them to escape. Because if any Israelite goes to any of their ungodly nations to hide from the Babylonians, if they have sense, they will treat them well, since those who do not treat them well would be punished as those who attacked them. For in mercy, the throne would be established, and someone would sit on it in truth in the tabernacle of David, judging, and seeking justice, and hastening righteousness. Though the nations would rush in like running water to attack the Negroes of Israel, GOD said, HE would rebuke them. For look, they would have walked into a trap, and before "The End Times" starts, they would be destroyed, because that is the portion of those who plunder the righteous Negroes, and the lot of those who rob them.

Chapter 18

So, woe to the land shadowed with buzzing wings of military helicopters in The End Times.

Some Terms:

"Beyond the rivers of Ethiopia" - This is west of the Jordan and beyond. It is the zone from where the Promise Land border ends, which leads into Babylon. That means, west of The Gaza Strip into European lands.

In The End Times, at first, Babylon will send ambassadors by ships, and even by vessels of reeds to invade The Promised Land (which is The Gaza Strip). Then further in the future, they would send planes, and helicopters to do the same thing in modern times (our time), and when Babylon send their men to the Negro people of Israel, they would say to themselves, "Go swiftly to the nation with people who are tall, and are of smooth skin, because they are terrible (strong), and since the beginning, they have taken all the land East of the Euphrates River, which is Gaza Strip, their Promised Land."

Some Terms:

Tall - is to be of greatness, or power
Smooth skin - is brown skin which does not show the blood flowing through it
Terrible - is to be strong, powerful, or prosperous
Yet even though it sounds bad, that is the goodness of GOD, because GOD would be allowing the Babylonians to punish Israel, as HE sits back and

watch, so that the chastening would cause many of them to turn from their sins and change to worshipping HIM again.

Some Terms:

People tall and smooth of skin - people of color

A Nation powerful - The Nation of Israel

Whose land the river divide - The Euphrates River divides Europe from Africa and The Jordan River divides east from west in the Gaza Strip

GOD WILL PUNISH THE REST OF AFRICA
Isaiah 19

As for Egypt, they better know that they would get punish. Because they enslaved Israel, even though they knew they are Negroes from Noah's lineage, like them. The only difference is that they are from Japheth, who has light brown to brown skin descendants, and Israel is from Shem, who has brown to dark brown skin descendants.

Symbolisms:

Israel – is symbolic of the righteous Negro people of GOD

Egypt – is symbolic of the unrighteous Negro people of the world

GOD is disappointed in Negroes, and HE said that Egypt better know that they would become a weak nation as their punishment, and they would be afraid of the people of Israel. But after that, their Egyptian people would compare the truth they know of Isreal and would reason with people who are seeking truth in white nations. Then they and those white people would also start to praise, and worship YAH, the GOD of Israel. At this time, Jesus would come, and the gentiles would have their Savior, Jesus, the mighty one, and He would deliver them. After that, GOD HIMSELF would punish the Negro people of Egypt, and the white Assyrians. Then eventually the colored Egyptians and the white Assyrians would come together with the Negro people of Israel, and GOD would bless them all, and in that day, Israel would be one of three with Egypt, and Assyria, and be a blessing in the land of Africa.

Isaiah 20

Time frame - In the year that Chief Tartan came to Ashdod.

One day, while Isaiah is mourning, GOD tells him to take off his sackcloth and to walk about naked and barefooted, and Isaiah takes of his sackcloth and walks around naked and barefooted. Ater three years walking around barefooted and naked, like a demented fool, GOD tells him, "Just as he walked about naked and barefooted for three years like HIS servant, it is a sign and a wonder to show what would happen to Egypt and Ethiopia, because they are two Negro African nations that are not seeking HIM. And many times, the white Babylonians would use them to help them destroy and plunder the ones of Israel who serves HIM. And though Ethiopia and Egypt are blessed and powerful, because of their location, and though they are a refuge to the people of Israel and many white Babylonians believers, HE wants them to know that when they see the Assyrian Babylonians coming, it would be time for their punishment from HIM for being unbelievers, and the Assyrians would take their Egyptians and Ethiopians people as prisoners, and make them slaves. And when it happens, they would expect it, and they would know that they would not get any help, and they would not be so beautiful and prosperous anymore, and then the people of Israel would be ashamed to ask them for help again.

Isaiah 21

GOD is angry, and HE shows Isaiah the burden against the "Wilderness of the Sea", and Isaiah saw a lot of devastating things that happens in the world, because of unrighteous practices.

Symbolisms:

Wilderness – is a barren place or a waste land

Sea - is symbolic of the world, or multitudes of people

Whirlwind in the south – is a spirit force from the south (symbolic of coming from hell)

Yet even though Isaiah is waiting for the wicked to be punished, he mourns, and becomes sick, and in his sickness, he realizes that because of the haste to make a profit, the people of the world do not wait on the fruits of the earth to ripen. Therefore, it is human beings that are destroying the earth.

Later that day, GOD shows him a vision of things after the devastation on the earth, and he sees that his Negro people of Israel would repent, and turn back to GOD to live a righteous life again.

Some Terms:

"Army of north" - This can be GOD's army from heaven (north is symbolic of heaven), or it can mean that GOD is using the white Babylonian nations (north of the globe) to punish the world.

East - is symbolic of the godly region of the globe (all of Africa, including Iraq and Iran)

West (America) - is a wilderness that is undiscovered. It would be a refuge for the godly people during this time of prosecution in the East, where the godliest people would be sent, so they would not get killed by the devious wicked white people of The Roman Empire.

ESAU'S PEOPLE
The Burden against Dumah:

Fact:

Dumah - is the land that belongs to the people of Esau (Jacob's brother)

From the start when Esau separated from his brother Jacob (Israel), Esau went to dwell in the land of Seir to live amongst the Sons of Seir, which are ungodly white people. But Esau also inherited other lands, which are known as the land of the Edomites, and the Edomites, who are descendants of Esau, are always in contention against the Israelites, because of the loss of their birthright to receive the world's blessing from YAH, their GOD, that Jacob tricked Esau to receive. In their contention, Esau's red skinned Negro descendants had been at war with Jacob's dark skinned Negro descendants of Israel out of anger, and GOD said they would be punished for harassing Israel, but HE would also invite them to receive the gift of salvation when Jesus comes.

Facts:

Jacob's descendants are the Israelites. They are Negro of brown to dark brown complexion

Esau's descendants are the Edomites. They are Negro of red to yellow complexion

Esau and Jacob are twin brothers, who are sons of Isaac, but because GOD knew how things would be, even though Esau (Edom) was born first, GOD made it so that Jacob (Israel) would be the heir to the blessings.

Arabia (the land of the Arabian Desert) would also be punished, because the Arabians are colored people in African that are ungodly.

Isaiah 22

The Day of The LORD will come. Surely, because of this iniquity there would be no atonement for the world, even to their death, said the LORD of Hosts.

Facts:

"Surely for this iniquity" - The iniquity is the injustice and the unrighteous on the earth, which causes the just, and the righteous to suffer more than the wicked.

Though GOD allows the wicked to make the righteous suffer, HE would turn the tables, and HE would not be done until HE is good and ready, and when HE is done, HE would give the righteous all the glory they deserve.

Isaiah 23

Therefore, Tyre and the white lands along the Mediterranean Sea would be punished, because they are guilty of using their ships to enter the nation of Africa to destroy and plunder the Negro people along The Gaza Strip.

WHITE PEOPLE AND WHITE LANDS

People of Tyre:	*People of Babylon:*
Sidon	*Hittites*
Tarshish	*Jebusites*
Cyprus	*Sidonites*
Land of Canaan	*Girgashites*
Land of Chaldeans	*Amorites*
	Assyrians

These white people of Tyre, and Babylon are some of the descendants of Canaan, the son of Ham, known as the Canaanites. They are associated with each other to find ways of destroying people of color that are not like them, and they would travel back and forth from their white lands to do crooked deals with all the people west of the Nile River in Africa, at "The Harvest of the River", which is the marketplace.

Facts:

"The harvest of the river" - This is a marketplace at the "Nile River" where the world comes to trade.

"The Nile River" - runs south to north in the Continent of Africa and divides the countries of Egypt and Sudan into two sections: east and west.

As wicked deceivers, the Babylonian made friends with all the merchants in the world, especially with those nations that were west of the Nile River, and when they make a deal, they get plenty for cheap. Then they go home satisfied, but they leave the righteous, and fair dealers to struggle, and die, and for that practice, GOD said, Tyre would be forgotten for seventy years (from 1 A.D. to 70A.D.), according to the days of one king. Then at the end of the seventy years, Tyre would look like a country that no one ever knew, and they would try to recover, but they would be crooked merchants again, and they would be crueler than ever before. But they would not get away with the crookedness, because other nations would plunder them, and give their riches and treasures to the righteous people for them to enjoy.

GOD WILL EMPTY THE EARTH
Isaiah 24

"Who would get punishes?

The people

The priests

The servants

The masters

The maids

The mistresses

The buyer

The seller

The lender

The borrower

The creditor

The debtor

In "The Last Days", which is also the time of the rule of The Roman Empire, everyone would get punished, because they transgressed the LAWS of GOD, and changed the ordinances (rules), and broke the everlasting covenant. Therefore, the curse would devour the earth, and everyone would suffer, and nothing would make people merry, and people would have to cry to GOD, and give HIM HIS glory for HIM to bring them through **"The Great Tribulation"**, which is the beginning of HIS wrath that will end The Roman Empire.

Isaiah 25

Then all the people that are saved during "The Great Tribulation" would exalt the name of the LORD, GOD, because HE would have done wonderful things, and HE is faithful and true. Even the heathens would worship GOD, because HE is good to the poor, strength to the distressed, a refuge from the storm, and a shadow from the heat. So, GOD would destroy racial discrimination, swallow up Death, wipe away tears, and get rid of the wicked, and all the righteous people would say, "Behold, this is our GOD. We waited for HIM, and HE saved us. This is our LORD, we waited for HIM, and we are glad, and rejoice in HIS salvation".

Isaiah 26

At that time, Judah will sing, because the white folks would fear them, while the righteous gentile people come to enter through the gates of Jerusalem (whether they looked black, white, or in between), and GOD would keep them in perfect peace, because they want to obey HIM, and want to trust in HIS WORD. At that same time, the remnant of Judah would be ready to share the truth with others, because they would be like a woman who is pregnant with the truth to full term, ready to give birth, and the righteous gentile would leave from all over the world and go to Africa to learn the truth from them. And as they learn, they would be able to escape the torment of the wrath, while GOD continue to punish all unbelievers by pouring out HIS anger on them. Even on some of "The Chosen Ones" of Israel, who belongs to HIM that refuse to obey.

LEVIATHAN, THE SERPENT
(The god, Satan)
Isaiah 27

In the book of Job, the LEVIATHAN represents GOD, and the behemoth represents man. Here, the "Leviathan" is the fleeing serpent, which is Satan, who is pretending to be GOD, but he is always on the run from punishment. And the reptile at the end of verse one, is the behemoth (which is man) of the sea, and sea is the world. Here, GOD is saying, that HE would destroy Satan, and all the wicked human beings in the world who follow him and praise him.

"The Day of THE LORD" is a period for the wrath of GOD appointed to start during the time of The Roman Empire (which is The Last Days), and it will end in 'The End Times', which is in modern times, after The End time prophecies are completed, and GOD says, "It is done". Whereas The Great Tribulation of The Day of THE LORD is the beginning of the wrath of GOD that will start after Jesus die during the rule of The Roman Empire. It is the time that GOD appointed to use HIS great strength to destroy the satanic system of The Roman Empire world government. At the same time, GOD will kill all the people in the world that serves Satan through the Roman government, and amid the chaos, the gentiles would be able to come to the righteous Negroes of Israel to learn the truth, and when they are taught, they would believe and become fruitful. Then the people of Israel would look beautiful again, and their sins would be forgiven, but their main cities would remain desolate for animals to graze there, and after all the gentiles are taught, GOD would gather the people of Israel that are still captives in ungodly nations, from the

Euphrates River to the Brook of Egypt. Then the trumpet from heaven would be blown, and one by one HIS people would come from the white lands of Assyria, and from Egypt, and other ungodly colored nations to worship HIM in their own land.

Isaiah 28

Woe to the fools in Ephraim, because the tribe of Benjamin, from the Negro people of Israel, are there practicing witchcraft, and worshiping idols with the ungodly white people, and GOD said, HE would destroy those who turned against HIM, but HE would save those who change, and decides to obey.

Can anyone understand what GOD said, and learn from it?

It seems like only the new believers believes what GOD is warning the world about. That is **"The Rest"** that GOD talked about, when HE said, the weary believers would believe and rest from worrying about things they need to live in the flesh and about going to hell. But no one listened, even though they were told what would happen, day by day, and year to year, because they felt they had the spiritual power over those things by themselves.

Symbolisms:
"Adults" - Those are people who were taught the WORD, but are disobedient

"Infants and Babes" – These are new believers in the WORD, who are obeying

That is why GOD promised that HE would send Jesus, The Stone, Who would come from the Negro people of Zion, and Jesus would be precious, because He would be the foundation of all truth, and if anyone believes in what Jesus says, they would not be so quick to do evil, because Jesus would be teaching on justice, and righteousness, and about Satan, and his lies, so that everyone would understand that they do not have to die and go to hell. And Jesus would keep on repeating the same message, so that no one would end up in hell.

So, do not mock anyone, if they tell you those things would happen, unless you have a way of escaping the punishment, because destruction is determined, even upon the whole earth during the wrath of GOD. People must start doing the right things, because GOD is not going to keep on telling people how to act right, and HE is already destroying the wicked, so the righteous ones could flourish and live their lives in peace, and HE would punish HIS Negro people for as long as HE has to, so that none of them would end up in hell.

GOD WILL PREPARE US

The Black Cummin

(A poem about the chosen Negro Israelites):

The black cummin is not threshed with a threshing sledge, nor is a cartwheel rolled over the cummin.

But the black cummin is beaten with a stick, and the cummin comes forth with a rod.

Bread Flour

(A poem about the gentiles of the world):

Bread flour must be grinned.

Therefore, GOD does not thresh it forever.

Which means that GOD does not break it with HIS cartwheel or crush it with HIS horsemen.

Note:

These two poems describe the effort it takes for GOD to break the people of Israel compared to the gentiles for them to believe the truth in the WORD. This also comes from the LORD of Hosts, WHO is wonderful in counsel and excellent in guidance, because HE will smooth off the rough edges to bring us into HIS righteous kingdom.

"Black Cummin" represents the Negro people of GOD that are like the black pepper seed, which needs force to break it. But with too much force the cummin

can slip away without being broken. So, GOD chasten them by beating them with just enough force for them to become what HE wants.

"Bread of Flour" represents the gentile people of all colors and nations in the world that are like the wheat grain that is used to make flour for bread, which is softer than the black cummin, and easier to crush. When GOD chasten them, HE does not have to be as harsh on them like HE has to with the Negro of Israel.

Isaiah 29

Woe to Ariel, the city where David dwelt, because the people of Israel in Ariel would get punished, because they were righteous people in a righteous city, with a righteous king ruling over them, and yet they turned, and are following unrighteousness like the rest of Israel that are being ruled by an unrighteous white man, and for their punishment, they will become useless prophets, and they will hunger, and suffer to the degree they deserve. Just like the rest of the world.

Negro, are you blind?
Pause and wonder!
Blind yourself and be blind!

The Negroes of Israel are drunk, but not with wine, and they are staggering, but not with intoxicating drink, because their GOD poured out on them a spirit of intoxication, and they are in a deep sleep, and HE covered their heads, especially the heads of the seers.

Terms:
"Cover your eyes or heads"- This is a term means that GOD took away your understanding

The whole vision has become to the unbelieving Israelites like they are blind to the truth. Like the words of a book that is sealed, which men deliver to one who can read, saying, "Read this please", and he says, "I cannot read it!", because they are in deep sleep, since GOD closed their eyes, especially the eyes of the prophets. Therefore, GOD said, as much as they draw near to HIM with their mouths, and honor HIM with their lips, they have removed their hearts far from HIM, and they only fear HIM according to the commandment of men, and HE would do a marvelous work amongst them, and a marvelous wonder, and the wisdom of their wise men would perish, and the understanding of the prudent man would be hidden.

Woe to the Negroes of Israel who seek deep to hide their counsel from GOD by their use of sorceries and wizardry to gain their success like the atheist and devil worshippers who are fooling themselves, though they think they are right.

Can they answer these three questions?

1) Shall the potter be esteemed as the clay?

2) Can the thing that was made say to the one who made it "You did not make me?"

3) Shall the thing formed say to HIM who formed it, "HE has no understanding?"

No! That is why Lebanon would be punished. But they would replenish and turn into a fruitful field someday.

Note:

Damascus the capital of Lebanon will be destroyed, because it is ruled by wicked white people, but the country would be renewed, because it is part of the "Promised Land" region that GOD wants the righteous to have.

In those days, many different types of people would believe in the truth, and the meek, and the poor would find joy in GOD, because the wicked white people, and their wicked rulers who rules over the world would be destroyed.

And since the wicked white people are the ones that used the Roman law to unjustly punish, and torture people, when they are destroyed, the Negro people of Israel would not be ashamed of themselves anymore. Nor would they be oppressed. Then everyone in the world would be happy when they see that the wicked white people are gone, and everyone would respect GOD, and praise HIM, and they would also love the Negroes of Israel, because those who erred in truth would come to understanding, and those who believed and were mourning would learn the true doctrine and mourn no more.

Isaiah 30

Woe to the rebellious children of Israel, because they seek counsel from many sources about their sins, but they do not seek it from GOD, since they do not want to change their ways.

Woe to South Africa also, because they would also be punishment, since they are being ruled by wicked white men who are against the native Negroes.

WARNING!

This is a letter to the sinners of the Nigro people of Israel.

The Letter:

This is a rebellious people. Lying children. Children who would not hear the LAW, or the LORD. They are those who say to those with visions, "Please do not see', and to the prophets "Please do not prophesy the right things to us", because they want the prophets to speak to them what they want to hear by prophesying deceits.

P.S.

Since they despise the WORD, and trust in oppression and perversity, and rely on them, this iniquity would be to them like a breach ready to fall, or a bulge in a high wall whose breaking comes suddenly in an instant.

GOD wants to be the strength of Israel, but they will not return to HIM, because they rather say, "No, for we will depend on horses". That is why HE said, they would run, and say their horses are swift, and those who chase them, their horses would be swifter, and HE is waiting on them to come to HIM, so HE could be gracious to them and exalt them and have mercy on them, because HE is a GOD of justice, and everyone who waits for HIM would be blessed. And if they are righteous, they would weep no more, because HE would be very gracious to them at the sound of their cry. And when HE hears their cry, HE would answer them, and though HE allowed trouble to come into their lives, HE would speak to them, and say, "This is the way. Walk in it." Then they would consider their graven images of silver, and their molded images of gold, and say, "Get away", and they would throw them away as unclean things, and HE would bless them abundantly, and cause all that they do to prosper, and tear down the proud for their purpose. Moreover, evil would not even seem like it exists, and the righteous would look even better than before, but that would be only when GOD starts to answer their prayers and heal them of their mental and emotional pains.

Isaiah 31

Woe to the people of Israel who do not trust in GOD, but trust in Egypt.

Terms:

"Those that go to Egypt"- Egypt is symbolic of the world

This phrase is referring to those who seek their provisions by man, evil, or by worldly means rather than by trusting in, or calling on YAH, THE LIVING GOD for it, and since the worldly people are usually successful in finding ways of providing for themselves, they would usually reject GOD, because of this, and they would only call on GOD when they are in big trouble.

By now, the people of Israel should know that the Egyptians are men, and not GOD, and their horses are flesh, and not Spirit, and they should know that when GOD stretch out HIS hands, both he who helped, and he who is helped would fall.

Chapter 32

They should know that The Righteous Kingdom would come, and it would be ruled by righteousness, and those who would not comply with the changes would not prosper in life. And they should know that some of their Negro women are at ease, because they can depend on a male figure in their life, but many of those men are not trusting in GOD, and they would eventually be punished for the ways in which they make their money, and sooner, or later, they would not be able to provide for a woman. Therefore, the women should learn to trust and depend completely on GOD, instead of on men, so when a man cannot give to them, they would still have all they need from GOD.

All women who are at ease by depending on their men should be trembling, and they should be troubled being complacent, and strip themselves, making themselves bare, by putting on sackcloth, secluding themselves in fasting and prayer. And all righteous people should keep on seeking the ALMIGHTY (GOD), until the (HOLY) SPIRIT is poured upon them from above, and they, and the earth would be prosperous again, and justice would dwell in the wilderness, and righteousness in the fields. Which means, there would be peace everywhere.

Definitions:
"Peace"- is the works of righteousness, and the effects of righteousness is quietness and assurance forever.

May our people dwell in peace, and may righteousness be on the earth. Blessed are those who sow besides all water who send out freely the feet of the ox and the donkey.

*** *This term means that those who share the TRUTH and help people of all races and nations to believe the truth would be blessed by GOD with everything, including peace.*

Isaiah 33-35

Woe to the plunderer, the thieves, even though no one steals from them, woe to them anyway, and they better beware, because when a person deals treacherously and steals, it always comes back to them when they get old, or after they become tired of the game. Instead, the thief should fear GOD, and let GOD be exalted, because HE is GREAT, and HE filled Zion with justice and righteousness, and made wisdom and Knowledge the stability of our time, and the strength of salvation.

That is why the fear of the LORD (GOD) is HIS treasure. Therefore, it is certain that everyone would cry like the people of GOD, who are hypocrites, and are sinning, while they are being punished. But the righteous ones would always laugh. For the LORD IS Our JUDGE, Our LAWGIVER, Our KING, and HE IS GOD, and HE will save the righteous from the unrighteous, and the righteous would be rewarded for keeping the faith. Even if they are killed because of it. So, these things will happen during the wrath over many centuries, because GOD is angry against all the nations, and everyone will get punished. Just search the book of THE LORD, and read it, because it said, not one of these prophesies would fail to come to pass.

When GOD is satisfied and ends HIS wrath, then there would be no more barriers, because though the wilderness, and the wastelands were necessary as barriers between the good and the evil nations, in the recreated earth, GOD would remove those barriers, and the wilderness, and the deserts would be filled with beauty and life. That is why GOD told us that HE would make those places rejoice. So, take my word for it, GOD would do as HE promised. Now be strong, and do not be afraid, because if you are righteous, our GOD would come with vengeance on your behalf.

THE HIGHWAY TO HOLINESS

The process of GOD taking HIS vengeance is so that those who do not understand would see and understand and be blind no more, and so that those who do not know would hear and understand and be deaf no more. And it is a process that those who are restricted by Roman laws would be able to walk about freely, and no one would consider them lame anymore. And it is for those who cannot speak out the truth to be able to sing it out loud and be considered mute no more. Because water would burst forth in the wilderness, and streams in the desert, and the highway would be there, a road that would be called "**The Highway to Holiness**", since it would be a highway for the clean, and the unclean cannot pass through it, and whoever walks the road, even if he is a fool, he would not get lost, since there would be nothing, and no one there that could hinder their walk. So, it would be easy for believers to reach GOD, and people would come to the HIM singing, being filled with joy, because there would be no more sorrow, or sighing.

BABYLON IS BOLD
Isaiah 36-37

Time frame – In the 14th year of King Hezekiah, King of Israel

Sennacherib – the King of Assyria

Eliakim – the priest of Israel (son of Hilkiah), also a king of Judah

Shebna – the scribe (records biblical records of the people of Israel)

Joah – the recorder who writes details of the lives and events of the people of Israel

Hezekiah – the king of Judah

One day, Sennacherib, the white king of Assyria, went to conquer the fortified (strongest) cities of the tribe of Judah, and he sent an army with Rabshakeh (a chief) to boldly ask Hezekiah (the king of Judah), who did he trust in so much for him to say that he had the understanding, and the strength for war, because he think that what he is saying are vain words, and he wants to know who does he trust, because it looks like he trusted in the law of the world, on which if a man depends on it, it would cause him harm, and if he says he trusted in GOD, then he wants to know if they did not already turn from HIM. Then with boldness, the Babylonians go to Hezekiah and read the letter. Afterward, they boast on, and on, about how GOD gave them the power to overcome Judah, and there is nothing they could do about it.

Facts:
Who speaks what?
Hebrew - spoken by the Negro people of Israel
Aramaic - spoken by the white people of Babylonian
Both people learned each other's language during the Babylonian captivity

Then Eliakim, Shebna, and Joah asks them to please speak to them in the Aramaic language, because they understood it, and not to speak to them in their own Hebrew language in the hearing of their people, who are on the wall, who the Babylonians placed in charge over them. But, ignoring their request, the Babylonians loudly said in Hebrew, "Hear what the great king of Assyria has to say, and do not let Hezekiah deceive you, because he would not be able to deliver you. Nor should you let him persuade you to trust in your GOD by saying your GOD would help you, because the city would be captured by the Assyrians. But after you are captured, the king of Assyria wants you to make peace with him, and you can buy a present to give him as a gift, and you can stay in your own land, and work for yourselves, and provide your own food and drink, until we come to take you to another land, which is blessed like your own. So, you better not let Hezekiah tell you that your GOD would save you, because no other gods of any other nations had been able to save themselves from the king of Assyria."

After hearing what the white men said, Eliakim, Shebna, and Joah goes to Hezekiah, the king, and in great sorrow, they tell him what they heard.

And Hezekiah tear his clothes and goes into The House of THE LORD and fast and pray, pleading with GOD for help, and because of the boasting, and blasphemy of the Babylonians, GOD tells him not to worry, because HE would cause the Babylonians to destroy themselves in the battle. Meanwhile, as GOD assures Hezekiah of the victory, Tirhakah, the king of Ethiopia, sends a message to Hezekiah, stating that he is deceiving himself to think that the Assyrians would not conquer them. And when Hezikiah heard what the letter said, he goes back to The House of THE LORD to fast and pray, and he plead with GOD for Israel to be delivered from the Babylonians, and GOD gives Isaiah, the son of Amos, a message to give to him to let him know that his prayers were answered.

The Message:
To Hezekiah.

Israel will defeat the Babylonians and would be blessed in abundance for the coming years, while you are still alive.

When Hezekiah received the message and read it, as soon as he read it, GOD sends angel to kill off the Assyrians soldiers, and they killed 185,000 that day. But Sennacherib, the Assyrian king escaped and returned to his home in Ninevah. Then one day, while he is worshipping his false god, his sons, Adrammelech and Sharezer kills him with a sword, and run to the land of Ararat, and his son, Esarhaddon, reign next in his place.

Terms:
Ninevah - this is an urban city in Africa with a mixed culture of people
Ararat - this is a mountain in N.E. Europe in the white nation of Turkey

Chapter 38

Shortly after that victory, Hezekiah gets sick, and GOD sends Isaiah to tell him that he needs to make some correction to his household before he dies. When Isaiah goes to him, and tell him what GOD said, he turns his face towards the wall, and weep in prayer, because he had been trying to follow the LAW, and wants more time to make more changes for the people of Judah. And because of his earnest prayer, GOD tell Isaiah to go back and tell him that he would recover to live for fifteen more years, and HE promise that the Assyrians would not defeat them, and HE would give him a sign for him to believe. Immediately, Isaiah goes back to Hezekiah and tell him that GOD said he would recover, and he would defeat the Assyrians, and HE would give him a sign by turning time backwards for him to believe. Right then, for the sign, even though it is dark in the night, time goes backwards, and a shadow is cast on the sundial after the sun went down, as if it was daytime. Then Isaiah tells some men to place some figs on Hezekiah's boil for him to recover.

What Hezekiah Plead:

In the prime of my life, I am about to die, and I am deprived of the remainders of my years and would not see you in the land of the living or anyone else anymore. Now my life span is gone, because it had been taken from me, and I wonder about my sickness all day and night, and I am begging YOU to help me to recover. And O' LORD, I know that I am sick, because I became bitter, but I am asking that YOU recover me and not let me die.

That is what Hezekiah was pleading for while he was sick, and was wondering if he would ever recover.

Chapter 39

When Merodach-Baladan, the son of Baladan, the king of Babylon, heard that Hezekiah was sick, he sent a letter with presents to him, and because he was pleased with the gesture, he invited Merodach-Baladan to come take a tour of his house. Once Merodach-Baladan gets there with his men, Hezekiah shows them all his possessions of precious things, and even the armory, and the spices. That day, Isaiah goes there, and Merodach

- Baladan and his men are still there, and Isaiah asks Hezekiah who they are, what did they see, and where are they from. Hezekiah answers, and said, "They came to me from a far country called Babylon." Then Isaiah question him about what they saw, and he said, they saw everything, and Isaiah tell him that all the things in the house that were acquired over generations would be taken away, because the same Babylonians he trusted would come and plunder Israel and take many of the children and turn them into eunuchs to serve their kings. Yet, Hezekiah tells Isaiah that whatever the LORD tells him to say is good, because at least there would be peace and truth in his days.

Isaiah 40

Then Isaiah leaves, and Hezekiah continue to pray, and he realize that GOD allowed him to be sick for him to see his bitterness, and he knows that GOD would heal him and keep him from death, and save his soul from hell, since he cannot praise HIM while he is dead, because only the living on the earth can praise HIM, as he is doing on that day. Then he speaks comfort for Jerusalem and cry out to her, and he asks GOD to forgive her for her sins, and to give her peace, because Jerusalem would receive for her sins double the punishment from HIM. At that moment, he thinks on the order of things that would happen according to the scriptures.

First John, the Baptist will come:

That means there is much hope, because the voice of John, The Baptist, would be crying out in the wilderness saying, "Prepare the way of the Lord (Jesus, The Messiah), and make straight in the desert and the highway that leads to our GOD (The FATHER), because all the lowly shall be exalted, and all the proud shall be made low. Then all confusion would be cleared up, and things would become easy, because the glory of the LORD, GOD, would be revealed through Jesus, The Messiah, and all flesh would see it together, because GOD said it would happen. Therefore, we should cry out with joy, because all flesh, and all loveliness would wither away like grass, but the

WORD of GOD stands forever, and though everyone is using idols, and are calling on false gods, there is only one GOD."

Then Jesus will come:

In knowing this, all the righteous Negroes must get up and shout out to the world the good news, and say, "O people of Israel, shout out, and do not be afraid to say to all your people, behold your God (Jesus), because many people (of flesh) could not accept a GOD (of spirit), since they cannot see HIM, and GOD HIMSELF, promised that HE would send Jesus (in the flesh) to represent HIM on the earth, so that many people could accept Jesus (The Christ). But GOD said, they would be fooling themselves, if they think that Jesus would accept them on any other terms, other than that of the FATHER (GOD)." For when Jesus come, He would require people to obey the LAW, and the righteous would carry out His TRUTH, and perform the works that He did once they live by the LAW. That's right! Jesus would live by the LAW for the righteous kingdom to come, and He would bring Israel back to serving GOD in truth and in praise, and since GOD did not need any help in HIS creation, and there is no spirit which can convince GOD of their plan, GOD would not take any counsel from anyone, because it is HE WHO made justice, and wisdom, and no one can understand HIM. And since the world is a small thing to GOD, then tell me who can make an image of HIM?

DID YOU EVER HEAR ABOUT GOD?

Do you know GOD?

If you never heard of GOD, then HE is THE ONE sitting above the earth, and to HIM we are as small as grasshoppers, and HE is the one who made the heavens and the earth, and HE will take royalties from their thrones, and HE will judge the judges as being guilty, and HE will never allow an unrighteous person to be at ease, because eventually, HE would allow them to wither away.

So, who else can be GOD?

No one! That is why those who wait on THE LORD would renew their strength and mount up with wings like eagles. They would run and not get weary, and they would walk and not faint. That's right! The righteous are strong, and prosperous, and they will endure to the end of their lives, because they live the righteous life without losing faith.

Isaiah 41

So shut up all you traders!

Which one of you can contend with GOD?

Who started it all?

It was GOD WHO started it, and HE would finish it, because everyone makes idols and worship false gods, and tell each other to have a good life, but the people of Israel are GOD's servants, and they must not do as the others, because they are descendants of Abraham, who was GOD's friend, and GOD chose them to live in The Promised Land region (The Gaza Strip), and HE never did stop loving them. Therefore, as righteous people, they should not be afraid, or confused, because GOD is with them, and HE would strengthen them, and use righteousness to defeat the wicked. Then all the black magic and the witchcraft that the wicked cast against the righteous would fail, which would cause those who practice those things to perish by their own works. GOD is their right hand, and HE would help them, and they must stop being afraid, because when they seek righteousness, GOD is there, and HE is the GOD of Israel WHO would hear the righteous when they call, and HE would open doors for them, and make them prosperous, and all the black magic and witchcraft that was cast against them will fail. Then the world would know and understand that GOD has done all things for them.

GOD is angry. So, HE tells the nations to present their case, and the people of the nations asked HIM, what case does HE have against them, and HE tell them to tell HIM the past, and the future, so maybe the world would consider them to be gods. That is, if they could make good things happen, or perhaps make bad things happen for the world to see and be amazed. But since they are all nothing, but fakes, and they cannot perform any miracles, those who trust in them are idiots, and are an abomination to the one and only GOD.

Terms:

"I have raised up one from the north and He shall come" - The "North" is heaven (in this case), and He is Jesus

"And He shall come on behalf of GOD to punish Israel for their sins - This He would be Jesus

**** When this happens, Israel and the whole world will be getting a physical correction from the north, which from Europeans in The Roman Empire, but when Jesus comes from the north, which is heaven, Israel and the whole world will get a spiritual correction from the north, which is The Kingdom of GOD in heaven.*

First, when Jesus comes, GOD will teach Him with heavenly wisdom. Then when Jesus is grown, He would be meek, but He would be strong, and He would use His authority to overcome those things that are contrary to the truth. Because it was declared from the beginning that Jesus would be righteous, and His righteousness would condemn the wicked people of their acts. It was also declared that Jesus would come from the righteous Negro people of Israel, through the dark-skin tribe of Judah, the tribe of David, because there is no one in the world, even amongst the righteous Negroes of Israel that can answer any question concerning the truth, since they are all vanity, and their works are nothing. Which means that their molten images are useless to them and cause them confusion.

JESUS IS THE MESSIAH
Isaiah 42

People would get to see Jesus, the servant of GOD, the one that GOD would be delighted in. And GOD would put HIS SPIRIT in Jesus, and Jesus would bring forth justice to the gentiles, because He would not yell out, or raise His voice in the streets to teach. His lifestyle would be His quiet way of teaching, and He would not destroy the last hope of someone, nor try to prove the truth by debating with another over the doctrine of men. And He would establish justice on the earth, and the gentile on the coast of Africa would wait for Him to teach them the LAW, because GOD called Him to righteousness, and GOD would guide Him through His mission, and protect Him, and give Him as a covenant to the people, so that He would be a perfect example to bring the gentile to belief. Then those who are blind by the lies would see and come to understanding, and those who are prisoners to false doctrines would be set free by the truth. Because YAH is the GOD of Israel, and RIGHTEOUS is HIS name, and HE would not give HIS glory to others, nor give HIS praise to graven images, and HE would tell you anything new before it happens, and would fight your enemies, and defeat them for you.

Listen, all of you that act deaf and like you cannot hear and look all of you that act blind and like you cannot see, and maybe you would see or hear something that you could understand.

Who is blind, but GOD's servants, the people of Israel?

Or who is as deaf as the prophets, whom HE sent?

The servants of GOD are acting like they are perfect, but they are blind. Because though they had many visions, they did not look to see them come to pass, and they had the truth, but they did not obey it. So, GOD is pleased with how HE is about to punish them for the sake of the few righteous ones there, and because GOD will not bypass the LAW, HE would punish those who do not obey it. Therefore, since unrighteous people rob and plunder righteous people, and righteous people are placed in prison, because of injustice, and are always preys that no one helps, nor does anyone ever return what was stolen from them, GOD is coming with justice.

Isaiah 43

Now do you know who created you, Jacob?

It was GOD, through the lineage of Adam (see Genesis genealogy of Adam).

Facts:

Jacob is Israel, and he is the Negro that started The Nation of Israel, and his descendants are the people of Israel who GOD calls "The Chosen Ones".

The Negroes of Israel should never fear anyone, because GOD redeemed them, and HE is calling them by their names, because they are HIS children, and when trouble comes, HE would be with them, since HE is their GOD, and HE would also save them for they are precious in HIS sight, and HE loves them. That is why HE honored them, and HE would make others have pleasure in serving them, because they are righteous as HE is. And HE promised that HE would bring all the righteous ones from out of any bondage they are in, and HE would make the pathway to bring them back to "The Holy Land" where they would be in the presence of all righteousness.

ISRAEL IS THE CHOSEN ONES

It's true.

The Israelites are the Negro people of the lineage of the Negro man, Jacob, who is through the linage of a Negro man named Isaac, who is through the lineage of a Negro man named Abraham, and they are the chosen people of GOD. Bring the blind who believes in the lies, who think they can see what is happening, and bring the deaf that believe in the lies, who think they can hear and understand the truth. Now gather them all together, and see if they can tell the past, or the future, and let them bring out their witnesses to justify that they are the chosen people of YAH. Let any others nation, or race say they are The Chosen Ones, and that it is true, and that GOD declared them as HIS witnesses, and servants, but do not believe them. Even if they say they believe that YAH is the CREATOR, and HE is the GOD WHO created the heaven and the earth. The Negro Israelites are the chosen people of GOD! They are GOD's witnesses, and HIS servants, whom HE chose to tell that before any other gods, HE is the only GOD, and there would be none after HIM, because HE is the only one that can save them, since no one can defeat HIM. Therefore, the people of Israel need to acknowledge YAH as their GOD, because HE would defeat the wicked white people for their sake.

YAH is the GOD of the Negro people of Israel. HE is their CREATOR, their KING, and THE HOLY ONE, WHO would destroy the wicked white people, and their unjust government for their sake, and for the sake of the rest of the world. Therefore, the people of Israel must stop thinking about what the wicked white people are doing to them, or about what they did in the past, because GOD said, HE would do a new thing that would confuse the white men and cause them to be defeated. Yes, GOD said, HE would do a new thing, and the Babylon system of injustice and unrighteousness would be destroyed, and things would change for the better, that even the animals would give honor to HIM, because the deserts, and the wildernesses would flourish, and the world would be nice to live in.

Yet, even with all that the people of Israel know, because of the system of things during the time of The Roman Empire, and because of the lies the Romans are infusing in everyone's mind, they still will not pray to GOD, or praise and commune with HIM. Instead, they are sinning, and it is making GOD weary. But if they turn to HIM, they will see that HE had already forgiven them of their sins. Therefore, HE wants them to come, and state their case, so they could be acquitted, because it was their forefathers that taught them how to sin and their people turned from HIM, and in their time, it is because all the leaders of their churches are profane, and they are causing the dark skinned tribe of Judah to be cursed, and all the Negro people of Israel to be a reproach.

The message that GOD wants them to hear is this. Whether they are of The Government of Judah, or of The Government of Israel, no matter if they are black skinned, dark brown skin, light brown skin , red skin, yellow skin, or white skinned, and no matter if they have nappy hair, curly hair, or straight hair, or have brown eyes, hazel eyes, green eyes, or even blue eyes, HE wants them to know that because HE created them, HE would help them, and they should not be afraid, because all they have to do is seek HIM.

GOD forgave the sins of Israel:

1. GOD will acquit the people of Israel of all the charges against them, because not even their forefathers were able to follow the LAW completely, because of the injustice and unrighteousness that was in the government.

2. GOD will not let the chosen people sin forever, and HE will curse them so that they would turn from sinning and be a blessing to the world again.

3. For the sake of righteousness, GOD will let HIS Negro people be the scorn of the earth for a while, but HE would redeem them, so they will be glorified for eternity.

CONSIDER YOUR GOD
Isaiah 44

Who would help the Negro people of Israel?

Fear not. GOD, THE KING of Israel, THE REDEEMER said, HE would help them, because they are HIS servants that HE chose, and HE would pour out HIS SPIRIT to help them in all things. Therefore, they should be glad to call HIM their GOD, and HE would bless any of them who seek HIM, and HE would bless their descendants, and their offspring, and they would be proud to be Negroes, and proud to be believers in HIM, because HE is the first GOD (the Alpha), and the last GOD (the Omega), and there is no other gods besides HIM.

If anyone think they can predict a thing like GOD can, then let them ask their idol, and predict it, and see if it comes true like when GOD predicts a thing. They cannot predict the future! Nor can any other spirit. Therefore, those who makes and worship images can see that they are useless, because their images cannot predict anything, but they are ashamed to say so.

So, who would worship a molten image that does nothing for them?

Surely, everyone who makes and worship idols should be ashamed, because even when they get together, they are still afraid, and the blacksmith should be ashamed too, because he carefully makes the idols, and yet at the end of the day, he is still hungry. Just like the craftsman that takes time to plant the tree to cut it down to craft his image to bow down before it, and worship it, even though he uses some of the wood to burn for warming himself, and some of it for cooking.

Idolatry is foolishness, and people do not know or understand things, because GOD keeps them ignorant, since they are worshipping idols, which are made by workmen, and craftsmen, as if they cannot see that it is pure foolishness.

"Shall a person bow down to a block of wood, or to a molded image when it does not understand, or have any knowledge?"

Can't people see that they burned half the wood for their use, and yet they bow dawn to the other half that they carved into an image?

Can't they see that if their god turned to ashes when it was burned, it cannot deliver them?

Remember this people of Israel. GOD made you, and you are HIS servants, and HE would never forget you. That is why HE forgave you for all your sins and is ready for you to return to HIM. So, believe it, and let all those in heaven, and on earth rejoice, and even in hell, because GOD is in control, and HE can make everyone who predicts something other than what HE said, look like idiots, because HE is telling everyone that HE is THE SHEPHERD over the Negroes that are governed by Israel, and HE is over those governed by Jerusalem, and for certain, the temple that was destroyed would be rebuilt.

Isaiah 45

There is only one GOD!

There is no other GOD!

Only YAH, the GOD of Israel is GOD.

Though GOD allowed Cyrus, and all the other white kings to come to Africa to take away the best people, HE said, HE would reverse the way things are going and give them the treasures that the wicked white folks gained by doing evil to them, because HE is GOD, and they are HIS. So, HE feels sorry for those who do not like belonging to their righteous Negro heritage, and HE also feel sorry for the ones that wish they are of some other race or wish they were never born.

Go ahead, and ask GOD about the Negro people, or about anything that was made on the earth, because GOD made the heavens and the earth by wisdom, and HE is guiding the Negro people of Israel, and HE is using them to build HIS city, so the colored people of the unrighteous nations of Egypt, Cush (Ethiopia), and the Sabeans would flee from all their white captives and come to live in righteousness with them. That is why Israel would be saved, because GOD wants to make the white people confounded when they see that all the people of color are taken out of their control. GOD did not create the Earth in vain, HE created it to be inhabited. And HE did not create the Negro people to follow righteousness in vain, because HE created them, so that HE has a reason to get rid of wicked white people. Then those who escaped the lies of the white man can get together and talk about their life experiences.

Wasn't it as GOD predicted?

Wasn't it just as the prophets said?

Didn't the white man treat you badly by using their power through the government?

Sure, it was what GOD predicted and what the prophets said. The white men do treat every colored nation badly by using the government. Therefore, colored people should look to GOD, because HE alone is GOD, and every knee would bow to HIM in reverence, or in fear, because in GOD, all the Negro people of Israel would be justified, and they will shine.

Isaiah 46

The people of Israel had been worried about the heathens burdening the beast to carry their idols around, even though their idols (Bel, Nebo, etc.) cannot walk, or stand, and they fall as they are carried about in their carriages, because they have no life in them. So, they cannot do anything, even if people worship them. Therefore, the people of Israel should listen, because GOD had been begging them to trust HIM, since HE kept them from birth, and would keep on keeping them, and deliver them, and they should give up the idols, since they cannot help them, because there is only one GOD.

That was why GOD asked them, who do people compare HIM to, and who did they make equal to HIM, or did they compare HIM to someone they said

HE was like, because it is like they do not know that things made are all idols. Since they are made from gold, wood, or other metals, and are carried around and worshipped, even though they cannot answer, nor save someone out of trouble. The Negroes of Israel should act like human beings, and remember that idols cannot do anything for them, and they should remember that in the past GOD punished idol worshippers, and HE would always punish them, because HE is GOD, and there is no one like HIM, and HE would do all that HE proclaimed HE would do. This is why all stubborn and unrighteous people should be listening, because GOD said HE would get rid of them, and their wickedness, and establish righteousness for HIS people, as well as for all the righteous people in the world. Then the righteous Negroes of Israel would be glorified, and it would happen soon.

Isaiah 47

Let all the white people cry, since they would no longer be considered prestigious, because GOD wants them to start doing some work for themselves, and stop pretending like they are The Chosen Ones, because HE is YAH, the GOD of Israel, and HE is ready to take vengeance on them, and HE wants them to be astonished, and shut their mouths, since they would no longer be in charge, because when HE was angry with HIS people, HE gave them over to their white nations, but they showed no mercy. Even the elderly they worked hard, and all of them puffed up themselves with pride as they practice their sorcery, and enchantments, and they go around saying, they are the greatest, and their children would not suffer any loss. Therefore, since they treat the righteous Negro people bad and they practice false worship, and are puffed up in pride, GOD said, HE would take power from them, and removed all the colored people from amongst them, and make them suffer the losses of their children, so they would know that HE did it.

Though the wicked white folks are trusting in their wickedness, and are saying no one sees what they are doing, and though they believe that they are the only ones that matters in the world, GOD is watching, and one day, suddenly, evil would come upon them, and they would lose everything they took from the colored people by use of their evil practices of sorcery, witchcraft, enchantments, etc. This the wicked white people know, and they are afraid. So, they are consulting their sorcerers, enchanters, astrologers, stargazers, and any wicked counselors they had been consulting since their youth, to find out how to prevent the evil coming to them from GOD. They are also weary and confounded, because they cannot find a way to prevent the evil that is coming to them. So, they keep on seeking answers from their wicked counselors to find a way to save themselves, and for centuries now, they had been seeking answers from their evil counselors, but no matter what, they would end up like stubbles in the fire, because they cannot save themselves.

That's it. That is what GOD said HE would do to the wicked white people, the ones that all the colored people worked for, ever since their youth, and when it happens, none of the colored people would care that it happened to them.

Isaiah 48

Still, the Negro people of Israel are being hypocrites, and they should listen, because they call themselves the children of GOD, and they pray to HIM daily, but they do not live in truth, or in righteousness, and even though they call themselves holy, and say they trust GOD, since they lived in The Holy Land, they are acting like they do not see that GOD is already punishing the white folks for their wicked ways, like HE promised, because they want to be like the white folks. So, even though they heard from the prophets over, and over again, they refuse to believe. But since GOD promised that HE would punish the wicked white people for their sins, HE is doing it, and HE does not want anyone to say that it was an idol that predicted it, because they heard about it, and are seeing it, and it is a new way of saving them by turning HIS anger from them to punish the white people that had been harsh leaders over them and all the colored people in the world. For HIS name's sake, GOD is doing it. Just like HE punished HE would do to the white folks for idol worship, and HE is also punishing Israel for their idol worship to refine them, so that HIS name would not be profaned, and so that no one, or nothing else would be praised.

Israel must listen, because YAH is their GOD, and HE is the only GOD, and HE made the heavens and the earth, and HE is still in control, and HE wants every nation to get together and consider which of them could have thought that HE loves the Negro people of Israel so much. That's right. GOD loves HIS Negro people of Israel, and HE is punishing the white people for causing them to suffer, so that they could prosper again. Now, if you are a Negro, then believe it, and draw close to GOD, since it is no secret to you anymore, because GOD promised that HE would tell you how to live life, and how to become a success, and HE promised HE would guide you the whole time.

Wow!

Only if the Negro people of Israel had been doing what GOD said, they would had been such a good example of righteousness and peace, and they would have been very numerous and blessed. They should have left the wicked white people to themselves, and run from all the pagans with joy, screaming out to the world that the GOD of Israel redeemed HIS people, since they did not thirst when HE led them through the wilderness, which proved that HE loves them, and for certain HE would take vengeance on the wicked white people for their sake. Therefore, there would be no peace for the wicked.

Isaiah 49

Listen gentile people of color, and gentile white people from afar. Take heed and realize that GOD chose the Negro people of Israel first, and HE gave them the WORD to preach and live by, and HE protects and strengthens them, and call them HIS servants, and they try to be a good example to glorify HIM, but after a while they felt they were wasting their time obeying HIM. And the GOD that created them begged them to obey HIM again, and HE promised them that any of the righteous ones of them that comes to HIM, even though the unrighteous ones are not serving HIM, if they continue to serve HIM, HE will strengthen them, and glorifies them, because it is an easy thing to be HIS servant. Therefore, the righteous ones try to convince the unrighteous ones of Israel to do the same things they do, so that all the people of Israel would be blessed and would be an example to the gentiles for them to also be saved and be blessed.

All the Negroes people of Israel who believes and obey knows that GOD said that, even though HE allowed people to hate and despise them, HE is their redeemer, THE HOLY ONE of Israel, and HE is using them to cause others to believe in HIM, and HE heard them crying out, and HE is helping them to show the gentiles how to also be saved, so when the wicked white folks are destroyed, their land could be divided amongst all the gentiles. Then HE would make a way through the mountains and the deserts for the gentiles to come from Europe, Syria, and Assyria to get the land of the wicked white folks in Africa to live in. And at that time, all the Negroes of Israel would leave the white nations and return to their native home in Africa to live in their own land, because HE wants everything on earth, and in the heavens to sing when HE comforts HIS people by HIS promises and is having mercy on them. Yet, they think that HE forgot about them.

Can a woman forget about her babies and not have compassion on them?

Yea, a woman may forget about her children, but GOD would never forget about HIS children, because HE wrote everyone's name in the palm of HIS hands as a reminder of them, and HE promised that the white folks would be taken from The Promised Land, and all the captives of Israel in the white lands would return to their native land. Then they would greatly multiply, and be happy, and all the gentile believers would also be happy, and they would praise the Negro people of Israel for showing them the way to get saved, because all those who remain would know that GOD is GOD, whether they are dark, light, or white skinned, and they would not be ashamed anymore.

Do you think that the righteous should be saved from the wicked?

Of course, yes! GOD said, all of them should be saved, because

HE fights against all those who are ungodly, and HE would kill them all, so all the other people could live a good life.

Isaiah 50

Where are the divorce papers that GOD gave to Israel for the reason, HE got rid of her, and who did HE lose her to, to pay a debt?

There are no divorce papers. GOD did not lose Israel to pay any debt. It was because they sinned and repeatedly transgressed HIS LAW and committed all kinds of abominations in the land, why they lost everything. You see, when GOD visited them, no one took time to see HIM, and when HE called to them, no one answered HIM, and HE wondered if they thought HE could not help them, even though they know of all HIS power. But not the righteous ones, because GOD made them wise, so they could tell others what to do in times of trouble, and every day, HE speaks to the righteous, and tells them what to do, and they listen, and obey HIM, and people hate them, and mock them, but they do not stop listening to THE ALMIGHTY GOD, and they are not ashamed, because they would keep obeying the words of GOD, and if GOD is on their side, then who is willing to contend against them.

Why don't all us believers get together and see who would be willing to fight against us?

Surely GOD will help the righteous person.

So, who would be willing to fight that person when they know that they would be defeated?

No one is willing to contend with a true believer, because everyone gets scared of GOD. That means, no witch, no law, or spirit will contend with the true believers. Therefore, if you fear GOD, and obey HIS WORD, or if you are sinning, and would like to stop, then you must trust in the WORD of GOD, and rely on HIM for everything. But if you do not want anything to do with GOD, and you want to keep worshipping idols and practice witchcraft, then you would suffer with all the torment in your life.

Isaiah 51

Listen to me Negroes of Israel around the world who follow righteousness. Those of you who are seeking GOD must look to YAH, the GOD that made you, and you must search for the truth of your inheritance, and seek the people who practice **"That Old Time Religion"**, which was taught by Abraham to his descendants in Africa, because YAH, GOD, would comfort all of you, and beautify the place, that even the deserts, and the wilderness would be like a flowered garden, and everyone would be happy while giving HIM praise.

Listen to me Negro people of Israel and all you different kinds of people in Africa. GOD said it, and you can be comforted by it, since HIS righteousness is near, and HE had already started HIS punishment on the wicked white people, which every colored nation is waiting to see the end of. Look up to heaven, and see what the earth is like, because things would be totally different from how they are now when the wicked are gone, and righteousness is ruling.

Listen to me all of you who know how to be righteous, and all of you that know the LAW. Please do not be afraid of what people are doing, or what they say they would do to you, because GOD would kill them all, and they would go to hell. GOD would always protect you. So, say it, "Finish them off! Finish them off my GOD, and show YOUR power, as YOU did in the old days, because YOU are the GOD that killed off the people of Rahab for their idol worship, and YOU are the one that dried up the Red Sea, so the people of Israel could pass over. Yes, YOU are. YOU are the only GOD, and YOU would do what YOU say, and YOU said, the Negro people of Israel would return from their captive lands in white nations and return to Zion (in Africa) with singing, and they would be happy, and they would no longer be crying." Now since they know this, they must remember that they knew it would happen, and they should not be afraid of the wicked white people, because YOU, said YOU would kill them all.

Why would the people of Israel let the oppressors make them forget about the GOD WHO made the heavens and the earth, and then they live in fear every day?

What can the wicked white man do to you?

O' my GOD, believe it or not, the wicked white people can do a lot of wickedness. But things are certain to happen like GOD said. Meanwhile, the Negro captives of Israel in the white lands are wishing they could be freed soon, because they are starving to death, and they know that the prophets said, the LORD, their GOD that divided the Red Sea for them to inherit The Land of Canaan (The Promised Land), said, HE would free them. Therefore, whichever one of them, who does not believe it, better believe it, and get up out of their depression over how bad things are now, because none of their tribes taught the truth to each other, nor did they stick together, and it caused ignorance and division to come upon them.

Who should feel sorry for them, now that desolation, destruction, famine, and death are all around them, and no one can comfort the next, and all the men are weary, as they hang around in the streets and act wild in the neighborhood, being angry at GOD, because of the oppression of the white man.?

Listen, all you angry, hurting Negroes, YAH, your GOD, understands your afflictions, and HE is no longer angry with you, and HE would not let things go on like that forever, because HE would punish the wicked white people, and everyone else that caused you problems, and used you as a door mat, the ground, or the street to walk upon.

Isaiah 52

Awake! Awake to the truth!

Be strong, Negro people of Zion.

Put on your beautiful garments, O Jerusalem, The Holy City.

For no longer shall the unrighteous live with the righteous in Jerusalem.

Just like how the people of Israel sold themselves for nothing, GOD said HE would redeem them without money, because as they settled in The Promised Land, after being freed from the Egyptians, the Assyrians white people oppressed them for no reason.

Should the people of Israel had been taken away for nothing?

"No."

Yet, they are crying out every day, and it is making GOD look like nothing, and HE promised that they would know that HE exists after HE completely free them from their oppressors. Therefore, it is a beautiful thing when someone come to tell them about the good life that GOD planned for the righteous, a time when there would not be any need to watch out for any attacks, and people would be happy, and joyful when everyone see the salvation (saving power) of GOD. Therefore, the Negroes of Israel must leave from amongst the wicked white people, and stop touching unclean thing, and be clean, because they are the vessel of GOD, and they do not have to sneak, or leave in haste, because GOD would set up the way, and HE would make sure they get through, and since many types of people were happy to see them looking scraggly and ugly, GOD would make sure people see it happen, even though they did not know that it was prophesied. Then they would shut their mouths.

ARE THERE ANY BELIEVERS?
Isaiah 53

"Who believed that GOD would redeem Israel?"

"To whom, did GOD reveal this secret to?"

GOD revealed it to those who obeyed, and HE decided to send Jesus to live the life, so that none of us would have an excuse for why we do not know.

Jesus the Savior:

For Jesus shall grow up before GOD as a tender plant which came up out of dry ground, and He would not be boastful, because He would be gentle, and meek, and the people of Israel would get to see Him. But when they see Him, He would not be to their desire, and they would not like Him. Therefore, the people of Israel would despise, and reject Him, and because they would be refusing the truth, He would feel grief.

Yes, that's right. It was prophesied that Israel would truly hate and reject Jesus, their Savior, and Jesus would grieve, and be filled with sorrow as they turn from the truth that He teaches, because no one wants to be like Him. Yet, He would still feel sorry for them, and He would want things to change. But they would want to kill Him, and GOD would want Jesus to be cursed, because all the people went astray by worshipping idols and false gods, and GOD would let Jesus suffer for their sins, instead of them. Therefore, Jesus would be oppressed and afflicted, and yet He would not say anything, and He would be innocent when they take Him to kill Him, and they would place Him in prison, and would not give Him justice in court, and would kill Him before He has any children.

Jesus is going to hell:

After Jesus dies, He would go to hell, where the evil and unrighteous people belong, even though He did no violence, and there was no deceit in Him. And everyone who died before him would be down there in hell, since the price for salvation had not been paid yet, and it would please GOD when Jesus' soul is made as an offering for sin.

Jesus is the perfect Lamb:

While Jesus is in the bottomless pit, in the grave of hell, He would see His Negro people, as well as all the people in the world of every race, and every nation, and all the government officials that had died from the beginning of time, since Adam to the two thieves on the cross who died with Him. Then He would preach to everyone down there about the truth and about the resurrection of life after death, and many of them would believe and walk out of hell, and walk about on the earth, and people that knew them would recognize them. Then they would resurrect to heaven. Meanwhile, Jesus would be walk with, and speak with other people, and He would eat with them, and then go up to heaven to eternal life to live with all the resurrected ones who are the children of GOD, which will include those who believed, and resurrected from hell. This would be by 33 A.D., and from heaven, Jesus and the resurrected righteous ones would work on the plan for the righteous kingdom that would come to the earth. At this time, Jesus would understand the reason why He had to suffer so much in life, and He would be happy that He died for His Negro people, and for all the righteous people in the world, because after He obeys GOD, and redeem the world, He would be great. Then He would gain many followers for living a perfect life until He died, and for going to hell as a sinner, so that we do not have to.

Isaiah 54

The barren are the Negro believers in the world, which seems like they are foolish for holding on to the faith, and they are scorned, and are told to give up on GOD. But GOD said sing. Sing you righteous Negroes who are not successful in the world, because there are more mixed colored people than there are Negroes, and combined, there are more people of color than there are whites, and GOD said, HE would make room for everyone of color, because the biracial believers are considered as part of Israel. That is why HE said, HE would give them the lands where the white people live after HE kills them all. So, sing, all you colored people, because you would gain it all in the end. Do not be afraid or feel confounded. Shut up, and let the wicked white people gain more lands, so all the righteous colored people could gain it in the end, because when it happens, the Negroes of Israel would not feel ashamed like when they thought they had no GOD, since by this time, they would know that GOD made them, and HE is with them, and HE is their redeemer, THE HOLY ONE, the GOD of the whole earth that shows HIS love for them, even after they rejected HIM.

It would only be for a short time that GOD turns HIS back on HIS people of Israel, by letting the white people take them as captives to their white lands, because HE promised that HE would bring them out of captivity to bless them in their native land, even though in HIS anger HE stopped helping them for a moment. And HE promised that HE would have mercy on them from then on. Just like how HE promised Noah that HE would never flood the whole earth again. Which HE is doing by reminding the world of it by randomly showing a rainbow. So, even though everything may change, GOD would never stop having mercy on the Isreal again, and even though they are afflicted, HE would pour out HIS kindness on them, and they would be rich again with much land, and they would know about HIM and live in peace, because they would be established in righteousness. Therefore, if they are believing, then they would never fear the terror of the white people, because they would not be able to do anything to them, and even when the white people gather together to fight them, they would never succeed, because no weapons formed against the believers of the people of GOD shall prosper, and everyone that speak negative against them shall be condemned, since they are the heritage of GOD, and they are righteous like HIM.

Isaiah 55

Now, all of you who are seeking THE LIVING GOD, come! Even if you have no money still come to eat and drink freely.

Why spend money on false doctrines?
And why work so hard, and still not be satisfied?

The witches and warlocks cannot tell you truth. The doctors do not know the body. Working hard will make you sick. Sickness will break you and kill you. Only GOD, THE ALMIGHTY knows all and can help. Negroes of Israel, listening carefully, and turn to your GOD, and live, and HE would be merciful to you. You must believe that your Negro Jewish people are a witness that the world would learn righteousness from, and other Negroes, and biracial people would believe GOD, because of you. You must seek after GOD while He can be found, and you must pray to HIM, while HE is near, and the wicked ones should stop doing wickedness, and the unrighteous ones should stop thinking bad things, and start obeying GOD, because GOD said, HE would have mercy on them, and pardon them, since HE does not think, or act like them.

As the heavens are higher than the earth, so are GOD's ways higher than their ways, and HIS thoughts high than their thoughts, and as the rain, the sun, and the snow comes from the heavens to bless the earth, so shall HIS WORD be that comes out of HIS mouth, and they shall not return to HIM void. Because what HE says will happen to whom HE said it would happen to, and it will happen how HE said it would happen. Therefore, the Israelites must believe that their Negro people would be freed from their white captives, and they would do it peacefully, and they must believe that the colored nations of the world would be happy for them when they see how joyful and prosperous they are in the land, and when that happens, then the world would see that GOD really exists, and GOD would be remembered for this forever.

Isaiah 56

Thus says the LORD:

Keep your opinion to yourself, and live a righteous life, because I am telling you that MY salvation is about to come, and MY righteous is about to be revealed, and the people who do not do evil and understand why Jesus, The Savior had to come will be blessed. So, you are warned, because I do not want anyone who wants to believe in ME saying, I forbid them from joining MY people. Please! Even if you are a eunuch, or if you do not believe that you are good enough, as long as you believe in The Savior, Jesus, and obey MY will, you can be saved, and all those who are saved would be able to come to the holy mountain to make acceptable sacrifices to ME as one people, because I would gather all MY people from white lands, and make them prosperous again, and the other colored nations, and biracial nations would befriend Israel, and believe in ME, and belong to ME.

Believe it!

All the white folks are ignorant. Their watchmen are blind and cannot see the signs. They are dumb, and love to sleep. They have greed, which can never be satisfied. They lead their people without any godly understanding. They do as they feel to gain what they have. And they are so lazy, and foolish, that every day, they have a party and drink themselves into a stupor while planning to have a wilder party for the next day. So please, all you believers, just continue to live a righteous life by not doing evil, and keep the Sabbath, and stop working yourselves to death.

Isaiah 57

Since the righteous perishes, and the merciful men are taken from the earth, and no one ask why, then consider this. Maybe it could be that the righteous are being taken, because they can enter peace after they are dead, and rest in their righteousness.

YOU WICKED SO AND SO!

Come here, you sons of B!^@*&$. Who are you laughing at?

You stick out your tongues at the Negro people of GOD, but are you not all sinners, and a bunch of fakes?

You worship everything and call them your gods. You even sacrifice your children to them in your hidden temples, and you make your sacrifices, but there is no benefit in it. You even call on other spirits and make covenants with "Death" and "Hades", and yet your spells can never destroy the righteous. That is why all you wicked people are weary in your ways. But you would not say "There is no hope", because you do not fear GOD, even though HE had been punishing you. Instead, you want GOD to accept your abominations, but HE will not do it. Let your idols deliver you, because GOD will not answer your prayers. HE will only ignore you when you are crying. Then when you are gone, it would be like taking all the stumbling blocks out of the way, and when there are no stumbling blocks, the righteous can prosper. Therefore, GOD would make sure there is no peace for the wicked.

Isaiah 58

Are you righteous?

Cheer GOD on when HE is punishing the wicked, because people are seeking their desires from HIM daily, and yet they are unwilling to turn from their sin, and GOD is especially disappointed with the Negroes of Israel, because they boast about being The Chosen Ones, and they practice the rituals, but they are no better than the rest of the world. In fact, Israel do not even observe the Sabbath any longer. They just use that day for their pleasure, and to hire laborers to do work around their houses, and they are fasting and praying, but they are only seeking vengeance on each other, and they will not get any answers from GOD this way.

THE ACCEPTABLE FAST

Fasting is not about afflicting the soul. It is not about bowing down in prayer for days, nor is it about crying and pleading for your causes.

Would you call that a fast and an acceptable way of presenting yourself to GOD?"

This Is the fast that GOD has chosen:

To loose the bonds of the wicked

To undo the heavy burdens

To let the oppressed go free

And that you break every yoke.

Doesn't fasting mean that you share your food with the hungry, and help the righteous when they are rejected by the world?

When you see the naked, clothe them, and do not hide yourself from any righteous person. If you help those who are seeking GOD, and comfort them in their afflictions, then the world would know that you are also righteous, and your works would glorify GOD. Then GOD would guide you continually, and HE would satisfy your souls in a drought, and make you strong, and you would never lack, and when you call on HIM, HE would answer you, and when you cry, HE would say; "Here I AM." By this point in time, the people Israel know that those from among them would rebuild and refurbish the place, and raise up the foundations of many generations, and they would be called **"The Repairer of the Breach"**, and they know that if they observe the Sabbath as a Holy day of rest, and honor THE LORD GOD, HE would bless them and honor them, and make it all good for them.

Isaiah 59

GOD's hand is not shortened that it cannot save, nor HIS ears heavy, that it cannot hear. The iniquities of the Negro people of Israel separated them from HIM, and their sins made HIM hide HIS face from them, and HE stopped hearing them, because they are murderers, and a bunch of sinners, and they also tell lies, and they talk about perverse things, and no one is seeking true justice, because they only seek to get away with their sins, and they are a bunch of vipers that are hatching out eggs, and when they do evil, they die, but before they die, they would make sure that they already corrupted someone else.

Didn't they know that whoever takes the way of unrighteousness would not have peace?

Yes, they do know that the unrighteous would not have peace, but they sin anyway, and it is because THE LORD, GOD, saw that there is no justice on earth why it displeased HIM, and since there is no righteous man, and no intercessor, GOD promised that HIS own arm would bring salvation for man.

Isaiah 60

Trouble would come, but keep the faith, because GOD would keep HIS promises to HIS Negro people, and to anyone else who follow righteousness. Then all the people of Israel would call their walls "Salvation", and their gates "Praise", because they would be righteous.

BEAUTY FOR ASHES
(This will be quoted by Jesus)

Isaiah 61

The SPIRIT of the LORD is upon me (Israel), because THE LORD (GOD) has anointed me to preach good tidings to the poor, and has sent me to heal the broken hearted, to proclaim liberty to the captive, open the prisons of those who are bound, proclaim the acceptable year of HIS punishment of the day of HIS vengeance, comfort all who mourn, console those who had been serving HIM, and give them beauty for ashes, the oil of joy for mourning, and the garment of praise for the spirit of heaviness, so that they are called The Trees of Righteousness, and The Planting of THE LORD (GOD) that GOD glorified, and GOD would call the men of Israel "The Priests of the LORD", and men would call them "The Servants of our GOD".

Isaiah 62

GOD will not rest, until the Negroes of Israel are glorified, and every righteous person gets their rewards, and we know that the Negroes of Israel would not always be forsaken, and their land would not always be desolate, and they would be called by a new name.

Israel's New Name:
You shall be called Hephzibah - which means "MY delight in her"
Your land will be called Beulah - which means "Married"

Believe it.

This is prophecy. The nation of Israel will return to her husband (GOD), and her children (the righteous Negro people of Israel) would come home to their own land, and be abundantly blessed by GOD, their FATHER.

ESAU IS RED
Isaiah 63

Who is this who comes from Edom?

Edom is the nation of the descendants of Esau, and they are called Edomites. Esau is Jacob's older twin brother. Jacob is also called Israel, and his descendants are the Israelites, who are "The Nation of Israel". Esau's skin and hair is red complected, and he, and his red skinned descendants are supposed to be the heirs of GOD's blessings according to his birthright. Jacob's skin and hair is dark, and his dark-skinned descendants are supposed to be second to Esau's descendants. Both Esau and Jacob grew up with their parents, Rebekah and Isaac as a righteous Negro family. But since they are small as a group, and because of Esau's red skin, he desired more to be amongst the white people in the region, and though Esau is the heir of GOD's blessings by birthright, since GOD knew that Jacob is the better man, and a person dedicated to his Negro roots, GOD caused it so that Jacob inherits the blessing by making Esau trade it to him for a plate of food.

Therefore, because Esau rejected his Negro heritage and birthright, and Jacob did not, Jacob became the heir. Then GOD changed Jacob's name, and calls him Israel, and Israel, and his descendants received the blessings of GOD. For that, Esau's descendants, the Edomite, are always anger and violent towards Jacob's descendants, the people of Israel, and GOD punish them for what they do, and GOD promised that HE would heal them, and HE would also offer them HIS salvation to save their souls. Then when that time comes, the Edomites would appreciate HIS correction, because HE would have saved them, even though they turned to sinning and turned against their brothers in Israel for living a righteous life, which helped caused the people of Israel to turn into sinners. Then after the chastening and the forgiveness of GOD, the Edomites would appreciate the grace of GOD, and they would say, "Doubtless, HE is our FATHER, even though Abraham our (earthly) father was ignorant of us and the people of Israel did not acknowledge us (as their brothers), GOD is our FATHER, and our redeemer." Then they would want to know why GOD allowed them to stray from HIS ways and allowed them to harden their hearts to not fear HIM to make them actually become like those who had no LAW, and like people who had no GOD.

Isaiah 64

Afterward, they would reminisce on how wonderful and kind GOD is.

(Please read this chapter in The Bible to see how Edom would appreciate GOD's love.)

Isaiah 65

Yet for the time, GOD talks about HIS frustration in chastening sinners, since it brings no change in their thoughts, and HE sighs. But in due time, HE would relieve HIMSELF, by redeeming the righteous, and by glorifying HIS people. Then after that happens, there would be a new earth, and a new heaven, and the former would not be remembered, or come to mind, and we would be glad, and rejoice forever in what GOD created, because The New Jerusalem, which is heaven, would descend to the earth, and her inhabitants would be righteous, and there would be rejoicing in The Holy City, because the people of Israel would be filled with joy. Therefore, there would be no weeping or crying there, and when this happens, a person who is one hundred years old would be considered a child, because they could live forever in the flesh if they want to. But the sinner who lives to that age would be completely scorned, and torment, until they change, or decide to die. Surely, at this time, before the righteous calls, GOD would answer, and while they are still speaking, HE would have already solved their problem.

Isaiah 66

Thus says the LORD:

"Heaven is MY throne, and the earth is MY footstool. You cannot give ME a house or give ME a place to rest. You cannot give ME anything, because everything belongs to ME. But it is for certain, you can give yourself to ME, by being poor and contrite in spirit, and by obeying MY every WORD. Do not deceive yourself, because I will not accept a proud sinner, and I would cause all those who rejects the righteous person to be ashamed. Glorified ME, so that you may see your joy, and when you see that righteousness and peace comes, you would rejoice and be glad. Because by the truth of the WORD, all flesh, all idol worshippers, and worshippers of false gods would be killed. Then after the earth is restored, the righteous would walk about, and look upon the abhorrent flesh of the living dead of those who still decides to transgress the LAW, because their flesh will be rotting and stinking from a sickness of their regret of choices, which would be like a worm in the stomach that cannot die, and from the anger of the results, which would be like a fire in the chest that cannot quench.

MICAH'S PROPHECY
Time period—in the days of Jotham, Ahaz, and Hezekiah
(the Negro kings of Judah, from 750 B.C.)

Chapter 1

GOD speaks through prophets, and while HE is speaking to others, HE is also speaking to Micah of Moresheth, throughout the reign of several kings about the sins of the people of Israel that lives in Samaria, and in Jerusalem. And Micah told the people of Israel all that GOD said, and he went out in the whole world, and told people, they better listen, because GOD is a witness against them from HIS holy temple in heaven, and HE is coming down to tear down all the places of false worship, since all the people of Israel are practicing false worship, like everyone else. Also, because the people of Israel in Samaria are idol worshippers, and most of their false places of worship are in Jerusalem (The Holy City) among the tribe of Judah. So, that is the reason why all the places of idol worship must be torn down, and GOD would do it by destroying the people in Samaria as a payback, because their idol worship ways affected the people of Judah, HIS favorite of all the tribes of Israel. Therefore, disaster would come from GOD to all the idol worshippers, because they caused GOD's people to do the same thing, and after HE punish the idol worshippers, HE would give their things to HIS people to make them the heirs of the things of the idol worshippers. So, all the unbelievers might as well start to worry, because their precious children will suffer.

Chapter 2

Feel sorry for those who lay in their beds at night thinking how to do evil while waiting for morning to come, so they could carry out their plots to look at properties, and houses they like, and take it by violence, not knowing that GOD would utterly destroy them, so they could see that they end up with nothing.

Tell me is the SPIRIT of GOD restricted?

Is it GOD who is really making people suffer?

Doesn't HE do good to those who are righteous?

GOD is good, and righteous, and people resist HIM, but they cannot restrict HIM, and HE would make people suffer, if they turn from HIS ways. Yet the Negro people of Israel are acting like enemies to each other, and they steal even the clothes from their closest friends, as if they do not already have clothes for themselves. They also cast out the women from their nice houses, leaving the children with no place to live. Which is the reason why GOD told them they may as well leave from their native land, since there is not the place where they can find rest, and it is defiled, and would be completely destroyed. So, if anyone say it would not be destroyed and the people would be happy and merry, then that person would be lying, and had gotten the information from a lying spirit. Because it is true that the few people in the land would suffer, and they would cry out in agony, since GOD would make sure they are punished for their idol worship.

Chapter 3

Once Micah was done telling the conworld what GOD said, he goes to the priests and the rulers of his Negro people in Israel and asks them if they know what it means to be just. Because he noticed that they hate good, and love evil, and it is like they stripped the skin and flesh from the bones of the people and then chopped them up like meat for the pot, and the people are crying to GOD. But GOD will not listen to them, because everyone is sinning, and turned from HIM to idol worship, and they strayed, because the priests and leaders told them they would have peace, while they took everything from them, and killed anyone who did not give them anything. So, because the priests and the leaders do not have any true understanding, they are covering their lips, and shutting their mouths, since GOD is not giving them any answers. And it was truly declared that the tribe of Judah, and the rest of the Negro people of Israel are sinners, and the leaders and priests hate justice, and they built up the nation with blood shed, and their head judges take bribes, while their priests teach for pay, and their prophets give answers for money. Yet, they still call on GOD, and they think that HE is with them, and they cannot be harmed, but GOD said, they better know that it is because of them why the place would become heaps of ruins, and the mountain where the temple is would look like a forest.

Chapter 4

Yet still, GOD promised that the day would come when the temple would be restored, and their Negro people would be established with a strong government. Then people from other nations would come to Israel to worship HIM, and when the many nations come, they would learn about HIM from the Negro people of Israel, and they would believe, and live by the WORD, because of what the Negroes of Israel taught them. After that, people would not want to fight anymore, and there would be no more war, and the Negro people of Israel would be at peace with everyone, as everyone learn from them. That is how GOD said it would be, since HIS people believed in HIM, while others were believing in other gods, and when it happens, HE would rule over HIS people from Mount Zion and continue to be with them forever. So, they better believe it, because they would get to see it and receive the blessings.

The Negroes of Israel need to stop crying.

Don't they have a KING?

Don't they have any priests to give them good advice?

Yes, they have kings and priests. Even better, GOD is their KING and Jesus is their High Priest, and they have other good men that are priests, but they are acting like a bunch of women crying out in labor, and GOD would let them be in pain, until they believe and are delivered. For the time, they would be running and hiding out in the fields from the Roman white men, and they would be captured, and taken to Babylon. After that, GOD would deliver them. Then the nations that wanted them to stay defiled to laugh at them would be shocked, because they did not know the thoughts of GOD, nor did they understood that HE was telling them that HE would destroy them for trying to destroy the Negroes of Israel. Therefore, the Negroes of Israel should be happy about this, because GOD said, He would make them strong to destroy many nations, and they would end up with everything.

Chapter 5

Since all the nations would gather themselves together to fight against the Negro people of Israel, GOD want them to realize that even though the tribe of Judah is the smallest group among Israel, and among all the nations of the world, someone would come from their tribe to rule the world forever. But first, HE would give them over to the world, until the time when Jesus, that someone is born. Then when Jesus is grown, He would teach them the truth, as the remnant of them return from their captivity. And Jesus would stand against the white (Roman) government and their laws, and He would teach the truth about GOD, and HIS government, and He would be great forever. And while He teaches the TRUTH, the Assyrian white people would try to take over the land of the people of Israel, but Jesus would defeat them and save all His Negro people from the severe attack. Then the remnant of the people of Israel would have a good life again, and they could go anywhere in the world without anybody showing them hatred, and they would not have to have wars, and they would not want to worship idols, because GOD would fight against anyone that does not like them for who they are.

Chapter 6

Did the Negroes of Israel hear what GOD said?

Yes, they did hear GOD.

Then why didn't they plead their case loudly to let GOD hear their voices, and let all the governments, and strong people know that they know that their GOD is against their enemies?

And why didn't they stop wondering why they hate this message, and the person that brings it, when they knew that GOD took them from slavery in Egypt, and led them by Moses, Aaron, and Miriam.?

Don't they remember how Balak tried to use Balaam (the wizard) to curse them, and how Balaam told him that he could not, because they were righteous?

Shouldn't they have gone to GOD, and bow before HIM with burnt offerings of calves and other sacrifices?

They refuse to plead their case, because they do not believe GOD, and so they keep hating those who bring The Good News, and they refuse to change, and though they know that GOD would save them, they are discouraged in their punishment. You may think that they should go to GOD with their sacrifices, but GOD does not love the sacrifices of animals more than HIS people, and HE would never ask them to give up their children for their sins, because HE showed them what is good, and HE told them that all HE requires is that they do justly, love mercy, and walk humbly with HIM. Now

HE is crying out throughout the cities wondering who is wise enough to seek wisdom and obey the LAW HE appointed to follow.

Would anyone of the people of Israel listen, or does GOD have to pour out HIS punishment on all the wickedness, and make them sick, and the place desolate?

If they do not listen, then they would eat, and not be satisfied, and they may live somewhere else, but it would not help, and whatever they save would be lost, and nothing they do would prosper, because they keep on worshipping their idols, and keep giving their children as a sacrifice to them from the time of Omri, and Ahab, their kings. Really, they should feel sorry for GOD, because HE is looking for faithful, and just people, but only finds one or two, here and there, and there are no more good people, and no one is trying to do right, and they all lie in wait, seeing how they could destroy their own people, and how to make themselves very successful. Plus, the priest, the princes, and all the nobles get together to carry out their evil schemes, and the best of them, and the ones that should be most upright are crooked and evil. But the day would come when they get punished, and GOD warned them not to trust in their friends, or to put their confidence in their companion, and to watch what they say to people who they think loves them, because sons would dishonor fathers, daughters would hate their mothers, and family members would be against each other. Since a person's enemies are within his own household.

Therefore, they must look to GOD, and wait on HIM, because HE said, HE would hear them and save them, and they should not be happy when any righteous person falls, because they would recover, and GOD would guide them with HIS wisdom. For the meantime, they must bear the punishment for their sins, until GOD plead their case, and execute judgment on their behalf. Then when their enemies see that they recover, and are prosperous, they would be ashamed for asking them, "Where is your GOD" while they wait to see them die in the streets.

Though the white people would come to take the people of Isreal as captives, the people of Israel must teach their people the truth in the LAW, because GOD said, HE would save them, just like when HE freed them from Egypt, and every nation would see it, and be amazed, as well as ashamed of what they did. Then they would not fear anyone, because YAH is their GOD, the one who delights in mercy, WHO forgave them their sins, and gave them the truth and the blessings, swore to their forefather, Abraham HE would.

NAHUM'S PROPHECY
Time period - 713 B.C.

Chapter 1

During that time, while GOD speaks through Micah to HIS Negro people, HE is also speaking through Nahum (the Elkoshite) against the people of Nineveh to let him know that HE is a jealous GOD that takes vengeance on HIS adversaries, and HE reserved a time when HE would punish HIS enemies, even though HE is slow to anger, and great in power, because HE would not acquit the wicked, since HE controls everything from rebuking the seas to drying up rivers, to destroying nations, and HE is going to punish them, even though they are safely located and numerous, because they are a bunch of wicked counselors that plot evil against HIM, that HE would destroy as they pass through the land to kill HIS people, and after HE destroys them, HE would set HIS people free from all the other oppressors, and HE would never allow them to be afflicted anymore.

That's it, but Nineveh repented, and that is why the mixed culture of Nineveh would be forgotten for being vile, because GOD forgave them and did not punish them. So, we should be glad to listen to those who are coming with the good news, that peace would come after all the ungodly nations are punished the same way they punished "The Nation of Israel".

Chapter 2

Though the wicked people in every ungodly nation are boasting against the people of GOD, GOD said, they better get ready for war, because HE is ready to restore the people of Israel, since the wicked people took everything from them, and left them to look like nobodies, and they killed many, and were covered in blood as they came rushing in on chariots, running over whoever was in the way. And with flaming torches, they rushed through the streets, while swinging them at anyone, and they took the best of the people of Israel that were left alive, because it was decreed that they would be taken as captives and be treated badly by their masters.

Though Nineveh was forgiven, and it is a great place to be, they are still sinning, and GOD said, they would get punished, and people are going to stay from there, and even though they might beg people to come there, no one would come. Then people would ask, "Where are all the people that made money, and lived in, and enjoyed Nineveh so much?", because GOD is against Nineveh, and HE would punish them for all their wrong doings.

Woe to the bloody city, Nineveh! It is full of liars and thieves, and there is no end of them victimizing people, and there is nothing but noise from the whips, the rattling wheels of the chariots, and of the galloping horses with the horsemen holding their shiny swords, and glittering spears. Oh, what a multitude of dead Negroes, a great number of bodies, countless corpses, which the invading Ninevites stumbles over as they slaughter them. So, GOD is angry with Nineveh for copying the ways of the white pagan people of harlotry and sorcery, that they use to oppress the godly Negroes of Israel, and because GOD is against them, HE is going to make all the people of their unbelieving, mix culture, ashamed of themselves, by making their city desolate, so everyone would wonder what happened to them. Then people would not want to live in the city anymore, not knowing if it would ever recover.

The people of Nineveh must think that they are better than the ungodly white people of Amon who have the ungodly colored people of Ethiopia, and the ungodly colored people of Egypt as friends that always helped them. And they must think that they are unbeatable, because the ungodly colored nations of Put and Lubim also help them. Or it must be that they forgot that when GOD was ready, HE caused the ungodly white people of Amon to be defeated and carried away as captives, while their children were killed in the streets, and their honorable men sold to the highest bidder, and the best men in the community carried away in chains. By now Ninevah should have believed that the same thing would happen to them, and though they may seek help from their friends, they still would be defeated, because GOD said, HE would cause their enemies to overcome them, and surely enough, the people, and their leaders would look no stronger than women after being defeat.

Therefore, GOD is telling them to prepare themselves for war, because they increased their riches by stealing from others, and running home with it, and the commanders and the generals of their army are thieves who spy on others in the least expected ways, and they do ungodly things, because they are wicked, and do not want to change, and because of their wickedness, their people would be severely hurting, and would not be healed, and when people hear about their pain, they would be glad, because which one of them had not been affected by the works of the wicked.

ZEPHANIAH'S PROPHESY

**Time period - In the days when Josiah,
the son of a black man named Amon,
the king of Judah, from 630 B.C.**

Chapter 1

Dring this time, GOD tell Zephaniah, of the royal seed of Judah, from the son of Cushi, the great grandson of Hezekiah, HE would completely destroy everything and everyone of false worship in the land and consume everyone in the tribe of Judah who worship false gods, along with their idol priests, and their pagan priest. Even those who worship only angels, as well as those who worship HIM, if they also worship false gods and evil spirits. So, if they turned their back on HIM, the true GOD, then they better shut up, because it is "The Day of THE LORD", and HE is ready to kill those who are against HIM, and against the righteous people, and HE would also kill all the royal seed of the other nations that rules over them, and kill those who invaded their land to marry them and teach them violence and deceit. Then there would be mourning all over the place, because all the false worshippers, and their merchants, and all those who handle money would be killed. Then after the invading false worshippers are killed off from the land, HE would closely examine HIS people in Jerusalem and punish anyone that is not completely dedicated to HIM, so that they would know that HE wants them to always be good and never be evil. Which is why HE is warning them that

"The Day of THE LORD" is near, and because HE is angry, it is going to be a time of trouble and distress, devastation and desolation, darkness and gloom: a time of war with HIM in which HE would bring distress upon human beings for sinning against HIM, and no amount of money could deliver anyone from the wrath, because HE is jealous that we are worshipping idols and evil spirits, instead of worshipping HIM.

Chapter 2

Talk it over together, all you GOD haters, before GOD kill you off in HIS wrath. And all you righteous people that have always been good, you must continue to be good, and maybe GOD would keep you protected in the time of HIS anger, since no matter where you are, destruction would come.

GOD said, The Gaza Strip (The Promised Land for the Negro people of Israel) would also be forsaken, and Ashkelon would be desolate when the idols of Ekron, and Ashdod are destroyed, and the white (Canaanites) and the brown skinned Philistines, who lives there on the seacoast of Chereth would be destroyed. Then the believing Negro people of Judah would use the seacoast for pasturing their flocks, and HE would intervene for them against the ungodly people of Moab and Ammon, because of how Moab, and Ammon had been threatening to take their land. Therefore, Moab would be destroyed, like the white culture of Sodom, and Ammon would be destroyed, like the white culture of Gomorrah, until their nations are overrun with weeds and are desolate. Then the few people of Israel that are in their land would plunder them, and take over what they have, and it would happen, because they made arrogant threats against the people of Israel. Yes, GOD would be awesome. HE would get rid of all false ways of worship, and people would worship HIM from any part of the earth. But first, HE warned the colored nation of Ethiopia, and the white nation of Assyria that they would be killed for their wickedness, just like the mix cultured nation of Nineveh. Then wild beasts and birds would take over their capital building and the streets, because the places would be desolate, since they feel secure, and feel that no one can defeat them.

Chapter 3

People are feeling sorry for the multi-cultured people of Nineveh, because they are rebellious oppressors that still refuse to change, and they do not obey GOD, and do not want to, and the leaders are violent, the judges are corrupt, the prophets are crazy and wicked, and the priests corrupted the church with their violence. Everyday GOD tries to tell them about their wicked ways, but they know no shame, and that is why GOD must punish them severely. Because at first, HE punished them some, by destroying their cities, but every day, they get up, and still do evil. Now HE is angry, and ready to pour out HIS wrath, not only on Nineveh, but on all the wicked nations, so that HE could restore communication with the righteous people of Israel that serves HIM. Then when HE is done, all the wicked ones that encouraged them to be proud of idol worship in the mountains would be gone from the land, leaving only the meek, and humble ones that trust in HIM, and they would not tell lies, or be deceitful, because there would not be any wicked ones in their land around them to cause them to do wrong.

Sing Negro women! Negro people of Israel, sing, and be glad, and rejoice with all your hearts. GOD said HE forgave your people for their false worship, and HE promised that HE would get rid of your enemies from amongst your people. And since HE forgave you, and does not like your enemies, HE is with you, and you do not have to worry about problems anymore, and you should not be afraid, if you are righteous, because HE is in your midst, and is the mighty one that would save you, and HE would rejoice over you with singing when HE gets rid of the people that turned you to false worship. Then at that set time, HE would be dealing harshly with all those who afflicted you, and HE would save the lame, and bring back those who were taken captive, and you would be famous, and be praised around the world, because of how you were freed.

JEREMIAH'S PROPHESY
Time period - In the thirteenth year of Josiah,
the son of Amos, reign over "Judah", around 629 B.C.

Chapter 1

Shortly after GOD spoke to Zephaniah, HE starts to speak to Jeremiah, the son of Hilkiah, the priest in Anathoth, in the land of the tribe of Benjamin in the 13th year of Josiah reign, and HE told Jeremiah about how HE would punish their Negro people of Judah. Later in time, GOD speaks to Jeremiah again, during the reign of Jehoiakim, the son of Josiah, and again during Zedekiah (another son of Josiah) reign, and each time, Jeremiah warned the people of Judah for all those years, until GOD was ready to finally start the punishment on them.

As prophesied, in the end of the 11th year of Zedekiah's reign, the white people invade the land and carry away the best of the people of Judah from Jerusalem to their white land as captives. Just like they did with the rest of Israel. But they left Jeremiah, and others that are either sick, or poor in the land, and while they are in distress, GOD tells Jeremiah, "Before I formed you in the womb, I knew you, and before you were born, I sanctified you and ordained you to be a prophet to the world." Then Jeremiah said, "I do not know what to say, since I am still a boy", and GOD tells him not to call himself a boy, because HE will use him to speak to whomever HE wants, and say whatever HE wants him to say, and he should not be afraid, because HE will protect him.

Then GOD touch his mouth and tell him that HE placed HIS words in his mouth, and from that day, HE is setting him over the nations to root out and pull down, to destroy and throw down, and to build and plant. And GOD shows him a vision, and asks him what he sees, and he said, he sees a bunch of almond trees, and GOD tells him, he is seeing well. Then since GOD is ready to do what HE said HE would do, HE shows him another vision, and asks him what he sees, and he said, he sees a boiling pot facing away from the North. To explain the vision, GOD said, "From the Northern region of the world where the white people live, the white people would come and bring calamity upon the land of the people of Judah, because I Am calling all the white leaders of the North to come, and set up their thrones in Jerusalem all along its borders, and in all the other cities of Judah, because I Am ready to punish them for all their wickedness, and for forgetting about ME by burning incense to idols and to false gods." Then GOD tells him to tell the people everything HE said, and not to be afraid of them, because if he is ashamed, HE would shame him before them, which is why HE made him strong, so he could stand against them, that when they fight against him, they would lose, because HE would protect him.

Chapter 2

Another time, GOD speaks to Jeremiah, and tells him to go and cry out to the Negro people of Jerusalem of the tribe of Judah, and tell them that, "HE remember their past when they first started to believe in HIM, and they were holy to HIM, and were The First-Fruit of all the righteous people that HE is calling to HIMSELF, and anyone that tried to kill them off made HIM angry, and HE caused disaster to come upon them. So, HE wants them to tell HIM what kind of injustice their forefathers told them HE did to them why they stopped seeking HIM, and became idolaters, because HE is complaining about how they forgot about how HE freed them from Egypt, and how HE led them through the wilderness with signs and wonders through a land of desert and pits, drought and shadows of death; a place where no one travels through, or lived in. And HE is also complaining about how HE took them to the beautiful Promised Land filled with fruits and goodness, which they defiled with their sinful ways. HE is also complaining about how the priests started to doubt that HE is amongst them, and how the leaders do not obey the LAW, and how the prophets are saying that the false god, Baal, gave them the understanding they have, even though the information does not benefit them. That is why HE is bringing charges against them, and against their children, and their children's children for generations, since nowhere in any other nation they ever change their god, even though they are not real gods. Yet they went from worshipping HIM, THE LIVING GOD, to worshipping idols, and they should be astonished at this, and be afraid, because they committed two evils. One is, they forsook HIM, the fountain of living water, the provider of everything, and two, they started to worship the idols they made with their own hands, which cannot do anything for them.

Are the people of Israel servants, or are they slaves?

The answer is "neither".

Then could you tell me why they don't have anything?

Well. All the young white leaders are raised to treat the Negro people of Israel harshly and destroy their land to leave it empty and leave them looking like servants, instead of like royalty. But the Negro people brought this on themselves when they forgot about YAH, their GOD, even after HE proved HIMSELF to them. Now GOD said, they might as well take the punishment, and forget about running off to the unrighteous colored folks of Egypt, or to the unrighteous white folks of Assyria, because HE would cause the poverty to correct them for their wickedness, and for turning from HIM, since it was an evil thing, they did when they did not want to listen to HIM anymore. Even after HE freed them, and called them holy, and after they said they would not sin, they are worshipping idols all over the place, and though they were made to be holy kings and priests of their nation, they are sinner and are considered strangers to their GOD. So, even though they still say they worship HIM, HE considers them sinners.

So, how can they say they were still holy, if they worship false gods?

It is as if they do not see all the idols they set up throughout the place, or what they are doing. They are just wild, and they like to act crude to get what they want, and they run to anyone that wants them to do something wrong for them, because they love ungodly nations, and want to be like them.

Do you know what is wrong with the people of Israel?

Poverty. That is what is wrong with them. The poverty makes them ashamed, because it shows that GOD is punishing them for being ungodly, and for not being holy kings, prophets, and priests in their government and church. That is why they are still saying to a tree "You are my father", and to a stone, "You gave birth to me", since they turned their backs on GOD. Yet whenever they are in trouble, they call HIM to save them.

What about the gods they made for themselves?

Why don't they call on those gods in times of trouble, if they could save them?

The have many gods, so why do they still pray to YAH, the living GOD, if they are sinning against HIM?

In vain GOD punished HIS children, and it brought no change, because they killed off all the prophets that tried to tell them what HE said. My goodness!

Did they hear what GOD is saying?

Hasn't HE provided for them and instructed them in the past?

Yes, they heard what GOD says, and HE did provide for them. Yet, in their unrighteousness they are saying, they are great, and they do not need HIM anymore.

Would someone forget the things that made them beautiful?

Yes, because the Negro people of GOD forgot about HIM, and they are trying to make other people love them for the bad things about themselves and they are teaching others that godly people like to intermingle with the ungodly. Plus, they even kill innocent people. Yet they say they are innocent, and GOD would not do anything to them. But GOD is against them, even though they insist they are not sinning.

So why were the Negroes so confused about why they must change their ways?

They are confused about change, because they should be ashamed of the ungodly colored people of Egypt, as well as ashamed of the ungodly white people of Assyria, but they are not. And since they are not ashamed of ungodly people, no matter what race or nationality they are, like prisoners the Negro people of GOD would be, because GOD rejected them, and HE also rejected their allies, and therefore, they cannot help them.

Chapter 3

If a man leaves his wife and she marries another man, should the man go back to his wife?

Of course not! Because she would be with two men. That is nasty, sinful living. Yet, the Negro people of Israel are playing around with many gods of other nations, while YAH, their GOD is still around and is begging them to be with HIM. That is why GOD wants them to look all around and tell us which country they went to and practiced what they did that made them want to wait for other countries to call them to come to them to do wrong things. For that, GOD said, they are going to get punished for being whores since they are not even ashamed of it, and they should start to cry out to HIM, and say "FATHER, YOU are the ONE that always helped us, so help us", because HE said, HE would not be angry with them forever.

On another day, GOD ask Jeremiah, did he noticed the people of "The Kingdom of Israel" had been everywhere playing a whore by worshipping idols, even though HE begged them to stop and come back to HIM and they refused, and if he noticed that the tribe of Judah is doing the same thing. And HE said, it was because the people of Israel turned from HIM to idols worship why HE is acting like HE divorced them and why HE sent them away from HIM. Yet the tribe of Judah did not fear HIM and ended up doing the same thing as the rest of the tribes of Israel, and because all the people think it is nothing to worship idols, they end up worshipping carved stones and trees. So, even though the tribe of Judah wants to change, they did not turn back to HIM with their whole heart. Instead, they are just pretending, and though most of the tribes are more ungodly than Judah, Judah is still treacherous.

After saying that, GOD tell him to shout out in the direction of the North to the people of Israel that were taken into captivity, and tell them, HE would not punish them, because HE is merciful, and cannot be angry forever. If they just acknowledge that they turned their backs on HIM to worshipped idols everywhere, since they belong to HIM, and HE wants them back, HE will accept anyone of them that come back to HIM, so they could be with HIM in Zion. Then HE would give them teachers who would give them knowledge and understanding, and when it happens, they would not need to talk about "The Ark of The Covenant" of THE LORD, and they would not visit it anymore, because they would not remember it, and they would not make another one, since they would already have knowledge and understanding. Then at that time, Jerusalem would be called "The Throne of the LORD", and all the nations would come to visit there to know about being righteous, because they would not want to do evil anymore. At the same time, the tribe of Judah would join back with the rest of the tribes of Israel, and the captives would return home from their white captors and all the people of Israel could live in their inherited land again. But first, HE wants to ask them why HE should bring back all the captives and give them back their inherited land if they do not want to call HIM FATHER, or want to be with HIM, though they are the ones that left HIM, and are crying after forgetting about HIM, because of the perversion of their ways. That is why HE is telling them they should return to HIM, and HE would heal them, because they truly hoped in vain to be saved by their idols, but with HIM they could be saved. So, HE is wondering, if they do not see that all the things their forefathers built are destroyed, and HE is also wondering, if they are ashamed, since they go to bed ashamed every night, and hold their heads down during the days, because they, and even their forefathers sinned against HIM by not obeying HIM.

Chapter 4

If they return to HIM, and put their trust in HIM, no one would be able to oppress them, and they would be able to testify that HE lives by truth, judgment, and in righteousness, and the world would be living in happiness, because of HIS blessings. That is why HE had been telling them they could be angry, but they must stop sinning, and trust HIM completely, and HE would save them from HIS destruction for the evil they did. But they keep refusing to do as HE says. Now HE is telling them to blow the trumpet, and gather themselves, because it is time for war, and they should take refuge, and not delay, because HE would cause the white people from the North to come to bring disaster upon them, and HE chose the white people to punish them, because they are the destroyer of nations, and they would leave from their nation to make the land desolate, and the cities laid to waste.

HE is YAH, their GOD, and HE is fiercely angry, and is ready to punish them. Therefore, they need to stop being surprised when they hear that they would be punished, and they need to stop saying that HE deceived them by promising them peace, but instead giving them troubles, because it is time for them to be punished, and the white people are coming to take them and destroy everything. Now they wish they had repented before, because a prophet from the tribe of Dan prophesied about it to them, and they should have told the whole world that the white people are coming from a far place to show the tribe of Judah that they have no one to protect them, because they rebelled against truth, and it is their ways, and their wickedness that brought those things upon them, and the punishment would be bitter, because sin is deep in their hearts.

O' my soul, my soul. The righteous are troubled, and they want to scream out the truth since the punishment already started, because the people of Israel still need to change, and there would be destruction upon destruction, and in the blink of an eye, another Negro would be destroyed.

How long would the destruction of the Negroes continue?

O' when would it stop?

It will be destruction after destruction that will only stop when GOD says so, because the Negro people of Israel are acting foolish, and they are acting like they do not know their GOD, and like they are silly children that do not have any understanding, since they do not know how to do good, just how to do evil. Just think about what the earth would eventually look like. It would be void, dark, and without form, and there would be no birds, or animals, and no human beings, and the cities would be broken down, because of the fierce anger of GOD in HIS wrath as He punish not only HIS Negro people, but also every nation in the whole world, even though HE would not completely destroy everything and everyone. But for now, the earth mourns, and the heavens are dark, since GOD spoke, and will not change HIS mind, or shorten the time, and the punishment will start with the Negro people of Israel when HE allows the white man to plunder them.

What can the Negroes do?

There is nothing they can do, after lightening their complexion, widening their eyes with makeup, and changing their styles to look like the white people, just to have their white friends despise them, and always be on the prowl to kill them.

What a travesty!

It is a travesty to hear the voices of the Negro people of Israel crying out from all the anguish they feel, and a travesty to know they are ready to give up, because their souls are weary from seeing themselves die off.

Chapter 5

If they run through their neighborhood of the Negro people of Jerusalem to see if anyone execute righteous justice, or if anyone is seeking the truth, and they see any, then GOD would pardon them. So, even though they swear that GOD is on their side, GOD knows the truth that HE has stricken them. Yet, they do not feel bad for what they did, and even though GOD killed many of them, they still refuse correction, and are more stubborn than ever, because they still refuse to return to obeying GOD. Now, they are poor and foolish, because they do not know how to please their GOD. It would have been nice to speak to the great ones amongst them, but they too completely turned from GOD, and therefore, every people of every ungodly nation would come and kill many of them, and take leadership over their land, because GOD cannot just ignore what HIS people are doing to HIM, ever since they forgot about HIM and started to worship idols, which are not even gods. So, even though GOD treated them so well, and even though they were like well-fed stallions, they acted like wild horses that lusted after ungodly ways.

Shouldn't GOD punish them for these things?

And shouldn't HE satisfy HIS anger by punishing them for it?

Yes, GOD should punish them and satisfy HIS anger. That is why HE said HE would destroy their land, but HE would not destroy all the people, and HE would send some from each tribe into captivity, because they do not want anything to do with HIM, since they do not want to obey HIM anymore. Also, they tell lies on HIM by saying HE would not punish them or kill them by hunger, or war. As if they do not realize that the prophets could not give them any answers anymore, because HE stopped talking through the prophets since they kept talking smack. So, that is the reason why HE said HE would not change HIS mind about punishing them, and the fierce white people far from the nations of Africa, whose language they do not know or understand, would come and eat up all the harvest, the flock, and the fruits, and drink up all the wine, and destroy all the cities.

Nevertheless, HE said, HE would not let the white people completely destroy them, and if anyone asked them why HE forsook them, they should say, "They forsook their GOD and served gods of foreign nation is the reason why their GOD made them captives in foreign lands to serve their gods there, instead of in The Holy Land."

By now, they should know that they are foolish, and they do not understand a thing, because they saw things, and did not understand what they saw, and they heard things, and did not understand what was said.

Shouldn't they fear GOD?

Shouldn't they have been trembling at HIS presence, since HE is so powerful and mighty?

Yes. They should be trembling in fear in the presence of GOD. Yet, they do not fear HIM, and they are defiant, and rebellious in their hearts, and they do not obey HIM, and they do not consider fearing HIM, even though HE blessed them with everything at the appointed time. So, it is because of their sins, why GOD does not bless them like HE used to, and because they are wicked like the ungodly people, and they set traps to kill human beings to get rich and fat, and they have houses filled with stolen goods. Just like HE does not bless ungodly people in other nations, HE stopped blessing them for their ungodliness in their nation. Even worst, the Negro people of Israel are more wicked than the ungodly people in the world, because even if they are prosperous, they do not help the fatherless children, or any needy person.

Shouldn't GOD punish them for these things?

Shouldn't GOD punish them for turning to idols and making HIM angry?

Of course, GOD should punish them, because there was an astonishing, and terrible thing that was committed by the people in the land in which the prophets prophesy falsely, and the priests say whatever they want to say, and people seem to like it that way. So, that is the problem.

What decision would they make to save themselves from the punishment in the wrath of GOD?

Chapter 6

Too late! They cannot save themselves. They must bear the punishment, and since the tribe of Benjamin was first to invite the white people into their inherited piece of land to practice evil, GOD tell them to pack up their things and leave from amongst the people of Judah in Jerusalem, and announce war, because the white people are coming from the North to fight them, since they are looking weak. And the white people would surround them and be ready to fight day or night to destroy the place, as HE told them to, and they would cut down the trees, and build mounts against Jerusalem to fight them, because they deserve to get punished for oppressing those who are being godly in their own land. Then when it happens, all of them would know that HE, their GOD, does not like them sinning, because HE is ready to make their land desolate, and a place not inhabited, by completely destroying it.

Which one of them is going to listen to the warning?

Ah! It looks like no one will listen. It is like they are deaf, or like they just do not like to obey GOD, and GOD is tired of it all, and is ready to pour out HIS fury upon all their houses to tear them down, and give their women to white men, because all of them are sinning. Even the prophets and the priests are sinning, and they do not help the situation at all, because they keep telling the people they would have peace when destruction is coming to them.

Were they ashamed when they were sinning?

No, they had no shame. They did not even blush. That is why GOD said, they would be killed during the wrath, and if they think about it, and start to follow HIM like righteous people supposed to, they will find rest for their souls. But they do not want that, because they do not want to do what GOD say. That is why HE sent the white men to be as watchmen over them, who threatens them with war. Yet, they still would not obey, and they need to believe, and realize that GOD is not listening to them, and it is HE who caused them to be confused about reality, and HE who caused a lot of calamities to fall on them. So, they should stop bringing their gifts, and sacrifices to GOD, because HE said, HE does not want their gifts, nor does HE like what they are doing, and HE would make them ashamed by making the white people destroy everything. Now, since they heard what would happen to them, they need to be scared, and they better not go outside, because they might just get killed. So, they need to start crying, because the most holy of them are going to be stripped of everything they have, because their GOD placed the wicked white man over them to see if they would ever turn back to HIM. But since they are all stubborn rebels, living against the truth, and are corrupt, that is the reason why they are being punished so harshly, and it does not seem to be working, and they are being called reject silver, because their GOD rejected them.

Chapter 7

Still, GOD loves them, and to help them, HE tells Jeremiah to stand in the gates of The House of THE LORD and tell the people of Judah that enters through the gates that they must worship HIM, and amend their ways and their doings, and then HE would allow them to survive and live there. Therefore, they are not supposed to trust in idols, or call their temples the temple of GOD, and if they thoroughly amend their ways, and their doings, and execute righteous judgment between a man and his neighbors, and stop oppressing the fatherless, the widow, and strangers, and stop shedding innocent blood, and walking after other gods, then HE would change HIS plan to punish them and allow them to stay in the land and live, and HE would come to live there with them. But all HE sees is them trusting in lying words that cannot benefit them, and they steal, murder, commit adultery, swear falsely, and worshipped false gods. Yet they have the nerves to stand before HIM in The House of THE LORD, and say, because they were chosen by HIM, it means that HE gave them permission to do all those things. But if they go to Shiloh, the first piece of holy land, they will see what HE did to the people of Israel there for their sins. Because HE got up early every morning to instruct and correct them, and they would not listen, and HE called them, and they did not answer. Which is why Judah would get punished too, and the plan would be carried out to destroy The Holy Land, and the white people would take the people as captive to their white lands to cast them from HIS sight. Just like what HE would do to the tribe of Benjamin of Mount Ephraim, the first tribe that allowed the white people to join them in the land to practice false worship. Therefore, the righteous ones of Israel should not pray, cry, or make intercession for the disobedient ones, since HE would not listen to what they have to say.

Didn't they see the sinful things they do in the holy cities of Judah, especially Jerusalem?

Yes, they saw how they were corrupting The Holy City. But amongst the people of Israel, the whole family works together to serve their idols, because the children gather the wood, the father light the fire, and the women prepare the food they sacrificed to their goddess, "The Queen of Heaven". That is what they are doing to make YAH, the almighty GOD angry, and HE told them not to provoke HIM to anger anymore, because HIS anger and fury would be poured on them, and their land, and HE does not want sacrifices and rituals, because not even their forefathers HE demanded it of when HE brought them out of Egypt. But what HE did tell their forefathers is that HE wants them to obey HIM, so HE could call them holy, and HE wants them to do as HE says, so they could be healthy and prosperous. Yet, from the days of their forefathers, they refuse to listen to HIM, and obey HIM, and year after year, they follow their evil hearts, and remember less, and less about HIM. Even when HE sent them prophets, it did not help them much, because they kill the prophets when they tell them they are wrong, and this generation of the Negro people of Israel (during the Roman Empire Era) are worse than anyone before, and they are a nation that do not obey their GOD, or receive correction, and they no longer know the truth, because they do not want to do the right thing anymore.

Therefore, they need to stop trying to look good, because it makes no sense, and they should look around to see how the wrath of GOD caused destruction for them, because of the evil they did in HIS sight, and for setting up idols in

The House of THE LORD. Plus, they polluted the holy places, and they built up high places in the city of Tophet, which is in The Valley of the Sons of Hinnon, so they could sacrifice their daughters to idols by telling them to jump into the fire and burn up. That is a terrible thing, because GOD never ordered them to sacrifice their daughters to HIM. Nor did it ever come to HIS mind. So, for that, GOD said, the day would come when that place would no longer be called Tophet, or "The Valley of Hinnon", because it would be called "The Valley of Slaughter" when HE is done killing off every unrighteous person there. And when HE is done, it would be so many dead bodies there that there will be no more room to bury them, and the corpses of the dead would be food for the birds and the wild beasts, and no one would run them away. After that, all the people in the cities of Judah would stop being so happy when they see how destroyed and desolated the places become.

Chapter 8

Then the people of the tribe of Judah would bring out the bones of their king, priests and prophets, and all the inhabitants that died there in Jerusalem, and they would be able to spread them out before the sun, the moon, and all the angels in heaven, which they love and serve as their gods, because they would not be buried, and they would be as refuse on the earth. And the few evil ones that are left alive and driven to desolate conditions would choose death, instead of life, and people would tell them, "They have fallen, and cannot get up", and would wonder if they would turn back to YAH, their GOD.

Why do the Negro people of Israel continue to go farther and farther away from their GOD by holding on to their deceit, and refusing to turn back?

Listen carefully, and you would not hear anyone repenting for their sins, because they are all wondering what they did, and everyone is doing what they want, while the enemies of every nation invade them by war. Yet they say they are wise, and GOD is with them. But look how the scribe (secretary) writes all sorts of false reports, and how the wise men (the seers or prophets) are ashamed and dismayed, since they rejected the WORD of GOD. Now they are void of wisdom, because they are all wicked and greedy, and because they keep saying they would have peace is why no one would change. So, that is the reason why GOD gave their wives to men of other nations, and their fields to whoever wanted them. Leaving them with nothing while HE continued to warn them the whole time.

Were the Negro people of Israel ashamed when they were sinning?

No, they were not ashamed. That is why GOD said, they must be punished, and HE would consume them, and take back everything HE blessed them with.

Why does the Negroes of Israel sit and do nothing?

They should go into the city and look silently, since GOD has put them to silence with this bitter life, because of their sins. For though they are looking for peace, none comes, and they are looking for a time of health, but there is nothing, but trouble, and they are all trembling, because not only did GOD already consumed most of them by the white men, and other ungodly nations, HE is ready to send the wickedest white people among them to bite them, and finish them off. Then when they come, they have to comfort themselves in sorrow, while their hearts fail them, because the white people cannot be charmed.

Now listen!

Do you hear the voices of the Negro people of Israel crying all over the world?

Isn't GOD, THE KNG of HIS Negro people?

Yes, GOD is their KING, but they made HIM angry with their carved images, and there is no more time to waste, or time to relax, because they are still in the same problems. Since they are hurting so much, it is mournful, because it is shocking, and it is like there is no balm in Gilead, or any physicians in Jerusalem, "The Holy City" of the tribe of Judah, and it is like GOD cannot heal them, why they are so sick and cannot recover.

Chapter 9

Therefore, the righteous one suffers as they watch their disobedient people suffer under the white men in Jerusalem, and they mourn while they wish that their heads are full of water, so they could cry for their people every day, and night, because all of them are being killed. Yet, the righteous ones are also wishing that they could go far from the unrighteous ones, because they are idol worshippers, and friends to treacherous people, and they are liars that do not seek the truth. Which is why the righteous ones only speak to other righteous ones like themselves, and they tell each other to take heed to their brothers, because they might be against them, since everyone walks in slander, deceives their neighbors, tell lies, and weary themselves by doing evil all the time. That is why GOD brought them trouble to refine them, and test them to see if they would turn back to HIM, and GOD wants the righteous ones to know that the tongue is an arrow that is shot out, and it can come with deceit, because someone can speak peace to his neighbor, but in his heart, he is waiting to kill him.

Shouldn't GOD punish HIS people for those things, and avenge HIMSELF?

Yes, GOD should punish HIS people for doing wrong. That is why there would be desolation of the land of all the Negro people of Israel, and whoever is wise and can understand this, should tell their Negro people that the land is perishing, and it would burn up like the wilderness, so no one could travel through it. Because their GOD said, they forgot about the LAW, HE gave them, and they did not listen to HIM, or were they willing to do as HE said, and they did whatever they wanted to, and sought after the false god, Baal, as if they did not know HIM, their GOD. Which is the reason why HE called all their women to scream out to wail for all the dead by screaming with their eyes gushing with water to show that they are ashamed of being plundered, and cast out of their land, and they would be ashamed when they see that most of their men are dead, and they would remember that their people are being punished. Therefore, the women must teach their daughters, and all their neighbors to cry about this matter, because death has come to make them widows, and kill off their children to leave them dead on the streets with no one to gather and bury them.

If they think they are wise, then they should not depend on their wisdom. If they think they are mighty, then they should not depend on their strength. If they are rich, then they should not depend on their richness. But if they want to depend on something, they should depend on the fact that they know GOD, and on the fact that they understand what HE wants, and they know that HE wants them to be loving and kind, and to exercise fair justice, and live in righteousness on the earth, since that is what HE likes. Because the days would come when not only their Negro people would be punished, but also everyone who sins. That means everyone. Not just the people of Israel. From the ungodly Negro people of Egypt to the ungodly Negro people of Judah, to the red skinned ungodly Negro people of Edom, to the ungodly Negro people of Ammon, to the ungodly mixed cultured people of Moab, to all the ungodly white people of Babylon, and even to the ungodly people in the most remote parts of the world. No matter what color they are, or what nation they are from.

Chapter 10

That was why GOD warned them not to do as the gentiles, because they would also get punished for their sins, even though they did not see it coming, since their customs are futile, because they carved trees, and decorated them, and say they are gods, and they stand them upright with nails and hammer, so they would not topple over, and they are carried, and cannot speak. Which was why HE is begging them not to be afraid of the gentiles, especially since their gods cannot do any evil to them, nor can they do any good to them.

Which nation would not fear GOD, if HE has the right to do as HE pleases to anyone, and there is no one like HIM?

Do the people of Israel see that all gentiles are fool when they worship, and speak to worthless wooden idols, even though YAH, GOD, is the true and living GOD, and the everlasting KING, and at HIS hands the earth would tremble in HIS wrath, and the nations would not be able to stand it?

That is why the people of Israel should be telling the ungodly people in the world that the gods that did not make the heavens and the earth would perish, because YAH, their GOD, made the earth by HIS power and established the world by HIS wisdom, and HE controls everything. Then they should remind themselves that GOD said, "All idol worshippers are without knowledge, and are put to shame by the falsehood of their idol gods which has no life in them, and HE is not like idols, since HE is the maker of all things, and Israel is HIS inheritance, and HE is pissed, because HE does not like idol worship, which is why HE is telling all the idol worshippers to gather their stuff, because HE is ready to throw them out of The Mother Land, and put them in distress.

In such harsh time, the righteous ones of Israel are also feeling sorry for themselves, because they are also being severely punishment, but they will bear it, even though they have no house, no business connections, and no one to help them, and all their leaders turned from GOD, and their people would not prosper, and would be scattered. Therefore, GOD tells the righteous ones in the land to listen out for the reports of the great commotion when the white people come from the North to make the cities of Judah desolate, and

HE tell them that since they know that human beings do not have any sense, they should pray to HIM to please correct them with justice, so they would not end up as nothing. And they should pray that HE pours out HIS fury on the unbelieving gentiles who do not know HIM, and on the families that do not call on HIS name, because they are the reason why they are destroyed, and their land became desolate.

Chapter 11

Since GOD remembered the words of the covenant HE made with Israel, HE tells Jeremiah to tell the people that the person who does not obey the words of the covenant would be cursed. Because HE instructed them from the time their forefathers were delivered from Egypt to listen to HIM, and obey HIS words to be HIS chosen people, so HE could establish the promise HE made to their forefathers to give them a land flowing with milk and honey. When Jeremiah heard that, he tells GOD he would tell them exactly what HE said. But first, GOD tells him to say out loud in the streets of the cities of Judah, especially in Jerusalem, "GOD exhorted your forefathers, and delivered you from the Egyptians, and HE got up early every day to tell you that you must obey HIM, and still, you are not obedient up to this day. Which is why you are being cursed, and there is a conspiracy among you, because you broke the covenant, and turned back to being sinners, because you do not want to obey GOD. And because you are gone to other gods is why calamity would come upon your cities, and you would not be able to escape. And though you cry to GOD, HE would not listen to you, and HE does not want any of the righteous ones to feel sorry for you, or even pray for you, because HE would not listen. And because the tribe of Judah, HIS beloved ones are lewd, and their holy flesh is gone from them, and they do evil and rejoice, even though HE call them The Green Olive Tree that is lovely with good fruit, HE is punishing them, and there is no hope for them, because though HE established them,

HE pronounced doom against them for the evil they did against themselves by giving offerings to false gods.

Those are the facts that GOD presented to Jeremiah, and when GOD was done speaking, Jeremiah immediately goes to the people of Jerusalem and tell them exactly what GOD said, and he tell them they better believe it, because GOD gave him knowledge of it by showing him what they did. Then he said, he was stupid to try to warn them, because he did not know that they were scheming to kill him for living righteously, and even though they did not want anyone to remember him anymore, GOD, the righteous judge, the one who knows the mind, and the heart of a person would let him see that HE is protecting him, because he only wants to help them. At that very moment, GOD tells him to tell the people of Anathoth who wants to kill him, "They would be punished severely, and their sons would be killed in battle, while the women and children die off from starvation, leaving nothing left of them."

Chapter 12

Immediately, Jeremiah realizes that GOD is righteous each time he pleads with HIM, and he talks to HIM about HIS judgment, since he wants to know why the wicked prosper, and why the treacherous are so happy. Because even though he knows that GOD made everyone, it seems like the wicked multiplied, and get cleaver, and rich, and they talk about GOD, but they refuse to obey HIM. And since GOD know him, and tested his heart towards HIM, he pleads with GOD for Him to destroy all the unrighteous ones. Then he asks GOD, how long the earth would suffer desolation, because of the wicked, and how long would the animals, and everything be gone, while the people of Israel keep saying, it does not matter what they do, as if they do not realize that if they were unable to defeat the regular white men in the streets, they would not be able to defeat the white soldiers on horses that would come against them. Or perhaps they do not realize that if they are worried in The

Holy Land about the white people, then they would be much more worries when the white people take them to their wicked lands.

The people of Israel were warned about dealing with their own people treacherously and about telling others to fight against their own people. That is why they should not believe their enemies, even if they speak things they want to hear, because GOD forsook them, HIS dearly beloved ones, and gave them over to their enemies for turning against HIM. But GOD hates it, because now they are like the ugly duckling that all the other ducklings hate, and it is HE, WHO turned the world against them, and allowed rulers of other nations to destroy their land and their Negro people and made the place desolate. Now the place is mourning to HIM, because no one could see that HE was serious, and they kept saying they were alright, though everything they did turned to nothing, even after they put themselves in pain trying to accomplish it.

Do you think you should laugh at the Negro people of Israel?

Go ahead and laugh at the Negroes of Israel! Laugh all you want, because GOD said, all the nations that invaded their land, and destroyed their people, then took over the land, would be taken from it. Then after all the invaders are taken from the land, HE would return to them, and have compassion for them by bringing them back, and giving them the land they inherited. Then if the rest of the people in the world turn from their false ways of worship, and learn about HIM, and obey HIM, they would be as blessed as the Negro people of Israel, but if any of them refuse to change, that nation would be destroyed.

Chapter 13

On another day, GOD tells Jeremiah to get a linen sash, and tie it around his waist, and wear it every day as a belt, but never to wash it. Then Jeremiah gets the sash, and ties it around his waist, and GOD tells him to take the sash to The Euphrates River (near the white man land) and hide it in a hole in the rock. Jeremiah did that. Then after many days, GOD tells him to go back to The Euphrates River and get the sash, and he goes back to The Euphrates, and gets the sash, and it is ruined, and good for nothing. And GOD said, "That is how HE is going to ruin the pride of the people of the tribe of Judah, since they are evil idol worshippers that turned from HIM, who became worthless, because when HE asked them to cling to HIM, like the sash around the waist, so HE could call them HIS people that are blessed, they would not listen. Which is why HE is going to make them dumfounded by making them kill each other, since HE has no more pity for them, and if they have sense, then they would give HIM glory before HE starts the punishment, but if they are dumb, HE feels sorry for all that would happen to the ones left in the land, and to the ones that are taken as captive. Which is why HE wants all the officials to humble themselves, because they would be punished, and they would lose their position for allowing evil things in the land. So, it is pronounced that they would be carried away as captives, and HE wants them to open their eyes and notice which white leaders are preparing to come from the North to destroy them, and take over, because HE does not know what they are going to say when the white men take control of them, since it was them who taught the white people to be leaders, and chiefs over them. So, let them look at themselves screaming out like women in labor, and let them wonder why those things are happening to them, even though they know they are being punished for their sinning.

Can the black Ethiopian people change the color of their skin?

Or can the leopard change his spots?

No, they cannot, even though bleaching can lighten the pigmentation of skin, and genetic and hormonal manipulation can change a being temporarily. So, a person that is accustomed to doing evil can never change his ways. That is why the lands of the people of Israel are desolate, and most of the people were taken captive. It is also why GOD would scatter the remnants that are left in the land, since it is what they deserve for turning from HIM. Then they would be shame of their adultery, their lustful neighing, their lewd harlotry, and their false ways of worship, and there is no way they can escape it.

Chapter 14

The people of Judah mourn, because the city gates are languished, and the place is destroyed. There is not even water to be found, and the ground is parched, because there is no rain. Therefore, the farmers are ashamed, and the animals still give birth in the fields, but they leave, because there is no grass. O', even though all those things look bad for the people of Israel, GOD had to do it for the sake of HIS name, because they are sinners, and they sinned against HIM, their SAVIOR, in times of trouble.

For the moment, the Negroes are like strangers in "The Holy Land", or like travelers that are only visiting for the night, and they are astonished at their troubles, since they are acting like THE MIGHTY GOD cannot save. Yet, YAH, their GOD is in their midst, because they are called by HIS name, and HE would never leave them, even though they like to wonder from HIM and HE does not like it. That is why HE is punishing them for all their sins, and why HE said not to pray for any good to come to them right then, because HE would not listen, since HE does not want anything to do with them.

When Jeremiah heard what GOD said, he asks HIM did HE know that the prophets told the people that there would be peace for them, and GOD said, the prophets are lying, because HE did not tell them to tell the people that, and the ones that lied, they, and the people that believe their lies would be killed, and no one would bury them. Which is why HE wants him to tell them that they might as well start crying, and cry day, and night, because they are going to be severely punished by war, sickness, and famine, and the prophets, and the best of them that are not killed would be carried away into captivity. Then Jeremiah asks if HE really rejected the tribe of Judah, because HE is disgusted at how they are acting in Zion, and if HE struck them, leaving them without any healing, looking for peace when it would not come, and for healing when they cannot be healed, because there is nothing but trouble around them. Then in great sorrow, he repents for the people, and said, "We acknowledge YOU, my GOD. We know that we sinned against YOU. So, for YOUR namesake, please do not hate us and shame us. Please remember YOUR covenant and do not break it. There are no idols of other gods of any other nations that can cause it to rain. Just YOU. So, we will wait on YOU, because YOU made everything, and YOU are in control of it all."

Chapter 15

To that, GOD replies, "Even if Moses and Samuel stood before ME, and pleaded for the people, I still would not change MY mind about punishing them", and HE tells him to go, and tell them to stay out of HIS face, and get away from HIM. So, he asks GOD, what if the people asked where they should go, and GOD said, "Tell them I said, they could all drop dead, and whoever die in war, so be it. Whoever dies of starvation, who cares. And whoever is taken as captive, oh well! Because destruction is ordered to come, and the sword would kill, and dogs would drag the bodies, and the birds, and the wild beast would devour the bodies, and the best of them that are still alive would be taken as captives to many white nations, leaving only the lame, the dumb, and the weak in the land. Therefore, I want them to tell ME which nation would have pity on them to plead their cause, or stop to ask how they are doing, since not one soul would pity them, because I forsook them, and the young, the old, and the new, would all be punished, leaving only widows, orphans, fools, and the weak."

Then Jeremiah said, "I feels like my life has always been terrible, and I am always thinking about how the people do not like him, and how I could not befriend anyone to talk things over with." To that, GOD replied, "Few good people are in the land, and I would treat them well, and keep the white people from bothering them, but everyone else would suffer when they feel the harshness of the white man destroying everything, and the captives taken. Then after hearing that, he asks GOD to remember him, and to be with him, and not to kill him, because he is suffering by the hands of the people for what HE told him to say and do. Yet, he tells GOD that he is happy to know the truth, and is willing to take the time to learn, because the truth gives him joy, and made him rejoice when he found out that he belongs to HIM, which is why he does not hang around sinner, or laugh with them about sins, because he feel bad about those things, since he fears HIM. Then he asks why does he always feel so much pain like he has a perpetual wound which cannot be healed, and if he would be punished like anyone else, and GOD said, "If you completely return to ME, and separate yourself from the people, I would protect you while I use you to warn them, and whoever likes you from now on, and join with you, that would let you see who is righteous, or not. But you should not return to them, because they are going to fight against you, even though they would not prevail, because I will be with you to save you from all their schemes."

Chapter 16

On another day, GOD tell him that he should not take a wife, or have children there in Jerusalem, because the children that are born there, and the mothers, and fathers who have them would all die a gruesome death, and no one would cry for them, or bury them. Then the birds, and the wild beast would eat them, and when it happens, HE does not want any righteous person from Israel to cry, or pray for the ungodly ones, because HE took away their peace. And no other nations would come to them and mourn, or comfort them over all the dead, or help them out, and no one would be their friends, because HE will make sure they come to nothing. And when the people ask him why

HE is going to do those things to them, and what did they do to deserve it, he should tell them, "It is because their forefathers did not obey HIM, and they served other gods, and since they are worse than their forefathers, HE would send them into exile to another land that they do not know. And HE will stay away from them, so they could serve the gods there. But the day would come when they would not be saying, the GOD who brought us out of Egypt lives, but they would be saying, the GOD who brought us out of the North from the white man lands lives, because HE would bring them from captivity, and take them back to their native land. But first, they must be punished, and many white men would come to them, and be glad to punish them for HIM, because of their ungodly ways. Then HE would repay the white people double for what they've done, and for defiling the land, and filling it with their detestable and abominable idols.

When Jeremiah heard that, he said, "Oh my GOD. Now the gentile people would come from all over the place and say that our Negro people inherited lies as a doctrine, because it was worthless to them." And GOD asks him, if people should make gods for themselves that are not GODS, and since the answer is no, GOD said, "This one time, I will cause MY Negro people to know how mighty and powerful I AM. Then they would know that I AM the only GOD."

Chapter 17

Since the sins of the people of Judah are deep in their hearts and minds, while they worship their idols under every green tree, GOD said HE would cause the white people to invade their land, and take everything, and whoever is left would eventually want to be in the white man's lands. Because cursed is the person that turned from HIM, and trust in another human being, since that person would have nothing but problems in life. But, blessed is the person that trusts in HIM, since that person would be well stable, and all his needs would be provided, and that person would not be afraid when trouble comes, and that person would not get sick, and would not worry about what is needed when without anything, nor would that person stop being joyful. Then GOD tells him that HE wants them to know, that the heart is deceitful more than anything and it is desperately wicked, but who would have known it. Which is why HE searches the heart, and tests the mind, so that HE could bless or punish anyone according to what they deserve. Therefore, if any Negro of Israel is getting rich by some unlawful, or ungodly way, that Negro better expects to be punished, and in the end to feel like a fool, because even though "The Throne of GOD" where they worships was glorious and high from the beginning, it is ruined. Which is why all the people who forgot about HIM, their GOD, should be ashamed, since HE is the ONE that can provide all their needs.

That revelation astonished Jeremiah, and he repents for the nation. Then he asks GOD to heal him, and save him, because he praises HIM, even though his Negro people are asking, where are the promises HE made to them, and why doesn't it come then. And since he never turned from GOD, nor did he ever want the people to be punished, he said, that was the reason why he warned them like GOD told him to. Then he asks GOD not to hurt him too much, since HE is his only hope in that time of doom, and he also asks to let everyone who persecutes him be ashamed, and confused, while HE keeps him sane.

Then GOD tell him to stand in "The Gates of Jerusalem" where the kings of Judah come and goes, and tell them they and all the people better start to observe the Sabbath, and not do any work at home, or anywhere in the city, because that is what HE told their forefathers they should have been doing, but they did not do it. And if they obey HIM, HE will not destroy the city, and HE would give them great kings through the lineage of Judah to lead them. Then all the people of Israel would come from the different parts of their land with offerings to gather in Jerusalem with sacrifices of praise to The House of

THE LORD. But if they do not observe "The Sabbath Day" by not doing any work, HE would allow the white people to come to destroy Jerusalem, The Holy City, and no one could stop it.

Chapter 18

On another day, GOD tells Jeremiah to go down to the potter's house, and HE would speak to him there. So, Jeremiah goes to the potter's house, and the potter is there making something at the wheel, and the vessel he is making was marred in his hands, and the potter makes the vessel into something good, other than what he had intended to make before. Therefore, GOD tell him to ask the people of Israel, if HE could do the same thing to them, because as the clay is in the potter's hand, so are they in HIS hands. And GOD tells him that if HE speak about destroying a nation for their sins, the instant they turn from their evil, HE will change HIS mind about destroying them, and if HE told a nation that HE would bless them, the moment they do evil, HE will change HIS mind about doing them any good. Therefore, HE is devising a plan against them, and all of them better decide to change from their evil ways, even though they are telling themselves that it would not do them any good to change why they continue to do things their way, hoping they could get some enjoyment out of their evil ways. So, HE wants them to go and ask any gentile person, if any of them ever turned away from obeying their god, like how they turned from HIM and did evil things. And HE also wants them to go and ask anyone, if they would leave a clean source of water, which run from the top of the mountain to go to a place that has stagnant polluted water, just like how they left HIM, their GOD, their nourishing provider, by going to gods that are polluted, and cannot do anything for them. So, that is the reason why their land is going to be desolate, and people would be disgusted at them, and shake their heads at how shameful they, and the place looks, and they would also be scattered throughout the white man's lands as servants.

Immediately, Jeremiah leaves to tell the people what GOD said, and when he told them everything, they want to kill him, because they do not want to change, and they feel like they would not get in trouble, if they killed him, since none of them, not even the priests, the judges, the lawyers, or any citizen are law abiding. Now Jeremiah is concerned for his life, and he pray to GOD to protect him from those who are against him, and he also pray that they would suffer to the full extent of GOD's punishment.

Chapter 19

Then GOD tells him to get an earthen flask from the potter, and take some of the elders, and the priests to "The Valley of The Sons of Hinnon" to the entrance of Potsherd Gate and tell the tribe of Judah that HE would bring such a catastrophe on the place, that when they hear it, their ears would tingle. Because they forgot about HIM and they made The Holy Land a place where idols are worshipped, and a place where the killing of innocent people is regular. Plus, they are worshipping the false god, Baal, in the mountains, and they are burning up their children as sacrifices to him, which is a thing HE never asked them to do, because it is awful, and HE would never think of such a thing. That is why HE said the day would come when the lands of the tribe of Judah would no longer be called, Tophet, but it would be called "The Land of Slaughter", because HIS counsel would be taken away from them to cause the white man to kill them, leaving the birds and wild beasts to eat their dead bodies, and the cities desolate for people to scorn when they see those that are alive are reduced to eating their own children.

Then GOD tells him that after he tells the people those terrible things, he must break the flask in front of the elders, and the priests that goes with him, and say, "Just like this flask is broken, so shall this city, and these people be broken, which cannot be made whole again, and they would be buried in Tophet, until there is no more room to bury them, because they created such a terrible city such as Tophet." W So, without hesitation, Jeremiah goes to the people of Judah that lives in the city of Tophet and tell them what GOD said HE would do to them. Then he breaks the flask, and explain the reason for it by the parable, and he leaves from there, and goes to the courtyard of The House of THE LORD, and tell the people there, that GOD said HE would still bring doom upon them, because they are stubborn, and would not change.

Chapter 20

After Pashhur, the son of Immer, who is priest, and the head of the church, heard what Jeremiah prophesied about them, he hits Jeremiah upside his head. Then he locks Jeremiah up in the stocks, in the land of the tribe of Benjamin, which is by The House of THE LORD (the church). The next day, he takes Jeremiah out of the stock, and Jeremiah tells him that, GOD does not call him Pashhur, instead, HE calls him Magor-Missabib, which means a wicked white man, since he acts like a wicked white man, which is why the white men would come from the Babylonian lands to kill them, and carry some as captives to their white lands and take over their lands. Moreover, all the wealth, the produce, and all the precious things would be taken, and he (Pashhur), and all the people in his family of priests would go into captivity in white lands, and die, and be buried there, because they told the people nothing but lies.

After that, Jeremiah cry out to GOD in prayer and complain to HIM about convincing him to talk to the people, even though before he said he was willing to, because they are mocking him, and they make him afraid every day, and he has to shout out, saying "Violence, and plunder!" to get help, and they try to harm him for telling the truth. But even though he said he would not prophesy anymore, he tells GOD that he would prophesy, because the message is burning inside of him, and he could not hold it in, and he must prophesy, even though they continue to mock him, and look to harm him from every direction. Then he asks GOD to take vengeance on them, because he pleaded for them, but they refuse to change, and he tell GOD that he wishes that his people would sing to HIM, and praise HIM, because HE delivered the life of the poor believers from the hands of those who gained their riches by doing evil. Then he thinks about how bad his Negro people are at the time, and he curse the day he was born, and wish that day was not blessed when his mother had him, and he wish that the doctor that told his father that he just had a son was cursed, and would suffer, because he did not kill him in the womb, so that he would not have to see such terrible things about them to be ashamed of.

Chapter 21

After many years passed, the people continued to suffer. Then Nebuchadnezzar, the white kings of Babylon start his attack on the people of Judah. Just like how GOD said he would. Scare to death, Zedekiah, the king of Judah, goes to talk to Pashhur, and Zephaniah (the priests) and he beg them to ask GOD what he should do about the attack from Nebuchadnezzar. Wishing that maybe GOD would be nice to them, and make the white king leave them alone. Then with some hope, Pashhur and Zephaniah pray to GOD for the answer, and instead of answering them, GOD gives the answer to Jeremiah, and tells him to tell Zedekiah (the king) that HE personally would go in the midst of the battles to help the Chaldean (Babylonian) white people to defeat them, and afterward HE would let Nebuchadnezzar take him, and his royal family, and all the people that are still alive to Babylon as captives. So, it is about life and death, and if they are not killed, and are left in the city, they would be captured and taken to the white man's land to live there and serve them, because HE is against them, and so, HE recommends that he, and all the royal lineage, and all the leaders get up in the morning, and start to punish the people that are doing evil. So, they could save the ones they are doing it against. Then if they do that, HE will not destroy them for their own evils in their leadership, because it is the idol worshippers that HE is against for thinking that HE does not care, and HE would do nothing. Which is why HE is telling them that HE would punish them according to all the evil they do, and destroy them, and everything around them.

Chapter 22

GOD continue to speak, and HE said, since Zedekiah and his family are leaders, HE wants them to rule righteously, and not to do any wrong to the visitors, or the fatherless, and the widows, or murder anyone, because if they do what HE says, then they will have great kings from their own people (Judah) to lead them. But if they do not do what HE says, then they will become desolate. And even though they are his favorite people, HE would make their land like the wilderness, and everyone who pass by would wonder why HE did it, and people would say, "HE did it, because they forgot about the covenant HE made with them, and because they worship and serve other gods". So, HE does not want them to weep for the dead, HE wants them to weep bitterly for those that are taken captive, because they would die where they are taken, and return to The Mother Land no more. As for Shallum, the son of Josiah (a king of Judah), he is going to be captured, and he would return there no more, and all those who got rich by some unjust way would also be captured, because they are unjust, and they should not be rulers, just because they enclose themselves in cedar houses. Now HE is asking them, if they did not know that their forefathers had to do the right things to be blessed, because it seems like their hearts, and eyes are for nothing except for killing the innocent, and for practicing oppression, and violence. As for Jehoiakim, the son of Josiah (the other king of Judah) he is going to die, and will be buried with the dead donkeys, and get dragged, and cast out beyond the city walls, and no one would feel sorry for him. And the people of Israel that are in Lebanon (which is a white city inherited by Israel) that are in the town of Bashan, they should know that all their allies are gone, because when they were prosperous, they were being corrected, but they refused to listen. So, they are going to lose their greatness, and be ashamed, and even though their houses are made of cedar, they would not look so great after they are punished. Also tell Coniah, that he needs to know that HE likes him, even though he is a white man, and is the son of Jehoiakim, who rules over all the people of Judah that lives in Lebanon, but he would still be cast out of the land, and Nebuchadnezzar, the king of Babylon, and all his Chaldean (white) people would come, and take them into captivity to their white land.

Is Coniah a despised broken idol, something which people have no pleasure in?

No, he is not.

Then why would he and his white people be cast out of their inherited land?

I can only guess that it was, because GOD has judged his leadership as a white man, and HE does not want him, or any of his family to rule over any of HIS Negro people anymore.

Chapter 23

That is why GOD told Jeremiah to tell Coniah that they should feel sorry for those who are teaching, and preaching to their people, because HE is against them for not teaching the right things, because it makes the people disobey HIM, and only few of them that are righteous would be saved and get to return home after they are captured. And only those few would be blessed to have good kings and priests that would teach them, and they would not be afraid anymore, or be dismayed, because they would not suffer any lack. Then the world would know that the people of Judah are saved, because they would increase from the few, and they would praise HIM, their GOD, and call HIM "THE LORD OUR RIGHTEOUSNESS", and as long as HE lives, HE is promising that HE would bring them out of captivity from the white nations in the North, and from any other white nation in the world.

Yet, after hearing that promise, Jeremiah's heart is broken, because all the prophets would be taken into captivity as GOD pronounced, and the land is full of idol worshippers, and it is cursed, and the pleasant places of the wilderness are dried up. Which shows that they are evil, and their priests, and prophets are profane, and only wickedness is found amongst the people, even in his own family. And his heart is also broken, because his people would suffer much, and they would be taken from The Mother Land (Africa), because GOD is bringing disaster on them to punish them. Even in Samaria among the people of Israel, there is a lot of foolishness, because they prophesy in the name of the false god, Baal, to curse their own, instead of wanting to change from their evil ways. Which is why GOD would punish them, and why HE said not to listen to the prophets, since they made the people worthless by telling them anything, instead of telling them what HE said, and they continually tell those who hate HIM that they would live in peace.

Which one of the people of Judah took time to stay in prayer before GOD to know what HE wants?

Which one heard what GOD said, and understood it?

Very few.

That few included Jeremiah, who took the time to know what GOD was saying, because he wanted the people to know that GOD is angry, and is ready to punish all their wicked people, and HE would not change HIS mind, because later in time, everyone would understand why HE did it. Jeremiah also took the time to know GOD, since the people needed to know that GOD did not send all the prophets they had been listening to, even though they prophesied in HIS name, because if the prophets took time to talk to GOD, and heard what HE wanted, then they would have told the people the truth, and the people would have changed by then.

Was GOD near, and under their arms?

No, HE was not.

GOD is far in the heavens, and no one can hide from HIM, because HE sees everything, and HE saw what the prophets did, and HE heard what they said against HIM. Now HE is tired of the prophets, because they are trying to let HIS people forget about HIM, and they claim they have dreams, and claim HE spoke to them, when HE did not. So, HE said, they can keep on thinking that, but HE wants anyone who knows the truth to speak the truth faithfully, because HE is against the lying prophets for telling the people lies, when HE never sent them, and yet they keep telling people HE did. Therefore, anyone that prophesied, saying, **"The oracle of the LORD"** as the lying prophets say when they prophesy, that person would be punished, along with everyone in their family, and they would look shameful, because HE does not want them to prophesy saying HE said anything to them anymore.

Chapter 24

Next thing you know, Nebuchadnezzar, the king of Babylon comes and carried away Jeconiah, the princes, and the craftsmen of the people of Judah from Jerusalem to their white lands. And GOD shows Jeremiah a vision with two baskets of figs before HIS temple. One basket had very good figs, nice and ripe in it. The other had bad figs, which could not be eaten, because they are so bad, and GOD asks Jeremiah what he sees, and he said, he sees figs, and some of them are very good to eat, and some are so bad, they cannot be eaten. Therefore, GOD said, just like those good figs, so would HE acknowledge the good people of Judah that were taken to the white people's land for their own good, because HE would use the bad situation for good, and then bring them back to their native land, and build them up again, and they would want to know HIM as their GOD, and they would be HIS holy people. But as for the bad figs, such as Zedekiah (the king of Judah) and his princes, and the unbelieving ones that are still in the land, and those that ran to Egypt to save themselves, they would have trouble, and look cursed, no matter where they are, and they would starve, and get sick, or be killed in war, until all of them are dead.

Chapter 25

Then in the fourth year of Jehoiakim's reign over Judah. Which is in the first year of Nebuchadnezzar's, the king of Babylon reign, Jeremiah speaks to the people, saying, from the thirteenth year of Josiah's reign, for twenty-five years, he had been getting up early in the mornings to warn them about what GOD said HE would do to them, and GOD sent them other prophets, but they also refused to listen to them, and because they do not want to listen and change from their evil ways, all the white nations, and their armies would come to invade them, and they would not be happy anymore, because they would be serving the white people for seventy years. But when the seventy years are passed, GOD would punish all the white people for being harsh on them, even though HE allowed them to take them as captives, and HE would make their land desolate, because HE wants to let all the white nations take the bait, since HE sat a trap for them, that they would not be able to escape. So, all other nations are also being warned, because after the white folks are punished for what they do to them, the other nations would also be punished for making them suffer.

Even some of the Negro folks of Israel are going to be punished for making their own people suffer, and even Pharaoh, the king of Egypt, and his ungodly Negro people, and all the mix-cultured people of the land of Uz, and all the ungodly colored people of the Philistines, mainly in the cities of Ashkelon, Gaza, Ekron, and a remnant of Ashdod. And all the red skinned Negroes of Edom, and the Negro people of Moab and Ammon, which are the descendants of Lot. And all the ungodly people of the different cultures amongst them, especially the pure white people of Tyre, the pure white people of Sidon, and all the white people in Europe on the coast across the Mediterranean Sea. As well as Dedan, Tema, and Buz, and all the nations that are in remote areas, along with the white people who are ruled by Zimri, and Elam, and the white people of Medes, and all the white people of the North. All of them would be punished for mistreating the Negro people of GOD.

So, GOD said, let them be. Let them mistreat HIS people all they want, because they are going to get punished, and if they think they are not going to get punished, they are making a sad mistake, because if HE punished HIS people for destroying themselves, why would they not think that HE would punish everyone else that helped to destroy them. Yes, everyone would get punished for what they did to the Negro people of Israel. That is why everyone was warned that GOD is against them, and from nation to nation, disaster would come, and GOD would kill people from one end of the earth to the other, and the dead would not be buried, because they are oppressors, and GOD is angry with them.

Some notes:

*The **Moabites** and the **Ammonites** are Negro people that are descendants of Lot that came from incest that his daughters had with him, while he was drunk. Therefore, the land of Moab and Ammon are black lands, but white people went to those lands and stayed there, and they also call themselves Ammonites and Moabites, because of the country of origin, and when the white people came there to live with the Negro descendants of Lot, the descendants of Lot allowed them to teach them , and to practice idolatry, and they also marry each other, which cause them to have biracial children that are also idol worshippers. Then the land of Moab and Ammon became inhabited with ungodly Negroes people of Israel, ungodly white people, and ungodly biracial people that worships idol.*

Chapter 26

When Jehoiakim first started to reign, GOD told Jeremiah to stand in the courtyard of The House of The LORD before the people of Judah that came there to worship, and tell them what HE said, so maybe they would listen and stop doing evil, so HE would not punish them by the white people as planned, and if they do not listen and change, HE has to follow through. Then Jeremiah goes to the priests, and all the people that are in The House of THE LORD, and tell them what GOD said, and they seize him, and said they are going to kill him for saying they are going to be captured, and the city would be desolate. Then when the princes heard about the commotion, they go to The House of THE LORD, and sit in the entry of the gate, and the priest, the prophets, and all the people tell them that Jeremiah deserves to die, because he said they are all going to die off. And Jeremiah said GOD sent him to prophesy against the tribe of Judah, and all the people in their cities, and he wants them to change their ways and obey GOD, and maybe GOD would change HIS mind, and they can do whatever they want to him, but if they kill him, they would be killing an innocent person.

After hearing that, the princes said he does not deserve to die, because he is only warning them as GOD told him to. Then one of the elders said, "In the past, Micah (a prophet) prophesied the same thing in the time when Hezekiah was king of Judah, and Hezekiah did not kill him, and when the people changed from their evil doings, GOD did not do what HE said HE was going to do to them." Then the elder tells another story, one of a man named Urijah, who also prophesied in the name of GOD against Judah and all of Israel during Jehoiakim's reign, and when Jehoiakim tried to kill him, he ran to Egypt to save his life, and Jehoiakim sent to Egypt to get him, and they went and got him, and killed him, and buried him with the common folks, instead of with the prophets. Then the elder said, nevertheless, forget all that, because

Ahiham, the son of Saphan is watching over Jeremiah, and the people cannot kill him, because GOD keeps him protected, always."

Chapter 27

Also, in the beginning of Jehoiakim's reign, GOD tells Jeremiah to make bonds, and yokes, and put them on his neck. Then send them to the kings of the ungodly nations of Edom, Moab, Ammon, Tyre, and Sidon by the hands of a messenger, because they oppressed HIS people when Zedekiah was king of Judah, because HE made the earth, and everything in it, and gives power to whomever HE wants to, and HE gave the earth and everything in it to HIS white servant, Nebuchadnezzar, the king of Babylon, so that every nation would serve him, and the nations that do not want to serve Nebuchadnezzar and his white people until HE is ready to punish them, they would be punished with war, disease, and hunger. So, they better not listen to their so called prophets, diviners, dreamers, soothsayers, or sorcerers that tells them that they would not serve the white people of Babylon, because if they subject themselves to the white people of Babylon, they could remain in their own land and live off what they have there. And it is the same thing that HE told Zedekiah, that if he, and the people of Judah served Nebuchadnezzar, and his white people in captivity in Babylon, then they could live. Because none of them should want to die by war, famine, and diseases, just so they do not have to serve the white people. So, Zedekiah, and his people of Judah better not listen to anyone that says they would not serve the white people, because it is a lie, since they are not sent to say anything, and they are only false prophets that are telling lies, so they would not believe the truth, and change, because they want them to be punished for not changing.

Therefore, the good priests and prophets, better not listen to their lying priests, and prophets when they say that the rest of the tribes of Israel are about to return from captivity in Babylon, and they better decide to serve the white people of Babylon when they come to take over the land, so they could live. Because if they are really good prophets and priests, they would have prayed to make intercession that all the holy, and royal treasures in the land would never had been taken to Babylon. Which is why Nebuchadnezzar, and his army would be allowed to come back and take whatever treasures that were left from the first time. Yea, that is what would happen to all the treasure that remains in The House of THE LORD, and in the king's palace, but they should not worry, because even though they are carried away to Babylon, the day would come when the white people would be punished, and the treasures, and the people would be back to the holy land.

Chapter 28

When Jehoiakim's reign ended, Zedekiah (also known as Mattaniah) become the new king of Judah, and in the 4th year, and 5th month of his reign, Hananiah (the prophet), the son of Azur, from the city of Gibeon speaks to the people while they are in The House of THE LORD, and said, GOD broke the yoke of the king of Babylon, and within two years the treasures of The House of THE LORD that Nebuchadnezzar took would be brought back, and Jeconiah, the son of Jehoiakim, and all the people that were taken captive with him would also be brought back. Then Jeremiah sarcastically said, "Amen! Let GOD do what HE said. Let HIM bring back all the treasures of The House of THE LORD, and all who were taken captive to Babylon. All the prophets before me prophesied against many countries and governments, and about wars, disaster, and diseases. But some prophets prophesy about peace, and when you see there is no peace, then you would know which prophets were prophesying the truth." Persisting in his prophecy, Hananiah takes the yoke that Jeremiah has on his neck, and breaks it, and said, 'Within two years, that is how GOD would break the yoke of Nebuchadnezzar from the necks of all the nations in the world.' That was another false prophecy. One to cover the other. So, Jeremiah leaves from there to let them believe whatever they want to believe. Then GOD tells him to tell Hananiah that he broke the yoke made of wood, and made things worse, since now it is a yoke made of iron, because HE placed a yoke of iron on all the nations, so they would serve Nebuchadnezzar, and his white people in Babylon, and they would serve him, because HE gave him the whole world, and everything in it. Right away, Jeremiah goes back to Hananiah, and said, "GOD did not send you to prophesy. Yet you made the people believe your lies, and within this same year, GOD is going to let you die, because you taught the people to rebel against HIM." Shortly after that, in that same year, in the seventh month, Hananiah dies.

Chapter 29

To continue with the message, Jeremiah sends a messenger named Elesah from Jerusalem with a letter to give to the priests, and all the people that were carried away as captives from Jerusalem to Babylon by Nebuchadnezzar. Then when Elesah gets to Babylon, he reads the letter, which said, "GOD said, it was HE WHO caused them to become captives, and they may as well build houses there, plant gardens, eat, get married, and have children, and they could intermarry with the white people there, so that they may increase in numbers and not die off. And they are to seek peace in Babylon, no matter where they are, and pray for Babylon, because they could still live in peace there. So, they better not listen to any prophets or diviners that tell them they would not be there long, because they would be in captivity for seventy years. Then after the seventy years, GOD said, HE would be good to them, and they would return from captivity to have peace, hope, and a good future, and they would pray to HIM, and HE would answer them, and if they seek HIM with all their hearts, they would find HIM, because by that time, they would believe, since HE would give them prophets in Babylon. As for the people that are left in their inherited land that are not in captivity, they would die off by war, famine, and diseases, since they are so bad, and every nation would fight against them, because they did not listen to HIM, and because of that, Ahab (the king), and Zedekiah (the priest) would be killed in captivity by Nebuchadnezzar.

Then whenever someone would want to curse someone, they would say, "May GOD make them like how HE made Zedekiah and Ahab, whom the king of Babylon roasted in the fire". Yes, they would be punished, because all of them did disgraceful things in their land by committing adultery with their neighbor's wives, and they speak lies in the name of GOD when they know that GOD knows about it. And Shemaiah would also be punished, because he sent letters to the people in Jerusalem to Zephaniah (the king), and all his household of demented priests to tell them they are the priests, instead of Jehoiada and his family, which caused the people to lock up Jehoiada in the stock, and yet, he would not rebuke, and lock up his false prophet, Zephaniah for prophesying by a familiar spirit, and saying, they would not be captives in Babylon. So, they may as well build houses and plant gardens to stay there, because GOD did not tell him anything. That is why GOD told him to send them the messenger with the letter to let them know that HE would punish Shemiah, and his family, because he lied to them, and caused them to be captives."

Chapter 30

On another day, GOD goes to Jeremiah and tells him to write down everything HE told him in a book for himself, because the days would come when HE would bring back the captive of the tribes of Israel, including Judah, and give them their inherited land again, because HE heard the voices of trembling, and fear, and not of peace, since the way it sounds, it seems like it would be less painful if a man is in labor. And HE sees every man with his hands on his loins, and his face pale like a woman in labor, and it is a terrible time that none was like it before, because it is a time of trouble for them. But they would be saved from it, because the day would come when HE would break the yoke, and no foreign nation would be able to enslave them again, and they would serve HIM, and there would be kings through the lineage of David (the tribe of Judah) on the throne. Therefore, HE does not want them to be afraid, or dismayed, because they are HIS people, HIS servants, and HE would bring them from their captivity to be at rest, and in peace, and no one would be able to make them afraid, because HE would be with them, and HE would save them. And though HE would completely destroy any nation that enslaved them, HE would never completely destroy them, and HE would correct them of their sins with justice, and punish them, even if they are badly wounded, and afflicted. And since there is no one willing to help them, HE wants to know why they cry about their affliction, when they know that they are being severely punished for increasing in sin. And though HE is allowing the nations to devour them, HE wants them to know that afterwards, HE would devour the nations for them, and HE would restore their health, and heal their wounds, because the world called them an outcast by saying, "These are the people of Zion, that no one sees." Which is why HE would bring them back from captivity, and be merciful to them, and make their land look like how it should look. Then they would be happy, and thankful, and they would be great in number, and have healthy children, and have nobles that are honest, and HE would want to be near them, and would want them to be HIS people. Therefore, the wicked people better watch out, because HIS fury would fall on them for what they did to HIS people, and HE would not stop being angry, until HE does it, and they would see.

Chapter 31

So, because HE loves the people of Israel, HE would build them up again, so they would be adorned with tambourines while singing and dancing, and much would grow in Samaria, and the people of Israel there would be glad to worship HIM. Therefore, HE wants them to sing with gladness, and shout out to all the nations, and tell them they would be freed. And HE wants them to start giving HIM praise, and ask HIM to save them, because HE would bring them from the countries in the North, and from anywhere else, no matter if they are blind, lame, or a woman with child, or whatever, HE would make sure they return. That is the reason why HE told all the nations they better listen, and why HE said someone should tell it to the people on the islands far away, that the same GOD that scattered HIS people all over the world is the same GOD that would gather them, and keep them as a shepherd keeps his flock, because HE redeemed them, and ransomed them from people more brutal than them.

Then there would be singing in Zion, which would be filled with HIS goodness, because the people would have food, wine, and oil, and their souls would be well satisfied, and everyone would be rejoicing, because their mourning would turn to joy after HE comforts them. So, even though there is so much crying amongst them over the loss of their people, they should stop crying, since there is hope in the future, because HE heard them repenting, and praying to come back to HIM to be restored from this severe punishment. And since they are HIS dear children, and they are pleasant to HIM, even though HE spoke bad to come to them, HE remembers them, and yearns for them, and HE would have mercy on them. That is why HE wants them to set up signposts, and make landmarks, and get ready to travel down the highway back to their cities, and not to turn from HIM anymore, because HE is doing a new thing in the earth in which the weak would overcome the strong. Then they would no longer have to speak the white man's language, and they would be holy, and they would administer justice, so that their farm would bear much, and HE would satisfy their weary souls, and take away their sorrows. So, even though things are bad for them, it would be good for them later.

Now Jeremiah knows the plan, and he wakes up, and looks around, because he could sleep without any trouble that night, knowing that his people would recover, even though they would have to go through a lot of hardship to get to that point. He also knows that they would stop saying they are being punished for their forefather's sins, and they would start saying that all of them are being punished for their own sins, and the days are coming when GOD would make a new covenant with them. Not the same one HE made with their forefathers, where they had to read words, or listen to speeches to know what HE said, but a new one, in which HE would make them automatically understand the LAW with their mind and heart. Then GOD would be their GOD, and they would be HIS people, and no longer would anyone have to teach another, because everyone would know what GOD wants. By then, GOD would have forgiven them of their sins, and forget about what they did, because HE is the creator of the stars, and the heavens above, the one that controls everything, and HE would never throw away HIS children, since HE wants to live with them in their inherited land after it regains its original borders to make the whole place holy. Therefore, that is why HE promised that it would never be destroyed again.

Chapter 32

Then in the tenth year of Zedekiah's reign over Judah, which was in the 18th year of Nebuchadnezzar's reign over Babylon, Nebuchadnezzar and the Babylonian soldiers go back to Africa, and set up siege against Jerusalem. Meanwhile, Jeremiah is still locked in the courtyard of the prison of Zedekiah's palace where Zedekiah put him for saying GOD is going to give their city over to the people of Babylon, and he would not be able to defeat, or escape from the Chaldean Babylon soldiers, and would be taken into captivity. Then one day, during the siege, Hanamel (Jeremiah's uncle) goes to visit Jeremiah in the courtyard of the prison to see if he would be willing to buy a piece of land, according to their custom in the LAW of GOD, because he felt that GOD sent him there. And Hanamel beg Jeremiah to buy his field in Anathoth in the country region of Benjamin for himself, hoping that he would buy it, so that he would know if GOD really sent him there, or not. When Jeremiah buys the field for seventeen shekels of silver, signs the deed, and makes a copy of it, then sealed one, and leaves the other unsealed, and takes possession of the land, according to the LAW, Hanamel is sure that GOD sent him there to make the deal.

Afterwards, Jeremiah prays to GOD, and tells HIM, that there is nothing too hard for HIM. Then he gives the deeds to Beruch, the son of Neriah, in the presence of Hanamel, and all the others who witnessed the transaction in the court, and he pray again, telling GOD how great HE is, and how HE sees everything. Then he complains to GOD about how HE freed them from Egypt, and gave them the white man lands, which is "The Land of Canaan" as their inheritance of "The Promised Land", because the white people were wicked, and how because of their disobedience, the white people came back to take it again. He also complains that he does not know why HE told him to buy the field, even though the Chaldeans (white people) already has it. That moment, GOD tells him that HE is the GOD of everyone on the earth, and nothing is impossible for HIM, and GOD remind him that HE promised them that the white people would come to take over the city and burn down the houses where they burn incense to their false god, Baal, and to other gods to provoke HIM. GOD also remind him that HE would bring them back from captivity, and allow them to live in their inherited land to be HIS people, and HE be their GOD, and HE would never leave them again, because just like how HE brought calamity on them, HE would also do good for them, and they would be able to buy, and sell land amongst themselves, and GOD is done speaking. Then immediately, Jeremiah tell Beruch to put the deeds in an earthen vessel, so they would last long, because GOD said that houses, fields, and vineyards would be owned again in their land.

Chapter 33

On another day, GOD speaks to Jeremiah while he is still locked up in the courtyard of the prison, and GOD tells him he could call to HIM, and HE would answer him, and show him great things, and even though the people of Judah fought with the Chaldeans (Babylonian soldiers) and died off for their wickedness, HE would give them back their land and renew them, and the place would not be desolate anymore, and then the whole world would praise HIM when they see it happen. And the days are coming when HE would bring them from captivity in the white people lands, and give them righteous leaders from their tribe, Judah, the lineage of David, to rule over them, and no one would be able to break the covenant HE has with Judah to be righteous leaders, or with the Levites to be priests to HIM. Then HE asks, if they heard what people are saying that HE did to them (Judah), and to all the other tribes of Israel? Because people are saying that HE cast HIS two families away, and they are despising them as if they should no longer have the right to exist. But HE is telling them they better believe HE would never cast them away, especially those of the tribe of Judah, and HE would have mercy on all of them, and bring them from captivity, and give them back all their land.

Chapter 34

As GOD was done speaking, Nebuchadnezzar (the king of Babylon,), and his army, and all the kings of other white nations, and their armies under his dominion goes to fight against Jerusalem, and all the other cities of the tribe of Judah. At that moment, GOD tells Jeremiah to tell Zedekiah (the king of Judah) that it is time for them to be given over to the white folks, and he could escape all he wants, but eventually he would be caught and taken into captivity, but when he dies, he would die in peace and have a decent burial as a king. So, Jeremiah goes to Zedekiah, and tell him what GOD said, and at that moment, the white armies came there to fight against them, and they take over the land, and the people, and Zedekiah makes a covenant with them, that he, and his people would live with them as peaceful as they could. And GOD tell Jeremiah to tell Zedekiah that even though the white people took over, HE would cause every white man to set his slave free, so that no one would think they could keep a Negro of Israel in bondage. Immediately, Jeremiah goes back to Zedekiah and tell him what GOD said. Then when the news got to the white people, by the time it got to them, it got mixed up, and they thought it said that every white man should set their Negro slave free. So, they freed the Negroes. But afterward they changed their minds, and made them their slaves again, and put them under subjection.

That moment, GOD reminds Jeremiah that HE made a covenant with their forefathers when HE freed them from the ungodly colored people of Egypt, and HE told them, if they used any of their colored people as servants, they should only serve them for six years, and yet they did not listen to HIM. So, even though the new generation changed, and tried to do right by freeing their servants after six years, they changed again, and enslaved the servants they freed, and since they changed from not enslaving their own people for more than six years as HE commanded them in the LAW, and they kept on worshipping false gods, that is why HE is punishing them like that by the white men.

Chapter 35

Again, GOD speaks to Jeremiah in the days of Jehoiakim (the king of Judah), and tell him to go to the Rechabites, who are people of unknown genealogy, that claim they are also people of Israel. Then he must take them into the church (The House of THE LORD), and go deep within the chambers, and give them wine to drink. So, Jeremiah goes for a Rechabite named, Jaazaniah, and he takes Jaazaniah, and his entire family to the other Rechabites. Then he takes all of them to The House of THE LORD, deep within the chambers, where Hanan (the priest) stays, above where Shallum, the gate keeper stays, and sit wine before them, and tell them to drink. But they say they will not drink, because their forefathers taught them never to drink, build houses, plant farms, or vineyards, or have any of those things, and they must live in tents to live in the land for a long time. Therefore, the Rechabites does not drink, according to the custom of Israel, which is practiced by the Nazarites, and they do not try to possess earthly things, according to the LAW that Abraham followed, and they obey their forefathers by not doing what they commanded them not to do, even though they are not truly Israelites. Therefore, Jeremiah realizes that the Rechabites are obedient to the LAW, even though they are not children of GOD, but the people of Israel are rebels against the LAW, though they are the LAW givers.

After that, Nebuchadnezzar and his armies goes to Africa again, and they go to where Jeremiah, and some others are, and Jeremiah and the others leave from there and goes to Jerusalem, because they feared what Nebuchadnezzar and all the white soldiers would do. While they are in Jerusalem, GOD speaks to Jeremiah, and GOD tells him to ask the people of Jerusalem why don't they listen to HIM, and obey the LAW like how the Rechabites listen to their forefathers, and obey, even though HE got up early every day to instruct them, and even sent prophets that also got up early to tell them to turn from evil and false gods, so they could continue to live in the land. Yet they still would not listen. And because of that, they may as well stop hoping HE would change HIS mind to punish them. But first, Jeremiah goes back to the Rechabites, and tell them that GOD is pleased with them, because they showed that they are obedient to the LAW when they turned from the wine, and for that, GOD said HE would never cause their people to die off.

Chapter 36

Suddenly, Jeremiah is remembering the past, in the days of Jehoiakim when GOD told him to take a scroll and write on it what HE said HE would do to the people of Judah, from the time HE spoke to him during Josiah's rule, up until that present day, that maybe they would realize all the things that was said against them, and turn from their evil ways, and be forgiven. He also remember when he got a scroll, and GOD told him what to write on it, and he remember when he called Baruch (the scribe), and told him to write the words which GOD spoke to him on the scroll, and he told him to go into the church (The House of THE LORD) on the day the people are there fasting, and read it to them, because he was afraid they might want to harm him.

So, he remembered when Baruch wrote on the scroll what he said GOD said. Exactly the way he said it to him. Then in the 5ᵗʰ year, on the 9ᵗʰ month of Jehoiakim's reign, the people proclaimed a fast, and Baruch went to the gathering, and read the words on the scroll to them, and when Michaiah, the scribe, the son of Gemariah heard what Baruch said, he went to the scribe's chamber in the king's house where the princes are, and tell them everything that Baruch said. Then the princes sent Jehudi, the son of Nethaniah, to get Baruch to come to them with the scroll, and Jehudi went for him, and took him to the princes, and they told him to sit down, and they read what was written on the scroll to them. And when Baruch sat, and reads it to them, they were surprised at what it said. So, they said they would let the king know about it. Then they asked him how he knew about those things, and he said Jeremiah told him what to write in the book, and they told him that he, and Jeremiah should hide, and not tell anyone else.

Then Baruch left, and the princes went to the king in the court, and they told him what was said on the scroll, but they did not show him the scroll, because they hid it in Elishama, the scribe's chamber. Then Jehoiakim (the king) sent Jehudi to bring the scroll to him, and Jehudi went for it from Elishama's chamber, and took it to the king, and started to read it to him, and the princes that were there. It was in the 9ᵗʰ month, which was in the winter, and the king was sitting with a fire burning on the hearth before him. Then after Jehudi read about three or four columns, the king got furious, and grabbed the scroll, and cut it up, and was ready to throw it into the fire. So, Elnathan, Delaiah, and Gemariah tried to tell him not to burn it up, and he threw it into the fire anyway, and it was completely burned up. Except for Elnathan, Delaiah, and Gemariah, none of them worried about what the scroll says, not Jehoiakim (the king), not Zedekiah (the priest), or Elishama (the scribe), or any of the princes.

While in his fury, the king commanded some of his men to seize Jeremiah, and Baruch, but GOD kept them from sight. Then GOD told Jeremiah to get another scroll and write everything on it that was on the previous scroll, and go back to Jehoiakim (the king) and tell him that since he burned the scroll, because he did not want to hear that the white people of Babylon would come to destroy the land and cause the place to be desolate, for that, when he die, none of his sons would become king, and he and his family, and his servants would be punished for their wickedness, and all the pronounced doom would still come upon all the people of Jerusalem. Right then, Jeremiah got a new scroll, and GOD told him what to write on it, and he gave the scroll to Baruch for him to write the words which GOD said on it. So, Baruch writes exactly what he said GOD said. Which was everything that was on the first scroll. Plus a few extra lines were added to it to tell Jehoiakim (the king) what is going to happen to him for what he did with the first scroll.

Chapter 37

Let's recap some more. Nebuchadnezzar and his fierce white army went to the land of the people of Judah, and they took Jehoiakim and his family as captive to Babylon, and instead of Coniah (a white man) ruling next, Zedekiah, the son of Josiah starts to rule over Judah. But Zedekiah and his army were not GOD fearing men, and it caused the people to remain in their wickedness. Then things got really bad. So, before they locked Jeremiah up in the courtyard of the prison at Zedekiah's palace, Jeremiah was going back and forth to the people prophesying, and Zedekiah told Jehucal, and Zephaniah (the priests) to ask Jeremiah to pray to GOD for them, and at that time, the Pharaoh of Egypt, and his army shows up in Jerusalem to help them out, because Zedekiah asked him to, and when the Chaldean white people that besieged Jerusalem heard that Pharaoh, and his army are there, they left, and Zedekiah thought he had the answer to his prayer.

But GOD told Jeremiah to tell Zedekiah, though he prayed for help, Pharaoh, and his army cannot help them, and they would return home, and then the white men would come back to burn the place down, and he need to stop deceiving himself, saying, the white people would leave them alone. Immediately, Jeremiah left Jerusalem and went to the land of the people of Benjamin to speak to Zedekiah, and as he entered the gates, Irijah, the head guard, seized him, because Irijah thought he was there to help the Chaldean white people. So, he told Irijah that he was not there to help the white people, but Irijah did not believe him. Then Irijah took him to the princes, and when the princes saw him, they were angry with him, and they struck him, then locked him up in the prison at Jonathan, the scribe's house, because they made that place a prison also.

After Jeremiah had been in the dungeon for several days, Zedekiah sent for him, and they went for him, and took him to Zedekiah's house, and Zedekiah secretly asked him if he had any message for him from GOD, and he told Zedekiah that GOD said he would be taken captive by the Babylonians. Then he asked what he did so wrong, why he locked him up in prison, and where his prophets were that said that the Babylonians would not come against them and the land, and he told him that he would die if he went back to the prison at Jonathan's house and begged him not to send him back there. And Zedekiah did not send him back to that prison. Instead, Zedekiah placed him in the courtyard of the prison of his palace, and that is how he ended up in the courtyard of Zedekiah's palace, placed under the watch of prison guards. *(See chapter 32-34).*

Chapter 38

When Shephatiah, Gedaliah, Pashhur, and Jucal heard the doom that Jeremiah prophesied against them, that all the people would die, if they do not serve the white people, they told Zedekiah (the king) they think Jeremiah should be killed, because he was making the people, and the remaining men in the army scared, and Zedekiah told them to do to him as they please, because he agreed with them. Then they took Jeremiah and let him down by a rope into a dungeon that belonged to Malchiah, the son of Zedekiah, and the dungeon was muddy, and Jeremiah sank down into the mud, and when Ebed-Melech, an Ethiopian eunuch, who works for Zedekiah, heard they placed Jeremiah in the dungeon, he goes to Zedekiah while he was sitting out by the gate of Benjamin, and told him that the men that locked Jeremiah up did wrong by throwing him down in the dungeon without food, and water, and he was about to die. Then Zedekiah told him to take thirty men with him to lift Jeremiah out of the dungeon before he dies, and he took the thirty men to the dungeon, and they tied old clothes, and rags together, and pulled Jeremiah out of the dungeon. Then they told him to put on some of the old rags, because he was naked, and after he put on the rags, they placed him in the courtyard of the prison to be guarded there.

Later, Zedekiah sent for Jeremiah to come to him at the third entrance of The House of THE LORD, and when Jeremiah went there, Zedekiah asked him to answer him honestly, and he told Zedekiah, if he told him the truth, he would kill him, and if he gave him advice, he would not listen to him anyway. So, Zedekiah swore to him that he would not kill him, or allow anyone else to, and he told Zedekiah that GOD said, if he surrendered to the king of Babylon, then he and his family would live, and the city would not be burned down, but if he does not surrender, then the white people would take over the city, and burn it down, and he would not be able to escape. Now Zedekiah said, he is afraid of their own people that turned against them, and joined with the

Chaldean white people, because they might catch him, and turn him over to them to abuse him, and Jeremiah told him they would not abuse him, because if he obeys GOD, he will live, but if he refused to obey, then all the women, and children would be captured and taken to Babylon, and those same women would say that he surrendered all of them over to the white men, even though he would be captured too. Hearing that, Zedekiah told him not to tell anyone what he just said to him, and if the princes heard that he spoke to him, and asked him to tell them what he said by promising him they would not kill him, then all he has to do is tell them he came there to ask him not to send him back to the prison at Jonathan's house to die. After that, Zedekiah sends him back to be guarded in the courtyard of his prison, and sure enough, all the princes went to him, and asked him why he was speaking to the king, and he said what Zedekiah told him to say to them, and they did not say anything more about it after that. But they kept him in the courtyard of the prison, and even after Jerusalem was taken, he was still locked up.

Chapter 39

In the 9th year, and 10th month of Zedekiah's reign over Judah, Nebuchadnezzar and his armies go back to Jerusalem, and besiege the place. By the 11th year, the 4th month, and 9th day of Zedekiah's reign, the city is completely penetrated by white soldiers, and they also sit in the middle gate, and when Zedekiah, and his army see them there, they run and leave the city through the king's garden during the night. So, the Chaldean army chases after them, and they catch up with Zedekiah in the plains of Jericho and capture him. Then they take him to Nebuchadnezzar in the land of Hamath where Nebuchadnezzar pronounce judgment on him, and they kill his sons, and all the nobles of Judah in front of his eyes. Then they gauge out his eyes and take him from Africa to Babylon as a captive.

Afterwards, the solders burn down the city and carry away those who were left in there. They even take the ones who turned from their own Negro people for them, but they leave the poor who has nothing, and gives them vineyards, and fields, and Nebuchadnezzar leaves Nebuzaradan there to be a chief guard over those left in the land. But Nebuchadnezzar tells him to take care of Jeremiah, and not to do him any harm, and to do whatever he tells him to do. Afterwards, Nebuzaradan, the chief guard, sends Nebushasban, Rabsaris, Nergel-Sharezer, Rabmag, and all the top white officers to where Jeremiah is, and when they get there, they tell someone to take Jeremiah from the courtyard of the prison to let Gedaliah take care of him, so he could live among his people. Meanwhile, Jeremiah is in the courtyard speaking to GOD, and GOD is telling him to tell Ebed-Melech, the Ethiopian, that trouble would come upon the city, and he would get to see it, but HE would save him, and stop the Babylonians from taking him captive, because he believes the prophecy and trust in HIM.

Chapter 40

When Nebuzaradan, the chief guard, gets to the courtyard, he tell Jeremiah he is letting him go from the prison in Ramah, and he is freeing him, because his GOD pronounced the doom on their people, and his GOD is doing what HE said, because they sinned against HIM, and if he wants to come with him to Babylon, he would take care of him, but if it seems wrong to come, then he could stay there, and it is up to him to choose what he wants. Yet Jeremiah says nothing. So, Nebuzaradan tell him to go back to Gedaliah, who is one of the Negroes of Judah, that Nebuchadnezzar made governor over the people of Judah who are still in the land, so he could live with his own people, or he could go anywhere he wants. At that moment, Nebuzaradan gives him food and gifts, and let him go. Then he goes to Gedaliah in Mizpah to live with his own Negro people there, and shortly after he gets there, Gedaliah gathers all the people in the land in Mizpah, and tell them they should not be afraid to serve the white Babylonian people, because if they serve them, they would not be killed, and as for him, he is going to serve the white people in Mizpah, and those who do not want to serve the white people there in Mizpah, they should gather some food and wine from there for themselves, and go back to wherever they lived before, and serve them there.

You see, ever since the white people invaded the Negro people of The Kingdom of Judah, all the Negro people of The Kingdom of Israel that lived in Moab, Ammon, Edom, and all the other ungodly Negro nations were thrown out by the people in those nations, because they thought they would also be invaded by the white Chaldeans (soldiers), just because of the few people from Israel that lived with them in their land. So, because the people of Israel were thrown out, they hid in many places to survive, and when they heard that Nebuchadnezzar, the king of Babylon, did not kill all their people in Judah, and he made Gedaliah, one of their own, the governor over those that are left in the land, they leave from where they were hiding, and go to Judah to Gedaliah in the city of Mizpah to get food and wine to survive. Even Johanan, the son of Kareah, and all the captains of the army in the fields, come out of hiding, and goes to Gedaliah to get food. Then after getting there, Johanan, and the men of the army tell Gedaliah that Baalis, the king of the white people of Ammon, sent Ishmael, one of Israel's own to murder him. But Gedaliah does not believe them. Then Johanan takes Gedaliah aside and secretly tell him that he would kill Ishmael for him, and no one would know, because if he dies, then all the people that came to him for help would scatter again, and the remnant of Judah would perish. But Gedaliah tells him not to do it, because he thinks what he is saying about Ishmael is a lie.

Chapter 41

By the 7th month, Ishmael, who is an officer from the royal family of Judah, goes to Mizpah with ten men, and Gedaliah fed them. Then Ishmael, and the ten men that are with him get up, and kill Gedaliah, and all the white men that are there ruling over the people with him. They also kill all the people of Judah that his brother, Gedaliah, is governing over, that are there with him, and he even kill the white soldiers that are there. Two days later, no one even knew about it yet. Meanwhile, eighty men from Shechem, Shiloh and Samaria which are other city of Israel, are looking for Mizpah to sacrifice to GOD in The House of THE LORD. At the same time, Ishmael was traveling to go there too, and while on the way, he was crying the whole time. Then when he sees the eighty men trying to find their way, he tells them to let him take them there to Gedaliah, and they let he guide them, and he led them to the middle of the city, and starts to kill them, and ten out of the eighty men beg him not to kill them, and tell him they have treasures and food supplies they would give to him. So, he did not kill them. Then he throws the dead bodies of the ones he killed into a pit, which is the same pit that Asa (a past king of Judah) dug to hide in when he was running from Baasha (a past white king over the people of Israel), and he took the men he did not kill, and the king's daughter to make them captives in the land of the Ammonites white people. When Johanan and the other men of the army hear what he did, they go to look for him to fight him, and they see him by the pool in Gibeon, and when the people he captured see Johanan and his men coming, they are glad. So, they leave from beside him, and run to Johanan, and he escape with the ten men he did not kill and goes to the white Ammonites. Then Johanan and his men leave with the people of Mizpah who ran to him, and go to Chimham, which is near Bethlehem, because Mizpah was destroyed, and then the people said they want to go to Egypt, since they are afraid of the white people that took over their people in the cities of Judah, because they are convincing them to kill each other.

Chapter 42

Right away, Johanan and the men in the army, and all the people with him goes to Jeremiah, and ask him to please pray to GOD to help them, and show them what to do, because only a few of them are left, and Jeremiah tell them he would pray to GOD for them, and whatever GOD said, he would tell them. So, they were glad, and they said they would do everything he said. Then Jeremiah prays for them, and after ten days, GOD speaks to him and tell him what to tell them, and he called Johanan, and the rest of the people, and tell them that GOD said, if they stay there in their land, because they are righteous, HE would bless them, and they should not be afraid of the king of Babylon, because HE is with them, and HE is sorry HE caused so much bad things to happen to them, but if they refuse to stay in the land, and decide to go to Egypt where there is no war, then the white soldiers would follow them, and kill them there, because HE is angry with them, and if they go to Egypt to save themselves from the wicked white men, HE would make them look like fools, and so they better not go, because they are being warned, and if they do try to escape, then they are hypocrites for asking HIM what to do, and then do what HE said not to do.

Chapter 43

Jeremiah tells them what GOD said, and after hearing what he said, Azaria, Johanan, and all the proud men said he is lying, because GOD did not tell them not to go to Egypt. Then they said, Baruch sent him to tell them lies, so they would get captured by the white people, or killed when they decide to stay in the land, and they were not going to believe what he said. And since they said that Johanan and the men of the army chose to take only Jeremiah, and they leave with all the people who went there with him and Baruch and go to Tahpanhes in Egypt where Pharaoh lives.

While they are in Tahpanhes, GOD tell Jeremiah to get some large stones, and hide them in the clay bricks of the courtyard, which is at the entrance of Pharaoh's house, while the people watch him, and then tell HIS people who lives there, that HE said, "Nebuchadnezzar would come and set his throne above those stones that are hidden, and spread his royal pavilion over them, and start war in Egypt, and kill off every one of them that are appointed to die, and take as captive those who are appointed to be taken, and the Babylonian soldiers would burn down their false places of worship they built there in Egypt, and the Egyptians would also be taken as captive, and Nebuchadnezzar and his army would leave from Egypt with them, as happy as a lark."

Chapter 44

GOD also tells him to tell the people of Israel that are hiding and were already in Egypt in the city of Migdol, Tahpanhes of Noph, and Pathros, that HE had to cause the calamity on their people in Jerusalem, and in all the cities of Judah to make them desolate, because they are wicked, and they are worshipping other gods, and though HE sent them prophets to warn them, they would not listen, and HE wants to know why they would not listen either, because they keep worshipping false gods, which caused their people to be taken, and for false worship, everyone has to be punished, even if they are hiding out in Egypt.

Immediately, Jeremiah goes to Egypt and tell the people of Israel who lives there what GOD said. Then all the men of Israel who knew that their wives worship false gods, stood up in the crowd, and said they would not believe him, and they would continue to burn incense, and pour out drink offerings to "The Queen of Heaven", because that is what they always did, and they had plenty of food, and were well off without trouble, and since they stopped burning incense, and offering drink offerings to the idol, "The Queen of Heaven", they lack everything, and are being killed off by war and famine. Then the women say they worship The Queen of Heaven and sacrificed to her with their husbands' permission, and Jeremiah tell them that GOD did not tell them to do that, which is why HE is so mad at all of them, and because GOD cannot stand the false ways of worship anymore, HE is punishing them by making the land of Judah desolate, and since they all said what they had to say already, they better realize that GOD is great, and no one can hide from HIM, and if they think they are hiding out in Egypt, they would be found, but a small remnant would return to the land of Judah, and they should know that

Hophra (the Pharaoh, who is the king of Egypt) would be kill by his enemies, because of his false ways of worship, just like how Zedekiah, the king of Judah was killed by his enemy, Nebuchadnezzar, the king of Babylon, because of his false ways of worship.

Chapter 45

From the 4th year of Jehoiakim's reign when Jeremiah told Baruch to write the words on the scroll, and read it to the people, Baruch had been feeling sorry for himself, because of all the suffering he had been going through in the land, and GOD tell Jeremiah to tell him that he might as well stop all the belly aching, because HE would build up, or tear down whatever HE wants, and HE is going to tear down all the land of Judah, and he should not look for anything good to happen special for him, but HE would keep him alive, and his life would be a prize to him where ever he goes.

Chapter 46

GOD also tell Jeremiah that HE wants him to tell the nations what HE would to do to all of them, and HE wants him to tell the army of Necho (the Pharaoh, the king of Egypt) that rules by the Euphrates River in Carchemish, who Nebuchadnezzar (the king of Babylon) defeated in the 4th year of Jehoiakim (the king of Judah's reign), who thinks they are acting like soldiers, and think they are strong, they should know, "They are already defeated, and even if they call their ungodly colored allies, like Ethiopia, and Libya to help them, they cannot win, because it would be HIM punishing them when they see Nebuchadnezzar, the king of Babylon come and destroy Egypt, and then the people of Judah that are hiding there from HIM would decide to run back to the land of Judah to deal with HIM in their native land, and so, he may as well know that Nebuchadnezzar is mighty, and HE, THE MIGHTY GOD gave him the power to take over the world, even though he is a wicked white man, because HE is using him to punish the world for all the wickedness they have been doing, and HE wants him to know that Nebuchadnezzar thinks that he is weak, and way past his time, even though he and his people of Egypt had been the strongest nation in the past, and he better believe that the white army would come to destroy Egypt, even though it is a strong and beautiful place, and then the women would be ashamed when their soldiers are defeated, and they are all taken by the white soldiers, but HE does not want the people of Israel that are there to be afraid, because even though HE is punishes them, HE would save them, if they just turned back to HIM, because HE is only destroying all the nations, so that everyone would know that HE does not like false worship, and HE just want to save HIS people from all the nations that practice falseness.

Chapter 47

Then GOD tell him to tell the colored people of the Philistines that lives in the Northern portion of The Promised Land near HIS people of Israel, that the white soldiers of Babylon are coming to get them too, and the white armies of Tyre, and Sidon would be helping them to destroy their cities, and Gaza, and Ashkelon would become desolate. So, without hesitation, Jeremiah goes to the people of the Philistines (Palestine) and tell them what GOD said. Right then, Pharaoh (the king of Egypt) attacks the northern region of Gaza. But that was not the punishment for them yet, because it is the white people that would completely destroy the ungodly colored nation of the Philistines, which is Palestine.

Chapter 48

After that, GOD tells him to tell the colored nation of Moab that allowed the white people to live with them that taught them ungodliness, and taught them how to mix their race, and culture in unrighteousness, "They better feel sorry for their city, Nebo, which they named after the Pharaoh of Egypt, who showed them how to mix unrighteousness with people of color, because they are going to be punished. Then they would not praise the Egyptians anymore, and in Hebron, Luhith, Nebo, Dibon, Kerioth, Beth-Meon, Horonaim, and all the cities of Moab, there would be crying, because Moab would be destroyed, and so, they better flee and hide to save themselves, because HE has spoken, and that is why someone should give wings to the people of Moab, so they could flee, because cursed is any nation that does godly work with deceit, and cursed is anyone that tries to fight HIM back, for though they had a good life all along, they lost their way a long time ago when they accepted the white people to live in their land, and yet they have the nerve to think that their breath does not stink, even though it does, and that is why they would be punished to make them feel ashamed of false worship, just like how the Negro people of Israel are being punished for their idol worship to make them ashamed.

Does the people of Israel look shameful to the people of Moab?

Of course, they do. Because every time the people of Moab saw them, they would shake their heads in scorn.

So, what makes the people of Moab think that they could get away with false worship when the people of Israel are being punished for the same thing?

The people of Moab are fooling themselves, and that is why HE said, the Moabites better leave their nation, and go to live in rocks, because they are proud, lofty, haughty, and arrogant in their hearts, and their lifestyle is wrong, and does not make anything right. So, they may as well cry, because their land would be destroyed, and they would be taken captive by the white people, as a punishment for their false ways of worship, and though they would come back from captivity to their own land later, for now, they would be punished.

Chapter 49

As for the Ammonite white people, HE wants to know, if they think HIS Negro people do not have any sons, or anyone to give their inheritance to, why they came and took over their land while they were still living there and then took them to their land to live, and so, because of that, HE would punish them, and then all their white people in the Negro lands of Rabbah, Heshbron, and Ai, would cry out, because of trouble, and they would be taken captive, and the place would be desolate, but afterward, HE would bring them out of captivity and send them back to their own white land. As for the people of Edom, the red skinned Negro people of Esau, council is gone from them, and they are no longer wise, and for that, they would be punished, because they are of the righteous Negro lineage of Isaac, and yet they turned from righteousness to foolishness. Which is why Bozrah, Teman, and all the cities of Edom would be destroyed since they were deceived by their fierceness. Then they would look shameful. Just like when Sodom, and Gomorrah, and their neighboring countries that were destroyed. Now, if they look, they will see that the people of Damascus, Hamath, and Arpad are worried, after hearing that everyone would be punished who worship false gods and taught it to the people of Israel to deceive them. There would be trouble everywhere along the borders of the sea, and they would not be able to run anywhere, because they are going to die in their own land, and Kedar, Hazor, and all the cities in Damascus would be burned, because Nebuchadnezzar and his white army would come to destroy the place and take what they want. And the people of Elam would also be punished, and they would be totally consumed, and many of them would go into captivity by the white people, but since HE, is their GOD, HE would set up HIS throne in their land and bring them from captivity back to their own land.

Chapter 50

As for the Babylonians, HE is definitely against them and all their white Chaldean people, and HE said out loud, "Babylon would be taken, Babylon would be taken, and they would be ashamed of Bel-Merodach, and all their idols when they see them broken, because out of the North, another great white nation would conceive a plan and come against them and make them desolate, which would cause them to leave their land in Africa, and at that time, the Negro people of Israel that are in Babylon would be able to return home from captivity back to their own land, and they would ask, which way to Zion, and they would return home ready to serve HIM, their true GOD."

The Negro people of Israel had been lost, because their priests and kings allowed them to do the wrong things, which caused them to not know the right way. Then every nation that knew about them, devoured them, and said they did nothing wrong, because they were punishing them for being disobedient to HIM, their GOD, and because of that, HE said the Negroes should move from among the Babylonians, and be strong in HIS name, YAH, because HE is going to cause other white nations to come plunder the white Babylonian people for their sake, since they were so glad to punish them, and get rich from it when HE was angry at them, and then everyone would hiss at Babylon when they see the place destroyed and desolate from the wrath, because Babylon would be fought against, and their rain would be shut off, so they would not have anything to harvest, and every nation would learn from it and leave the Negro people alone in peace.

For now, the Negro people of Israel are scattered all over the world (during the time of The Roman Empire), because everyone came and took from their land, and they even took the land. First the white Assyrians devoured them. Then every other nation. Finally, the white Babylonians were glad to completely finish them off when GOD allowed them to punish them. That is why GOD said, HE would punish the Babylonians in The Great Tribulation of HIS wrath for trying to finish off HIS people. Just like how HE punished the white Assyrians for thinking they could finish them off in the first place. Then the people of Israel would return home from wherever they are, and they would live happily in their own land, and will be satisfied with everything. At that time, people would look to see what kind of sins the people of Israel would be doing, and there would be none, because they would be living right, after seeing what GOD did for them.

GOD sounded the alarm against Merathaim, Pekod, Leb-Kamia, and all the Babylonian cities to let the world be astonished at how the nation that beat up on everyone would be destroyed without even knowing that it was coming. So, Babylon was found, and would be caught, because they contended with GOD, thinking that HE could not defeat them, and since GOD remembers what they did, HE prepared the weapons to destroy them, and for now, people can feel sorry for the Babylonians all they want, but when it is time for their punishment, every nation would be glad to help out to repay them for what they did to the Negro people of GOD.

Yet, for the time, the people of Israel are oppressed in their Babylonian captivity, because the Babylonians are treating them badly, and they refuse to free them. But their GOD is strong, and HE would plead their case, so that the land could rest when the white people are gone from it. That is why the white folks in Babylon, and the white folks anywhere in The Mother Land better get scared, because GOD is against their witches, their warlocks, and their soldiers, and HE is against the horses they use for war, and against those mixed (biracial) white looking people that are of them. Just like how HE destroyed the white people of Sodom and Gomorrah, that is how HE would destroy the white people of Babylon, and since they already heard the news about what would happen to them, they are scared, and the ones in The Mother Land are already leaving, because there is no one like GOD, and no one can tell HIM what to do, and when HE destroys Babylon, everyone would know how mighty HE is, and they would fear HIM, and want to know HIM.

Chapter 51

Babylon would be punished, and no one would feel sorry for them when they see them killed, and thrown into the streets, because the people of Israel are not forsaken by their GOD, especially the tribe of Judah, even though they polluted The Holy Land by worshipping idols. So, everyone better leave from Babylon, to save themselves, because they would be killed with them as they are being punished for their sins, because Babylon is a nation that gained from witchcraft, and false worship, and they taught the world to do the same thing, which keeps people from following the ways of GOD. That is why everyone should leave from there, and go back to their own countries, because GOD prepared the white people of Medes to destroy the white people of Babylon in vengeance for teaching HIS Negro people to worship idols, and for being so harsh on them when HE used them to punish them for doing it.

Didn't the Babylonians know that GOD is great, because HE is the one WHO made the earth by HIS power and HE established the world by HIS wisdom, and stretched out the heavens by HIS understanding?

Most definitely, every Babylonian knows that GOD is great, but they are rebels, and that is why everyone who worship idols like they do are dumb to worship things that cannot walk, talk, or do anything, and they should be ashamed of themselves and should be killed. But not the remnant of Israel that GOD would save, because they are not like the rest of the world, since they are GOD's inheritance, and HIS name is YAH, and HE is THE ALMIGHY ONE that would use the righteous Negroes to teach others the WORD and punish anyone if they do not obey.

Yes, GOD is against Babylon, because they and their false ways of worship destroyed every nation in the world, which caused everyone to be against them. Therefore, everyone would join with the Medes to destroy them, and messenger after messenger, Nebuchadnezzar, the king of Babylon would hear how the place is being destroyed, and how all his mighty men are afraid, and are acting like punks while they are getting punished for how he completely destroyed the lands of Israel to make Babylon rich.

That would be a dream come through for the Negro of Israel, because they had been wishing for the same violence to come to the Babylonians as they did to them, since GOD promised them, HE would plead their case and take vengeance for them. But first, GOD would let the white men roar and have their feasts, and while they are in their excitement with drunkenness, GOD will kill them all for corrupting "The Holy Land", and for deceiving everyone in the world. Then people would see that their Babylonian god, Bel, cannot do anything. Which is the reason why GOD warned the Negros of Israel who loves Babylon to leave from there, because they would be afraid when they see ruler, after ruler coming to destroy Babylon. So this is the promise, after Babylon is destroyed, everyone would be happy, and the world would be beautiful, since it was the wicked white people of Babylon that were causing all the problems in the world in the first place. Therefore, the Negros of Israel should stop loving the Babylonians, and they should be ashamed of how they allowed them to come to Africa and pollute The House of THE LORD, because the time would come when the Babylonians would be destroyed, as a punishment for what they did.

That's it. That was what Jeremiah told Seraiah that GOD said HE would do against the nations, just before Seraiah was captured with Zedekiah and taken to Babylon. And Jeremiah told Seraiah to write all that he said in a book, and when he gets to Babylon, he must open the book and read it to all the captives, then say, "O GOD, YOU have spoken against this place to make it desolate forever". Then when he is done, he must tie a stone to it and throw it into the Euphrates River (which runs from Europe to Africa), and say, "That is how Babylon would sink after all the catastrophe GOD brings on them."

Chapter 52

Let's recap again. The story is that Zedekiah, the king of Judah, was twenty-one years old when he started to reign, and he ruled eleven years from Jerusalem, and his mother's name was Hamutal, and because he was evil like

Jehoiakim, the previous king of Judah, GOD promised that the Babylonian white people would come to punish them by taking them from the land. So, as soon as Zedekiah started his reign, slowly, but surely, the white people of Babylon came, and became squatters, and leaders over them in the land, and because Zedekiah rebelled against Nebuchadnezzar in the 10th month, on the 10th day of his reign, Nebuchadnezzar and his army came against Jerusalem, and built siege against it, up until the 11th year of Zedekiah's reign. Which ended his reign. And within that time, by the 4th month, and 10th day, there was a severe famine in the city, and there was no food for the people, and Zedekiah, and many of them left through the broken walls, even though the white Chaldeans were camped all around. That was when the white soldiers decided to chase after Zedekiah, and they found him in the plains of Jericho, and his men ran off as they captured him. Then they took him to Nebuchadnezzar at Riblah in the land of Hamath, and Nebuchadnezzar pronounced judgment on him, and they killed his sons, and the princes of Judah in Riblah, right in front of his eyes. Then they gauged out his eyes, bound him, and put him in prison, so he could die there.

Then in the 5th month, on the 10th day, which was the 19th year of Nebuchadnezzar's reign, Nebuzaradan, the chief of Nebuchadnezzar's army, and his team went to Jerusalem, and burned down The House of THE LORD, and they also burned down Zedekiah's palace, and all the great houses that were there, and they broke down all the walls to the city, and carried away as captives the rest of the prestigious people who did not run, and also some of the poor people, and even all the ones that were helping them to fight against their own kind, and they left most of the poor people there to stay there to grow vineyards and farm. Plus, they broke up all the bronze pieces that were in The House of THE LORD, and they carried the bronze to Babylon, and the pots, the bowls, the shovels, the twelve bronze bulls, the carts, and even the pillars with carved pomegranates they took. Yea. They took everything. Then they took Seraiah (the priest), Zephaniah (the second priest), and the three doorkeepers that were at The House of THE LORD, and they also took the soldiers of Judah's army, seven of the Zedekiah's close associates, the scribe of the army, and sixty other regular men to Nebuchadnezzar at Riblah, and killed them. Therefore, 3,023 people from the tribe of Judah were taken from their land to Babylon in the seventh year of Nebuchadnezzar's reign, and 832 in the eighteenth, and 745 in the twenty-third year, for a total of 4,600 people. Then in the thirteenth year of Jehoiachin's captivity, Nebuchadnezzar was no longer the king of Babylon, and Evil-Merodach became the king, and in the first year of his reign he decided to let Jehoiachin (the previous king of Judah) out of prison, and he treated him as a friend by letting him eat regularly with him and providing for him until he died.

OBADIAH'S PROPHESY

Chapter 1

One day, Obadiah had of vision of GOD, and HIS angels talking about how they heard about the red skinned people of Edom, the descendants of Esau, and how bad they are, and they said, they would be punished for their pride, and for their violence against their brothers, the people of Israel, and they should get ready for war, since many nations would come to take what they want from them, until the place is desolate. He also heard them say, "The Day of THE LORD" is near, and Edom, and all ungodly nations would be severely punished during this time, because they were all glad when the people of Israel were taken captive by the white people, and they entered the land and took whatever they wanted afterwards, and even took as captives those who escaped from the white people. But they better know that the people of Israel would return from captivity, and they would be the government that rule over the colored nations and correct them, and they should also know that the white people of the south would get the mountains region of their land of Edom, while the biracial people of Philistia get the lowlands. And the people of Israel would get the fields of Mount Ephraim, where the tribe of Benjamin lives, and they would also get the fields of Samaria where the white people took from them, because this way, they would be amongst their own people of Israel. By this time, the tribe of Benjamin would have returned to their inherited land, and the white people of Samaria would be gone, leaving the

12 tribes of Israel in the land, along with their red skinned Negroes of Edom, their brothers, that come to replace the white ones that are gone.

Not only that. By this time, the wicked white people would be so scared of the righteous government of Israel that is ruling over them, they would want to be far away from all the colored people, and they would migrate out of the regions (of Africa) to the Northern region of the world (Europe). Then the Negro people of Israel would take over the land they left behind, and because the Greeks are good white people in the Southern region of Europe, the Greeks would get the land on Mount Seir that belonged to the red-skinned Negroes of Edom, and they would live with the white people of Seir, and share the land of Mount Seir with them. Then the land of the people of Greece would also be taken over by the Negro people of Israel, and after the wicked white people move to the cold Northern lands of Europe to be as far away as they can to rule themselves, the Negro people of Israel would start to rule all the people in the world with colored skin, and they would also rule all the white people who are willing to comply with the LAW of YAH, their GOD. By the time this happens, Jesus would have already been born, killed, and resurrected to heaven. Then Jesus would come back from heaven to the earth to determine which of the people of Israel, and which of the people of Edom deserves to stay in the land, and at that time, Jesus would become the head of the government that is ruled by the people of Israel, which rules over the obedient people in the world.

HABAKKUK'S PROPHESY

Chapter 1

The wrath had been going on for a while, and when the prophet, Habakkuk saw how bad things were for the righteous Negro people in their own land, and all over the world, he cried out to GOD to find out if things would get any better. But GOD would not answer him, and he kept crying out to GOD to know why such terrible things are happening, and if there were any solution. But GOD still would not answer him. Then he start to feel like a righteous person is powerless against the law, and there was no justice, because the wicked people seem to be in charge over every judgment. So, while he is in distress, GOD finally answers him, and GOD tell him to look at what HE is already doing to the unbelieving nations in HIS wrath, and it will so bad, he will not believe it when HE is done, even though HE told him what would happen, since HIS plan is to use the white Chaldean people that lives far away (in the North) to come and fight against the white people that invaded the land and are still living there, because the Chaldeans are wicked people that are quick to go anywhere on the earth to take land that is not theirs, and they are puffed up in pride, and have horses that are faster than leopards, and fiercer than wolves, and they would come with violence and take many captives, because they do not care about authority figures when they set up their attack to seize land, and when they conquer land, they act ignorant against the natives of the land, and do all sorts of terrible things, and say their gods gave them power to do so. Then since Habakkuk realizes that his people would not die, and only the ungodly people against them would be punished, he tells GOD HE is powerful, holy, and mighty, and since he is a righteous man, he asks GOD, why it seem like HE does not care when people are sinning against the righteous ones, and why the righteous people does not seem to get justice when the wicked people snag them with nets and laugh about it. Then he asks, if HE knew that he is tired of it, and said, at least he realizes that HE is already punishing the wicked in HIS wrath, even though they continue to do evil, because that is how they make their money to survive, and most of all, he know that HE would not let this continue forever.

Chapter 2

So, he decides to wait patiently for whatever GOD has to say, and to wait to see what HE wants him to do. Then one day, GOD speaks to him and tell him to write down the vision that he would see, so that when anyone read it, and believed it, they could run, and take cover, because the wrath is set over a period of time, but at the end of it, things would end up for the wicked, just like how HE said, and it is only because the wicked are proud why they refuse to believe that it would happen, but because the righteous ones believe, their faith would make them survive it all. And since the wicked people lives by deceit, they are proud, and they are never in their countries where they belong, because they are always somewhere else taking someone else's land, and they are like "Death" that cannot be satisfied, because they take all the nations and the people for themselves. Which is why people should speak a parable against them to taunt them by saying, "They feel sorry for people that like to take things that does not belong to them, and for people that like to be master over others."

Don't the wicked know that their creditors would come and take all their things?

Don't they think the people they took from would someday realize it, and come take their things back, since they have violently taken the food and land from every nation by killing many of the natives?

No, the wicked do not think, and they do not think of the consequences of their actions. Now the only thing the remaining natives of the land want is their things back. So, start feeling sorry for those people that stole from people, then tell other people in their family to do the same thing, because everyone in the world testifies against them, since the bloodshed, the poverty, and hard labor caused people to see it clearly. Yet the wicked people drink and laugh with them, pretending to be friends, just to find out things about them to use it in their favor, even though they are filled with shame on the inside, instead of glory, but they do not have enough sense to even know that they are sinners. That is why GOD does not like them, and why HE wants to shame them, so that everyone would know their shame just by looking at them.

So, what was the use of all their idols which could not speak?

None whatsoever, because idols cannot do anything.

Now you know that the wicked people are wasting their time speaking to carved images of wood, and stone, overlaid with gold, and silver when the images cannot even speak back to them. Therefore, they better remember that GOD is in heaven in HIS holy temple, and HE is judging everything they do. As for the righteous ones, they can just be quiet and wait to see what GOD would do to the wicked.

Chapter 3

That's it.

That was the vision that Habakkuk had, and it was clear to him, and he became afraid, but he wants it to go as planned, and he would like GOD to have mercy on him, because HE is the GOD that came from Mount Teman, which is the top of Mount Paran, and the earth is filled with HIS praise, and HIS brightness is like light, and rays flashes from HIS hands, which hides power in them, and HE controls everything, and HE measured the earth, and divided it, and gave to each family as HE wished. Even the mountains, the sea, the sun, and the moon obey HIM when HE uses them to correct the nations that took land from other nations, and HE even uses the mountain, the sea, the sun, and the moon to save HIS people of Israel from the wicked people that came in like a whirlwind to take them all over the world as captives, while they rejoice secretly and live off the poor that are left in the land.

It happened just like GOD said. The wicked white people came across the sea to put fear in the people of Israel, and even though all the godly people in the land prayed, they were still defeated, because that was their punishment for worshipping idols. And though the trees in the land were stripped of their fruits, and no one could make any money, not even to eat, they still rejoice in GOD, and they continue to pray, because HE is the one that would save them by HIS strength, and the only one that would provide all their needs and make them happy.

THE BOOK OF DANIEL

Chapter 1

Let's recap a little. it was in the third year of Jehoiakim's reign, when Nebuchadnezzar went to Jerusalem, and took the king's lineage, the priests, and all the best people captive, and Nebuchadnezzar and his army instructed Ashpenaz, the master of the eunuchs to also take all the good looking, gifted, and wise Negro children that are quick to learn, and had no blemishes, who had the ability to learn the white man's language to know how to serve their kings. When the people of Israel got to Babylon, the best looking, and smartest Negro children were given daily provision of all the best food and wine the king offered, and they were trained for three years the language, and how to serve them, and four of the wisest, most handsome young boys were Daniel, Hananiah, Mishael, and Azariah. But Ashpenez, the main eunuch, renamed Daniel and his friends. Daniel is Belteshazzar, Hananiah is Shadrach, Michael is Mechach, and Azariah is Abed-Nego.

While all the other wise children of Israel were enjoying the good treatment from the king, Daniel did not want to defile himself with those things. So, he asked Ashpenaz not to give him those things, and because Ashpenaz liked him, he gave him his request, since he was getting bony, and he did not want the king to punish him for letting him get that way. Afterward, Daniel asked the steward that Ashpenaz appointed over him and his three friends, Hananiah, Mishael, and Azariah, to give them vegetables and water for ten days to see if they would be as healthy as the others that were eating the king's delicacies, and if they are not as healthy as the others, then they could feed them what they want. So, according to Daniel's request, the steward gave them vegetables, and water for the ten days, and during those ten days, GOD gave Daniel and his three friends the knowledge and skills in all things. HE also gave Daniel the understanding of visions and dreams, and at the end of the ten days, Nebuchadnezzar (the king) requested to see all the wise young Negro children of Israel, and Ashpenez took them to him. Then after Nebuchadnezzar interviewed them, he found out that Daniel, Hananiah, Mishael, and Azariah were the smartest ones, and he kept them as his personal servants, and as they served him, he found out that they were ten times wiser than his white people that used magic and astrology in Babylon.

Chapter 2

In the second year of Nebuchadnezzar's reign, Nebuchadnezzar has a dream that troubles him so much, it woke him up. Then he call the Babylonian astrologers, magicians, and sorcerers, and all his army to tell them the dream, and when they go to him, he tells them that he had a terrible dream, and he is anxious to know what it means. So, they tell him to tell it to them plainly in their Aramaic language, and they would interpret it for him, and he tell them that when he tell them the dream, if they cannot interpret it, he would cut them up into pieces, and burn down their house, but if they can interpret it, he would give them gifts and rewards and honor them. Anxiously, they tell him to just tell them the dream and they will interpret it. But he tells them, they are stalling, because they know that he is serious about killing them, and they know they cannot reveal the dream to him, and he refuse to tell them the dream, and demand that they tell it to him instead, since they are supposed to be so good at revealing things. They replied, "No one on earth could interpret a dream without ever hearing it. Which is why no other king had ever requested such a thing, because only the gods could do that." That response angered the king, and he gives a command to kill anyone in Babylon that said they could interpret dreams and visions and give understanding to things they do not know about. Right on the spot, his men kill the wise men that are there, and they are ready to kill any man that is wise, and because Daniel and his three friends are wise Negro captives in Babylon, they are also considered to be wise men, and they are after them too. Then Arioch, the captain of the king's army caught Daniel, and since Daniel is wise, he asks, why the king is so quick to send out a decree to kill the wise men, and Arioch tells him why, and with the understanding, Daniel goes to the king and asks him to give him time to figure out the dream. Then he goes to his place, and tell Hananiah, Mishael, and Azariah, his three friends, to agree with him in prayer, so GOD would reveal the dream to him.

That night, the dream is revealed to Daniel in a vision, and Daniel thank GOD for the understanding of it, and praise HIM. Then he goes to Arioch and tell him not to kill any more of the wise men of Babylon, because if he takes him to the king, he could tell him the interpretation of the dream. Right away, Arioch goes to the king and tell him that he found one of the Negro people of Judah that could interpret the dream. Then he presents Daniel to the king, and the king asks Daniel (Beltchazzar), if he could tell him the dream and interpret it. Daniel said, "Though none of his Babylonian astrologers, magicians, or wise men could interpret it, there is a GOD in heaven that reveals things, and GOD is trying to tell him what would happen in the future, and GOD gave him the dream, so he could know the future, and it is not because he is wiser than the other men why he was given the ability to interpret it, but it is for him to tell him how terrible he is, so that maybe he would change for the sake of all the Negro captives. After saying that, Daniel starts to interpret the dream, and said, "There is a great, awesome image in the dream that is standing before you with a head made of fine gold, the chest and arm of silver, the belly and thigh of bronze, the legs of iron, and the feet part iron and part clay. And a stone hand struck the feet of the image and broke them into pieces, and the entire image crumbled like dust to the ground, and the wind blew away the dust, leaving no trace, and the stone hand became great all over the world."

Here is the interpretation:

Daniel said, GOD made you the king of Babylon, and HE gave you The Babylonian Empire, and power and strength to rule as head of a world government over every nation in the world. The gold head is symbolic of you, and The Babylonian Empire would be destroyed, but there would be a second world government that would come that would be weaker than it. Then there would be a third world government, which is symbolized by the bronze. Then there would be a fourth world government (The U.K.) that would be as strong as iron, and it would have many smaller governments that would crush all the other governments in the world. The feet and the toes that are part clay, and part iron, means that the fourth world government would be divide (into The U.K. and The U.S.) but it would remain strong like iron, just as if it was not divided. As the toes of the feet of the image were part iron, and part clay, so would this fourth world government be part weak and part strong. And as you see the clay mixed with iron, so would the officials of this fourth world government mix with other officials of other governments in the world, but they would not like each other. Then after that time pass, GOD would set up the everlasting world government on earth, and Jesus, and all the righteous ones would govern it, and no one would be able to destroy this government, or take it over, because it would take over all the present governments and be the only government, which would remain forever. The stone hand that crushed the feet of the image that caused it to crumble is symbolic of GOD telling you what would happen to The Roman Government that you rule in, up until the future governments, to when enough is enough, and Jesus is given permission to complete end all world governments and start the eternal world government.

That was the end of the interpretation, and Daniel tells Nebuchadnezzar that the dream is certain, and the interpretation is sure to happen. Then when Nebuchadnezzar heard what Daniel said, he falls flat on the floor on his belly and gives a command to make an offering to GOD. Then he tells Daniel that YAH, the GOD of the Negro people of Israel is the GOD of all gods, THE KING of all kings, and a revealer of secrets, since HE revealed what his dream meant, even without him telling the dream. After that, he promotes Daniel and gives him many great gifts. Then he makes him the ruler over the white people in the whole province of Babylon, and chief administrator over all the white wise men, and Daniel asks if his three friends, Shadrach, Meshach, and Abed-Nego could help him rule over the white people in the province, and he said, "Yes". But Daniel decides to make his three friends rule the province instead, while he just sit every day watching at the king's gate.

Chapter 3

A short time after, Nebuchadnezzar makes a great big image of gold and sits it in the plains of Dura in the province of Babylon. Then he sends a message to all the important people of the government to come to a dedication of the image. When they get there, they gather in front of the image, a messenger cry out saying, "When you hear the symphonic sounds of all kinds of instruments playing, you should fall down and worship the gold image, and the ones who does not do it would immediately be thrown into the burning furnace." Since people do not want to die, from that day on, every time they hear the music, they fall before the gold image and worshipped it. But many of the Jewish Negro people would not bow to it, and some of the Babylonian soldiers decide to tell the king, specifically that Shadrach, Meshach, and Abed-Nego, the Jews that he placed in charge are not bowing down to the image, and are not respecting him, because they will not worship the god he made. This enraged the king, and he commanded that they bring Shadrach, Meshach, and Abed-Nego to him, and they bring them to him. Then he asks them, if it is true they are acting as if they do not hear the music and is it true they are not worshipping the image as they were told, because he wants to know which god would save them from the hot furnace. They replied, "We do not need to answer you, but if you need an answer, then the answer is, our GOD would be able to save us from you, and if our GOD does not save us, we still want you to know that we do not worship idols, and we will not worship yours."

That answer angered the king even more, and he command his men to heat the furnace seven times hotter than usual, and he tell some of the strongest men from his army to tie Daniel, and his friends up, and throw them into the furnace. With the flame of the furnace very hot, the men throw Daniel and his friends into the flame, and the flame kill the men that threw them in. Meanwhile, the king is looking astonished, because he sees four men in the furnace, and so he asks his counselors, if it was three men thrown into the furnace, and they said, yes. Then he tells them to look down into the furnace, because he saw four men down there, and the fourth one looked like an angel, and he goes to the edge of the furnace, and yells out, Shadrach, Meshach, and Abed-Nego, and tells them to come out, and come to him. Then they come out to him, and when the people there realize that the flames did not harm them, and they do not smell like smoke, Nebuchadnezzar said, "Blessed be the GOD of Shadrach, Meshach, and Abed-Nego, WHO sent HIS angel to deliver HIS servants who trust in HIM when they refused to worship idols, and were willing to die instead." After that, he makes a decree throughout the whole world that says, no one should speak against YAH, the GOD of the Negro people of Israel again. Then he promotes Shadrach, Meshach, and Abed-Nego to a higher position in the province.

Chapter 4

Now Nebuchadnezzar thinks that it is a good idea to tell people about GOD. So, he sends good cheers to everyone and declare to the world that GOD worked some signs and wonders by power and might, and GOD gave him a dream that none of the wise men of Babylon could interpret, except for Daniel, who did it by HIS HOLY SPIRIT. On another day, he had another dream that bothered him, and he tells Daniel that in the dream, "He saw a great big tree with lovely leaves, and abundant fruit that feeds everyone in the world, Which shelters the wild animals with shade, and provides branches for the birds to live in, and it provides in some way, or another for everyone, and everything on the earth. But someone came down from heaven, crying out "Chop down the tree", so that it would not provide for anyone, or anything anymore. Yet the person said to leave the stump bound with a band of iron, and bronze, so it would be watered by the heavenly dew, and eat from the earth with the beasts, and grass, that after a while it could change into something wild."

Daniel is astonished at the dream, and he wonders what it means. But Nebuchadnezzar tells him not to worry about it. Then Daniel tells him that his enemies would want to know the interpretation of it, because the tree represents him, who grew to be strong and great, ever since GOD gave him the Babylonian Empire to rule over the world, and the person he saw coming down from heaven is GOD, WHO gave the angels permission to destroy him and his government, so that everyone in the world would know that GOD gives power to whomever HE wants, and takes it back whenever HE is ready. And GOD would drive him away from his kingdom to live in the wild as an animal for as many years as it takes for him to change his heart from being evil into acknowledging that GOD gave him the Babylonian Empire, not because he is strong, great, or good, but because GOD is the one that is strong, great, and good. Then once he acknowledges GOD, he would get back his kingdom, which is represented by the stump left with the roots.

With that interpretation, Daniel advises him to change his ways by becoming righteous, and merciful to the poor, so that maybe GOD would give him more time to rule without having to punish him. Yet, Nebuchadnezzar did not heed the warning of the dream, nor did he take Daniel's advice, and a short time later, as he walks about his royal palace, boasting about how Babylon is great, and how he built it with his power and might to live there as a king, while he is speaking, a voice comes from heaven tells him he just lost his kingdom, and would be thrown out of the palace to live in the wild, and someone else would rule the kingdom until he knows how to respect GOD. That same hour, Nebuchadnezzar loses his kingdom and goes to live as an animal in the wild. As time passed, his body got wet with dew, and his hair grew wild like eagle's feathers, and his nails looked like bird's claws. Then one day, while he drinks from a puddle, he sees the reflection of himself in the water, and said, "What a mess!" Instantly, he gets his senses back. Then he looks up to heaven, and bless, and praise THE MOST HIGH GOD, and honors HIM, and said, GOD lives and rules forever, and GOD does what HE wants with HIS heavenly army, and no one can stop HIM from punishing them for their sins. From that time on, Nebuchadnezzar, the white king of Babylon praises the GOD of the Negro people of Israel, because their GOD is truth and just, and HE can correct anyone that needs correction.

Chapter 5

Once Nebuchadnezzar changed, he gets his kingdom back, and he continues in it with mercy and justice. Then when he died, his son Belshazzar became the king of Babylon, and one day, Belshazzar had a great feast, drinking wine with thousands of his men, his wives, and his concubines, from the vessels that were taken from The House of THE LORD in Jerusalem, while praising their idol gods. Within that same hour, a finger of a man's hand appears, and writes on the plaster of the wall, which is opposite of the lamp stand in the palace, and Belshazzar saw it, and is bothered by it so much, he gets weak at the knees and cries out for the astrologers, his soldiers, and the fortune tellers (soothsayers). Which he considered to be the wise men of Babylon. So, they hurry to him, and he tells them if any of them could read, and interpret the writing on the wall, that person would get a gold chain, and be clothed in royal clothes as the third ruler in the kingdom. For the prizes, the men try to interpret the writing, but they could not, and the king is disappointed. Then the queen, and some of his men tell him not to worry, and the queen tells him, in the days of his father, there was a wise man named Daniel that his father promoted, who could interpret dreams, and solve riddles, whom he called Belteshazzar, and she suggests that he should send for him.

Then they go for Daniel (Belteshazzar), and stood him before Belshazzar (the king), and Belshazzar asks him, if he is Daniel, the captive, whom his father, Nebuchadnezzar brought from Judah that he heard is wise and has THE SPIRIT of GOD in him, and he tells Daniel that all the wise men of Babylon could not interpret the writing for him, but he heard that he could do it, and if he does, he would get a gold chain and would be dressed in the royal clothes to be the third ruler in the kingdom. Then Daniel tells him to keep his gifts, or give it to someone else, but he would tell him the interpretation of the writing anyway, and Daniel tells him about how his father, Nebuchadnezzar was blessed with the Babylonian Kingdom by GOD to rule the entire world as he pleased, and how he got proud, and was thrown out of the kingdom to live as a wild beast, and how when he changed his heart, and humbled himself, and respected YAH, THE LIVING GOD, he got his kingdom back. And Daniel asks him why he would not humble himself, even though he knew about his father. Yet, Belshazzar (the king) did not care about what Daniel (Belteshazzar) said to him, because he became proud. Then one day, while he is having a big party with all his guests drinking from the stolen vessels that his father stole from The House of THE LORD, as they drink to their idol gods, it makes GOD upset, and YAH, the GOD who can keep him alive, or kill him, promote, or demote him, wrote on the wall "MENE, MENE, TEKEL, UPHARSIN".

Interpretation:

Mene - GOD has numbered the days of your kingdom and will finish it.

Tekel - You have been weighed in the balance, and you are coming up short.

Peres - Your kingdom has been divided and given to the Medes and Persians.

Upharsin- is the conjugated form of Peres

After seeing that, Belshazzar, the king, immediately gives command to put the royal robe, and gold chain on Daniel, even though Daniel told him he wanted nothing, and he tells everyone that Daniel is the third ruler of the kingdom. That same night, they killed Belshazzar, the king, and Darius, the king of the Medes received the Babylonian kingdom at about sixty-two years old.

Chapter 6

Once Darius starts to rule, he gets rid of Daniels friends as leaders, and replace them with Daniel, and 120 white men to rule as governors, and head of the whole province in charge of everyone. After a while, Darius decides to make Daniel the sole ruler over the kingdom, and over everyone, because he distinguished himself above the 120 white governors, and because of jealousy, the 120 white governors try to get Daniel into trouble. But they could not, because he is faithful, and precise in his work. Then they decide to trap him by the law, and they go to Darius, and said they, and the rest of his men got together and decided to make a decree that says, "Anyone who talks to any god, or man, except to him in the next 30 days, would be cast to the lions." Then Encouraging him to establish the decree, and sign it and put it into effect, so it cannot be changed according to the law of the Medes and Persians, and he established the decree, and signed it, and when Daniel found out it was signed, he go to his place, kneel three times that day in front of an open window faced towards Jerusalem, and pray, and give thanks to GOD, like he always did, ever since he was a little boy. +

Once the governors saw that Daniel was still praying to his GOD, they tell the king that he was not giving due respect to the law, because he is praying to his GOD three times a day. That news disappoints the king, since he must kill Daniel for breaking the law. So, he procrastinates about killing Daniel all night. Then his men go back to him and remind him that the law said the offender should be killed. So, the king gives the command to bring Daniel to him to throw him into the lion's den, and they brought him, and cast him into the lion's den, and with compassion, the king whisper to Daniel, and said, "I know that the GOD you continually serve would deliver you." Then they roll a stone in front of the mouth of the den. That night, Darius, the king, goes to his palace, and could not eat, or sleep, and he did not even want to be cheered by music. The next morning, he goes out to the den very early, and he cry out to Daniel, 'Did your GOD saved you?", and Daniel said, "GOD sent his angels to shut the mouths of the lions, so they would not hurt me, because I am innocent." Immediately, Darius command some men to take Daniel from the den, and when they took him out, no injury was on him, because he believes in THE LIVING GOD. Then Darius command that the men that falsely accused Daniel to be killed, and they throw the false accusers, and their wives and children into the lion's den, and the lions break their bones into pieces before they even hit the bottom of the den. Later, Darius writes a letter to the world, and greets everyone in peace, and makes it a decree that everyone in every nation should fear Daniel's GOD, because HE is the living GOD that live forever, WHOSE government would last forever.

So, that's it. The same little Negro boy named Daniel, who was captured by Nebuchadnezzar, the white king of Babylon, grew up to be wise, and he prospered throughout the time of Darius, the king of Medes reign, when he took over Babylon, and throughout the time of Cyrus, who reigned after Darius.

Chapter 7

Let's go back to the past, in the first year of Belshazzar, the son of Nebuchadnezzar reign, before Darius's reign when Daniel had a dream that woke him up, and while he sat in the bed, he had a vision of it, and he got up, and wrote down the main facts, which said, "He saw four winds from heaven, stirring up the Great Sea (which is the Mediterranean Sea), and four beasts (or government) came up from the sea, and each one was different from the other.

OUR GOVERNMENT THE BEAST

1. The first beast was like a lion, and it had eagle's wings, and he watched it until its wings were plucked off. Then it was lifted from the earth and was made to stand on two feet, like a human being, and it was given a human heart.

2. The second beast looked like a bear, and it was raised up on one side and it had three ribs in its mouth between its teeth, and it was told to eat more.

3. The third beast was like a leopard, that had four wings like a bird on its back, and it had four heads, and the power to rule.

4. The fourth beast (The U.K.) was dreadful, and very strong, and it was different from the other beasts, and it had ten horns (which are ten other leaders on its side), and it was devouring things with its huge iron teeth. Then as he thought about the horns, he notices there was a little horn (The U.S. Government) coming up among them that plucked three of the ten horns from the roots (which was with The U.K.), and in the little horn were human eyes, and it was pompous.

After seeing those beasts (which are governments), he said, he noticed that everyone was criticized, and put in their places, because of how they ran their government. Then he saw (GOD) THE ANCIENT OF DAYS, clothed in clothes as white as snow, having hair like wool, seated at HIS throne, and thousands upon thousands were ministering to HIM, and the people in the court were seated, and the books were opened to judge. Yet, the little horn (The American Government) with the pompous ways kept acting up. Then it was destroyed and thrown into the flames of hell, and all the powers of the rest of the beasts (or governments in the world) were taken away from them, but they were allowed to continue for a little longer. Then he saw a figure (Jesus) in heaven that looks like a human being, and the being came down from heaven, and GOD gave Him power over all the governments, so that everyone would serve Him forever, because His power would be everlasting, and His government would never be destroyed.

That dream troubled Daniel, and he could not interpret it. Eventually he decided to ask someone who was beside him what it meant, and the person interprets it for him, and said, "The great beast are four kings in four governments, and the people that believed in GOD would receive the governments and have power over them forever." Then Daniel asks him to tell him about the fourth beast that was different from the others, that had the iron teeth and the ten horns on its head and was pompous and fought with the saints and prevailed against them, until GOD, THE ANCIENT OF DAYS came, and judgment was made in favor of the saints to receive the government. To explain, the man said, "The fourth beast (**The United Kingdom**) would be the fourth world government on the earth, and it would be different from the others, because it would try to destroy all the people that believes in GOD. And The Ten Horns are ten rulers in other governments that would become powerful in this government. Then another government (**which is The United States of America Government**) would come after that one, that would be different, and it would take three of the ten rulers of that nation to form another government (which is **The United Nations**). Then The

American Government would use The United Nations to subdue the other governments, and this new government (The United Nations) is **The New World Order Government** that would be against GOD, and speak pompous things, and persecute the believers, and they would change even time, and the law, and GOD would allow those in The U.N. to kill the believers for a set time. Then when that time is up, GOD would be ready to judge the situation, and the people in the heavenly court would be seated to hear GOD judgement to destroy this government forever, so that GOD could give all the power and leadership of the world government over to HIS Son, Jesus, and all the resurrected believers.

That was the dream that bothered Daniel, and when he understood it, he kept on thinking about when all of it would happen and be over with.

Chapter 8

Yet still in the past. Go back to the third year of Belshazzar's reign. Daniel (Belteshazzar) also had another dream that bothered him, and in the dream, he is in Shushan, which is in the province of Elam by the Ulai River, and beside the river is a ram with two horns, and one of the horns is higher than the other, and the higher one came up last. Then he saw the ram pushing Westward, Northward, and Southward, but not Eastward, and no other animal could defeat him, and the ram does whatever it wants to do. Then a male goat with a horn between its eyes came from the West without touching the ground, running furiously at the ram with the two horns, and the goat confronted the ram, and attacked it, and broke its two horns. Then the goat trampled on the ram, and the ram could not defeat it, and the goat grew great, but after it became strong, the large horn is broken. Then to take the place of the broken large horn, four notable ones came up towards the four winds from heaven, and out of one of them came a little horn that became great towards the South, the East, and towards The Mother Land, which is central to the earth, and it get so powerful, it defeats some of the angelic hosts. It even made itself a ruler over the defeated angels, and it stopped the sacrifices to GOD, and tore down the churches. And because the little horn is evil, it has an army that goes about to attack the righteous people, and it twists the truth and casts it to the ground, and it prospers. Then two holy people spoke to each other, and one asked the other how long would it be that there would be no sacrifices to GOD, and how long would the sanctuary be polluted, and the other answers, and said, it would be for 2,300 days (about 6 years) before the sanctuary would be cleansed.

Daniel could not interpret this dream either. Then one day, as he thinks about it, someone suddenly appears before him, and he hear a man's voice coming from the Ulai River saying, "Gabriel, make the man understand the vision". Suddenly, Gabriel appears next to him, and he gets scared, and fall face down to the ground. Then Gabriel tells him that the dream was showing him what would happen in **"The End Times"**, and as Gabriel is speaking, he touches him, and stand him up, and tell him, he is there to let him know what would happen far into the future. Gabriel then explains that "The ram with the two horns represents the kings of Medes and Persia (those who would start The U.K.). And the male goat is the kingdom of Greece (those who will start The American Government), and the large horn between its eyes is the first king. As for the broken horn, it means that four kings would come from that nation, but they would not have as much power, and in the far future when the governments get totally wicked, a new ruler would come that would look mean, and he would be full of schemes that would make him prosper, and he would destroy the mighty, and those who believes in GOD. Yet, he would be destroyed by human hands." That was the dream that bothered Daniel, and when he also understood that dream, he fainted and was sick for days. When he finally recovered, he went back to the work he did for Belshazzar, the king of Babylon.

Chapter 9

By the time Darius, the son of Ahasuerus (from the Medes) took rule over the Chaldeans white people of Babylon, Daniel understood by Jeremiah's prophesies that they must stay in captivity in Babylon for a total of seventy years. Therefore, every day he fast and pray to GOD, and confess to how the people of Israel sinned against HIM, and to how they rejected the prophets when they tried to warn them. He also confessed that even while in captivity, the people still would not change, and he said he is waiting for the day when GOD's anger turns from them. Then one day as he is praying and confessing his sins, Gabriel (the angel) flies by swiftly, and meets him at the time of the evening offering, and Gabriel tells him that he come to give him understanding, because he is greatly loved, and he wants him to know that "It would be only seventy more weeks (a little more than 1 ½ year) before they are freed, and their problems ends, because a way was made for the forgiving of sins to bring everlasting righteousness to earth, and he should be patient, and he would see prophecies come to pass and the anointing of THE MOST HOLY, because from the time he hear that his people are being freed from captivity, and are going back to Jerusalem to rebuild it, until the time Jesus, The Messiah is born, it would be seven weeks (a little more than1 ½ month later). Then in sixty two weeks (a little more than 1 years after Jesus is born) the streets, and the wall of Jerusalem would be completely rebuilt, even though the wicked white people would still be there. Then after the sixty-two weeks, when the streets and the wall are completed (about 2 ½ years after the captives started to return), the white people would want to kill Jesus as a child (less than 3 years old), and His parents would have to leave with Him to Egypt to save His life. Then the white people would destroy Jerusalem and the sanctuary again, and they would keep destroying the place, and Jesus would return from Egypt with his parents before He is a teenager to see the place destroyed. Then after Jesus is grown, He would make a covenant with the believing people in the world for one week, and in the middle of the week, He would tell them they do not have to make sacrifices and offerings anymore, and when the white people hear that no one has to make sacrifices and offerings anymore, they would get furious and try to destroy all the believers.

Chapter 10

It was in the third year of King Cyrus' reign over Persia when Daniel received more understanding of the vision, and he realized that though it was a short time before the captives start to return home, it would be a long time before all the wicked governments end and mourns. After that, he did not eat anything tasty, or drink any wine, or look good for three weeks. Then on the 24th day of the 1st month, while he is by the Tigris River, he see a (spirit) man clothed in linen, and his waist is girded with gold of Uphaz, and he has dark glowing skin, eyes like a torch of fire, arms and feet like bronze, and a strong deep voice. Yet, no one, but him saw the vision that came after, because the men that were around him ran and hide when they saw the spirit man in the linen. Only he alone saw it, and he became weak, and fell out cold on his face. Then as he feels a hand touching him, he gets on his hands and knees in fear, and the (spirit) man tells him not to fear, because he came to give him more understanding, and he had been trying to get to him, but the evil spirit that influences the mind of the king of Persia held him back for twenty-one days, and Michael (the archangel) came to help him get away, and he is finally there to help him know what would happen to his Negro people in the future, because it is a long time away. Hearing that made Daniel speechless, and the spirit man touch his lips so he could talk again, and he tell the spirit man, he is weak, and overwhelmed, because of what he saw in the vision. Then the spirit man touch him, and strengthens him, and tells him to be at peace, and be strong, because he has to go back to Persia and fight the controlling spirit there, and when he leaves, the controlling spirit from Greece would come there to Babylon where he is, but he should not worry, because no one could prevent him from coming back there to him, except for Michael, the archangel, who is chief over him.

Chapter 11

Also in the past, before King Cyrus, when Darius was still king, Darius was frightened at what he saw happening, and Daniel wanted him to understand that all those things were prophesied, and to give him understanding, Daniel said, "Three more white kings from Persia would arise, and the last one, which is the fourth white king (in The U.K.), would be richer than all the others, and he would stir up everyone against the white people of Greece, and their king would agree to do everything the king of Persia says. Then the king of Greece will lose power to the king of Persia (in The U.K.), and his kingdom would be divided to the four corners of the world, but not in his favor, because others would be ruling it the way they want. Explaining further Daniel said, "The king of the South from Greece would rise in power (in America) and he would have a great kingdom, and after a year, the king of the South (from Greece in America) would make an agreement to join with the king of the North (from Persia in Europe) to be neutral to each other, and to marry each other. But this is a trick, because from the king of the South (the Greeks in America) someone would start an army against the king of the North (the Persians in Europe), and the army will go to the North (to Europe) to fight them, and they will win. At that time, the king of the South (the Greeks in America) would take the idols, and vessels of silver and gold of the Persians of the North (in Europe), and their white royal lineage to Egypt. Then the king of the South (the Greek in America) would return home and continue to rule, and be the stronger kingdom, and the king of the North (the Persian in Europe) would be subjected to the authority in the South (to the Greeks in America). But after a while, the king of the North and his army (of Persian people in Europe) would stir up strife and come to America to fight against the king of the South and his army (of Greek people in America), and the king of the South (in America) would become enraged, and fight against them and win, and he will take their soldiers to join his army. With this victory, he would get full of pride, and will go about killing many Europeans, but this will not make him become any stronger. Then after many years, the king of the North (in Europe) will gather a greater army and more equipment than before, and go to America to stand against the king of America, and like robbers they will put up mounts and take the best cities, and there would be nothing that the king of America could do about it.

Then when the king of the North (from Europe) is established in the big cities of America, he would use honest people to help him gain his kingdom in America, and he would capture the coastlands, but after a while he would be forgotten about. Then a person that works for him would start to impose taxes in his kingdom in America, but within a few days he would be destroyed, and after him, there would be a vile person who would sneak in, and take the kingdom that he established in America, because he would not be honorable enough to gain it honestly, and he would act deceitfully, and increase his followers, because he would share whatever he gets deceitfully with them. That man would start war in America, and he will fight with the king of the South (which is with the king in America) and he will defeat him. At that time, two kingdoms will be in America; one from the North with Persians, and one from the South with Greeks, and the two kings will live together in America and lie on each other while they eat together, but they will not prosper in their efforts at this time, because it is not the end of prophecy yet. After a while, the king of the North will leave from America with great riches and great hate against the holy covenant. Then at the appointed time, as prophesied, the king of the North would gather his army in Europe to come to America to fight again. But this time it will be different, because as he is on his way, a ship from Chittim (which is in Cyprus) will join with America, and fight against them, which will cause them to return home hating the holy covenant even more.

Being full of hate, the king of the North will join with other nations that also hates the holy covenant, and because the king of the North was defeated by another white nation weaker than them, he would become angry, and will defile the sanctuary of the Negro people of Israel in Africa, and stop the daily sacrifice, and place **"The Abomination of Desolation"** there. Which is when a wicked white person calls their defiled white things of worship holy and then place them in the holy sanctuary of the Negro people of Israel in Jerusalem, The Holy City, and say their defiled white people in Africa are "The Chosen Ones" of GOD, instead of the Negro people of Israel.

Daniel also explained our time in The End Times, and he said, "Once The Abomination of Desolation" happens, the king of the North (in Europe) would treat the ungodly people good, and the godly ones bad, and the good ones would get such little help that they would decide to join with him. But those good ones that do not join him would have time to refine and purify themselves until "The End". He also explained our present time and he said, "The king of the North (the Persian in Europe) would deny all gods, and will even blaspheme YAH, THE LIVING GOD while having his own idol gods in the fortresses, and he would not want any women, because he will only love himself, and he would continue to prosper until The Wrath ends. At that time, GOD would send him to hell, because he would have been getting his information from his gods and using it to have power over the nations. Daniel also explained our future time, and he said, "Just before **"The End"**, the king of the South (the Greek in America) would attack the king of the North (the Persian in Europe), and the king of the North would retaliate with great force, passing through to America to get the king of the South and his army as they attack other nations on the way. At that time the red skinned godly Negroes of Edom, the mixed culture godly people of Moab, and the prominent godly Negro people of Ammon (the descendants of Lot) would escape from all their captives. But the ungodly Negro people of Egypt, the ungodly Negro people of Libya, and the ungodly Negro people of Ethiopia would not escape, and their precious things would be taken. Still, it is all good, because someday, the kingdom of the North in Europe, which is ruled by the descendants of the wicked white Babylonian people of Persia would come to an end.

Chapter 12

Daniel knows that his time is not the end yet, and he knows that when "The End Times" is ready to start, Michael, the archangel, the guardian of the Negro people of GOD would be ready to use great force to take down the king of the North, which is the Persian ruler in Europe, and his wicked government to deliver the Negro people. Then many dead people would rise, and they would be judged, and some of them would be forgiven, and they would get everlasting life, but some would not be forgiven, and they would be put to shame and contempt. Then at that time, those who are wise, and those who turned others into believers would shine.

That was how Daniel explained the prophecies of the governments to Darius, the white king of Babylon, that would come after The Roman Empire in his time, even up until the present governments of our time, and Daniel tells him not to tell anyone else, because it would not happen until far into the future, and by then, many people would run back, and forth, and gain some understanding. Then Daniel tells him about a vision he had while he was with the spirit man in the linen. He says he saw two angels; one was on one side of the riverbank and the other on the other side. Then one of the angels asked the spirit man that was with him to tell him when those prophesies would happen, and the spirit man held up his hands to heaven, and swore it would happen a long, long time from then when all the righteous people feel hopeless while GOD completely finish off the wicked.

Yet even though Daniel heard what the spirit man said, he still did not understand when it would be, and the spirit man tell him to just live his life, and forget about it, because by that time, many people would be purified and become righteous. But because the truly wicked would always do wickedness, they would not understand, yet the wise would understand. Then Daniel tell him, from the time the people of Israel cannot sacrifice daily to their GOD to when his white people place the idols in The House of THE LORD, which is "The Abomination of Desolation", there would be 1,290 days (a little over 3 ½ years), and those who can wait to make it to the1,335th day (which is 45 days after The Abomination of Desolation start) would be blessed. But for the time, the spirit man said, he should go and live his life, because he would die, and resurrect to inherit his place in the kingdom of GOD before that time.

EZEKIEL'S PROPHESY

Chapter 1

Ezekiel was one of the first captives of Israel, and while he is in captivity in Babylon, in the 13th year, in the 4th month, on the 5th day, which is five years after Nebuchadnezzar took the first captives, he is at the Chebar River and sees a vision of GOD in heaven at HIS throne in all HIS glory. Then he sees a whirlwind coming from heaven, and the brightness of fire is around it, and four living creatures come out of the fire that looks like human beings, but each one has four faces, and four wings; two on each side, which they hide their arms behind. And their legs are straight, and their feet looks like the feet of calves, and their entire body sparkles like polished bronze, and a halo is over their head, and beside each creature is a beryl colored wheel with rims full of eyes. Each wheel turns about like it is a wheel inside a wheel, and whenever the living creatures walk, or fly, the wheels go with them, because the spirit of the living creatures controls each wheel. Then when the creatures fly about, the sound of their wings sounds like a rushing army, and when they stand still, they hide their wings, and it seems like they are being controlled by a voice coming from above their heads. And the appearance of the person speaking is like a human being, and from the waist up is amber colored fire within HIM, and from the waist down is bright fire, instead of amber, and it is GOD WHO is sitting at HIS throne, and it was GOD speaking to those four living creatures, and the brightness of HIS glory around HIM looks like a rainbow in a cloud on a rainy day.

Chapter 2

Awestruck by the splendor, Ezekiel falls to his face, and then he hears a voice speaking to him. It is GOD speaking to him, and GOD tells him to stand on his feet, because HE wants to speak to him. Then THE HOLY SPIRIT of GOD enters him, and stood him on his feet, and tells him HE wants him to go to the people of Israel, and not to be afraid to tell them they are rebellious, whether they think so, or not. Suddenly a hand stretches out with a scroll, and opens it to Ezekiel, and it has writing on the inside and on the outside is writing of lamentations and mourning.

Chapter 3

Then GOD tells him to eat the scroll, and he opens his mouth, and GOD cause him to eat it, and GOD tell him to fill his belly with it, and as he eats it, it is sweet in his mouth. So, GOD tells him to go and talk to the people of Israel, and because they are his people, they should understand, and listen to him, but since they are going to be stubborn, and hardheaded, HE would make him look mean, and strong, and he should not be afraid of them, even though they are rebellious. Right then, he lifted into the air, and hear a voice saying, "Blessed is the glory of GOD from heaven". He also hears the noise of the wings of the four living creatures, and the noise of the wheels beside them. Then the SPIRIT of GOD fly him away, and leaves him by himself, and he gets bitter as he considers what GOD said to him. Then he goes to the captives at Tel Abib by the Chebar River, and as he sit around them for seven days, he is astonished at the things he see them doing, and GOD appear to him, and tells him that HE made him a watchman over the people, and HE wants him to tell them they are being warned that the wicked ones would surely die, and if he does not warn them, and anyone dies in their sin, he would be blamed for it. But if he warns them, and someone dies in their sin, he would not be blamed for it, and it would be his fault if a righteous person starts to sin, and he did not warn that person, because as the person is being punished, that person would die by the punishment, because someone did not warn that person to change, and that person would suffer in hell, as if he never did anything good. So, if someone warns the righteous person that is sinning, and that person changes, then the person that warned them would be blessed, and the person changes and stops sinning, that person would be blessed, because they heed the warning. Then GOD stood him on his feet and tells him to go to the plains where HE would talk to him, and he goes to the plains, and GOD was already there, and is looking as glorious as the way HE did when he first saw HIM at the Chebar River. So, he fall flat on his face, awestruck by the beauty, like before, and GOD stood him on his feet, and tell him to lock himself up inside his house, because the people are ready to kill him, and HE is going to make his tongue cling to the roof of his mouth and make him mute, so he would not be able to cuss any of them, and when HE is ready for him to speak, HE would free his tongue for him to tell them, if they want to listen, they can listen, but if not, then they can continue to be stubborn and hard headed.

Chapter 4

After that, GOD tell him to take a piece of clay, and draw Jerusalem on it, and then lay it before himself, and place battering ramps against it, as if he took siege of it, as a sign to the people of Israel. Then lay on his left side for 390 days to represent one day for each year that "The Kingdom of Israel" turned from being godly, and after those 390 days, lay on his right side for 40 more days to represent one day for each year since "The Kingdom of Judah" turned from being godly. And he would not be capable of turning from one side to another, until the appropriate time, and he must make sure that he has wheat, barley, and other foods to eat for those days, so he would be able to cook a serving of 20 shekels per day (about 22 grams), fueled by human poop in front of the people of Israel, and eat it, and wash it down with 1/6 of a hin of water (almost 8 liters) to show them how they eat their small portion of defiled foods, and wash it down with lots of water among the ungodly white people they live with. That is not a pleasing plan with Ezekiel, and he complains he never defiled himself that way by cooking with human poop before. Then GOD change HIS mind and tells him he could use cow dung, instead of the human poop, and HE would cut off the food supplies in Jerusalem, and the people would barely have anything to eat, and they would die off from starvation.

Chapter 5

Then after he does those things, he must take a sharp sword and use it as a barber's razor and cut off his beard, then weigh the hair he cuts, and divide it, and take a small amount of it, and bind it to the edge of his clothing. And after that, take some of the hair, and throw it into a fire, and burn it as an example that from there, a fire would burn through the houses of the people of Israel, because their GOD located Jerusalem in the center of the world, but the people rebelled and are worse than all the nations surrounding them. So, for that, GOD is against them, and HE would punish them, so everyone could see it, and they would devour each other, and be scattered all over the world, and their native land would become a wasteland, because GOD is so angry with them.

Chapter 6

On another day, GOD tells him to look toward the land of the people of Israel and prophesy towards the mountains and tell the people, even the mountains, the hills, and the ravines would be destroyed, because of all the idol worship throughout the land, and the altars of false worship would also be destroyed, and their children would lay dead before them, and then they would know that YAH, is the only GOD, but HE would leave a remnant of them alive that would remember HIM, and they would not want to sin anymore. So, they could pound their fists, and stomp their feet all they want, but they would die off, and the dead would lie among their idols, and then they would know that YAH is the only GOD.

Chapter 7

GOD also tells him to tell the people of Israel that it is time for the sinning to stop, because HE is too angry, and the disaster would come, and HE would not spare them, and the trumpet was blown for war, and everyone would be afraid, and would be in sorrow when they see that they cannot be delivered from the punishment, and they would mourn, and then they would know that HE, YAH, GOD, THE ONE that created the heavens, and the earth is the only GOD.

Chapter 8

Then in the 6th year of captivity, in the 6th month, on the 5th day of the month, while Ezekiel is in the house with the elders, the SPIRIT of GOD appeared to him in HIS glory, and grabs him by the hair, and lifts him up into the air, and shows him a vision of Jerusalem, and he see through the north gate into the inner court of the sanctuary, and in the sanctuary is a seat for the image of jealousy. Then GOD tell him to look North toward the white people land, and he looks, and GOD asks him what he sees, and he said, he sees the image of Jealousy, which causes people to become jealous, and GOD says HE hopes he realizes that HE had to punish the people, because they ran HIM away from HIS sanctuary. Then GOD tells him to turn again, so HE could show him something else, and he turns, and GOD takes him through the courtyard of the sanctuary, and there is a hole in the wall, and GOD tells him to dig into the wall, and when he dug into the wall, he sees a door, and GOD tells him to go in so he could see the kind of things that people are doing in there. When he goes in, he sees every kind of creeping things, beasts, and idols, displayed around the place, and seventy of the elders, and Jaazaniah (the priest) are there with their censers burning incense to their idols, and GOD tells him that even though the people are doing those things, they are still wondering why they are being punished so harshly. Then GOD tells him to turn again, so HE could show him something worse than what he already saw, and when he turns, GOD takes him to the north gate of The House of THE LORD, and he is shocked to see women there in the church crying out to the idol, Tammuz. And GOD tells him to turn again, so HE could show him more, and he turns, and GOD takes him into the inner court of The House of THE LORD, and at the door of the temple, between the porch and the altar, are about twenty-five men facing towards the East with their backs to the temple as they worship the sun in the East. And GOD asks him if he ever saw any people do such terrible things to their gods and filled their land with violence to provoke their gods to anger, and HE sighs, because HIS people did it to HIM. Which is why HE is furious, and why HE would punish them without having any pity on them. Then GOD speaks out loudly, and said, "Let the rulers of the city come with their weapons." Suddenly, from the direction of the upper gate, facing North, six (spirit) men comes with their battle ax, and one of them is in linen, and has a writer's inkhorn at his side, and they stand before the bronze altar. By that time, GOD had already left from beside the carved cherub (angel) that is in the temple, and HE call to the man in linen to HIM, and tell him to go throughout Jerusalem, and put a mark on all the people that are sorry for all the sins that is in the land. Then HE tells the other spirit men to go behind the one with the linen and kill everyone that he does not put a mark on, and they are to begin at the sanctuary. Immediately, the spirit men leave, and they kill the elders that are at the sanctuary, and GOD tells them to throw the dead bodies outside in the courtyard of the temple to defile the place, and they throw the dead bodies in the courtyard. Then GOD tells them to go out to the city and kill, and they go out to the city, and kill, and while they are killing, Ezekiel is left alone, and he fall on his face, and cry to GOD, asking HIM if HE would destroy all the people of Israel, because HE is so angry that the tribe of Judah also failed HIM. In great anger, GOD replied, "All the sins of Israel, even the sins of the tribe of Judah are great, and the land is full of murdering, and the city is full of all sorts of sexual perversity, and they are saying that I AM the one that forgot about them and the land. So, that is the reason why I will not spare them, or have pity on them, until I punish them for what they did." Right at that moment, the man in the linen with the inkhorn reports back to HIM and said, he did as commanded.

Chapter 10

All that was seen from the temple on the earth in Jerusalem. Then from the temple on earth, Ezekiel sees into the 2nd heaven, where the Cherubim (angels) lives, and he sees up into the 3rd heaven, where GOD and the Seraphim (angels) lives, where there is a throne that sparkles like sapphire stone, and then GOD tell the (spirit) man in the linen to go to the 2nd heaven among the wheels, and fill his hands with coal from the Cherubim, and scatter the coal over Jerusalem. Then the spirit man in the linen leaves to do as commanded. Meanwhile, as Ezekiel and the cherubim (angels) are standing by the south side of the temple on the earth seeing all that is happening in heaven. Then the courtyard of the temple on earth is filled by a cloud of the brightness of the glory of GOD, and the sounds of the wings of the Cherubim is heard throughout the place. Then GOD leaves from the Cherubim in the courtyard, and pauses over the threshold of the temple, and inside the place is filled with the cloud of the brightness of HIS glorious light, and Ezekiel can hear the sound from the wings of the cherubim from inside. Then from the threshold, GOD commands the man in the linen to take the hot coals, and one of the Cherub among the cherubim stretches out his hand and takes some of the hot coal from the fire, and gives it to the man in the linen, and the man in the linen leaves with the coal. At that point, Ezekiel noticed that the cherubim (angels) have hands under their wings, and they also have the wheels that he saw before with the four living creatures that had four faces, and he realizes that the cherubim (angels) are kind of like the four living creatures that he saw at the Chebar River.

The Cherubim (angels) has:

1. The face of a cherub (angel)

2. The face of a human man

3. The face of a lion

4. The face of an eagle

**** Cherub is a single angel, and Cherubim is the plural form of the word Cherub. These are angels that have amber light, while the Seraph (singular), or Seraphim(plural) angels has bright white light.*

As the cherubim goes about, the wheels follow them when they move, and GOD leaves the temple, and stands over the cherubim, and then the cherubim, and GOD floats up and go to the east gate.

Chapter 11

From the east gate, GOD and the cherubim appear above Ezekiel. Then GOD floats Ezekiel up into the air and takes him to the east gate of The House of THE LORD, which face eastward, and at the door of the gate are twenty-five men, including Jaazaniah, and Pelatiah, who are leaders of the community. And GOD tell him, those are the men that caused all the people to continue in sinning, because they told them there is no need for them to build houses, since the city is a pot, and they are the meat, and HE wants him to tell the people that HE know they are bad minded, and it is because of them why their city is the pot, and they are the meat, and HE would fix things for them someday, but for the meanwhile, HE would drive them out of the city, and the city would not be the pot, because they would die off outside the borders. Right away, Ezekiel goes to tell the people what GOD said, and as he speaks to them, Pelatiah dies, and Ezekiel falls on his face in sorrow. Then Ezekiel asks GOD if HE is going to kill off all the people of Israel, and GOD said, his brethren, his family, his friends, and all the people of Israel said they did not want anything to do with HIM after they inherited the land, and yet, HE would protect them no matter where they are in the world, and HE would bring them back to their own land again to be united, and happy while they are praising, and obeying HIM, because HE is their GOD, and they are HIS people. Then GOD, and the cherubim floats into the air with him, and they leave the city, and go to stand on the mountain on the east side of the city, and GOD shows him a quick vision of the people that are in captivity by the Chaldeans (white people) in Chaldea, and even though he did not see much, he goes and tell what he saw to those that are being held captives around him in Jerusalem.

Chapter 12

On another day, GOD tells him that he lives with rebellious people that do not understand anything, and HE wants him to prepare to act like he is going into captivity by taking his belongings in the mornings to the walls, and in the evening dig through the walls in front of them, and day after day, doing the same thing. The next morning, he takes his belongings to the wall, as if he is going into captivity, and in the evening, he digs through the walls with his hands, as if he is trying to escape from the captors. Then the next day GOD tells him that HE noticed that no one even bothered to ask him what he was doing, but if they ask, then he should tell them, "It is a sign to them that they would also be carried away as captives like the rest of the people of Israel, and their princes would dig through the wall to try to help them get away, but they would be caught and taken to Babylon as captives, where most of them would die, and yet a few of them would be spared, so they could tell the gentile people about all the terrible things the wicked white people did to them in Babylon."

Then GOD tells him to eat, and drink in fear, and to go, and tell the people of Judah, they should eat, and drink with anxiety, and fear, since they would die off, because of all their sins, and the land would become desolate. And

GOD asks him about the proverb the people say when they talked about how the place looks a mess, and what they say when they complain about how they are tired of waiting for it to change, and GOD tells him to tell them that the people can stop saying the proverb, because it is time for the place to be destroyed completely, because HE is tired of them and their false worship there, and it would no longer be postponed. On another day, GOD tells him that the people of Israel are saying that the vision he saw them going into captivity is false, because it would not happen until way into the future, and HE wants him to tell them that none of HIS words would be postponed any longer, and they better expect it to happen immediately.

Chapter 13

Shortly after that, GOD tells him to tell the prophets of Israel that tell lies, they are foolish, because they follow their own spirit, and they do not see anything, and they do not help the people to know the truth, so they could know what to do, and HE wants them to know that HE is against them, and HE would severely punish them. As for the prophetess, they are liars too, because they use charms to tell lies to the people, so they would die off, and they kill those that should not die, and help the ones that should. And since they killed off HIS people, HE wants to know if HE should not do something about it, because they know that HE is against anyone that use magic charms as a way of killing people, and they know that HE would reveal their evil ways by allowing those who are trapped by them to escape, because they make the hearts of the righteous people sad, and they help the wicked people to benefit from evil, which cause them to not want to change.

Chapter 14

While GOD is speaking to him, some of the elders come there to talk to him about what to do, and when they asked him what to do, GOD alerts him that they came there looking for answers, even though they worship idols, and HE does not want him to let them know anything, and so HE wants him to tell them that any prophets that come there to ask him what HE said, they would be punished according to how often they worships idols, because that way, HE can control them by what is in their hearts, and since they turned from HIM with their idols, they must repent, and turn from their idols if they want to save themselves, because anyone that turn from HIM to worships idols, and then asks HIS prophet what HE said, that person would be punished, and if HIS prophet tell them anything when HE told him not to, then the prophet, and the one that asks him for answers would be punished, so they would learn to stop turning from HIM.

On another day, GOD tells him that when a nation sin against HIM, HE would cut off their supplies of food, and cause famine and destruction to the place, and even if Noah, Daniel, and Job were still living, and were living there, only they alone would be saved, because of their righteousness. Which is why the sword, famine, wild beasts, and pestilence is the severe judgment against Jerusalem, but a small amount would be saved, and they would be treated well after it all happens, and then they would see that HE does nothing without having a good reason.

Chapter 15

Then GOD asks him, if the wood from a vine is better than any other wood in the forest, and could it be used to make anything, and since the answers are no, then the wood from a vine is useless, and it can only be used to burn in a fire, and once it is burnt up, it is really good for nothing. So, as the vine is used for fuel, that is how HE would give the people of Jerusalem as fuel when HE turns from them, and they would go out as fire, and the land would become desolate, because they persisted on being unfaithful.

Chapter 16

After not speaking to Ezekiel for a while, GOD speaks to him again, and tells him that HE wants to let the people of Jerusalem know about their sins, and HE wants to tell them that they are acting like they were born from the wicked white people that were born as natives in The Land of Canaan, instead of acting like the white people being born from them, because they are acting like their father is a white Amorite man, and their mother is a white Hittite woman, and it seems true, because on the day HE chose them, they looked so slimy, and were unattended for, that no one pitied them, or had compassion to do anything for them. But when HE passed by and saw them struggling in the blood of their birth, HE had compassion for them, and HE told them to live, and HE made them strive, and they grew to be mature, and they were beautiful. Then later when HE checked on them, they were not only beautiful, but also righteous, and HE protected them, and made them HIS, and HE completely forgave them of their sins, and gave them understanding by HIS HOLY SPIRIT, and they were beautifully dressed, and had fine jewelry, that every nation in the world was saying how beautiful they were. Then things changed, because they trust in their own beauty, and they start to look for everyone from every nation to compliment them when they see them and start to use the things HE gave them to worship idols with. They even took their gold and silver to make the idols, and they covered the idols with the beautiful, embroidered garments HE gave them, and the pastries, the fine flour, the honey, and all the food HE gave to them, they put before their idols that cannot even eat. Then they gave their children, which belong to HIM to the idols, by burning them as a sacrifice, and yet they act like they do not even remember when HE cleaned them up and chose them to be HIS example to other people in the world, because they are building shrines to idols, and are offering themselves to everyone that passes by. At first, they committed harlotry with the Egyptians colored people, their neighbors, by worshipping the same false gods as they do. Then they acted like the whore to the white Assyrian people, and still they were not satisfied with just that. So, they acted more like a whore with the white Chaldean people, and still, they were not satisfied, until they were worse than everyone else, and had a degenerate heart. Yet, they were not even good whores, because they whored themselves out to strangers without asking for money, and they paid their lovers to come to them from all over the world.

As a matter of fact, they are opposite of any other whore, because no one solicited them to be a whore, and they pay their lovers to whore around with them, instead of getting paid, and that is why HE would take pleasure in getting rid of all the people from every nation that are in The Promised Land whoring around with them, so it could be to them as a punishment for a wife that whores around on her husband, because HE is jealous. Then after the land is destroyed and desolate, and everyone hates them, HE would be satisfied and would not be angry with them anymore. So, like mother like daughter, like sister and sister, is what people would say about their Negro women, because they would see how they hate their children, and despise their husbands. And others would say that their people are that way, because they learned it from their white ancestors, since they believe that their mother is a white Hittite, and their father is a white Amorite, and they believe that their eldest sister is one of the white women from Babylon in the North that took over Samaria (which belongs to Israel), and they also believe that their younger sister is a white woman that lives in the South with the white people of Sodom. Even if that was true, they are worse than those wicked white tribes, though they were better than any white group. But since they wished to be like the detestable wicked white people, instead of being like their own righteous Negro people, people are thinking they are worse than any wicked white clan. As a matter of fact, the white people of Sodom were better than what the Negro people of Israel turned out to be. Though Sodom was destroyed for being full of pride, for eating too much, for being too lazy, and for not helping the needy, and though they always had plenty food and drinks to have parties, while they committed their sins and worshipped idols, they were not as bad as what the people of Israel turned out to be.

Chapter 17

At that moment, GOD tells him to speak against the people of Israel in a parable, which interprets to say, "A great number of different kinds of white people from Babylon came into the land and took the best of them as captives, and they set up merchants, and sold them as slaves to other white nations, and left some of them in the land with white dictators to rule over them, so they would have to obey them if they want to live. Then they even turned their Egyptian friends against them, and that is why GOD is going to make the white people powerful, and the land looking good while they ruled them, so that some of them left in the land would mix with some of the white people, and have biracial children that would be faithful, and increase, and become prosperous. Then there would be a great number of biracial people in the world that would want to be godly that wants to know the truth from the righteous Negro ones that are in the land, so they could do the right things and prosper."

Shouldn't GOD destroy the wicked white nation and leave them to diminish, so HIS Negro people could teach the truth to those who want to know it?

Chapter 18

Yes, GOD should destroy the wicked white nations, so others could learn from HIS people about HIM. That is why HE asked Ezekiel what he meant when he said the people of Israel are being punished for the sins of their forefathers, and since it is not a truthful statement, GOD said, "As long as I lives, I do not want to hear you say that again. Because everyone in the world belongs to ME, and if a man is righteous and does not turn from ME, he would live, but if he is unrighteous and turned from ME, he would die, and if an unrighteous person has a child that is righteous, that child would not be punished for their father's sin, because each person is being punished for what they did. And if an unrighteous man turned from his sins and become righteous, he would not be punished, and if a righteous man turned to sinning, he would be punished, and yet some people say that a child should suffer for what its parents did. But I do not have pleasure in killing people, and I just want the wicked ones to change so they could live righteously. Yet some people are still saying that I am unfair, but I am fair, and it is you that are unfair.

Listen to this! When a righteous person changes, and starts to sin, and then dies, it is because of his sins why he dies. So, when a wicked person changes, and starts to do the right thing, he preserves his life. Yet, the Negro people of Israel say that GOD is not fair. Which is why HE would judge them according to their sins. Therefore, it would be wise if they repent, so HE would not punish them, because HE has no pleasure in killing all of them, and HE does not know why none of them refuse to stop sinning, and why they do not turn back their heart to loving HIM, and to the spirit of loving their Negro heritage.

Why should the Negroes die?

They do not have to die. All they need to do is turn from following the white people ways and live GOD's way, because GOD has no pleasure in killing them.

Chapter 19

But they refuse to do that. That is why GOD tells Ezekiel to lament over the princes of Israel and tell them that, "Their mother is a lioness that lies down among the lions to nurse her cubs, and one of them became a young lion that learned to catch preys and devour men, and when the other nation heard of it, they captured him and took him to Egypt. And when the mother saw that he would never return home, she took another one of her cubs and raised him to be a young lion that also learned to catch prey and devour men, and the other nations also captured him, but this time, they took him to Babylon, and that is what it is like for the Negro people of Israel, a nation that is strong that joined themselves with the world, and was deceived by them to be enslaved, and devoured, until they are left with nothing."

Chapter 20

Then one day, as one of the elders is on his way to Ezekiel to ask him what GOD is telling him, GOD tell Ezekiel to tell the elder HE has nothing to say to him, and HE wants him to judge the people, and tell them that they are nothing but a bunch of sinners, because HE choose them, and gave them the best land in all the world, and told them to get rid of all their idols, and false ways of worship, because HE is their GOD, but they rebelled, and did not throw away all their idols, or stopped worshipping other gods, especially those of Egypt. Which is the reason why HE sent them into slavery in Egypt. But HE delivered them from there to the wilderness where HE gave them HIS rules and regulations, and they rebelled again. Then HE punished them by killing them in the wilderness, and the next generation obeyed HIM, and HE gave them back their land again. Plus, The Land of Canaan, which is The Promised Land. But since HE knew they would rebel again, HE told them they would be scattered all over the world as punishment for that, and because they rebelled as HE predicted, they were scattered all over the world throughout other countries that traded them to the white people in Babylon. Yet those that were still in the land continued to sin, even when they saw what was happening to them, and they were even impressed by the evil ways the white people got their power. That is why HE gave the white people of Babylon the boldness to go take as many of them as captives as they want, since they do not want to serve HIM. So, they can go serve their idols all they want, since HE does not want them to profane HIS name anymore with their gifts, and idols, and only when they worship HIM the right way on the holy mountain, HE would accept them and their offerings and deliver them from all the people that enslaved them. Then they would remember what happened to them when they defiled themselves, and they would not do it anymore, and they would know that HE is a good GOD when they realize that HE punished them to save them.

Right after saying that, HE tells Ezekiel to speak against the South (Greece) and tell them, "HE would kindle a fire that would devour the white people there (in Greece), and also devour the white people of the North (in Persia), and they would scorch, so the whole world would see it, and no one would be able to help. Then after hearing that, Ezekiel said, "The people would think I am talking nonsense if I tells them that."

Chapter 21

GOD is hot with anger, and HE tell Ezekiel to tell the people of Jerusalem, HE is against them, and feels like just taking HIS sword and kill off all of them, whether they are wicked, or not, but instead HE is going to kill off all the invaders in their land, whether they are wicked or not, and everyone would know that HE alone is GOD. Then GOD tells him to sigh when he tell them what HE said, and when they ask him why he sighed, he should tell them, "It is, because everyone would sigh when it happens, and it is going to happen soon, because a sword was sharpened and polished to make a dreadful slaughter against them, because their GOD despises them for their sins, just like how HE despises other nations for their sins."

Then GOD tells him to make a sign that has two arrows on it, which points to the ways they could get to Babylon, and put the sign at the head of the road, pointing to Jerusalem, because the king of Babylon is hiding out at the fork of the road, consulting with his images by use of divination, and is shaking the arrow, and looking at the liver as a practice of his witchcraft, so he could find out from the evil spirit how to besiege Jerusalem. Then after he placed the sign at the fork of the road, he must go to the priests and tell him, they may as well remove their turbans and go and tell the royal families they may as well remove their crowns, and start doing the right things, because nothing is going to be the same when HE exalts the humble and humble the exalted. After that, he must go and tell the Amorite white people in the land, they are going to be punished too, and because their ancestors were from there, just like the ancestors of the Negroes who were from there died there, they would also die there in their native land and be completely forgotten about.

Chapter 22

Then when he is done telling the Amorite white people what HE said, he must go back to the people of Jerusalem and tell them they are murderers, and idols makers, and it is time for them to be punished, and other nations would mock them, and say, the reason why they are being punished is because they do not care about their parents, and they oppress their visitors, and mistreat the orphans, and the widows, and their leaders became murderers, ever since they started despising the holy things, and stopped observing The Sabbath. But even though people would say that they need to know it is because their HE, their GOD despises them, and HE would scatter them in every nation to remove them far from the filthiness they made in the land to let them stay defiled in the other nations for all HE cares.

On another day, GOD tell him to tell them, they are like dross of tin, iron, or some type of molten metal to HIM, and HE would gather them in the middle of Jerusalem and put them in the furnace to melt them like metal, because HE is so angry with them, and the reason why they have not been blessed in a long time is, because they will not change, even though HE is begging them to, so HE could stop punishing them, but they all continue to be liars, murderers, and thieves, and everyone is against each other, and they oppress each other, and mistreat the needy, and the poor, and HE had been looking for someone to stop sinning, and start to pray for the nation, but no one would change and stop sinning, and that is why HE is punishing them so severely.

Chapter 23

Another day, HE tells Ezekiel a story about two women that were the daughters of the same woman that were whores from their youth, and they whored around, pressing their bosom against the Egyptians, and one of the women is named Oholah, and her sister's name is Oholibah, and they were holy people that should have had children that were holy. Therefore, Oholah, the oldest, represents all the people of the tribes in The Kingdom of Israel that practice unrighteousness like the ones in Samaria, and Oholibah, the youngest, is Jerusalem, which represents the tribe of Judah in The Kingdom of Judah that stayed righteous. At first when Oholah (The Kingdom of Israel) started, they were dedicated. Then they start to practice witchcraft, and black magic like the white Assyrian people, but the darkest skinned ones that were Oholibah, who are of the tribe of Judah, held on to their beliefs, and stayed dedicated HIM, their GOD. And though Judah was strong, and holy, they became friends with the ungodly white Assyrians, and start to worship idols and defiled themselves, and they even worship the idols of Egypt, because they never stopped loving the Egyptians after they were delivered from slavery from them. That is why HE is allowing the white Assyrians to take them as captives and take over the land, and even though her sister, Oholibah, the people of Judah, saw the rest of Israel suffering when they turned to idol worship, they decided to do the same thing, and became more corrupted, and then started to inter-marry with the wicked white Assyrians that got them into idol worship in the first place. So, once that happened, it made all the people of The Nation of Israel defiled in their native lands. But the dark skinned tribe of Judah are worst, because they looked on the portraits of the Chaldean (white) soldiers on the walls, and admired them, and then they sent to Babylon for more of them to come to them, because they admired their look so much, and they even dress like the white people, and wear their turbans flying loose on their heads like bandits, just like them.

That is why at first, HE left the people of Israel, but HE stayed with the tribe of Judah which is of the royal lineage that ruled the government and is of the lineage of the prophets and priests that ruled the church, who are to teach and lead the people in godliness. Then when the tribe of Judah did what the rest of Israel did, HE got very angry that all HIS people turned from HIM and are trusting in the gods of ungodly nations. Now HE wants the nations to hate the dark skinned Negroes of Judah, just like how HE made them hate the rest of the Negro people of Israel, and HE wants all the white Chaldeans, and the white Assyrians, and every white nation to come against Jerusalem, and kill some, and take some to Babylon. HE also them to place white leaders over those that are left in the land that would deal with them fiercely, because it seemed right to use the white people that hates them to punish them for HIM, and with the harsh treatment, maybe they would hate the white people, and their ways, and turn back to HIM. Therefore, the tribe of Judah would be punished like the rest of Israel, because the whole nation has become a bunch of idol worshippers, and lovers of shameful people in other nations. Then they would be laughed at, and be scorned, until their lives feel like nothing but sorrow, because all the rest of Israel that are still in the land still commits adultery, and they are murderers, since they commit the adultery with their idols, and they sacrifice their children to them by burning them up in the fire. They even defiled the holy sanctuary, and profaned The Sabbath, because after they killed their children for the idols, on the same day, they go into the sanctuary and profane it. Not only that, they also sent for the white men to come way far from their white nations to come to them, and they clean up for them, and dress up, and put on make-up, and jewelry, and sit the white people on a comfortable coach, and push a table in front of it, which is the table from the sanctuary for the holy incense and oil, and they place bracelets on the white people's wrists, and crowns on their heads, and laugh with them, as if they are their long-time friends. So, for that, they would be punished with captivity to make the land clean again. Then they would know that their GOD, is THE MOST HIGH.

Chapter 24

Again, in 9th year, in the 10th month, on the 10th day, GOD speaks to Ezekiel, and tell him to write down a certain date, because that day would be the first day Nebuchadnezzar, the king of Babylon come and make siege against Jerusalem, and he must tell the people, and HE would cause him not to be able to cry tears to show sorrow, but he would be able to mourn quietly while he goes about with his turban bound on his head, and his sandals strapped on his feet (like a true priest). Then in the morning, Ezekiel goes to the people and tells them what GOD said. That same evening his wife dies, and he did not mourn, or cry. Then the next day, people ask him why his turban is girded on his head, and why is he not mourning, or crying, and he tell them that GOD told him HE is going to destroy them, since they profaned HIS sanctuary, and it is GOD WHO caused him not to feel any sorry, and caused him not to be able to cry, because GOD does not feel sorry for them, and they would be crying, and he is a sign to them to know that when they are suffering in their sorrow, GOD is not feeling any sorrow, or pity for them.

Chapter 25

Then GOD tells him to prophesy against the white Ammonite people again, and tell them that because they laughed when HIS sanctuary was profaned, and when the land became completely desolate after the tribe of Judah was taken into captivity, HE would cause the people of The East to punish them, and take over the land they are living in. Then HE tell him to tell the mixed cultured people of Moab, and the white people of Seir that, because they were so quick to say the people of Israel were like the rest of the ungodly people in the world, they would be punished, and the people of The East would come and take their land, just like how they would take the land of the white people of Ammon. After that, HE tell him to tell the red skinned Negroes of

Esau that lives in Edom in the land of Seir amongst the white people, they would be punished by the people of Israel, because the people of Israel are their brothers, but they hate them and treat them badly after they inherited the promise to be "The Chosen Ones". And tell the Philistine people (the Palestinians), they would be punished also, because after the people of Israel inherited The Promised Land, which is The Land of Canaan that belonged to the white people of Canaan, the people of Israel allowed them to stay North in the land, but because they get jealous every time they see the people of Israel prospering, they became spiteful and destructive to cause trouble for them.

Chapter 26

Almost two years later, in the 11th year, on the 1st day of the of the year, GOD tell Ezekiel to tell the white people of Tyre, because they laughed when their white people took captives of the people of Israel to prevent them from being an example to the world, HE is against them, and HE would cause many nations to fight against them and destroy them, and then they would know that HE is THE MIGHTY GOD, and all the white nations on the coastline would become afraid when they see them destroyed, and they would lament for them, and say, "O' how Tyre had been perished, the ones that other fishermen on the coast feared", and those white nations would wonder who caused it to happen, and they would start to tremble, because they would know they are next.

Chapter 27

Therefore, GOD laments for the white people of Tyre, and HE tell Ezekiel to tell them, "They are an island, which is located at the entrance of the sea, and their border is beautiful, and they used the finest of wood to make their ships, because even wood from Lebanon they used to make the masts, and oak from Bashan to make the oars, and their Ashurite friends always gave them ivory from the coast of Cyprus to inlay the planks, and they get fine embroidered linen from the coast of Elishah they get from Egypt to make the sails, and the white men of Sidon and Arvad are their oarsmen, and the astrologers and witches of their own people became their pilots, and all the nations on the coastline are there to buy from them to encourage them in business, and all the world is in love with them, because they and the white nations around them controls the fishing and shipping business, and because of it, other nations became allies and started to trade with them. Now people from Persia, Arvad, Gammad, Lydia, and Lybia joined their army, and Tarshish trade silver, iron, tin, and lead, and Javan, Tubal, and Meshech trade human beings and bronze, and Togarmah trade horses, steeds, and mules, while Dedan trade ivory tusks and ebony, and Syria trade emerald, rubies, and fine linen, and Judah and all the people of Israel trade wheat, honey, oil, balm, and other produce, and Damascus trade wine and fine wood, while Dan and Javan trade wroth iron, cassia, and items made of cane, and Arabia trade lambs, rams, and goats, and Sheba and Raamah trade spices and all kinds of precious stones. But even though the world loves them, HE hates them, and HE is going to punish them, because they are a wicked set of white people that gain from others through witchcraft, and devil worship."

Chapter 28

HE also tells Ezekiel to tell the prince of Tyre, even though he is so proud, and said he is a god on his throne, HE wants him to know that he is just a man, whether he thinks he is a god, or not, and even though he think that he is wiser than Daniel, and no one could hide a secret from him, and he think that he gained his riches from his wisdom in trade, there would be strangers who fight against him, and kill him, and the one who kills him would know he is not a god. For the tragedy coming to Tyre, HE tells Ezekiel to lament for them, and tell them, they were perfect in beauty and wisdom, because their land broke off from "The Garden of Eden" when the earth divided, and was filled with precious stones, like Sardis, topaz, diamond, beryl, onyx, jasper, sapphire, turquoise, emerald, and gold, and they were like angels, and were good, until they turned to evil, because their beauty filled them with pride, and that is why HE would punish them. Then HE tell Ezekiel to tell the white people of Sidon, HE does not like them either, and HE would punish them too, and then they would no longer hate, or bother the Negro people of Israel, because they would realize that HE is the only GOD, and HE would gather all the people of Israel from wherever they are and bring them back to their own land to build houses, live safely, and execute judgment on all the people in the world that hates them, so that the world would know that HE is the only GOD.

Chapter 29

Then in the 10th year, in the 10th month, on the 12th day of the year, HE tells Ezekiel to tell Pharaoh, the king of Egypt, that HE is against him and his ungodly colored people, because they are a bunch of monsters that think that the Nile River belongs only to them. Which is why HE would cause the nations to fight against him, and snare him like a fish on a hook, so they would know that HE alone is GOD. Then the land of Egypt would become desolate, but at the end of forty years, HE would gather all the people of Egypt from wherever they are, and bring them back to their land, and from then on, they would be one of the smallest governments in the world, and they would never rule over other nations again, and the people of Israel would not run to them for help any more, and then everyone would know that HE is the only GOD.

Many years later, in the 20th year, in the 1st day, HE tell Ezekiel that in the past, Nebuchadnezzar, the king of Babylon, and his army helped the people of Egypt to fight against the white people of Tyre without being paid for it, and it is the reason why HE is going to give the land of Egypt to Nebuchadnezzar, and Nebuchadnezzar would take away all the wealth, carry off the spoil, and remove the pillage, as the payment for helping them, and during that time, the righteous people of Israel would start to prosper again.

Chapter 30

Again, HE speaks to Ezekiel and tells him to tell the world they would cry when they see the day when HIS wrath starts, because it would be a time when all the ungodly people are punished, and Ethiopia, Egypt, Libya, Lydia, Chub, and all the ungodly colored nations would be punished, along with all the white nations they helped to make the Negro people of Israel suffer. Then in the 11th year of captivity, in the 1st month on the 7th day, HE tell Ezekiel Egypt is already being punished, and they would be scattered among the nations.

Chapter 31

Few months later, in the 11th year of captivity, in the 3rd month, on the 1st day, HE tell Ezekiel to tell Pharaoh and his colored people their nation is great like the nation of the white Assyrian people, and everyone likes them, and trade with them, and many people go there to run away from the problems in their own countries, and they are great, because everyone loves them, and nowhere is as beautiful as it, except for The Garden of Eden, and so, all the nations envy them, but HE is against them, because they are idol worshippers, and they are proud. Which is why they would be destroyed, just like the other nations that refuse to stop worshipping idols and false gods and acknowledge that HE IS THE ALMIGHTY GOD.

Chapter 32

A little over a year later, in the 12th year of captivity, in the 12th month, on the 1st day, HE tells Ezekiel to take up a lamentation against Pharaoh and tell him he is like a young lion among the nations, and like a monster, bursting fort from the sea that is bothering other nations and polluting the world. Which is the reason why he, and his colored people would be thrown from Egypt to live among the other nations, and it would cause them to look like nobodies, and the white Babylonians would come, and destroy the land and take them as captives, and all the animals would be removed from the Nile River, so that it would not be muddy from them always walking in it, and then the water would be clear, and the river would run like oil.

About two weeks later, in the 12th year of captivity, on the 15th day of the month, HE tells Ezekiel to cry for the people of Egypt, because of what HE would do to them, as he tell them "They are going to be in poverty, and they could run to all the ungodly nations to save themselves, but not even the strongest of the ungodly nations would be able to help them, and if they run to Assyria, Elam, Meshech, Tubal, Sidon, Edom, and any other ungodly nations, there would be their graves, because they would be ready to welcome them to live there, so they die there with them, because that would be the time of The Day of THE LORD, the time when HE punishes every nation in the world for their ungodliness, as well as the people of Israel. So, not only would the people of Israel be captives in the white man's land as their punishment, but every nation would also be captive in some land, or another for their sinning, and war would be fierce, and all the wicked people that die during that time would go to hell. Which would include all the leaders, the government officials, the soldiers, and the people that refuse to stop their false worship, and seek righteousness, because they are wicked people in unbelieving nations."

Chapter 33

On another day, HE tell Ezekiel to speak to his people and tell them when war comes, if they choose a watchman, and he blows the trumpet to warn them, then whoever hears the sound, and does not heed the warning, and dies, it is their own fault, because they could have saved their lives, but if the watchman did not warn them, and they die, then it is the watchman's fault. Then HE tell him that HE made him the watchman over the people of Israel to warn them, and to tell them they would die, and if they do not listen, and they dies, then he would not be blamed for their death, because they could have saved themselves, but if he does not warn them, and they die, he would be blamed for their death, and would be considered as a murderer. Therefore,

HE wants him to tell them that if they keep on sinning, they would not live, and even though HE does not have pleasure in killing the wicked ones, they have to change if they do not want to die off, and if they do not believe it, they must think it is the righteous ones that would die in The Wrath, and the wicked ones would live. Or though HE said it would be the righteous ones that would live, because of their righteous works, they must think that none of the works of a righteous person would be remembered during the wrath, and so, HE wants them to remember that it is the unrighteous person that would die, but if they turn from their sin, then none of their sins would be remembered, and they would not die. Yet they are still saying HE is unfair.

Towards the end of the 12th year of captivity, in the 10th month, on the 5th day, someone escapes from captivity in Jerusalem and goes to Ezekiel and tells him that the city had been captured. Then GOD tell him that the people in the land inherited ruins, and yet they are still saying, since Abraham was one man and was able to inherit the land, because they are many, they should be able to stay there, and possess it, but HE wants him to tell them, since they eat meat with the blood, and worship idols, and they rely on their swords, and defile each other's wives, and commit murder, HE wants to know why should HE make them stay there, because as HE lives, HE swears that those who inherits the ruins would die, so the land would become desolate, and the arrogance cease. After that, HE tells him that the people are talking about him, and are telling each other they should come to him to know what to do, and some of them came, and heard what he said, but they still refuse to listen, and it must be because they love the way his voice sounds, why they come to hear, but not to do, and HE wants him to let them continue to be fools, so when all their punishment come upon them they would know they had a prophet that was telling them the truth, and yet they would not believe.

Chapter 34

Then HE tell him to speak to the shepherds of Israel, and tell them they would be punished, because they fed themselves, and did not feed the people, and they did not do anything to heal the sick, and broken hearted, and the people scattered, and became prey for every nation out there, and as the shepherds wonders on every mountains to worship idols, they forgot about taking care of the people, and that is why HE is against the shepherds, which are the pastors, the priests, and the leaders of the community, and they would be punished. Then they would no longer be an example for the people to follow, and HE would search for HIS people HIMSELF, and bring them back from all the places they are scattered, whether rain, or shine, and HE would feed them, and strengthen them, and determine who is good (which are the goat) from who is real good (which are the sheep), because the real good ones would be obedient to HIS HOLY SPIRIT. Then HE would choose the real good ones to be leader over them to govern them right, and HE would be their GOD, as they lived in peace, and safety in the land, and the trees would be flourishing with fruits, because they are HIS flock, the flock of HIS pasture, and they are human beings, and HE is their GOD, the one, and only true GOD.

Chapter 35

Then HE tell him to prophesy against the people on Mount Seir, and tell them, they would be destroyed, because they always hated the people of Israel, and they were willing to kill them in war, and would say they would take over the land, since it should had been theirs, and for that, they would be killed, and the place would become desolate, because they laughed, and talked about the people of Israel when they were killed, or taken captives, and when they became desolate, they said they would take over their land. Which is why the whole world is going to rejoice when they see Mount Seir destroyed, just like how the people of Mount Seir rejoiced when they saw the land of Israel desolate. So, they better prepare themselves for punishment, because not only the white people of the Seir's would be killed, but also all the red skinned Negro people of Edom, the descendants of Esau, which are Israel's brothers, and everyone else that lives up there on the mountain with them.

Chapter 36

Then HE tells him to prophesy to the people of Israel, and tell them, because all their enemies laughed at them, HE would give them the greatest government, and demote all the others, since it was the ungodly nations that took them as captives, and made them desolate, and kept talking about them. And HE wants them to know that the desolate places would flourish again, and they would not be a mockery to the rest of the world, because HE is jealous that everyone deceived them, and took all they had. Which is why HE would make them prosper again, and since HE is on their side, HE would make sure it happens, and even though the other nations said it was because they killed their own people why they became desolate, they would not be saying that about them anymore, nor would they stumble again, because HE is concerned about the reputation of HIS holy name, and HE would give them a heart to be righteous, and give them HIS HOLY SPIRIT to teach them, and guide them, and HE would make the place be like The Garden of Eden, and make the wastelands fortified and inhabited, so when the world sees it, they would know that only HE could rebuild a ruined place.

Chapter 37

On another day, by HIS HOLY SPIRIT, GOD takes Ezekiel, and sit him in the middle of the valley, and it is full of dry bones, and as Ezekiel looks around, he sees many dry bones, and HE asks Ezekiel if the bones could live again, and Ezekiel said, only HE knows. Then HE tells Ezekiel to tell the bones to hear the word of the LORD, and HE would cause them to live again by putting flesh on them, and breathing breath into them. So, Ezekiel tells the bone to come alive again, and the bones start to rattle, and then start to come together. Then muscles and flesh come upon them, and skin covers them, but they are still dead. Then HE tells Ezekiel to tell the breath to come from the winds of the four corners of the earth and then breathe on the dead bodies to bring them back to life again, and Ezekiel speak to the breath, and then breathe, and the breath goes into the dead bodies, and they come alive again, and stood on their feet as a great army. Then HE tells Ezekiel, that the dead bones represent the people of Israel, because they said their bones are dry, and their hope is lost, since they no longer get any help, but HE wants him to tell them HE would help them, and give them life again, so they would know that HE is their GOD.

Another day, GOD tells him to take a stick and write on it "For Judah and for the children of Israel." Then take another stick and write on it "For Joseph, the stick of Ephraim, and for all the people of Israel", and put the sticks together in one hand, and the sticks would become one. In obedience, Ezekiel gets the sticks, and he place them together, and the sticks become one. Then GOD tells him HE wants him to demonstrate the act to the people, and when he demonstrates it, they would ask him what it means, and he should say, "GOD would take the people of Joseph that lives in Ephraim with the white people and join them back with Israel. Then HE would join all the people of Israel back with the tribe of Judah, so the nation of Israel would be as one again, and HE would guide them, and protect them, and gather all the captives, no matter where they are, and bring them back to the land. Then they would no longer be two nations (Israel and Judah), nor would their government ever be divided again, because they would never worship idols, or do bad things, or deal with ungodly nations again, and they would be glad to be HIS people, since there would be an everlasting covenant between HIM and them, and they would be holy, and HE would be in the sanctuary. Then the other nations would know that HE helped them when they see the glorified sanctuary there in their midst."

Chapter 38

Then GOD tells him to tell the white people of Gog, Magog, Rosh, Meshech, and Tubal, HE does not like them, and HE would put hooks into their jaws, and lead them, and their armies out of the land of Israel, because they are ungodly, and Persia, Ethiopia, Libya, Gomer, Togarmah, and their armies that joined with them would also have to go. So, HE want them to know that HE knows that after the people of Israel returns from captivity back to their land, and are living in prosperity, all of them with their ungodly armies would come back to kill them, and take over the land again, but they may as well forget it, because HE would punish them so badly, they would never know when the people of Israel return from captivity. And the people of Israel would live peacefully for a long time, while they keep on thinking about when to attack them, but after a while HE would put it in their minds to come against the people of Israel again, and then HE would show them a thing, or two, and they would respect HIM as THE ALMIGHTY GOD. So, even though the people of Israel would know that it was prophesied long time ago that they, and their wicked armies would come against them, HE wants the people of Israel to know that when the time comes for it to happen, He would be angry with their enemies, and when they come, HE would show them HIS fury, and there would be a great earthquake, flooding, rain, hailstones, fire, and the smell of burning sulfur in the land that would destroy them, because HE is jealous, and protective over HIS people, and HE wants the whole world to know it.

Chapter 39

GOD also tell him to tell the white people of Gog and all their allies, HE would surely destroy them for what they did to HIS people to cause them not to know HE loves them. Then HIS people would not want to be friends with any ungodly nation anymore, and if that is not enough punishment for them, later on, when they try to destroy the people of Israel again, HE would make the valley in the land of Israel their burial place, and for seven months the people of Israel would be burying their bodies, and it would be so many bodies buried in the valley, it would obstruct visitors from passing through, and people would call it "The Valley of Hamon Gog". Then after the seven months, the people of Israel would hire a search party that would employ them for a long time, and they would search through the land to see if there are any more dead white bodies around, and if they find any, they will put a marker beside it, and the buriers would come, and get the dead bodies to cleanse the land, and they would take the bodies to The Valley of Hamon Gog to bury them with the others. So, for that coming slaughter to them, GOD tell Ezekiel to tell all the birds, and the wild beasts to get ready, because HE prepared a great feast for them, and they would eat the flesh of horses and riders, and of mighty men, until they are full. They would also drink the blood of princes, even of rams, goats, and bulls, until they are drunk, because HE would set HIS fury against all the ungodly nations, so HIS people of Israel, and the rest of the world would know that HE only punish HIS people for their unfaithfulness to HIM, and since HE loves them, HE would bring them back from captivity to their own land, and make them lovely, and prosperous again, and HE would never stop helping them.

Chapter 40

Then in 25th year of the captivity, on the 10th of the 1st month, exactly 14 years after Jerusalem was seized, GOD takes Ezekiel in a vision to the land of Israel and sit him on a mountain, and when Ezekiel looks towards the South, he sees something that looks like the structure of a city. Then GOD takes him to the city, and there is a man in the gateway with bronze colored skin that has a line of flax, and a measuring rod in his hand, and the man tells Ezekiel to pay close attention to everything he tells him, and shows him, because he was brought there to see, and hear, so that he could go back, and tell the people of Israel about it. Then the man measures the gateway that face east. He also measures the fixings around it. Then they go into the outer court, and there are chambers, and pavements all around the court, and the man measures from the lower gate to the front of the inner court. He also measures a gateway that is facing north that is accessed from the outer court. Then he measures a gate that is opposite of the north gate, and he goes towards the south, and measure the gateposts, and the archways, and they go to the inner court, and the man measure the gateway that face south, and its gate chambers, the gateposts, and the archways. Then they go to the north gate, and the man measures it, and as they walked through the place, Ezekiel notice all the furnishings, the utensils, and the tables, and how everything is set up, and the man tell him that the south chamber is for the priest that takes care of the temple, and the north chamber is for the priest that takes care of the altar, and they are the sons of Zadok (the chief priest) that descended from Levi (the tribe of the Levites), and they are there to serve GOD. Then the man measures the court and then measures the doorposts.

Chapter 41

From there, the man takes him into the sanctuary, and the man measures the doorposts, and the entryway, and goes inside, and measures the doorposts there. Then he measures a 20 cubit length by 20 cubit width space beyond the sanctuary, and said, it is "The Most Holy Place". Then he measures the walls of the temple, the chambers, the doors, and the terrace, and he goes, and measures the building that faces the separating courtyard, and he measures the width of the eastern face of the temple and measures the length of the building behind the temple facing the separating courtyard, its galleries, the doorposts, and the windows. Then he measured even the space that is above the inner court, and as they walk through the place, Ezekiel notices all the beautiful cherubim, and palm trees that are carved on all the walls. He also notices that the doorposts are squared, and the altar is made of wood, and it is a place of beauty, and splendor.

Chapter 42

Then the man takes him to the outer court towards the north, and he goes into the chamber that is opposite the separating courtyard, opposite to the building on the north, and measures all three stories of the building. Then he measures a wall that runs parallel to the chamber, and measures all the chambers, and the walk areas, and he tell Ezekiel that the north, and south chambers, opposite the separating courtyard are the holy chambers where the priest goes after meeting with GOD to eat the holy sacrifices in his holy garments, and when the priest is done, he takes off the holy garments, and leave it there, and then go back outside, because he cannot wear the holy garments outside. Then since the man is done measuring inside the temple, they go out to the gateway facing east, and he measures it.

Chapter 43

Then GOD appear in HIS glory from the East, and goes into the temple, and by HIS SPIRIT, HE takes Ezekiel into the inner court, and Ezekiel can see the beauty of GOD in the temple, and a man is standing beside GOD, and GOD tell him, that is the temple where HIS throne is, and where the sole of HIS feet sits, where HE lives among the people of Israel, and HE does not want them to defile HIS place anymore by their unholy practices, because it is like a wall between HIM, and them, which caused HIM to destroy them, and HE wants them to be ashamed of how they defiled HIS place. Then GOD tell him HE wants him to describe the place to them of how it looks in the vision, so when they compare it to what it really is, they would be ashamed of how they ruined it, and HE also wants him to explain everything to them, from the use of each room, to each piece of furnishing, and utensils, to the reasons for the sizes of each room, and the positioning of the rooms, to how to make the sacrifices on the altar, and for how long.

Chapter 44

Then by HIS SPIRIT, GOD takes Ezekiel to the outer gate of the sanctuary, which faces towards the east, and it is shut, and GOD tells him it would remain shut, and no one else would be able to enter through it, because HE entered it, but the prince could sit, and eat with HIM at the entrance, and has to come in, and leave out by way of the vestibule of the gateway. From there, GOD takes him to the north gate in front of the temple, and goes in, and the place is filled with the light of HIS glory, and it looks so beautiful, he fall to his face in praise, and GOD tell him to make sure he tell the people exactly what he saw in the temple, and about all the things he heard about the laws, and ordinances to run it, and that they need to stop bringing foreigners into HIS temple, and allow them to practice their abominations there, because no foreigners should enter the temple, not even the foreigner that became citizens amongst them. He must also tell them that the tribe of Levi, which are the Levites that should minister to HIM in HIS house would no longer be able to minister to HIM anymore, because it is their punishment for turning from HIM, and worshipping idols, but they would be allowed to minister to the people instead, and though they would not be able to go near the holy things, or go into The Most Holy Place, they would be allowed to take care of the temple, and do all the work that has to be done for it, and because things have change, the family of Zadok, of the tribe of the Levites, that stayed dedicated to HIM when the rest of the Levites worshipped idols would now be the priests that are allowed to put on the holy garments, and go into the temple, and talk directly to HIM and offer sacrifices on behalf of the people. Therefore, the family of Zadok should know they should not drink before they enter, and their hair must be well trimmed, not long, or bald, and they can only marry a woman who is a virgin.

Chapter 45

GOD also tell him to tell the people they should divide the land according to their inheritance, and set apart a holy section, which would be a district for HIM, and in it would be a sanctuary, which is **"The Most Holy Place"**, and it would be where the priests lives so they could be near, and minister to HIM. Then GOD tells him where, and how much land the prince should have, and to tell the prince to remove violence and plundering, and execute righteousness and justice, and stop depressing the people, and deal with them the right way. Then GOD tells him about the ordinance concerning the oil, the bath of oil, and about the offerings that the people should give in the 7th month for 7 days according to the offerings, and HE tells him that the gateway of the inner court that faces east should be shut for the six working days, but on The Sabbath, and on the days of The New Moon it should be opened, and the prince as well as the people could stand by it while the priests offers the sacrifice at the threshold of the gate, and the priest could leave through the gate, and the gate should not be shut until evening. HE also tells him about what is involved with the burnt offering, the grain offering, and the offering for the day of "The New Moon", and how they should go about conducting the feasts, and HE tell him about how to keep the inheritance of their land in the family. Then HE takes him into the entrance at the side of the gate through the holy chambers of the priests, and show him a place at the western end of the chamber, and said, it is where the priests should boil the trespass offering, the sin offering, and bake the grain offering, so they do not have to cook them out in the court to sanctify the people. From there, HE takes him to the outer court, and walk him around it, and in all four corners is another court, and a row of stone building all around in them, and there are cooking hearths under the rows of stones, and HE tells him that is the kitchen where the ministers boil the food for the people.

Chapter 47

Then HE takes him back to the door of the temple, and water is flowing from under the threshold of the temple towards the East, which is from the right side of the temple, south of the altar, and HE takes him through the north gate to show him how the water flows out from under the temple to the right side. Then the man that measured everything takes him out one thousand cubits into the water, and the water is up to his ankle, and the man takes him another thousand cubits further, and the water reaches up to the knees, and they walk out another thousand cubits, and the water reaches up to the waist. Then the man takes him out another thousand cubits further, and the water is like a river, and it is so deep, they would have to swim. So, the man bring him back to the riverbank, and he sees many trees on both sides of the river, and the man tell him the water flows towards the east, and goes down into the valley, and enters the sea, and when it gets to the sea, it heals the sea, and fills it with life, and any living thing that drinks from the river along its path would be healed, and live, but the swamps, and the marches that extends from it, does not get healed, and they would be very salty. Right at that moment, Ezekiel notices the trees on the banks of the river are trees that grow all kinds of foods, and they never wither, because they are being watered by the river that runs from under the sanctuary, and they bear fruits every month to eat, while their leaves are used for medicine. Then GOD tell him how he should divide the land among the twelve tribes according to their borders, so they, and the other nations that join them could live equally, and comfortably, and GOD said, whatever land they give to the strangers would belong to them, because they are now part of them. Then for their border, GOD said, "The north side should be from The Great Sea (The Mediterranean Sea) going towards Zedad (between Damascus) all the way north to the border of Hamath. The east side should be from between Damascus and Hauran, and between Gilead, along the Jordan River and along the eastern sea. The south side should be from Tamar to the waters of Meribah by Kadesh, along the brooks of the

Mediterranean Sea. The west side should be from the Mediterranean Sea going southbound, until you get to the opposite side of Hamath.

Chapter 48

Then GOD tell him, when he divides the land, he should give the northern border to the tribe of Dan, Asher, Naphtali, Manasseh, Ephraim, Reuben, and Judah, and on the East of the border of Judah would be the holy district that is set aside for the sanctuary in the middle, and it would be where the priests of Zadok lives, and opposite the border of the holy district would be where the rest of the Levites lives, and they would not be able to sell, or trade any of that area, and the rest of the area of the holy district would belong to the prince. As for Benjamin, Simeon, Issachar, Zebulun, and Gad, they would inherit from the East side to the West, and Gad could also have the south side, going southward from Tamar to the Mediterranean Sea. HE tells him where to put the gates to exit the city, and said, "There should be three gates on each side that are named after the tribes of Israel. The gates on the North would be named Reuben, Judah, and Levi. The gates on the East would be named Joseph, Benjamin, and Dan. The gates on the South would be named Simeon, Issachar, and Zebulun. The gates on the West would be Gad, Asher, and Naphtali, and from that day, the name of the city would be called "THE LORD IS THERE."

NEHEMIAH'S PROPHECY

Chapter 1

While GOD is using Ezekiel over many decades to prophesy to the people in their own land, in the 20th year of the captivity of the people of Israel, while Nehemiah is in Shushan the citadel as a captive, Hanani, and some of the Negro men from Judah go to see him, and he asks them about some of the people that escaped from the captivity while Jerusalem was being attacked, and how the city is, and they said, those who survived, and are there are in great distress, and reproach, and the walls of the city are broken down, and the gates are burned with fire. After hearing what they said, Nehemiah sit down, and cry for many days, while fasting and praying to GOD.

The Prayer:

LORD GOD of heaven, YOU are the great and awesome GOD, WHO keeps YOUR covenant, and have mercy with those that love YOU, and obey YOUR commandments. So, please let YOUR ears be attentive, and YOUR eyes opened, that YOU may hear my prayer which I pray to you day and night, because the people of Israel have confessed their sins against YOU, and since, even I and my family sinned, and the whole nation acted very corruptly against YOU, and haven't kept the commandments which YOU commanded us to do by Moses. I know that we disobeyed YOU, and YOU scattered us like YOU told Moses that YOU would, but if we returned to YOU, and kept YOUR commandments, YOU said, even though some of us were cast out, YOU would gather us, and bring us back to the place that YOU had chosen for us, and now we need YOU to deliver us as YOU did before. So, please let YOUR ears be attentive to my prayer, and to all the prayers of those that believe in YOU, and grant us mercy, so the world can see, because I am the king's cupbearer.

Chapter 2

Nehemiah's prayer was heard by GOD, and GOD also heard the prayers of all the people of Israel that were willing to obey HIM. But the punishment already started, and it must last for 70 years, and the time has not passed yet, and the people of Israel would remain in captivity until the appointed time.

(We will pick up on chapter 2 of The Book of Nehemiah later and place the remaining parts of the story in the proper time)

LAMENTATION

Chapter 1

How lonely sits the land of Judah, which is full of people, and though the people there cry out, none of their allies can help them, because all of them have some time, or another dealt with them treacherously. Now the people of Judah are in captivity in many nations, and are servants to them, and they find no rest, because there is no justice for them, and the road to Zion mourns, because there are no Negroes traveling to their feasts, and all the gates are desolate, and those there are still afflicted, since the white Babylonians are their masters, and are prospering from them, because GOD allowed it to be so. Now all HIS Negro people of Judah can do is remember how they were blessed in the past, because they became vile, and sinned gravely, which caused all the people in the world that used to admire them to only scorn them as they sigh and give away their valuables for food to stay alive.

Is anyone concerned about The Mother Land?

Well, yes. The righteous people of Israel are concerned about Africa, The Mother Land, and they have much sorrow, because they are being afflicted too, and they weep, and their eyes are filled with water, because GOD, THE COMFORTER is not helping at the time, and their Negro people of Zion are looking for comfort from other nations, but GOD had commanded all of them not to help, and so, there is no help. But the righteous ones know that GOD is righteous, because HE is punishing them for rebelling against HIS commands, and the righteous ones call others to help them, but they deceive them. Now all the righteous ones can do is watch, and see the priests and the elders search for food to save their lives, and the righteous ones are troubled, because they had also been disobedient, and everyone hear them crying, and are glad that GOD did it, and so, the righteous ones are begging GOD to please remember that HE said HE would punish every nation and make them destitute like Israel.

Chapter 2

GOD destroyed the people of Zion, and HE destroyed their beauty without having any pity, and HE stopped other nations from helping them, while allowing their enemies to overcome them. Like a bow, HE bent HIS right hand, and slay HIS favorite people as an enemy, and all the people that are left in Zion are crying, because even HIS own alter HE allowed to be destroyed, and HE abandoned HIS sanctuary, leaving the gates sunk into the ground, and there are no priests, or prophets there to teach the LAW, and the elders are wondering where is the grain, and wine, and since the prophets only see deceptive visions, all the people who passes by hiss, and shake their heads at the people of Zion. But GOD did it, and the young, and old lay in the streets, and the soldiers are killed in battle, and many are taken by the enemies, because GOD is angry.

Chapter 3

The righteous people of Israel know the afflictions in The Wrath of GOD seeing that they have a miserable life, instead of a good one, and they feel bound, and like they cannot get loose, because even when they cry to GOD, HE just ignores them, and since they became the ridicule of the people, they are bitter, and without peace. But if they remember what GOD said, then they would have hope, and with great faith their hope would be new every morning, because GOD can do anything. And if they hope in GOD, they know that it is good that someone should hope, and wait on HIM to save them, and they know that it is also good for someone to take the punishment for what they've done when HE is correcting them. Therefore, they should shut up, and hope, and let their enemies do as they please to them, because GOD would not ignore them forever, and even though HE caused them to have grief, HE would have mercy and show compassion. Soo, they should pray to GOD, and HE would draw near to them, and hear their complaint, and save them.

Chapter 4

The gold in The Mother Land is fake, the stones of the sanctuary are scattered all over the streets, and the precious people are considered bums. Even the jackals can feed their young, but the Negro people of GOD cannot feed their children, and they are cruel, and forget about them as they starve. So, the punishments on them from GOD is greater than the punishment of the sins of the white people of Sodom and Gomorrah, seeing that their Negro Nazirites look like walking skeletons, and they are unrecognized, because they are so bony, their skin stick to their bones, and those that were killed are better off than those that were not, because women are killing their children, and cooking them to eat. Therefore, the red-skinned Negroes of Edom better be glad they did not become the heirs, and are being punished like that, but they should know they would also be punished, because GOD saw what they did. Yet still, the dark-skinned Negroes of Israel, the heirs, should be glad, because once GOD is done punishing them, HE would never send them into captivity again, and HE would always be with them to help them no matter where they decide to live in the world.

Chapter 5

All righteous people in the world should be begging GOD to please remember HIS Negro people, because they are looking very bad, and white people are living in their land, and in their houses, as if they have become people that do not have a GOD. And they pay the white people for the water they drink, and for the fuel they use to cook, and heat themselves with, and they rationed out the land to the Egyptians, and to the Assyrian ungodly people to get food, and it seems like they are suffering not only the punishment for their own sins, but for their forefathers' also. And their skin is hot, because it is dry, and the white people bother their women, hang the princes, and disrespect the elders, and the elders stopped going out with singing, and joy, and no one is dancing in the streets, and they are subjected to the enemies, and because of this, they are scared while the white soldiers walk about freely.

My GOD, YOU live forever.

So, why have YOU forgotten YOUR people so long?

Could YOU please turn back and restore YOUR people as they were before?

Well, maybe not. Not if YOU are too angry and have utterly rejected them.

THE BOOK OF EZRA
(The Jews begins to return from exile)

Chapter 1

When Cyrus became the king of Persia, in the 1st year of his reign, GOD caused him to make a proclamation throughout the world to tell people that HE gave him the world government, and wants him to rebuild The House of THE LORD in Judah, and whoever is from Israel from the tribe of Judah that are captives in Babylon may go back to Jerusalem to build it, and whoever is master over any of the people of Judah should let them go, and give them the supplies they need. Also, a freewill offering to help them out. Then immediately, Cyrus sends out the proclamation, and when the people of Israel heard it, the elders of the tribe of Judah, and the tribe of Benjamin, the priests, and all the Levites, and everyone that hoped in GOD, got up and were ready to go right then and there. And the rest of the people who are not of Israel encourages them, and gives them silver, gold, livestock, and all kinds of precious things, as well as the freewill offering they need to have. Then Cyrus goes into his idol's temple and bring out all the things that Nebuchadnezzar took from the temple of GOD, which is The House of THE LORD, and he gives them back to them.

What was taken from The House of THE LORD:
30 gold platters
1000 silver platters
29 knives

30 gold basins

410 silver basins

And 1000 articles of various things

Which gives a total of 5, 400 items

Chapter 2

To finish his good deed, Cyprus counts the Negro people of Israel, and there are 42,360 of them that were taken captive by Nebuchadnezzar, and he release them, and they leave with many gifts, and with the items he gave back from the temple. All 42,360 of them, plus their 7,337 servants, 200 singers, 736 horses, 245 mules, 435 camels, and 6,700 donkeys leaves to go to Jerusalem. Then when they get there, they decide not to eat anything until the priest consults with the "**Urim**" and "**Thummim**", which are devices they use to get answers from GOD, but immediately, they erects The House of THE LORD (which is the tent tabernacle that they carry around), and they offer whatever they could to GOD. Then they collect 61,000 gold drachmas (coins), 5,000 minas of silver, and 100 garments for the priest, and they go to live in their own cities with the rest of the people that were not in captivity but had been under subjection to the white people in the land.

(For the complete list of names of all the Jewish Negro people of Israel that left from their captivity in Babylon at this time, please read it in The Bible for yourselves.)

Chapter 3

Seven months after the captives that Cyrus released returned to the land, they gather in Jerusalem, and Jeshua, and Zerubbabel, the priests, builds an altar to offer the burnt offering on, as it was written in The Book of The LAW by Moses. But because they fear the white people that are in the land, they sit the altar on its bases, instead of lifting it up, and they offer their sacrifices that morning, and keep The Feast of The Tabernacle for the number of days as required. Afterward they offer the regular burnt offerings, The New Moon

Feast, and all the feasts that GOD told them they should observe. Then on the 1st day of the 7th month they start to offer "The Feast of the Uneven Bread", which is "The Passover", even though the rebuilding of the foundation of the stone temple is not laid yet, which is The House of THE LORD that Solomon made for GOD to live in.

In the 2nd month of the year, the priests and all the people of Judah that came from captivity starts to do their work on rebuilding the city, and they also appoint the work to the Levites they must do for The House of THE LORD. Then after the foundation of the temple was laid, all the priests stood in their priestly clothes in front of The House of THE LORD, and play music, and sing songs, and the people give praise, and thanks to GOD with joy. But many of the priests, and the older people that knew what the temple looked like, realize that it is the wrong measurements, and they stop shouting for joy, and start to cry, but the others that did not know, kept on shouting for joy, and there was so much noise that no one could tell the difference between the shout of joy from the shout of sorrow.

Chapter 4

When the white rulers in the land heard that the returned captives are rebuilding The House of THE LORD, they go to Zerubbabel, the head priest, and tell him they want to help them build, because they love their GOD just like how they do, from the time Esar-haddon, the white king of Assyria brought them there. But, Zerubbabel, Jeshua, and all the people tell them they do not want their help, because they would rebuild the House of THE LORD themselves, just like how Cyrus told them that GOD said they should, and the white people leave. Then afterwards, the white people start to harass the returned captives to discourage them from rebuilding The House of THE LORD, and they even hire people to frustrate them the whole time, while Cyrus is still king of Persia. Then after Cyrus die, Darius, become the king of Persia, and the white people in "The Mother Land" try to use Darius to stop the progress of the returned captives, but they had no success, because the returned captives let them know what Cyrus had in the records. So, because the white people could not get through to Darius, they decide to try Ahasuerus, his brother, who is to become the next king, and they send a letter to Persia to him, complaining about the people of Judah that are rebuilding the temple in Jerusalem, but they did not have any success with him either, and the people of Judah continue to rebuild. Then the white people decide to see if Artaxerxes would help them, because he will become the king after Darius and Ahasuerus, and they write Artaxerxes a letter in their Aramaic language and send it from Jerusalem to him in Persia.

The Letter:

To King Artaxerxes.

From your servants that you sent beyond the river, we want you to know that the Jews that returned from exile there in Persia are here in Jerusalem, the rebellious and evil city, and they are rebuilding it, and we want you to know that if the city is rebuilt, and the wall is completed, then the Negro people there won't pay any taxes, tribute, or customs, and the funds of your treasury would diminish, and because you pay our salary from your treasury, we thought that it would have been dishonorable if we did not tell you, and we want you to search the records to find out if anything in the books say that Jerusalem is a rebellious city, and if they fought with other nations that caused them to be destroyed, and we are warning you that if you allowed the city to be rebuilt, you will only have power in Persia, and none over the people in Africa.

After the letter was read to Artaxerxes, he sends a message back to his white people in Jerusalem, telling them he understands them clearly. Then he gives command to search the records, and when the search is made, they find out that Jerusalem had been a rebellious city, and was overthrown for it, and they had mighty kings that taxed the people, and made them pay tribute, and custom. Right away, Artaxerxes sends a message back to Africa, commanding the white men to tell the returned captives to stop rebuilding the city, and he said he wants them to make sure they make them stop because he does not want them to rebuild it, and overthrow him when he becomes the king. Then when the message gets to the white people in "The Mother Land" and read it to them, they hurry to Jerusalem and force the people of Israel to stop rebuilding the city, and because of that, the rebuilding of The House of THE LORD was ceased.

Chapter 5

Then in the 2nd year of Darius reign, Haggai and Zechariah, the prophets, prophesy to the tribe of Judah in Jerusalem, and Zerubbabel and Jeshua, the priests, get up and start to work on rebuilding The House of THE LORD again with the help of the prophets. When Tatnai, (the white man governing the region), and some of the other white men that rule over the people of Israel in the land goes there, they asks who told them they could rebuild the place, and they ask for their names, and while they kept working, they replied, "We are the owners of the place, and we have permission from Cyrus to rebuild it." With that answer, the white men let them be, because they could not do anything about it, until they report back to Darius, and get a response from him.

After that, Tatnai and his men sends a letter to Darius, telling him they went to Jerusalem and saw the returned captives rebuilding the temple with timber and heavy stones, and they asked the builders who gave them permission, and took their names, and the builders told them they are the servant of GOD, who are rebuilding HIS temple, because HE was angry with them, and HE gave Nebuchadnezzar permission to destroy it, and take them as captives, but Cyrus freed them, and gave them permission to rebuild it, and he also gave them back the things Nebuchadnezzar took from there, and from the time of Cyrus, they had been trying to rebuild it, and yet they still are not finished, and he wrote him the letter, because he wants him to search the records in

Babylon to see if Cyrus gave them permission to rebuild the place, and if it could be his pleasure to hurry up and send a response.

Chapter 6

When the letter was read to Darius, he made a decree to search all the records in Babylon. Then in the province of Media, they found a scroll that said, in the 1st year of Cyrus' reign, he was concerned about The House of THE LORD in Jerusalem, and Cyrus said, let it be rebuilt with three rows of heavy stones and one row of timber, and he would take care of all the expenses, and he is giving back the things that Nebuchadnezzar took from there. So, Darius send a message back to Tatnai and his men, telling them he is warning them to leave the Negro people alone, and let them rebuild their temple, and he want them to give them whatever they asks for, whether bull, ram, lamb, wine, salt, wheat, or whatever, and he would pay for it, and he want them to do it immediately, so the Negroes would not be hindered any longer, and he also wants them to know that he sent out a decree that said, if any of them try to do anything other than what he said, they would be killed, and he wish that the GOD of the people of Israel would kill them, if they try to destroy them, or pollute HIS temple again.

Once Tatnai read the message, he and the rest of the white people did what Darius told them to do, and on the 3rd day of the 1st month (Adar), which is in the 6th year of Darius reign, the people of Israel finished rebuilding the temple according to how it should look. Then they celebrate the dedication of the house with joy, and offer a sacrifice, with a great big feast, and they assigned the priests and the Levites their duties. Then on the 14th day of the month of Adar, the families of the priests, and the Levites purified themselves, and killed The Passover lamb, and they have "The Passover", and the priests and the Levites eat together, while all the other returned captives eat with those that remained in the land that kept themselves unpolluted from the pagan ways of the white people.

(We will also get to the rest of Ezra later, by placing it in the proper time according to the rest of the story)

HAGGAI'S PROPHESY

Chapter 1

In the past, a few years before the people finished rebuilding The House of THE LORD, while others of Judah are still captive in Babylon, in the 2nd year of Darius' reign, in the 6th month on the 1st day, Haggai (the prophet), and Joshua (the priest) are still in captivity, and GOD spoke to them, and told them HE heard people saying it is still not time yet to rebuild The House of THE LORD, and HE wants them to know that it is time for them to return to their beautiful homes, and time for Babylon to be destroyed, because they have been depriving them of everything, and when they get back to Jerusalem, they should gather wood, and rebuild the temple, which is The House of THE LORD, so that it would be beautiful again, because HE does not want HIS house in ruins when everyone else's house is fixed up, and if they do not fix up HIS house, HE would not cause the land to reproduce, and be glorified again, and they should know in the meanwhile the captives that Cyrus sent back just began to work on The House of THE LORD.

Chapter 2

Then in the 7th month, on the 21st of the month of the year, GOD speaks to Haggai, and tells him to go talk to Zerubbabel (the governor of Judah), Joshua (the high priest), and all the people with him in captivity that knows what The House of THE LORD looked like, and ask them, if they do not think it looks like ruins compared to what it looked like before, and tell them they better be strong and without fear, because they are going to be freed, just like how HE freed them from Egypt, and to also tell them that HE is going to punish all the nations, so they would know that HE is glorious, because the earth, and everything belongs to HIM, and HE would make the praise of the rebuilt temple more than that of the old one, and there would be peace.

Shortly after that, on the 24th day of the 9th month, in the 2nd year of Darius' reign, GOD tell Haggai to ask the priests, if someone carried holy meat in their clothes and the clothes touch other things would the other things become holy. So, Haggai asks the priest the question, and the priest said, "No", and a Haggai asks him, if someone dirty touches someone clean would the clean person become dirty, and he said, "Yes", and Haggai tells him that was what happened to their people of Israel, and even to the tribe of Judah, because everything they do is dirty, which is the reason why GOD allowed the temple that is HIS house to be destroyed, and GOD wants them to remember what the place looked like when it had trees filled with fruits, and the storehouse filled, because from that day, he would be blessed. Then later, that same day, GOD tell him to tell Zerubbabel, HIS wrath would start on the other nations, and HE would destroy governments, and armies, but HE would make him great, because HE likes him.

ZECHARIAH'S PROPHECY

Chapter 1

During the same time while GOD is speaking to Haggai, on the 8th month of the 2nd year of Darius' reign, HE speaks to Zechariah, the son of Iddo the prophet, and tell him to tell the people of Israel to return to HIM, and HE would help them if they stopped being like their forefathers by ignoring the prophets, because the forefathers, and the unbelieving prophets are dead, and gone, since they refused to change, and since HIS word, and statutes remains forever, and they know their forefathers died off for not obeying, and since they refuse to change like their forefathers did, HE would do to them as HE did to their forefathers.

Then on the 24th day in the 7th month of the year, GOD shows Zechariah a vision of a man on a red horse, standing along the hollow of a myrtle trees, and behind him are horses; A red one, a sorrel one, and a white one. Then Zechariah asks GOD what it means, and an angel that is with them tells him he would show him, and the man in the vision on the red horse among the myrtle trees said, he and the ones with him are sent to walk back, and forth throughout the earth. Then the other ones with him said, they walked to, and forth, and everyone in the world is resting quietly, and the angel asks GOD when HE would have some mercy on Jerusalem, and on all the cities of Judah, since they are being punished for about seventy years already. GOD replied, "It would happen real soon." Then the angel tell Zechariah to tell the people that are captives with him that GOD said, HE is really ready to set them free, and even though HE was a little angry with them, and HE used the other nations to help HIM punish them for their evil intent, HE is ready to show HIS mercy, and free them, and give them back their land, and make them holy, and prosperous, so they could be representatives of HIM again.

Suddenly there is a vision above, and Zechariah looks up to see it, and he see four horns that are symbolic of what would happen in the future, and he asks the angel what they mean, and the angel said they represent the governments that scattered all the people of Israel over the world. Then GOD shows him four craftsmen, and he asks GOD what they are coming to do, and GOD said, they are the ones that scattered the people of the tribe of Judah for them to feel ashamed, and they are coming to terrify the people of Judah that are left, so they could get rid of all governments, and make their government a world government, and throw the people of Judah out of their land.

Chapter 2

After that vision, Zechariah sees another vision of a man with a measuring stick in his hand, and he asks the man in the vision where he is going, and the man said he is going to Jerusalem to measure it. Then the angel with Zachariah gets close to talk to him, and another angel come out to meet that angel, and tell him, "Hurry up and tell the man with the measuring stick, that Jerusalem would be inhabited, and it would need wall and be well protected, and there would be many people and livestock there, because GOD would protect them and glorify them again, and therefore, all the white people in the land better know they should leave, and go back to the North, because if they do not, then GOD would make them run, and they would be scattered all over the world. And the Negro people that are captives in Babylon, better know that they should be ready to leave from there to return home, because they are the apples of GOD's eyes, and HE would punish anyone that treated them badly, and many white people would become the servants to them, because they would know that YAH is their GOD, and they are HIS righteous Negro people, and so, they should sing, and sing always, since GOD is coming to deliver them to live with them in the holy place of Jerusalem in their own land. So, everyone else better shut up, because GOD is angry, and HE is tired of waiting to go back to HIS house."

Chapter 3

After that vision, Zechariah sees a vision of Joshua, the high priest, in filthy clothes, standing beside an angel, and Satan is also there opposing what is being said, and the angel rebuke Satan, and tells him to go to hell where he belongs, because GOD chose Jerusalem as the place for the world government. Then the angel tells some other angels to remove the filthy clothes from Joshua, and they remove them, and the angel tell Jashua it means his sins are forgiven, and he is righteous in GOD's sight. Then the angel tell the others to put a turban on Joshua's head, and they place the turban on his head, then dress him in his priestly garments, and stand there admiring how he looks, and the angel tell him, if he obey GOD, and keeps the commandments, he would be a leader that judges the people righteously, and he would be THE BRANCH, which is the beginning of the righteous government that rules the whole world, because GOD, and all HIS angels would help them, and when it all happens, everyone would have parties and feel free to enjoy life.

Chapter 4

Zachariah is engulfed in the vision, and the angel snaps him out of it, and talks with him for a while, so he can come back to reality. Then he starts to see another vision, and the angel asks him what he sees, and he said, he is looking at a solid gold lampstand with a bowl on top of it, and on the stand are seven lamps, which are connected by seven pipes to the lampstand, and there is an olive tree on each side of the stand. Then he asks the angel what it means, and the angel said, "Don't you know?", and he said, he does not, and the angel asks him if he remember the scripture when GOD told Zerubbabel,

"Not by might, nor by power, but by MY SPIRIT", and when GOD asked him "Who did all the nations think they are, and if they knew they would lose their government", that is what the vision is showing him. Then GOD responded, and said, "Zerubbabel laid the foundation of the temple, and his sons would finish it, and when you sees that, then you would know that I AM THE MIGHTY GOD, because I do not forget about the good things people try to do, and so, the seven lamps represent MY eyes that are looking on all the seven continents of the world." Then Zachariah asks, "What does the olive trees on each side of the lampstand that drips oil into the receptacles of the two golden pipes that drains the oil represents?", and GOD asks him if he didn't know what they are, and he said no. Then GOD said, "Those are the two anointed nations, the Jew of Israel, and the Muslims of Iraq that lives, and preaches the truth to represent HIM on the earth.

Chapter 5

Right then, Zechariah start to see another vision; One of a flying scroll, and GOD asked him what he sees, and he said, he sees a flying scroll about the size of 20 cubits by 10 cubits, and GOD tells him, it is the curse that goes all over the world that would kill every thief, and every perjurer, so that everyone that are living contrary to HIS WORD would know HE is in charge. Then the angel tells him to look, and see what would happen, and he looks, and sees something like a basket, and he asks the angel what it is, and the angel said, it is a basket that is going about the earth, and to him, it looks like there is a lead disc-like cover on the basket that lifted up, and a woman is sitting inside the basket, and the angel tells him, it is symbolic of wickedness. Then the angel interacts with the vision, and pushes the woman's head back down into the basket, and covers it with the lead disc, and two women with wings like storks come flying towards them, and the women lift the basket into the air, and fly off with it, and he asks the angel where are the women taking the basket, and the angel said, they are taking it to Shinar to build a house for it, and when they are done building the house, they would set the basket on a base inside the house.

Chapter 6

Then he sees four chariots coming from between two mountains made of bronze; The first chariot is being pulled by red horses, the second chariot is being pulled by black horses, the third is being pulled by white horses, and the fourth is being pulled by dappled (spotted) horses, and he asks the angels what it means, and the angel said, "They are four groups that GOD sends out to check on things on the earth; The ones with the black horses are going to the North, the ones with the white horse are going after them, and the ones on the dappled horses are going to the South, while the red ones stay watch over The Mother Land, and they go on their horses out to walk about on the earth." Then GOD tell him that the ones on the black horses that goes to the North gives HIM peace of mind, and HE wants him to go to the returned captives, and receive the gifts from them, and on that same day, take some of the reputable men of the returned captives to Josiah's house, and set the crown on Joshua's head, and tell him he is a ruler, and a priest, and he would have peace, because he was chosen to be the one to finish the temple which his father, Zerubbabel, laid the foundation of, and all his sons would succeed as kings after him, and it would definitely happen, if he finished rebuilding the temple.

Chapter 7

Few months later, in the 4th year of Darius (the king of Persia) reign, on the 4th day of the 9th month of the year, when the people sent Sherezer with Regem-Melech and his men to The House of THE LORD to pray, GOD speaks to Zechariah, and tell him to go to The House of THE LORD and ask the priests and the prophets that are there, "If he should cry, and fast in the 5th month like he always did." Then Zachariah goes to them, and asks them if he should cry and fast on the fifth month like always, and while he is speaking to them, GOD speaks through him, and says, "If when you were weeping, and crying in the 5ᵗʰ month for the last seventy years, were you really pleading for GOD's help, and didn't you think you should have obeyed HIM when you, and all the places around you was prosperous, and the south and lowlands had people living there. GOD said, HE wants you to execute true justice, and show mercy and compassion to your fellow Negro people, and not to make the orphans, the widows, or the foreigners suffer, but you refused to do it, and you turn completely away from the LAW, and HE punished you so severely, because you would not listen to HIM, or to the prophets HE sent you."

Chapter 8

On another day, GOD tells him, HE loves HIS chosen Negro people, and wants to show them great favor by returning to them after they returned to their land, so that Jerusalem would be called The City of Truth, The Holy Mountain of GOD, and then even old women could walk about in the streets, and boys, and girls could play outside, because the place would be beautiful to them, since it would be beautiful to HIM. So, they better believe it, because the prophets had been telling them from a long time ago that the foundation of The House of THE LORD was started, and someday it would be completely rebuilt, because during their time they were slaves, and they had no money, or paying jobs, and they had no peace from their enemies, and knew they would not be able to finish it. Now HE is showing the remnant of them HIS mercy, so they could be freed to finish The House of THE LORD and be blessed in their own land. Which is why HE wants them to speak the truth to each other, give justice, and live in peace, and not to do evil, because HE hates it, and the days they take to fast on the 4th, 5th, 7th, and 10th month, year after year to symbolize their mourning on the days the enemies came and took them as captives, those days would no longer be a time of mourning, but a time to party. Therefore, HE wants them to love peace, and truth, because when it happens, people would travel to Jerusalem to learn the truth, and as they travel, they would stop from city to city, telling others to come with them, so they could learn, and when people see a Jewish Negro man somewhere, they would grab him by the sleeves, and beg him to take them to his country to live.

Chapter 9

Then GOD tell him that the white people in Damascus, Tyre, Ashkelon, and Ekron would be punished, and the king of Gaza would die, and then a mixed race of people would live in Ashkelon and Philistine (Palestine), and all the other ungodly nations would also be punished, but whoever survive from those nations would turn to worshipping HIM, and they would be like the people of Israel. And the Negro people of Israel would not be oppressed ever again, and they would greatly rejoice, because Jesus, their King would be coming to save them, and He would be a righteous man, but not so good looking, and He would be riding in on a colt of a donkey. At that time, the Babylonian leaders and their armies would not be in The Mother Land anymore, and Jesus would teach the world the truth, and how to live in peace, and He would be the head of the righteous world government which they are also a part of. That is why, if any of them have any hope, they better return to doing the right thing, and they would get double for their trouble, and be the ones to rule the world government, and they should also know they are divinely protected, and they would get all the blessings that was planned for them, because they would be like the Jewels of a crown that is praised by everyone.

Chapter 10

Therefore, HE wants them to ask HIM for a blessing in a time when HE is ready to bless them, and HE would bless them, even with more than they could imagine, because they are scattered like lost sheep, and everyone is telling them lies, and HE is not angry at the leaders anymore, because HE is ready to punish those that had been punishing them, since HE wants them back home, so they could be the leaders of the world government. Then they could tread down the enemies, and put them to shame, and HE would save them, and it would be like they were never cast from the land, and they would increase, and then they could move to other countries on their own to live with some of their children abroad, and they would be able to return home whenever they want, and would be free to go back and forth with HIS permission.

Chapter 11

As for the people of Israel in Lebanon, fire would devour their tall, beautiful cedar trees, and the people in Cypress would wail when they see all the cedar fall, and no more oak trees for Bashan either, because all the thick forests would be destroyed. Then all the shepherds, and the lions would wail when they see all the forests gone, and the whole place ruined. So, let them fatten themselves up, because HE is ready to slaughter them for not teaching the people the right thing, and for killing them, and then had the nerve to say, "Blessed be the name of THE LORD, for I am rich from killing HIS people, and I don't care." So, just like how they had no pity on the HIS people, HE would not have any pity on them either, and HE would cause their own king, and their own neighbors to destroy them, because it is a trap which will trap them by HIS two staves, "Beauty and "Bonds". For their "Beauty" was given with the "Bands" of THE LAW to bind them in righteous living. So, even though HE allowed the leaders and the teachers to use and abuse the people to get rich, and beautify themselves to look fat and wealthy, they disgust HIM, and HE is ready to tear them down by letting them destroy each other.

Chapter 12

HE is GOD, and HE punishes HIS people for doing wrong, and HE would definitely punish people for doing HIS people wrong, and that was why HE said, HE would make Jerusalem as a heavy stone, like one that is drunk and cannot move, and when everybody around them come to lay siege against them, HE would destroy them instead. So, even though everyone is against them, HE would strike the horses with blindness, and the riders with madness, and in his heart, the governor of the people of Judah would say "The inhabitants of Jerusalem, the people of Judah is my strength in the LORD my host, our GOD." And since the ungodly nations did not feel any guilt, and had the nerves to say, "Bless the name of the LORD" when they traded the people of Judah as slaves, HE would have no pity on the ungodly nations either, just like how they did not have any pity on HIS people, because it is HE WHO would save HIS people, although HE punished them, and made others tread them so badly to the point where they thought HE would no longer pity them. Especially after HE allowed the white people to take over the world government which made things bad for them and for every believer in the world. Therefore, since HE is THE LORD, GOD, HE would save Judah, and in that time when the nations seek to destroy the people in Jerusalem, HE would destroy those nations, and because of the grace HE would give Judah at that time, they would remember Jesus, the One they killed, and would mourn as one who cry for their son that was killed, or as one who grieves for a first born who died. So, every family would be mourning.

That was what Zachariah told the people, and because of that, they did not want anything to do with him, and they threw him 30 pieces of silver, and GOD tell him to throw the silver to the potter, and he throw it into The House of THE LORD for the potter to smelt down. From that time, he stops dealing with them. Then GOD tell him, HE wants him to act like a foolish shepherd, since HE wants them to know that when Jesus come to them, Jesus would be like a foolish shepherd, because He would not care for them, if they are not righteous, and He would keep hitting them with the truth and let them suffer.

Chapter 13

Then when Jesus comes, if anyone wants to be righteous, they will know how to be, because Jesus would make sure all the idols are gone from the land, and all the unclean spirits that tell lies to the prophets would be gone. And if those lying prophets still try to prophesy, their parents would tell them they are liars, and they need to die, because YAH, their GOD did not tell them anything. Then the lying prophets would be ashamed of their false visions, and they would stop saying they are prophets, and would say they are farmers, and if someone asked them why they looked so beat up, they would say their own friends beat them up (for lying to them). Therefore, the people of Israel need to wake up, because HE is YAH, their GOD, and would never have punished them, unless HE had punished the leaders of the church, and the government first for what they taught, and allowed. But even though 2/3 of them died off, the other 1/3 would be saved, and they would be tested, and would be blessed again. Then they would be proud to be HIS children, and HE would be proud to be their FATHER.

Chapter 14

As GOD continues to speak, HE said, after Jesus comes, The Day of THE LORD is coming, because the ungodly nations tortured the Negro people of Israel, and since HE IS their GOD, HE is ready to severely punish the ungodly nations for it, and the heavenly army would come and stand on Mount Olives, which faces Jerusalem on the East, and the mountain would split into two, from east to west, making a large valley for the people of Israel to travel through to flee from the destruction that is coming when the world is being punished. And there would be no light, because the lights in the heavens would diminish. But angel would guide the people of Israel through. Then after the destruction there would be light again on that very same evening, so the people of Israel could see as they return to their places where the living (healing) water flows from under the temple in Jerusalem, half towards the Eastern Sea, and half towards the Western Sea. Then all the land would be put back in their place in which they are lower than Jerusalem. At the same time, Jerusalem would be raised up even higher on the mountain in the center of the world above every nation, and the people of Israel who are there would live safely. But around the world there would be a plague that would come upon those that do not like the people of Israel that would cause the flesh, the eyes, and the tongues to dissolve, that would kill both humans, and animals while they are standing on their feet, so that the world would know they have to leave the land of the people of Israel. Then when all the ungodly foreigners leaves from the lands, the people of Israel would fight each other to get rid of the bad ones, and when the land is left with only the righteous ones, people from other nations that are seeking righteousness would come to Jerusalem to learn, and they could worship HIM, THE TRUE GOD, and keep the feasts with the people of Israel. From that time on, whoever does not come to Jerusalem to learn, and to worship HIM, HE would cause it not to rain in that nation, and the same thing would happen to the colored people of Egypt, if they decide they do not want to worship HIM either. Because at that time, "HOLINESS TO THE LORD" would be engraved on the belts of the horses of the people of Israel, and every pot in Jerusalem would be holy, whether they use them in The House of THE LORD, or not, and people from other nations would come and cook in them to make their sacrifices. But none of the white people from the people of Canaan would be able to come.

THE BOOK OF ESTHER

Chapter 1

After Ahasuerus became king of Babylon, in the 3rd year of his reign, he had a great big party with all his officials, his servants, and all the great important people from all over the world, and they enjoyed themselves for 180 days (4 ½ months). Afterwards, Ahasuerus decides to continue to celebrate, and he invites the people of Shushan the citadel, and enjoyed himself with them for seven days, while drinking as much as they could, and because his wife, Queen Vashti was left to herself for the 180 days of the first party, when he started the second party, she decided to invite all the women in the palace to have a party of her own. On the seventh day of the second party the king is having, after he is very drunk, he tells seven of his eunuchs to bring Vashti to him with her royal crown on, so he can show her off to the people at his party. Then the eunuchs went for Vashti, but she refuses to go with them, and the King get furious, and sends for the wise men of Babylon, and tell them what happened. Then he ask them what to do, and one of them said, Vashti, not only disrespected him, she also disrespected all the princes, and every man in the province, and when her behavior is known to the other women, they would not respect him, and would despise their husband, and he should send out a decree, and make it a law that Vashti would not be able to come to him anymore, and that all wives should honor their husbands. This suggestion made the king happy, and the king sends out the decree to keep Vashti from ever coming to him again, and he send a letter in every language throughout the world that said, each man should be master of his own house and only speak their own language.

Chapter 2

After a while, the king starts to long for Vashti, and he remembers she could never come back to him again. Then one of his servants suggests to him to look for another beautiful young woman by sending appointed officers to get some women and give them a beauty preparation to choose one for himself. That sounds good to the King, and he sends out the news about the contest for a new queen. At the time, there are many of the people of Israel that are still there in captivity, and a certain Negro man from Israel, that lives in Shushan the citadel, whose name is Mordecai, is a captive there. After Mordecai heard the news, since he raised his uncle's daughter, Esther (Also known as Hadassah) when her parents died from before Nebuchadnezzar came, and took them as captives, he takes Esther to enter the contest, because she is a lovely, and beautiful black woman.

Then they place Esther, and the other beautiful women of many nations under the care of Hagai, the custodian of the women, and Hagai really liked her, and he gives her more time, and preparation of beauty than the other women, and after the beauty preparation they chose seven of the most beautiful women, and Esther is one of the women chosen. After that, they move her, and the other chosen women to a more beautiful place, but they still did not know she is one of the Negro women of Israel, because Mordecai told her not to tell anyone. Every day, Mordecai would pace back and forth in front of the court where the women are, so he could check on her, and for 12 months of preparation, which is 6 months with oil, and myrrh, and 6 months with perfume and beautifying, each young woman prepares to be ready for their turn to go to the king, and they could take whatever they requests to take to him from the women's quarters.

One by one, each woman would be called, and they would make their request of what they want to take to the king from their quarters, and in the evening, she goes to him, and in the morning, she returns to where the other women are and wait there until all the women are called. Then once all the women are seen, the king would decide which one he wants. When it is Esther's turn to go to the king, she requests to take nothing, and in the 10th month, in the 7th year of King Ahasuerus' reign, Esther goes into his royal quarters, and he loves her more than he loved all the other women that came in before her. Without seeing the rest of the contestants, he places the royal crown on Esther's head, and makes her the queen, instead of Vashti. Then he gives a great feast, and call it "**The Feast of Esther**", and he invites all the officials, and servants, and proclaim that day to be a holiday. Still, no one knows that Esther is from the people of Israel, and every day, Mordecai continue to watch her to make sure she is ok, and he would admire her when she is out with the other women. Then one day, while he is watching her, he overheard two of the king's eunuchs saying they are furious at the king, and are going to harm him, and he tells Esther what he heard, and Esther tells the king, and said, Mordecai is the one that informed her of it. Then the king sends to find out if the rumor is true, and it is. Then the king has both the eunuchs hung, and they record it for the history books.

Chapter 3

After that, the king promotes Haman to be chief over all the white princes and decreed that all the servants within his gate bow to him, but Mordecai would not do it. Then day, after day they tell him to do it, he still would not listen, and the other servants ask him, why he would not bow to Haman like the king told him to, and he said, it is because he is a Jew. Then they tell Haman that Mordecai refuse to bow to him, because he is a Jew, which angers Haman, but since he is afraid of all the Negro Jewish people of Israel that are there, he does not just want to hurt Mordecai, instead he wants to destroy all the Negro people of Israel that are in the province, including Mordecai.

Then in the 12th year of Ahasuerus' reign, Haman, and the rest of the white people in the kingdom cast pur (which is to cast dice) to determine what day they should destroy all the Negro Jewish people that are in the province, and it falls on the 12th month. Then with haste, Haman goes to the king and tell him there are certain people there in the province that have different laws than everyone else, and they do not obey his laws, and he think he should kill them off by sending out a decree, and he would pay the men that does it from out of the treasury. Without a thought, the king takes his signet ring off his finger, and gives it to Haman, and tells him he could do whatever he wants with the money, and the people. Immediately the scribes are called to write the decree according to what Haman wants in every language in the name of the king, and the decree is written, and is sealed with the king's signet ring. Then it is sent out throughout the world, and it states that "The white people should kill all the Negro Jewish people of Israel on the 13th day of the 12th month, whether young, or old, man, or woman, and they want them to be ready for that day." Then the king and Haman sit down to drink. Meanwhile, all the white men there are wondering what the heck is going on.

Chapter 4

When Mordecai heard about the decree, he tore his clothes and went out into the middle of the city as far as the king's gate and bitterly cried out there, since he could not enter the gates, because his clothes were torn. And everywhere else where the news is heard, the Negro people of Israel were crying, and tearing their clothes to start a fast. When the eunuchs tell Esther what is happening, it depresses her, and she sends clothes to Mordecai to put them on, but he refuses them, and when she hears he refuses the clothes, she tells Hatach, one of the eunuchs, to find out from him if he knows why the decree was sent out. Then Hatach go to the city square, and talks to Mordecai, and Mordecai tell him what happened with him, and he said that Haman said he would pay men from the king's treasury to kill off all the Jews, because of it. Then he gives Hatach a copy of the decree to show Esther to explain to her what is happening, so maybe she could go to the king, and do something about it. Right then, Hatach takes the decree to Esther, and explain everything to her, and she tell him to tell Mordecai that the king has a law that says, no one could come to him, if he did not call them, or he will kill them, but if they go to him without being called, and he hold out his golden scepter towards them, they will live, and she had not been called to him in the last thirty days. Then Hatach goes to Mordecai and tell him what Esther said, and Mordecai tell him to go back to her, and tell her, she better not think that, because she is the queen why they would not kill her too, and if she keep quiet in such a time, relief would come to them from somewhere else, and her, and her family would die, and he wants her to know that she got into the kingdom for such a time as this. So, Hatach hurry back to Esther, and tell her what Mordecai said, and when she heard what he said, she tell him to go back to Mordecai, and tell him to gather all the Jews in Shushan, and fast for three days and nights, and she, and the women with her would also do the same thing, and then she would go to the king to fight against the decree, and if he kill her, then he kill her. Again, Hatach goes to Mordecai, and tells him what Esther said, and Mordecai leaves from the city square, and gathers the Jews in the region to fast and pray for three days and nights like she told him to do.

Chapter 5

After the third day of fasting, Esther puts on her royal clothes, and stands in the inner court of the palace, across from the king's house, while the king is inside the house, facing the entrance. When the king sees her standing in the court, since he wants to meet with her, he holds out his scepter towards her, and she touches it, and he tells her to tell him what she wants, because he would give it to her, and she tells him she wants him, and Haman to come to have a banquet with her. Immediately he calls for Haman, and when Haman come to him, they go with Esther to her house to the banquet, and while they eat and drink together, he asks her what she really want, because he would give her anything, even up to half the kingdom, and she tell him, if he really likes her, and wants to give her what she wants, then she wants him, and Haman to come to another banquet with her the next day, and she would tell him what she really wants. Since Haman felt like she is about to surprise him, and honor him, he gets full of joy, but when he leaves from there, and sees Mordecai outside, he realizes that Mordecai is not afraid of him, and for that, he wants to kill him. But he restrains himself, and when he gets home, he sends for his friends, and his wife, Zeresh, to come to him, and when they get there, he tells them he has a lot of money, and great children, but he cannot be happy, as long as he keeps seeing Mordecai sitting at the king's gate. Then his wife suggests that he makes gallows, and in the morning, suggest to the king to hang Mordecai on it, and then he, and the king could merrily go to the banquet, and eat with Esther. With that, they all agreed, and Haman makes the gallows.

Chapter 6

That night, the king could not sleep, and he asked his servants to bring the history books to him, and when they got them, they read them to him, and they saw that there was something written about Mordecai, sending warnings that two eunuchs wanted to harm the king. So, the king asks them what honor Mordecai got for it, and one of the servants said, nothing was done for him. Meanwhile, Haman enters the courtyard in the dark to request to see the king, so he could tell him he wants to hang Mordecai on the gallows he built, and when the king see the movement in the yard, he asks who is out there, and the servant said, it is Haman. Then the king tells the servant to let him come in, and the servant lets him in, and the king asks him what could he do for him, and because he think the banquet that Esther is having is to honor him, he said to the king, "For the man you want to honor, you should give him a royal robe, and one of the horses that you rode on, with a royal crest on its head, and parade him around, and tell the people, this is the kind of man you love." That sounds good to the king, and the king tell him to hurry, and get the royal robe, and the horse, and get Mordecai, the Jew, and do to him exactly what he said. In humiliation, Haman goes for Mordecai, and place the robe on him, and parade him around town, while proclaiming he is being honored, because the king likes him. After the parade, Mordecai goes right back to the city square and continues with his fasting and praying. Meanwhile Haman is hurrying home, crying, because he is so ashamed, and when he gets home, he tell his wife and friends everything that happened, and they tell him that Mordecai is one of the Jews of Israel that he would not be able to defeat him.

Chapter 7

When the king, and Haman goes to dine with Esther as planned, the king tell her to tell him what she wants, because he would give it to her, and she tell him, if he really likes her, then she wants him to help her, and her people, because they were taken into captivity, and were sold, and now everyone wants to kill them off, and if they are sold again as slaves, she would not mind so much, even though it would have been a big loss to him. Shocked at her words, the king asks her who would ever do such a thing, and she said, it is Haman. Meanwhile, Haman is sitting right there and is scared. Then the king gets up drunk, and angry, and goes into the garden. But Haman stayed right there with Esther, pleading for his life. Then when the king finally calms down, and returns to the room, he sees Haman laid out cold on the coach with Esther sitting beside him, and he gets even angrier, because he thinks Haman is making advances at his wife. In the blink of an eye, his men come running in, and they cover Haman's face, and tie him up, and one of the eunuch points to the gallows he made to hang Mordecai, and the king tell his men to hang him on it, and they hang him. Then the king cooled down.

Chapter 8

Afterwards, the king gives Haman's house to Esther, and by that time, she had told him that Mordecai is a Jew, and a relative of hers. Then one day, Mordecai goes to the king, and the king gives him the signet ring that he gave to Haman, and Esther gives him Haman's house. Then she falls at the king's feet, and pleads with him about counteracting the decree that Haman passed to kill all their people on the 13th day of the 12th month, and she said, if he really likes her, he would write a letter to revoke the law, because she could not stand to see all her people destroyed, and without hesitation, the king tells her, and Mordecai they could write the letter in his name, and seal it with the signet ring, and no one would say anything about it.

In the 3rd month, on the 23rd day, the king's scribes are called, and Mordecai tells them what he wants the letter to say, and they write it. That same day, it is sent out to all 127 provinces in their own languages, and it says, the Negro Jewish people could protect themselves by any means against anyone that try to kill them on the 13th day of the 12th month, and they could take all their possessions after they kill them. Then when the news was heard, all the people of Israel became happy, and when Mordecai comes out in his royal robe, the people in the city cheers, and everywhere the news was sent, the people cheer. After that, many other people of many different nations became Jews, because they fear the Negro Jewish people of Israel.

Chapter 9

On the 13th day of the 12th month as planned, all the white people in Babylon that planned to kill all the Jewish Negro people of Israel were ready to kill them. Even though they heard that King Ahasuerus gave Queen Esther, and her Negro people the right to protect themselves, and take all they got, they still go out to kill the Negroes of Israel. Then the Negro people of Israel, and the white officials who fear what Mordecai would do to them, combine forces, and fight against the racist white people, and win, and when they were done, they tell the king they killed 500 white men. Then the king call Esther, and asks her if she want anything else, and she said she wants permission for her Negro people to kill more of the white people the next day, and she also want Haman's ten sons to be hung on gallows. With great adoration towards her, the king gives her the request, and he commands his men to hang Haman's sons, and they hang them. The next day, the people of Israel go out, and kill 75,000 more white people, but this time they do not take their things.

Finally, the Negro people of Israel could have some peace in their captivity in Babylon. Then on the 14th, which is the next day, they rested and made it a day to celebrate in feasting with joy. But some of them also celebrated on the 13th, and on the 14th, because they were so glad. Afterwards, Mordecai writes them a letter, telling them they should celebrate the victory of that day every year as a holiday with feasting, and joy on the 14th and 15th day of the 1st month (Adar), as the day they were freed from the harassment of the Babylonian white people, while in captivity. Which are the same days within the time of their Jewish Passover that they celebrate to remember the day when they were freed from the Egyptian colored people, and from that time on, year after year, he wants them to celebrate on the days of the 14th and the 15th of Adar with joy and feasting when they celebrate The Passover as a custom. He also tells them that because Haman cast pur to determine the date to kill them, and Esther got the king to counteract it, he, and Esther wants to call those two days, **"Purim"**, and they should tell their descendants to celebrate those days every year according to the time, date, and the written instructions. Then after that letter, Esther and Mordecai writes another letter to their people to confirm that they agreed with what Mordecai said to them in the first letter about the reason, the date, and time of the ritual of celebrating "Purim", and it was confirmed that it would be so.

Chapter 10

Though Ahasuerus, the white king, continued to be king, he allows Mordecai to rule the province for him to be in charge of his Negro people, as well as the white Babylonian people, and they like him very much, and were happy, because he always looked out for their good, and always try to keep peace between everyone, and they were also happy with Esther being a black woman, and being their queen.

(*We will now return to the Book of Ezra and pick up where we left off at chapter 7*)

NEHEMIAH
(Starting with the second chapter)

Chapter 2

In the 20th year of Artaxerxes (the king of Persia) reign, Nehemiah (the king's wine bearer) is sad when he serves Artaxerxes the wine, and because he was never sad around him before, Artaxerxes asks him why he is sad, and if he is sick, and because Nehemiah feels nothing, but sorrow in his heart, he become full of distress, and said, he is sad, because Jerusalem, the place of his father's tomb was destroyed, and the gates were burned. Then the king asks him how he could help, and before he answers the king, he prays to GOD, then he tells the king if he likes him, he wants him to send him to his people of Judah in Jerusalem where his father's tomb is, so he could rebuild it.

With the queen sitting beside the king as a witness, the king asks Nehemiah, how long it would take him to get there, and when would he return, but before he even answers, the king said, he is glad to let him go, and he asks the king to give him a letter to give to the white governors that governs the people in the land, so they would not bother him, and to also give him a letter to give to Asaph (the keeper of the forest) to tell him to supply them with timber to make beams for the temple, the city walls, and the house he would live in. With joy, and without hesitation, the king gives Nehemiah the letters he requested, and Nehemiah leaves with some of the captains of the king's army, and with soldiers on horses, and when they get to Africa, they go to the white governors that are ruling over the people in the land, east of the Jordan River, and he gives the governors the letter from the king, and Sanballat and Tobiah (two of the white governors) are deeply bothered that someone come there concerned about the Negroes they govern.

Then Nehemiah and the men that the king sent with him goes to Jerusalem, and after three days, GOD tells him to inspect the place, and he arose in the night, and snuck away from the king's men that are with him, and goes out to the Valley Gate to the Serpent Well and the Refuse Gate and take a good look at the broken down walls, and the burned gates. Then he goes to the Fountain Gate and to the King's Pool, but there is no room even for an animal to pass, and he goes to the valley and looks at the walls from there. When he is done, he turn back, and goes back the way he came, without anybody knowing he left, and he tells the king's officials, the priests, the nobles, and all the other Negro people that are to do the work, that Jerusalem is in great distress, and the gates are burned with fire, and he wants them to start building the walls, so they would no longer be a reproach, because GOD, and King Artaxerxes are on their side. When they hear that, everyone was glad to do the work, and they start, and when Sanballat and Tobiah (the two white governor), and Geshem (the Arab) hear of it, they laugh at those doing the rebuilding and despise them. Then they go to them, and asks, what they are doing, and if they are rebelling against the king, and Nehemiah said, GOD HIMSELF would make them prosper, and they will continue to build, no matter what they say, since they have no right to be there in Jerusalem, because they are not from there.

Chapter 3

Without stopping, Eliashib (the high priest), and the rest of the priest continue with the rebuilding, and they build the Sheep Gate, consecrate it, and hang the doors. Then they rebuild to as far as "The Tower of The Hundred" and consecrate it. Then they go on to build as far as "The Tower of Hananel", and the men of Jericho rebuild that area, and Zaccur, the son of Imri rebuild his area, and the sons of Hassenaah rebuild the Fish Gate by laying its beams and hanging its doors with the bolts and beams. Family by family, they continue to rebuild their regions, until they reach The City of David (which is Zion), where Nehemiah makes repairs to as far as the tombs of David, to the man-made pool, then to The House of THE LORD. After that, the Levites under Rehum, the son of Bani, make repairs to their district. Then the Levites under Bavi, the son of Henadad, makes their repairs, and Ezra makes his repairs from the buttress to the door of Eliashib, the high priest. And the priests continue with the repairs of their areas, and the goldsmith do their works, and even other people from other nations that joined them, helps them.

Chapter 4

When Sanballat heard they are progressing with the rebuilding of the place, he gets furious and starts to mock them, and he asks the white men that are with him, and all the white men that are in Samaria, what does the Negro people think they are doing, because he is wondering if they are trying to fortify themselves to offer sacrifices to their GOD, and he is also wondering, if they think they could complete the work in a day by reviving the burnt stones from the heap of rubbish. And since Tobiah is standing by him, Tobiah tells him not to worry about the Negroes, because whatever they build out of that rubbish, would crumble, even if a fox climbed on it.

With such opposition, Nehemiah prays to GOD to help them by causing problems for the white men that are troubling them, and they continue to build, and they built the wall all the way around, but only halfway up, and they accomplished much, because the people are eager to work. Then Sanballat and the rest of his men heard about the progress, and become furious, and they conspire together to go to Jerusalem to cause confusion. Meanwhile, Nehemiah, and the rest of his people are praying to GOD, while they keep a close watch to make sure Sanballat and his men does not come to bother them. After a while, the people start to say they are getting tired, because there is too mush rubbish there, they do not even have room to build, and they are also complaining, because the white men are threatening to kill them if they did not stop rebuilding. Yet they continue with the work as they watch out for the white men. Then some of the people of Israel in other areas go there, and warn them that the white men are really furious, and after being warned about ten times, Nehemiah position men to guard the area with weapons ready to kill, and he tell the nobles, and all the people not to be afraid, because GOD is great and awesome, and would fight for them.

When Sanballat and his men heard that GOD revealed their scheme to Nehemiah, and the builders, he, and the other white men left them alone, and they continue with the work, but from that time on, only half of them continue to work on the rebuilding, while the other half continue by keeping guard with weapons in hand. It is so bad with the harassment of the white men, that some of the builders have to carry weapons as they build. At that point, Nehemiah tell the nobles they have a lot of work to do, and it is only a few of them that are spaced too far apart, and he wants them to know, whenever they hear the trumpet for war, they should come to him, because GOD would fight for them, and while they continue to work, and guard the place, Nehemiah suggests that, instead of going home, they should stay there as guards during the night, and they agreed. Then they work during the days, and guard during the night, and they do not take off their work clothes, unless they are being washed, and after a while, the people of Israel that were captives in their own land starts to complain against the returned captives that are rebuilding the place, because they are concerned that the white men would not feed them anymore, and some of them are saying they do not have any land, because they mortgaged it off to the Babylonian king to get money for food, and they are slaves, even though they are their brothers, and black like them.

When Nehemiah heard what they said, he became angry, and he seriously thought about it. Then he tells the nobles it is their fault, because they charged their brothers a percentage whenever they lent them money, and he complains about how they misused each other. But the nobles said nothing, and he tell them what they are doing is not good, and they should fear GOD, and do the right thing, so other people would stop laughing at them. Then he tells them he would give the people money to help them with food, because he wants them to stop using each other, and he tells them he wants them to restore the land to those who lost theirs, and he wants them to give them a percentage of the money they took from them. So, the people agreed to do what he said, and he call the priests, and tell them to make sure they do it. Then he shakes out the fold of his clothing, and said, "That is how GOD would shake out the person that does not return the land as promised", and all the people said, "Amen!" Then they leave from there to do as promise, and Nehemiah, and the builders continues to work, and they do not buy any land, because they are there just to work. So, they work, and work, and all their provisions are provided, and Nehemiah pray to GOD to remembers him for all the good work he is doing.

Chapter 6

When Sanballat and his men heard the wall was completely done, even though the doors for the gates were not placed yet, Sanballat sends message to Nehemiah, telling him he, and his men wants to meet them among the village in the plain of Ono, and since Nehemiah felt they want to hurt them, he sends a message back to Sanballat, telling him, he is doing something important, and cannot come, and he see no reason to stop his work to come to him. So, Sanballat sends another message, telling him he wants to come to him, and Nehemiah sends a message back, telling him he does not have time. Then Sanballat try three more times, and each time, Nehemiah rejects him, and last time, which is the fifth time, Sanballat sends a message, and the message said, "Everyone in the world heard you are rebuilding the place so you could rebel, and according to those rumors, it seems like once you rebelled, you would want to be king over the white people, and my men, and I also heard that you sent out prophets to tell the people there is a king in Judah, and we are going to tell our king what you are doing, and it would be good if you come to talk things over with us."

Since Nehemiah knew, they were just trying to make them afraid, and stop doing the work, he sends a message back to Sanballat, telling him, no such thing is happening there, and he is telling lies. Then he pray to GOD for strength, and goes to Shemaiah's house, and Shemaiah tell him they should go into The House of THE LORD, and close the doors, because people are coming to kill him. But Nehemiah tell him he is not afraid, and would not run, plus he should not be in The House of THE LORD, and he is not going to hide there. At that moment, he realizes that GOD did not send Shemaiah to help him, and he was hired by Sanballat and Tobiah to make him afraid, so if he hides in The House of THE LORD, he would have sinned, and they would have something to hate him for. Therefore, he did not hide in The House of THE LORD, and he pray to GOD to punish Sanballat and Tobiah for being against them, and to punish the prophets that keep trying to make them afraid. Then they continue to build the wall, and it is finished within 52 days, on the 25th day of the month of Elul. Then when Sanballat, and his men, and the rest of the haters in other nations heard about it, they could not understand how it was done so quickly, and they figured it was GOD WHO did it. After that, the nobles of Israel that were captives in the land continue to deal friendly with the white man, Tobiah, and they write to him, and he writes back to them, because many of them remain as his friend, since he is married to one of the women of Judah, and they would tell Nehemiah what Tobiah said, and tell Tobiah what Nehemiah said. But Tobiah never changed from being a wicked white man, and one day, he sends a letter to Nehemiah to try to make him afraid again.

Chapter 7

Finally, the doors are hung on the gates of the wall, and the gate keepers, the singers, and the Levites are appointed to their position. Then Nehemiah gives charge of Jerusalem over to his brother, Hanani, after leading for many years, because Hanani feared GOD, and is faithful, and Nehemiah tells the people not to open the gates until the sun is hot, and to appoint other men to stand guard to watch the station while someone else watch their houses. Then he decides to check the record of the people, and he finds a register of those that came back during the time of Cyrus, after Nebuchadnezzar took them captive. As he read out to the people, he sees that Jeshua, Nehemiah, Azariah, Raamiah, Nahamani, Mordecai, Nahum, and many others had returned. Which totaled 42,360 men. Plus, the women and men servants, which totaled 7,337, and men and women singers, which totaled 245. Not only that, but they also have hundreds of thousands of animals for work, as well as for their sacrifices. Plus, tons, of tons of gold, and silver, and other materials they needed to rebuild with, and he read how they did all they could, and read that in the 7th month, each one went back to their cities to live on their inherited land.

(For the complete list of all the names of the Negro captives that were first returned from captivity in Babylon, please look in The Bible.)

Chapter 8

After he read the records, all the people gather in an opened square at The Water Gate, and they tell Ezra to bring The Book of The LAW, and it is on the 1st day of the 7th month, and Ezra (the scribe and priest) gets the book, and when he opens it to read it, all the people stand up, and he read it to them from morning to noon, and they listen attentively to him, as he stands on a platform made of wood, which they made for the purpose, and standing beside him is Mattithiah, Shema, Ananiah, Urijah, and other believing priest.

That day, Jeshua, Bani, the Levites, and other men help the others to understand what the book says, and they cry, because of the words, and

Nehemiah, Ezra, and the Levites pronounce the day to be holy to GOD and say no one should cry. Then they dismiss the people, and tell them to go home, and live a happy life and to give to the others that have not settled in yet, because the day is holy to GOD, and GOD is their joy, and strength. Then since they know that they feel at peace, and they go their way to enjoy life with each other, because they understand what GOD is saying to them through the LAW.

The next day, the heads of the household goes to Nehemiah and Ezra to understand more of what the LAW says, and they see written in the LAW, that the people of Israel should live in booths during the feast of the 7th month, and they should tell all the people to go to Jerusalem, and bring olive branches, myrtle branches, palm branches, and branches of other leafy trees to make the booths. Then all the people that returned from captivity decides to do as the LAW said, and they go out and get the branches, and make booths, and each one place a boot on their roof top, in their yard, in the courtyard of The House of THE LORD, in the opened square of The Water Gate, or at The Gate of Ephraim, and everyone is glad. Then for 7 days they listened to the LAW being read to them while they kept the feast, and on the 8th day, they have a sacred assembly, according to what was written in the LAW.

Chapter 9

On the 24th day of the month, they assembled in sack clothes with dust on their heads in fasting and praying, and those that are truly born Israelites, separates themselves from all the foreigners that joined them to live with them. Then they stand up, and confess their sins, and their bad ways, and they read the LAW for about 8 hours. Then they confess their sins and worship GOD for another 8 hours. After that, Jeshua and some of the other priest stands on the stage, and shout out praises to GOD, and the Levites stands up and join in on the praise, saying, "Blessed GOD forever, and blessed HIS holy name, because HE is exalted above all the blessings, and praise."

Then the Levites tell the story of how GOD took Abram (Abraham) from the ungodly white land of , which belongs to the Chaldeans, and How GOD felt that Abraham was faithful that HE could make a covenant with him, and how GOD told Abraham that HE would give the white people's land of Canaan to his descendants, and though GOD promised that to them, they ended up in slavery in Egypt, and when GOD heard their cries, HE delivered them from their slavery, and showed them, and the world that HE alone is GOD. So the Levites continue telling the story, from when GOD gave them HIS LAW, and led them to The Promised Land, which is The Land of Canaan that belonged to the white wicked people that GOD promised Abraham HE would give them, and how it was good for them, but since they did not get rid of all the white people from the land, like GOD told them to, they ended up ruining thing for themselves, because they did what the white people do, instead of doing what GOD said in the LAW. And because of their disobedience, they made GOD angry, and after many years of patience, and trying to correct them, GOD decided to send them into slavery again, but this time by the white people that they listened to, and idolized so much, and because GOD loves them so much, HE delivered them from the white people. Then the Levites said, because of GOD's graciousness, all of them that returned from captives wants to do the right thing, and even though they, and their forefathers did not obey the LAW, they thank GOD for delivering them, and for always loving them, and that is why they are promising they would keep the LAW.

Chapter 10

Right then and there, they made a document of the covenant, and each one place their seal on it to show they agree to do as it says, and they placed themselves under the curse to follow all that was written in the LAW, because they want to do things, such as not marrying people of other nations, and not working on "The Sabbath", and things such as giving offerings on a set basis, according to the rituals.

(For the complete list of names of all the people who placed their seal on the covenant, please look in The Bible.)

Chapter 11

Then all the leaders of the people that lives in Jerusalem, and the rest of the people in their inherited lands decides to cast lots to see, if one out of ten of them would win the chance to also live there in "The Holy City" (Jerusalem) with the people of Judah, because whoever wins the chance to live there are considered blessed, since it shows they want to live holy. By right, the darkest skinned people of the tribe of Judah that GOD loves the most, which includes the Levites, the priest, the prophets, and the kings, all lives in Jerusalem, since it is their inheritance, and they show themselves to be holy. Then once the lot is cast, the tribe of Benjamin, which was the first ones that allowed the white people to corrupt them were chosen to also live in Jerusalem with the tribe of Judah, because they decided to be holy again, after living with a bunch of white pagan heathens.

(For the list of the names of all the families that live in Jerusalem, please look in The Bible.)

Chapter 12

After that, they make a dedication of the completion of the wall around Jerusalem with singing, and giving thanks to GOD, and they march all about the places while giving thanks. On that same day, they offer sacrifices to GOD, and rejoice, because they are so happy, and they are so loud during their celebration, people could hear them even from outside the city.

(For the complete list of the names of the priesthood, and the complete version of the celebration, please look in The Bible and read it for yourself.)

Chapter 13

Also on that day, they read the LAW to the people, and found out that no Ammonite, or Moabite white people should had been assembled with them, because they did not help their people of Israel with bread and water. Instead, they hired Balaam, the wizard to put a curse on them, and GOD had to turn the curse into a blessing. So, because of what the LAW said, they separate all the mixed people from them that are part Negro and part white. Meanwhile, Tobiah, the wicked white man is staying in the storehouse in the courtyard of The House of THE LORD where Eliashib, the high priest prepared a room for him, and when Nehemiah found out about it, it angers him, and he threw out Tobiah, and his things. Then he commands that they clean the room and put back the things of GOD that belong there, along with a grain offering with frankincense burning. At that moment, he realizes that the Levites, and the singers did not get their portion of land, and they are living in the fields. So, he argues with the leaders about it to put them in their place. Then all the people of Judah take their tithes of grain, wine, and oil to the storehouse, and people that are trustworthy are chosen to guard and distribute it to those that need, and Nehemiah pray to GOD to remember him for all the good things he did that day.

After some days, he notice that the people of Judah are still selling, and trading on The Sabbath, and he warn them not to do any work on that day. Even the white people from Tyre that lives there in the land are in Jerusalem doing their business on The Sabbath, and he goes to the nobles, and asks them why they allow The Sabbath to be profaned as if they do not know that GOD punished their forefathers for it. Then as it is about to get dark, he commands that the gates of Jerusalem should be shut, and not opened until after The Sabbath, and he place some of his men to guard the gate, so no one else could come in. Yet after that, the merchants and sellers still sell outside the gates for several Sabbaths, and he warns them, and tells them if they do it again, he would punish them. Then he tells the Levites to cleanse themselves, and go out, and guard the gates, so The Sabbath would be a holy day, and he pray, and asks GOD to remember him, and to spare him according to the goodness of HIS mercy. From that day, no one came back on The Sabbath to work again.

Shortly after that, he realizes that many of the Negro people of Israel are married to white people from Ashdod, Ammon, and Moab, and half of the mixed children born by them only speaks the white people's language, and they could not speak the language of the Negro people of Judah. Then he argues with the people about it, and curse some of them, and pulled out their hair, and made them swear to GOD they would stop marrying the ungodly white pagan people, and he tells them how Solomon was a great king, and when he sinned by marrying ungodly pagan women, he ended up with problems. He also tells them about how he got rid of Sanballat, the white man that married one of the women of Israel to become the son-in-law of Eliashib, the high priest. Then he asks GOD to remember him for what he is doing, because they defiled the priesthood by marrying pagans, and he run Joiada, Eliashib's son, away from him, because he is the son-in-law to Sanballat (the white man). Then he cleanses everything that is pagan, and tells the priests, and the rest of the Levites what they should do as their service to GOD, and how to bring the wood offering, and "The First-Fruit Offering" at the appointed time, and he prays to GOD again, and asks HIM to remember him for all the good things he did.

MALACHI'S PROPHECY

By this time, the people of the tribe of Judah are freed from their captivity in Babylon, and they are righteous. But the people of the other tribes are still in captivity in Babylon, and if they are not captives in Babylon, they are in captivity in their own land, and are governed by a white man, because of their unrighteous. But, while the returned captives of the tribe of Judah rebuilds Jerusalem, the walls, and The House of THE LORD, they are living good, and are being blessed, along with the tribe of Benjamin that lives in Jerusalem with them, just like GOD promised, and yet most of the other tribes of Israel still do not want to live a completely righteous life. Still, there are more prophesies to be fulfilled immediately, and even up to "The End Times", and Jesus did not come yet, nor did salvation, or the righteous world governments that was prophesied about.

Chapter 1

Then one day GOD tells Malachi, when HE told the people of Israel HE loves them, they kept on asking HIM how can HE say HE love them, and HE told them, the people of Esau is their brothers, and HE love them (Israel), but HE does not love (Edom) the people of Esau, and it is like they did not notice that HE destroyed the mountain of the people of Esau, and their inherited land is for jackals, and wild animals to live, and so they arrogantly insist they would return to their land. But if they return and rebuild the place, HE would tear it down, because HE is magnificent, even beyond the borders of Israel, and since the people of Israel are like the people of Esau, HE does not like the people of Israel either, and they could bring all the sacrifices they want, but HE does not want it, because they offer substandard sacrifices, and the priest are profaned, and they say HE makes them weary.

Chapter 2

What HE wants is HIS covenant with the tribe of Levi to continue, because HE made them to be righteous priests, but they profaned themselves, and HE would not stop punishing them, until HE is good and ready, because HE wants them to be wise, and HE wants them to seek the LAW, but they departed from HIS ways, and HE hates them, and yet they want to know why HE is against them, and why HE is treating them so harshly.

Chapter 3

Then to give them understanding, HE sent them prophets to prepare them for the coming of Jesus, so when Jesus comes they could learn from Him, and Jesus is coming soon, and HE does not know if they could stand Jesus when He comes, because He would come to correct them, so they could be pure, and be able to offer sacrifices to HIM again. Then at that time HE would be happy with their offerings, just like long ago in the past, and HE would be there to protect them from sorcerers, adulterers, and perjurers, and from those who exploit wages, those who exploit widows, and orphans, and those who turn away foreigners, because those are the unbelievers. Yet, from the days of their forefathers, they turned from the LAW, and HE wants them to return to HIM, and they have not returned, because they keep wondering when they left.

Would a man rob GOD?

"Yes, people would rob GOD."

And the people of Israel robbed HIM though HE is their GOD, and they are wondering how they robbed HIM, and HE wants them to know that they robbed HIM in giving their tithes, and offerings, and the whole nation is cursed, because of it, and HE wants them to bring all the tithes and offerings to the storehouse, so there may be food in HIS house. And if they do not know what that means, first of all it has nothing to do with money, or goods, it means, they should take time to know the LAW, and follow it, which is "**The Tithes**", and in following, they should, sing, laugh, dance, and give thanks, and praise, because these are "**The Offerings**", and these tithes, and offerings would be stored up in HIS heart as reasons for HIM to bless them. Therefore, if they gave all their tithes and offerings to HIM, they would see that HE would pour out blessings for them that would be more than they could handle, and HE would protect them from everyone that comes to devour their prosperity, so they would never be impoverished again. Then all the other nations would call them blessed. But their words had been harsh against HIM, and yet they are wondering what they said against HIM, and HE wants them to know that when they say, "It is useless to serve HIM, and it makes no sense suffering, and following the LAW", is when they are against HIM, and when they call the wicked good, they are speaking harshly against HIM. Now they are saying the proud ones are blessed, because they had been allowing all the wicked ones to do what they wanted to do without punishing them. Now, that is a good message. So, immediately, Malachi goes to the people, and tell them what GOD said, and after hearing what he said, those who fear GOD speaks to each another about making a change, and GOD heard them, and kept it in HIS mind to remember to favor them, so they would see that HE favors the righteous.

Chapter 4

Though they were warned over, and over again, some of them would not change. But it was prophesied that the day is coming, burning like an oven when Jesus comes, and all the proud and wicked people would be judged, and become the stubbles that would burn in hell. But those who believes what Jesus taught, and then change, they would be healed, and once they are healed, they would go on to live a good life, and would be able to defeat the wicked people, because GOD, THE HOLY SPIRIT would be with them, even after Jesus resurrect up to heaven. Therefore, they should remember that Moses wrote in the LAW book, and said, Elijah is John the Baptist, the one that would come before the coming of Jesus, The Messiah, and when Jesus comes, He would teach the truth to the whole world, and would turn their Negro people, and others who believe back to righteous living, and true worship, because if GOD does not send Jesus, The Savior, GOD would destroy all the people of Israel, because of the lies that cause them to continue in rebellion.

WHERE ARE THEY NOW?

(Jesus, their Savior is near)

By this time, most of the people of Judah are freed, but most of the other tribes of Israel are either dead, captives and in bondage in Babylonian lands, or captives in their own land under Babylonian dictatorship. And in the days when the white man, Herod, starts to rule over the people of Israel, Zacharias (the priest) is one of the builders of the tribe of Judah who always pray for righteousness to come on the earth. Then one day when it is his turn to burn the incense at the temple, while everyone is praying, Gabriel the angel comes to him, and tell him his prayers had been heard, and he would have a son, they should name John, who would bring them joy, and gladness, and many people would be glad, because he was born. But since Zacharias is old, and his wife, Elizabeth is also old, and had been barren for all those years, he could not believe the righteousness he prayed for would start with his son, John, and Gabriel gets angry with him, and makes him mute, because he came with good news, and he would not believe it.

Shortly afterwards, Elizabeth gets pregnant, and she keeps secluded with the pregnancy. Then in the 6th month of her pregnancy, Gabriel goes to Mary and tell her she would have a son by THE HOLY SPIRIT of GOD, who she should name Jesus, and He would be The Savior of the world, and Mary is honored to be the mother of The Son of GOD. Then Gabriel tells her, her relative, Elizabeth, is already 6 months pregnant with a son, and he leaves. So, Mary hurried from Nazareth (in Galilee) to go to Jerusalem to see Elizabeth, and when she gets there, and enter the room, the baby leaps in Elizabeth's womb upon hearing her greeting, and when Elizabeth greets her back, THE HOLY SPIRIT reveals to her that Mary was chosen to be the mother of The Savior, The Son of GOD. Then since it had been 6 months being isolated, she is glad for the company, and Mary stays with her for about 3 months, and just before she has the baby, Mary leaves. When she had the child, they circumcised him on the 8th day, and when they were ready to name him, everyone thought they would name him Zacharias, after his father, but they named him John. Then the people ask Zacharias, if that is really the name they are giving him, and because he is mute, he writes "yes" on a tablet, and when they read it, they were surprised at the answer, and immediately he could speak again.

Then Zacharias and Elizabeth raise John to be a godly man, and when John is grown, he goes to the desert to live until it is time to reveal himself to the people of Israel. By the time he is grown, most of the tribes of Israel had returned to their land from their Babylonian captivity and are doing well. But those that are still in captivity are far from knowing the truth, and are not so well, and even though Gabriel told Mary that she would have a son by THE HOLY SPIRIT when Elizabeth was only six months pregnant with John, now John is grown, and Mary just got pregnant by the power of THE HOLY SPIRIT of GOD without ever sleeping with a man. When she tells her fiancé, Joseph, she is pregnant, he wants to keep her secluded, because he is a respectable man, and does not want people to judge her for being pregnant out of wedlock. While he is thinking about it, an angel appears and tells to be happy to be Mary's husband, because she is pregnant by THE HOLY SPIRIT of GOD. After hearing what the angel said, he marries Mary, and they live in Bethlehem (in the land of the tribe of Judah) in the days when the white man, Herod, subdued the lands of Israel. Then when Mary had her son, they name Him Jesus, and many of the wise Negro men from East Jerusalem leave to see the baby, because they heard of him for so long. So, they travel to where Herod is ruling in Jerusalem, and they go to him, and ask him, if he knew where the child is, and since many of the people of Israel are there, when the wise men ask about the child, they start to wonder if prophesy is being fulfilled. With wicked intention, Herod question the wise men about what they knew about the prophesy of the child, and he tell them to tell him when they find the child, because he wants to worship Him. Then the wise men leave from Jerusalem, and a star leads them to a house in Bethlehem where the child, and its parents are, and when they see the child, they fall before Him and worship Him. Then they give Him gifts of gold, frankincense, and myrrh, and leave from there overflowing with joy. But since they were warned in a dream not to report back to Herod, they take a different route back.

Later, an angel visits Joseph, and tells him to take Mary, and the child to Egypt, because the Babylonians wants to kill the child, and immediately, he takes Mary, and the child to Egypt. Then when Herod realize that the wise men ignored him, he gets angry, and sends out a decree that says, the white Babylonian should kill all the male Negro children in the Bethlehem district who are 2 yrs. old, or less. Which is the age he came up with from the information given to him when he questioned the wise men. From then, the Babylonians starts to kill as many of Israel's infants as they can, and Herod even change time from the year they are in to 1 A.D., after more than three thousand years of history from the beginning of time, to start again with A.D. At the same time, reversing the noted date they are in, which started from the beginning of time to their present time, which should be about the year 3500. From his time backwards it became B.C., and forwards it became A.D. Which means they could set time in the pass from their time as 1 B.C. to as many years backward as they want. Even millions and billions of years, and from their time forward from 1 A.D. to the date we are in today, which is 2025 years later, and beyond. So, since they say Jesus was born in 1 A.D., and He started preaching at 30 years old, then it was in the year 30 A.D., and He was crucified after preaching for three years in 33 A.D., and so it had been 2025 years since Jesus was born.Nevertheless, Jesus was born before they started time again, and He was 2 or 3 years old when the decree started, and for many years the killing of the Negro children continued as they were born in their land under subjection to the white men. Then when Herod finally died, his son, Archelaus takes his place as ruler over the Negro people of Israel, and the slaughter of their male infants finally stops. By this time, Jesus is a young boy, and an angel visits Joseph in Egypt and tells him it is time for him to return to Israel, and when Joseph heard that Archelaus replaced Herod as the new ruler, instead of going to Bethlehem, he decides to go to Nazarene, which is another region of Israel. That is why they call Jesus a Nazarene, since He lived there, as well as a Galilean, since His people are from Galilee.

Finally, it is time for John, The Baptist to start ministering, and when he heard that Joseph and Mary are in the region with the child, he begins to cry out in the wilderness, telling people to repent, because The Kingdom of Heaven is at hand. Then people begin to go to him to get baptized in the Jordan River. But when he sees the Pharisees, and the Sadducees coming, he calls them a bunch of snakes, and asks them, who warned them about the wrath to come. Then he said, it is not because they are the Negro descendants of Abraham why they would resurrect after they die, because it is how righteous they lived, and because he knows that most of them are sinners, he would always tell them to repent, so they could enter into The Kingdom of GOD, and he would also tell them about Jesus, so when Jesus come to them, they could hear, and understand what He said.

After many years passed, finally, Jesus is grown, and is ready for His ministry, and at about the age of 30 years old (in 30 A.D.), He goes to John, who is about 77 years old at the time, to get baptized by him in the Jordan River. But John tries to stop Him, because he feels that Jesus should be baptizing him instead, and Jesus tells him to just do it, because it is the only way to bring back the righteous ones that are dead, and in hell where everyone who died ended up, because the price of salvation has not been paid yet. Then after hearing what Jesus said, John baptizes Him, and when Jesus comes up out of the water, the heavens open, and THE HOLY SPIRIT of GOD fills Him, and they hear the voice of GOD saying, "This is MY beloved Son in Whom I am well pleased." Afterwards, GOD leads Him to the wilderness to be tempted by Satan, and after fasting in the wilderness for 40 days, He is hungry. Then Satan comes there to tempt Him while He is weakened, but He takes authority over the situation, and resists Satan's temptation by quoting scriptures, until Satan decides to leave. At that same time, the Babylonians locked up John, The Baptist, because he told Herod incest and adultery is wrong. Then when Jesus heard about it, He decides to go back to Galilee to the town where He grew up, and when He gets to Galilee, He decides to leave from there, and goes to Capernaum, which is the region where the tribes of Zebulun and Naphtali dwells by the sea. From there He begins His ministry, preaching about The Kingdom of GOD. Then he goes back to Galilee to preach there, and He perform many miracles to those who know Him, and when the white Syrians people that are there see Him doing the miracles, they begin to bring their sick, and mentally tormented patients for Him to heal them, and He heal them. Then news begins to spread about Him, and many kinds of people take their sick to Him, and He heals them, and preach about the kingdom, and perform many miracles.

From that time, He begins to have many followers, and He choose Simon and Andrew, who are brothers, and are also fishermen, and James and John, who are also brothers, and fishermen. Then He preach "The Sermon on The Mount", and said, "The poor in spirit are blessed, because they are suffering for trying to enter The Kingdom of GOD, and those who mourned when they see injustice, and unrighteousness are blessed, because they would be comforted when The Kingdom of GOD comes. Also, those who live a peaceful, and quiet life are blessed, because they are meek, and would inherit the earth forever, and those who are hungry, and thirsty to see justice and righteousness on the earth are blessed, because they would be jurors at The Great White

Throne Judgment. And because the merciful lives in sorrow, and feel sorry for sufferers, GOD would make things good for them, since they are like HIM. And the pure in heart would see the kingdom come, because they live by the LAW in evil times, so they could see the righteous kingdom. And those that are peacemakers are the true sons of GOD. And those that are prosecuted are blessed, because they are suffering for living by the WORD of GOD. So, they are all blessed when people revile them, and prosecute them, and say all kinds of evil things against them, because they are living a good life. Therefore, they should rejoice, and be glad, because that was the same way all the prophets were prosecuted, and they would get a great reward in heaven, because they are the salt of the earth, and the light of the world, and so, He wants them to shine in the presences of all human being by showing them their good works, so they would give glory to GOD, THE FATHER, because He did not come to destroy the LAW. Instead, He came to do exactly as the LAW requires, and to do as the prophets spoke about Him, and He wants them to know that all that is written in the prophecies would come to pass, and the earth would be restored, and if anyone broke the LAW, and taught others to do so, then they could only have low positions in the kingdom. But whoever does and teaches others to follow the LAW would have the greatest positions in the kingdom. So, unless their belief goes beyond the written LAW, and quoting it, they would not enter The Kingdom of Heaven to have, love, peace, or joy, and the greatest is love, because when they have love, they can have peace and joy. Which is why He tells them they are not supposed to sin, and they are supposed to seek understanding, and the only way to understanding is to obey the LAW of GOD, as well as the law of man

Also, because GOD wants them to be merciful, kind, and compassionate, they should love their neighbors, even the ones they call enemies, and they should love to love, so they would become children of the GOD in heaven and be perfect like HIM. Then when they do everything according to GOD's way, they would see their reward. So, from then on, GOD wants them to pray, even though HE knows what they want, because HE wants them to know they would receive what they asked for. And to avoid any regrets, when they pray, they should acknowledge to GOD that HE is holy, and HE is their FATHER, WHO lives in heaven, and they should tell HIM they want HIS kingdom to come on earth, so HIS will would be done on earth as it is in heaven, and they should ask HIM to give them their need for the day, and forgive their sins, as they forgive someone else's sin, and to lead them away from temptations, and deliver them from evil, because the world belongs to HIM, and HE has the power, and the glory to do it. And when they fast and pray, they should keep themselves looking clean and healthy, and they should know that the treasures of the world are not treasures at all, and it is the good work they do on the earth their heavenly FATHER considers as treasures, that HE stores up in heaven for them. And they should realize that what a person sees is what that person does, and they should seek GOD, so their lives could be a light to the people of the world. They should also realize that they can only serve one master at a time, and they should choose to serve GOD, instead of choosing to serve Satan, because of greed, or material wealth, and they should not worry, because GOD would provide all the food, clothing, and clean water that they need, and they should believe it, and be happy, because they already have what they need. Therefore, they should not worry about their needs, because GOD would provide, and they should seek first The Kingdom of GOD, and HIS righteousness, and do all they can do for the day, and if they are tired, then they should rest, and refresh themselves, and the next day do whatever they can do. Plus, they should take time to live their lives right and stop wasting their time on people who do not want to serve GOD, because it would be a hypocritical thing if they tell someone how to enter the kingdom when they themselves cannot enter.

He also tells them that when they live godly, they could ask for anything they want, as long as it is pleasing to GOD, and they would receive it, and if they searched for answers in the truth, GOD would make them find it, because

GOD is guiding, and leading them by HIS HOLY SPIRIT, and whatever good thing they want someone to do for them, they should do for someone else, because that is what the prophets, and the LAW was trying to tell them to do, since the only way to enter into The Kingdom of GOD is by living a good life. And since there are many ways that lead to destruction, and there are many who decides to follow those destructive ways, they should not follow the crowd, and they should be careful, because people would come to them pretending they are godly, when they are not, and they should know that a person must do good works, as well as having faith in GOD, before they can say a person is really godly. They should also know that not everyone who calls Him Lord would enter The Kingdom of Heaven, because only those who obey the LAW of GOD can enter in, and some would be told to leave, because their works were already given credit by man, even though they themselves were unpleasing to GOD. Therefore, they should be wise to do what the LAW commands when they hear it, because that is how to build their lives on a solid foundation.

Then Jesus is done with the sermon, and the people are surprised at how gentle He was when He taught them, because they were so used to having the scribes screaming at them and shoving it down their throats. When He comes down from the mountain, the crowd follow Him, and He heal a leper, then heal a paralyzed servant of a Centurion white soldier, and because the Centurion believed his servant would be healed before even seeing it, He commends the Centurion for his faith. Then He preach throughout the region some more, and did many other miracles, and the white Centurion man convinced Him that the white people had more faith in His teachings, than his own Negro people. This makes HIM say, "The Negro people of Israel, which are the people of The Kingdom of Heaven, could get cast out, and there would be lots of crying throughout the world." Meanwhile, the Pharisees in the crowd are judging Him, and He heard what they said, and He tell them, a person that is well does not need a doctor, and they should learn what that means, because He desires mercy, not sacrifices, and He came to call sinners to repentance, since the righteous are doing just fine and do not need Him. Then John's followers go to Him, and they ask Him why they and the Pharisees always fast, and yet He and His disciples do not, and He tell them, the bridegroom's friend does not cry when they are with Him, but the day would come when the bridegroom would be taken away, and His disciples would fast, and "Even though no one can defeat the devil until THE HOLY SPIRIT of GOD come, when THE HOLY SPIRIT of GOD comes, when the believers fast and pray, they would get the understanding and wisdom from THE HOLY SPIRIT they need to destroy Satan, and his devils."

From there, He goes throughout the region to preach again, and He heal all the people who come to him that are sick, but it is too many people that are physically, and emotionally sick for Him alone to heal, and He pray to GOD, and chose more men to help Him with the teaching, and though He had thousands of disciples, He chose twelve special ones He called apostles. Their names are, Simon (Peter), Andrew (Peter's brother), James and John (the sons of Zebedee),Philip, Bartholomew, Thomas, Mathew (the tax collector), James (the son of Alphaeus), Labbaeus (also known as Thaddaeus, because it's his last name), Simon (a white looking black man, who was also called Zealot), also Judas Iscariot (the one that would betray Him), and John and James, "Boanerges", which means "Sons of thunder". Then He teach them the truth, so He could send them out to perform miracles, and preach to the lost Negro people of Israel, (which are the lost sheep), the ones that do not know their roots, so they could understand what the scriptures said, and so they would know they are "The Chosen Ones". And He tell them not to teach anyone who is not of the lost sheep of Israel, and not to go to the city of Samaria, even though it belongs to Israel, because the people there are white, or mixtures of white, who took over the land.

Once they learned, He sends them out as innocent men (sheep) amid the ravenous Babylonians (wolves), and tell them not to carry any money, or change of clothes, because He wants them to see that GOD would provide all their needs. He also tells them to be wise, because not everyone is going to be happy to hear about "The Kingdom of Heaven", and people would try to harm them, especially those in the churches, because that was the way they treated the prophets, and that is the way they are going to treat all the believers. And He tell them not to be afraid, and to tell others about Him, because when they do, He would speak to GOD in their favor, and they should know that He did not come to give people peace while they sin, but He came to discipline them to make a change, even if no one else in the family would change. He also wants them to warn the new believers that when they choose to make the change, it would be hard, because many people would turn against them, such as their church, their parents, and their children, and they should know that if they cannot let everything, and everyone go, they may lose their faith before they die, and would not make it into "The Kingdom of Heaven." They should also know that those who help them are believers like them, and everyone would get their reward eventually.

Then with great urgency, He, and His apostles goes out to teach the lost Negro children of Israel, and while they teach, all the other kinds of people in the world learned. Meanwhile, John, The Baptist is still locked up in prison, and when John heard about Jesus' teachings, and the miracles He performs, he sends some men with a letter to take to Jesus, which asks Him, if He is the Messiah, or should he keep on looking for one, and Jesus tell them to go back, and tell him about all the things they saw Him doing, and tell him the blind can see, the deaf can hear, and the poor are having the gospel preached to them. Then the men leaves to tell John what He said, and He turns to the crowd, and said, "John is the greatest man ever born in the world (since he was born with THE HOLY SPIRIT in him), but even the least in the kingdom of heaven could be greater than him.

Then He said, from the day John, The Baptist was born, the righteous Negro people that are truly of The Kingdom of Heaven had been suffering violence from wicked people, because the wicked people are taking away all their love, peace, and joy by force, because they know when the people of Israel realize that "The Book of Moses" and the prophets said, John would be born to prepare them for His coming. So, since He is the one who would bring forth the righteous kingdom, the wicked people do not want them to realize they are "The Chosen Ones", and they would regain their faith and power. Therefore, if they are ready to believe it is the truth, then they should believe that John, the Baptist is Elijah, who the scriptures said would come, and since they can hear, they better believe they just heard the truth.

After that, He goes to preach to many different types of people for a while, but they are not accepting the truth no more than the Negro people of Israel, and He tells them that correction is coming to them through "The Great tribulation", which is the beginning of "The Wrath of GOD", and it would come very soon on all the unbelievers (during their Roman Empire time), and if they had been working to find the truth and are tired of not finding it, then all they have to do is seek Him, and He would give them rest by telling them the truth. And because He is gentle and lowly in heart when He teaches, He would give them rest for their souls with the truth, and He does not want them to take Him lightly, because He require that they live by the LAW, and it is easy, and because He is the Lord of "The Sabbath" (the one that can give them rest), he wants them to have mercy, instead of giving sacrifices.

Then He heal a man, and because it is The Sabbath, the Pharisees try to kill Him, and He leaves the area, and as He leaves, He heals everyone that comes to Him. He even heals a demon possessed man that the people brought to Him, and the people were amazed, but when the Pharisees see it, they said, He is taking orders from the leader of the demons, Beelzebub. So, He tell them, there is no way, because if He is using demons to fight against Satan's kingdom, it would fall. Then because the Pharisees said they could cast out demons, He asks them who do they listen to when they cast them out, if He cast them out by Beelzebub, and He said, a demon cannot take over a strong person's life, unless the demon constrain that person, and once that person is constrained, then the demon would cause that person to lose all their blessings, such as their health, money, friends, and family, and they should realize that every sin can be forgiven, even rejecting Him, but rejecting GOD (THE HOLY SPIRIT) would not be forgiven. Because if a person believes that GOD (THE HOLY SPIRIT) would reveal all things to them, then that person would pray, and ask GOD to forgive their sins and HE would, and HE would tell them what to do when it comes to demons, and spiritual things.

So, if they do what GOD said, then they would say, GOD is good, and HIS children are good, or they could continue to disbelieve, and be like a bunch of snakes that say GOD is bad, and HIS children are bad, since they are evil and cannot speak anything good. That is why they should know that every human being would have to give account for every word they spoke, because what they say may condemn them, or justify them, and they should know that when a demon is cast out, it goes around looking for someone else to possess, and if it cannot find someone else, it would try to re-enter the person it left, and if it sees that the person is living a clean life, it would get more demons, and they would try to force their way into that person's life. And if they are successful by means of the person themselves, their job, or even through other family members, the person's life would be worse off than before they got delivered. And because Satan is trying to take people to hell with him, every time when someone hear the WORD about The Kingdom of Heaven, and does not understand it, Satan comes and twist the truth, so they do not understand it, and it is like throwing seed away. And it is like throwing seeds on stones when a person hears the WORD, and become joyous and hopeful, and Satan starts to cause a lot of troubles in that person's life, till eventually that person lose their joy, and have no more hope in the truth. And if a person heard the word and desires to live right, then Satan would let that person have just a little less than what they need to survive, and that person would do some unjust, or compromising thing just to make ends meet, till eventually that person completely turn from the word, because it is like throwing seeds amongst thorns.

But it is good ground when a person hears the word, and obeys it, because even if there are still a lot of problems and chaos in that person's life, they could prosper and live life abundantly, depending on the effort they put into their work. Then He said Satan would come to the earth, but he would go to hell afterward, and the parable of "**The Wheat and Tares**" is saying that the son of man (human beings), which includes all the looks and complexion of the human race, had multiplied after the flood in the earth (which is on the field), but out of all the different kinds of people that came from Noah's three Negro sons, GOD separated the good seed of Shem's Negro lineage for HIS kingdom (which is HIS government), and HE calls them HIS "Chosen" people. Then Satan try his best to destroy The Chosen People, because GOD chose them to be an example to the world, so the world would know HIM through them. But since they did not show a good example, it caused the world to doubt GOD, and GOD decided to let Him, HIS son, come through their Negro lineage to tell them, and the rest of people in the world the truth.

While Jesus is speaking those words, Satan is listening. Then Satan decides to influence the wicked white people in The Roman Empire to use their governmental positions to destroy all the believers. Yet, because Jesus is around, even while believers are being harassed, things are calm just as the prophesy said it would be, and the white Babylonian people in the world are at peace with the Negroes of Israel, and with the gentiles, and everyone are allowed to hear, and learn the truth that Jesus preaches, but because of that, Satan gets even angrier. Then after a while, Jesus goes back to His hometown to see his mother, his younger sisters, and His younger brothers, James, Joses (which is Joseph), Simon, and Judas, because He wants to perform many miracles and preach to them. But because they knew Him since he was a child, and they knew He did not have any special teachings, they refuse to believe He is "The Christ."

The whole time Jesus preached, John, The Baptist had been in prison for accusing Herod of committing adultery. Then when Jesus goes to his hometown, Herod cuts off John's head, because his daughter-in-law danced a pleasing dance to him, and at her mother's request, she asked for John's head as a token, and when Jesus hears about it, He leaves on a boat to isolate Himself in a deserted place. Then many people followed Him on foot, and when He realize that so many people came there for His help, He felt compassion for them, and He heal them, and as it was getting late, the apostles suggest to Him to send the people home before they get hungry, He tell them they do not have to send the people away, and He wants them to give them something to eat, and they tell Him they only have five loaves of bread, and two fish, which does not seem to be enough, and He said, "Bring it!" Then when they take it to Him, He takes it, and blesses it, and tells the crowd to sit and eat, and that day, more than 500 people sit to eat the two fish, and five loaves of bread, and their bellies were full.

After they ate, the apostles snuck away on the boat from the crowd to the other side to sleep, and Jesus sends the crowd away, and is left alone, and while the apostles slept, the boat drifts from the shores with them, and when Jesus awoke in the morning, He sees the boat far in the water. So, He walks out on the water to the boat, and when the apostles see the figure coming towards them on the water, they think it is a ghost and become scared. But Jesus assures them it is Him and tell them not to be afraid, and He tell Peter to come to Him, and Peter start to walk on top of the water, and the wind start to stir up, and he lose his faith, and begin to sink. Then Jesus stretches out His hand and grabs him and tells him he has little faith and asks, why he doubted, and they get on the boat to join the other apostles, and sail to the land of Gennesaret, and the people there are glad to see them, and they take their sick to get healed, and they even beg Jesus to be able to touch His clothes, and when they touch Him, that also heals them.

With great earnest, Jesus keeps preaching throughout the regions, but after a while He felt the people who followed Him around were only honoring Him with their mouths, yet their hearts were far from Him, and they were worshipping Him in vain, because they teach the laws of men as doctrine, as if they did not know it is not the food that a person eat that makes that person defiled, but it is the words that comes from a person's mouth that makes that person defiled in their heart. While, He is thinking, the apostles ask Him if He noticed that the Pharisees are offended by what He said, and He said, let them be offended, because they are hypocrites who lead people that believes lies and are lost.

Then one day, while He is in the Tyre and Sidon Region of the Canaanite white people, a white woman comes to Him pleading for help for her possessed daughter, but He does not say a word to her. Then His apostles come running to Him, urging Him to send her away, because she begged them for help already, and He tell the white woman He is only there for the lost sheep of Israel. But the woman begs Him even more for help, and He tells her, He should not take the Negro children of Israel blessings and give it to the dogs, and though that was a derogatory statement He made, the woman pleads with him more for help, and said, "True Lord. Yet even the white masters give their dogs the scraps to be blessed by them." Then He praises her for her faith, and deliver her daughter from the demon, and leaves from there to The Sea of Galilee, and when He get to Galilee, He goes to the mountain, and many people follow Him, and He heal them, and they glorify GOD, because of Him. Then they follow Him around for days, and because He knew they were hungry, He felt compassion for them, and He asks the apostles what they have to feed them, and the apostles said, they have five loaves of bread and five little fish. Then He takes the fish, and the bread, and said a blessing, and feed the crowd, and that day, more than 4,000 people ate, until their bellies were full. Yet there were still seven baskets filled with fragments that were left over.

Later, He tell His apostles about hypocrites. But they did not understand what He was trying to say. So, He asks them who do others believed He is, and they said, some people think He is Elijah, and others think He is Jeremiah, or some other prophet. Then He asks, who do they think He is, and Simon Peter said, "You are The Christ, the Son of the living GOD," and He tell Peter he is blessed, and would be the rock (foundation) of the church, because only those that believe He is The Christ could really be part of the church, and if they believe when THE HOLY SPIRIT tells them He is The Christ, they could stand against all the devils in hell, and whatever they bind on earth would be bound in the spirit realm, and whatever they loosed on earth would be loosed in the spirit realm, and they should remember that whatever they loosed from the spirit world would be loosed on the earth. Therefore, they must be careful not to call on spirits. Then He tell them not to tell anyone else what He told them, and said He must go to Jerusalem to suffer many things, because self-righteous people would torture, and kill Him, but He would resurrect in three days, and immediately, Peter takes Him aside, and said, it cannot be so. At that moment, He rebukes Satan, and said he is an offence to Him, because Peter was saying things contrary to the word of GOD, and He tell them if they want to be like Him, they must bear the pain, and prosecution, because they would be hated for believing the truth. Therefore, they must completely stop sinning to be like Him, and because many people decided to live a sinful life, and lost their good life for it, they would hate them for being believers that have gained an eternal good life through Him. Then He asks, "What would be the use of gaining everything in the world, if it meant going to hell forever, especially when there is nothing a person could give in exchange for their soul?" So, He said, since only the bad people would go to hell, that means the good people would never go to hell again, because after He resurrect, they would go to heaven to start ruling with Him in The Kingdom of Heaven.

Six days later, He takes Peter, James, and John to the top of a high mountain, and transfigure right before their eyes, and His face shines like the sun, and His clothing became like bright white light. Then Moses and Elijah appear, and talk to Him, and when Peter sees them, he wants to make temples for them. But while he is suggesting it, GOD speaks from heaven, and said, "This is MY beloved Son in whom I am well pleased. So, listen to Him, and do as He do", and when they heard what was said, they fall on their faces in fear. Then He touch them, and tell them to get up, and not to be afraid, and when they got up, Moses and Elijah were gone, and He tell them not to tell anyone else about what they saw until after He resurrect.

Then one day, He, and His apostles goes to Galilee, and He remind them He would be killed, and would resurrect in three days, and to make sure they pay their taxes, forgive each other, and keep living by the LAW of GOD. Then Peter asked Him how many times he should forgive someone, and He said as often as they ask for forgiveness, because that is how GOD forgives them. Finally, He is done teaching them all He could, and He leaves from Galilee, and goes back to Judea, and while He is there, the Pharisees try to test Him by asking Him if it is o.k. to get divorced, and He says, "GOD made male and female from the beginning, and they should get married, and start a family of their own, and when a man and a woman gets married, they should not get divorced unless their spouse cheated on them, because it is adultery, and if their spouse did not cheat, and they divorce their spouse, and marry someone else, then they are an adulterer." Then He said, they have to realize that some people should not get married, like those that are born with deformities of the sexual organs, those (like eunuchs and transvestite) who had their sexual organs removed, or surgically manipulated, or those who decided to remain as virgins, because those types of people would not be equipped (mentally or physically) to function fully in marriage to have a family of their own. So, if they want to have a family and have a good life, they must obey the commandments, and if they do not know what they are, then He is telling them, they should not murder, they should not commit adultery, they should not steal, they should not lie, and they must honor their parents, and love their neighbors as they should love themselves. And if they believe that they are doing those things already, and want to be perfect, then they should stop all they are involved with, and go preach the WORD to the poor sufferers. Yet still, the love of money would cause many of them to lose their way to having love, peace, and joy from The Kingdom of Heaven. So, He wants them to know that everyone who gave up everything, and everyone for truth sake would become rich in this life, plus, they would have eternal life, and many types of people would receive the same reward of eternal life, no matter how long they had been serving GOD, and the white looking (biracial) gentiles would receive the blessing of the kingdom first, then the colored (biracial) gentiles, and last, but not least, the Negroes would receive theirs blessings again when they believe the truth and do the things of GOD.

After that, they go on their way to Jerusalem, and while they are traveling, He remind them, He would be killed, but they should not worry, because He would resurrect in three days. Then He said, every believer would suffer like Him, and be killed, and He does not know who would make it to heaven and sit on the throne with Him, because GOD decides that, and though in the earthly government people place leaders over themselves, it would not be that way in the righteous government, and if anyone wants them to be their servants, they should make them their servants instead, and if anyone wants to be more important than them, they should make them their slaves, because it is time to act like kingdom believers, since He made them free.

Near Jerusalem, they stop at The Mount of Olives in Bethphage, and He tell them to go into the village, and they would find a donkey with her colt tied together, and to lose them, and bring them to him, and if anyone asks them any question, they should say, "The Lord sent us", and they would allow them. Then they go to do what He said, and they got the donkey and the colt, and takes them to Him, and they lay their clothes on the backs of the donkey and the colt, and sit Him on them, and many people start to spread their clothes on the ground, and others cut down branches, and spread them on the road. Then the crowd parades before Him, and start to sing out in praise, saying, "Hosanna to the son of David, blessed is He who came in the name of the LORD (GOD)! Hosanna in the highest heaven', and when they enter Jerusalem and the people see Him on the donkey and colt, they get excited, and ask, who He is, and some of them said, they believe it is Jesus from Nazareth. Then after arriving at the temple, He gets off the colt and donkey, and goes into the temple, and when He see that they are doing all sorts of business in there, He gets angry, and turn over all their tables, and starts to heal the sick. So, the crowd gets even more excited, and start to say, "Hosanna to the son of David', and the scribes became indignant about it, and they take the priest to Jesus, and asks Him, if He hear what the crowd is saying, and Jesus said, "Yes. Didn't you read in the scriptures that the new believers would have perfect praise." Then He go on His way to the city, and while He is on His way, He gets hungry, and He sees a fig tree in the distant and goes to it to pick some figs, and there are no fruits on it, even though the tree should have been bearing fruit. So, He cursed the tree, and immediately it withers, and He then tell the apostles to learn **"The Parable of The Fig Tree"**, because He wants them to know if a person said they are godly, and they look prosperous, and yet when another person goes to them for understanding they cannot give it, then the one who tried to get the understanding should curse that person, because they are just showboating, and are still unproductive. Then He said, if a person has faith, and does not doubt, then what they believe would happen, and therefore, not only would the person be able to curse the fakes, but they could also get rid of the problems in their life, because all the things they ask GOD for, and believe they would receive, they will receive.

On another day He goes back to the temple, and the chief priest, and all the elderly people go to Him, and ask Him who gave Him the authority to do all those things, and He ask them who gave John, The Baptist, the authority to do what he did, and because they think He is tricking them, they said they do not know. So, He tell them, He does not know the answer to their question either, and since He spoke so many parables to them before, He decides to tell them another parable, which translates to say, "Those who does what GOD said are good sons, and those who do not do what GOD says are bad sons, and because many of the gentiles does what GOD says, they would be accepted, and be part of **The Wedding Feast**, which is a good life after they die."

On another day, the Sadducees asks Him about marriage, and having children after the resurrection, and since there is no need for reproduction for spirit beings, which is the way of living forever in the flesh, He tells them, "No one would get married after they are resurrected, because they become spirit beings, like the angels in heaven, so they could live forever, because YAH is not a GOD of the dead, HE is the GOD of the living." Then the Pharisees asks Him what is the greatest commandment from the LAW, and He said, the greatest one is "You shall love the LORD GOD with all your heart, soul, and mind, and it is the first, and greatest commandment, and because you shall love your neighbors as you love yourself is like the first commandment, it is considered to be the second greatest commandment. Therefore, they should love GOD, and love others, because those two commandments contain all the teachings of the LAW, which was written by Moses, and was taught by the teachings the prophets preached about. Then He asks them what they think about The Christ, and whose son is He, and they said, "The Christ is the son of David", and He said, why would David call The Christ, Lord, if The Christ is his son, because it is quoted in Psalm 110:1, "The lord said to his son, sit at my right hand, until I make your enemies your footstool. And since He knew they, and all the scholars would always interpret the scriptures wrong, He knew that they do not know that Psalm 110: 1 is saying, "THE LORD (GOD) said to the Lord (Jesus, The Christ), HIS Son, sit at MY right hand, until I make Your enemies Your footstool." And since He also knew that they think His father is Joseph, who came from the lineage of David, and they believe He is David's son, He tell them, "The Christ could not be David's son, if David called The Christ Lord", and because none of them know the scriptures well, they were not able to answer, and they leave Him alone from that day on.

Right after that, He tell His disciples to watch out for the theologians, because they go around in long robes, and act like they are judges in a court room, and they like to be greeted in public placed, and want the best seats in church, and yet, He wants them to learn the LAW that the theologians teach, and obey it without doing as they do, because they are hypocrites that made up all kinds of rules for others to live by when they themselves would not live by them, and they do all sorts of godly things in public, so people would praise them, and call them teachers, or rabbi (Father), because they think they are righteous. So, He does not want them to call them **"Teachers or Rabbi"**, because He (Jesus) is their Teacher, and only (YAH) GOD is their FATHER, and they should not call anyone else their teacher, or father, because GOD is in heaven, and is their only FATHER, and He (Jesus) is their only Teacher. Therefore, they should keep themselves lowly, until GOD, THE FATHER, exalts them.

Then He said, "Woe to the hypocrites, because they prevent others from entering a state of love, peace, and joy, when they themselves refuse to love and have peace, and yet they want joy, and they go from countries to countries as missionaries, preaching the word, but when they convert a person, the person becomes more of a servant to Satan than before they were converted, because the hypocrite think the temple made of stone is greater than the living temple (the person), and they also think the value of things placed at the altar is more important than the anointing (the person) that is at the altar itself. They even think that giving tithes and offerings are more important than taking care of the poor, the widow, and the fatherless. Yet they want to be considered as righteous, even though their minds and hearts are corrupt. So, the hypocrites put in a lot of effort into looking strong and healthy from the outside, because on the inside they are losing vitality, but eventually people would see from the outside how their sickness had taken over them, and even though the hypocrites want to be like the prophets, they would kill a prophet if he corrected them. Therefore, GOD will hold them accountable for the deaths of all the righteous people, because their ways deceived the people of the world, and they are a bunch of snakes who are trying to escape being condemn to hell.

O' People of Jerusalem, the ones who killed off the prophets who were sent to them to teach them how to live together in peace, since they did not want that. Now look at how they look. They are broke and confused, and do not even know they would not be blessed again, until they believe YAH, their GOD, would provide all their needs. So blessed are those who come in the name of the LORD, their GOD.

THE END TIME PROPHECY
(Spoken by Jesus)

On another day, Jesus, and the apostles goes to The Mount of Olives, and the apostles asks Him to explain "The End Time" prophesy to them, and He tell them to make no one fooled them, because many would come and claim they are The Christ, and they would hear about wars, and rumors of wars, but they should not worry, because it must happen, and when those things happen in their region "The End" is still not yet, because there would be wars, famines, diseases, and earthquakes in other places around the world, and people would start to worry, and the believers would be taken to courts, and be prosecuted in every nation for believing in His doctrine. Then all the countries in the world would search through the scriptures of The Bible, but after they see the truth clearly, they would be offended and would hate the believers even more. At that time, the WORD would be preached again, and "The End Time" prophesies would start, and those who believe until they die, or until The End Times prophecies starts, would rapture up to heaven and be saved. But those who are not in the rapture would be left on the earth to continue to suffer in The Wrath of GOD" in "The Great Tribulation", which is the beginning of the wrath that would start in their time, which is "The Last Days", and it will end when "The End Time" prophecies start.

Therefore, when they see the white people being accepted as the godly ones, and they start their governmental church in Babylon, then it is time for The Great Tribulation, and The Wrath of GOD would begin, and they would have to run and hide, because things would be falling from the sky, and strange things would be happening for a short period of time. And many people of the world would fool others by saying they are The Christ, and false prophets would start to do many miracles by evil spirits, and the people of the world would be deceived by those things. Then immediately after The Great Tribulation, just before the beginning of The End Times, the sun would be darkened, the moon would not give any light, and the stars would fall from heaven, because the heavens would be shaken, and He (Jesus) would appear in the heavens, and everyone would start to mourn. Then at that time, He would only rapture up the 144,000 Elects, and it would definitely happen before all of them die. But no one knows exactly what day, or what time. Then after He raptured up the 144,000 Elects, the other believers would be left on earth to finish out their lives, and some of them would be wise, and some would be foolish, because some of them know the truth, but they would not seek GOD, and even when they see the wise ones gaining understanding from GOD's HOLY SPIRIT, they still would not have enough sense to call on GOD, and because GOD would allow the unjust system to continue, and delay the righteous kingdom from coming, many people would decide to live a life without fruitfulness. Then when it is announced that He (Jesus) is coming again, the foolish ones would start to do some good works, but life would be burdensome, and they would want to give up. Then the foolish ones would seek the wise ones to beg them for encouragement, but no matter what they hear, they would not be encouraged, and the wise ones would tell them to get away from them, and go to those who live by preaching, so they could tell them how to receive THE HOLY SPIRIT.

Therefore, life would go on as usual after the 144,000 Elects are resurrected, and even to the end of "The End times", and people would die, and the bad ones would go to hell, but the good ones would go to heaven. And many of the foolish believers would go to church, but while they are still learning,

He (Jesus) would come on His white horse with the Elects on their white horses, and all the wicked people, whether dead, or alive, would ascend to heaven to be judged by GOD at "The Great White Throne Judgment", leaving only the believers on the earth, which are the sheep, and the goats, and the believers that are filled with THE HOLY SPIRIT (the sheep) would turn to spirit, while the other believers (the goats) stay as flesh, and He would take the wise, HOLY SPIRIT filled believers (the sheep) to heaven, and the foolish believers (the goats) would want to be accepted into heaven, but He would tell them they cannot go, because He never knew them. So, He would shut them out, and they would have to continue life on earth in the flesh until they die. Then those that were judged by GOD to live in the flesh again would be living with "The Goats" on the earth as He rule from Jerusalem with the 144,000 Elects, ruling in the righteous world government over those on the earth, hoping to convince people in the flesh to do good, even if they have to make them live for hundreds of years, because if they do not accept the truth, and they die, then they would go to hell, but if they believe in the truth, when they die, they would turn to spirit and live in heaven with the righteous spirit ones.

That is why He wants them to know that GOD is the creator of the heavens and the earth, and GOD gave human beings the ability to be fruitful and multiply while living a righteous life, and since the people of Israel were living righteous before the LAW, GOD choose them to teach people the LAW to live by it, and be more blessed, so the world would know He rewards righteousness. Then GOD gave everyone talents; Some He gave one, and other HE gave many, and HE left people alone to see what they would do with their talents, and those who have a lot of talents are confident in themselves, and they produce much, but those with little talent, just sit back, and does nothing with their abilities up till the end.

Now He (Jesus) is here, and He came to see what people do with their talent, and he commends those that does much, but He condemns those who do nothing, and takes their talent from them, because they are lazy and unproductive. Then He gives the talent to those who are productive, and they increase more and more in life, and life is very pleasurable, because of their talents, but the others are poor, and they must beg for help to make ends meet, and a whole lot of people are crying, because the rich are enjoying life, and they are not. Then He said, when He comes back again in" The End Times" with the righteous one on their white horses, just before the judgment, GOD would be already sitting at "The Great White Throne" to judge the believers, and the (sheep) with HIS HOLY SPIRIT, and the (goat) without THE HOLY SPIRITS would be separated, because He (Jesus) would separate those (sheep) who are filled with THE HOLY SPIRIT from those (goats) who are not. And He would take the spirit filled ones to be with Him on the earth in the spirit, but the other ones would stay in the flesh to live out their lives, until they die. And it would be so, because the righteous, HOLY SPIRIT filled ones fed the hungry with food for the flesh, and told them the truth, which is food for the soul, even when they were seeking deeper understanding of things themselves, and they made people felt comfortable around them, and they encourage others to live a good life, and gave clothing to cover the physically naked, while they secretly pray to cover them in the nakedness of their sins.

When did the righteous do all those things?

Well, each time they practiced the LAW, and showed some mercy, they were doing those things.

Jesus is done speaking on The End Time prophesy, and afterwards, He choose Simon (the leper) to be an apostle, and since the others are gathered at Simons house, He goes there to meet up with them, and while He is sitting at the table, a woman come to Him, and pour some expensive perfume (oil) out of an alabaster box on His head, and the apostles whisper to each other that they could have sold the oil and given the money to the poor. But when Jesus heard what they said, He corrects them, and said the woman would be remembered forever, because GOD used her to show them that they need THE HOLY SPIRIT (oil) poured upon their heads to gain the understanding they need to overcome the world. Then since Judas Iscariot does not have THE HOLY SPIRIT, after hearing that, he goes to the best known priests and asks them what they would give him for Jesus, and without saying a word, they count out 30 pieces of silver and gives it to him, and from that time, he looks for the opportunity to betray Jesus. Then on the day of "The Feast of Unleavened Bread", which is "The Passover", the apostles ask Jesus, where they should set up The Passover table, so they could have The Passover supper, and Jesus tell them to go into the city, and meet a man who is carrying water, and they go into the city, and met the man, and the man takes them to a house, and the owner of the house take them to the upper room, and said they could set up the table there.

Later that evening, Jesus goes to the house and goes to the upper room to eat "The Passover Supper" with them, and while they are eating, He tells them that one of them would betray Him, and they are shocked. Then they start to wonder which one of them would do such a thing, and He tell them the one that dips his hand into the dish with Him is the one, and as He said those words, He dips His hand into the dish, and at that very moment Judas also dips into the dish, and cannot believe it would be him. So, he whispers to Jesus, and said "Teacher is it I?", and Jesus said, "You said it". Yet, the rest of the apostles still did not realize that Judas would be the betrayer, and they continue to eat. Then while they eat, He takes the bread and breaks it and give thanks to GOD for it, and gives it to them, and said, "I would die for all sinners, and I wants you to call on Me anytime." Then He takes the wine and blesses it, and gives each of them a cup of it, and said, "Drink it, because it symbolizes that after I am killed, a new covenant would start, and not only the people of Israel would be forgiven by Me, but all people would be able to come to Me for forgiveness, and I would not be happy, until the time when all the righteous people make it into The Kingdom of GOD. Then after that, they sing a hymn.

From there they go to "The Mount of Olives", and while they are there, He tell them they would be scattered, and would start to sin, but after He resurrects from hell (the grave), He wants them to meet Him in Galilee. And Peter said, even if everyone else sinned, he would not, and He tell him, by early morning, he would have already denied Him three times, and Peter said, he would rather be killed than to deny Him. Then the rest of them agreed they would do the same, and then they go to Gethsemane, and He tell them to sit, and wait while He go to pray, and He goes to pray, and while He is praying, knowing He would go to hell, He begin to feel deep sorrow, and He stop praying. Then He goes for Peter, James, and John, and tell them to watch over Him as He pray, and He goes a short distant from them, and fall on His knees, and begin to pray, saying, "O My FATHER, please do not let Me die if I do not have to, but if I have to, then do it." Then He go back to the men that are watching over Him, but they are asleep, and He wake Peter up, and asks Him, why they could not watch while He pray for just one hour. Again, He tells them to watch over Him. Then He goes to pray, and this time, an angel comes to encourage Him, and He pray so hard, His sweat drops like it is blood, and when He is done praying, He return to the men that were watching over Him, and they are asleep again. But this time, He let them sleep, and He goes to pray, saying the same prayer, and when He is done, He goes back to the men that are watching over Him, and they are still asleep. So, He wakes them up, and asks them why they were sleeping when he is about to be killed, and while He is still speaking, Judas comes with the chief priest, and many old people with swords, and clubs to take Him by force, and since Judas told them ahead of time, the one he kisses would be Jesus, immediately he goes to Jesus, and said, "Greetings Teacher", and kissed Him on the cheek, and Jesus asks him why he betrayed Him. Then they grab Jesus, and one of the apostles takes a sword and cut off the ear of the high priest, and Jesus tell the apostle to put the sword away, because if they live by the sword, they will die by the sword, and He says He could have prayed to the FATHER, and ask HIM to send angels to help Him, but He must die to fulfill the scriptures. Then He looks at the crowd and asks them how they could come against Him with swords, and clubs to take Him like a robber, and yet when He preached in the temple, they did not take Him. But since no one answered, He accepts the fact that all those things had to happen to Him to fulfill the scriptures and to make the words of the prophets true.

From that moment, all his apostles fled, and the chief priest and the elders takes Him to Caiaphas (the high priest), where the scribes, and the older people are also to judge Him. Meanwhile, Peter is following closely by, and he sneaks into the courtyard of the high priest, pretending to be one of the servants, so he could see what would happen. Then liar, after liar, try to find reasons to put Jesus to death by the LAW, but there were none, because He lived a sin free life according to the LAW, and so, they pick people that volunteers to lie on Him, and they pick two great liars that said, they are witnesses who heard Jesus said He would destroy the temple and rebuild it in three days. Yet, Jesus just stood there, and said nothing, and the high priest begs him to say something, and then asks Him if He is The Christ, the Son of GOD, and He said, "I am the Son of GOD, and you would see Me get glorified.' Then when the high priest heard what He said, he became indignant, and tore his clothes, and said Jesus spoke blasphemy, and they have no need for anymore witnesses. Then he asks the crowd what they think, and they said, Jesus deserves to be killed, and they spit in His face, and beat him, while all of them teased Him.

In the meantime, Peter is watching, and a lady recognize that he is one of the apostles, and she asks him if he is, and he denies it, and before that night is over, he had already denied Jesus twice. By the time the cock crows early in the morning, he denied Jesus the third time and remembers what Jesus said. Then he leaves the courtyard crying. That morning, during The Passover celebration, they take Jesus to Pilate, the white man that governs over them in their land, and ask him to kill Jesus for them, and Pilate asks Jesus if He is "The King of The Jews", and Jesus answers, "Yes". Even though He would not say anything to the chief priest, or to the elders. Then Pilate asks Him, if He heard what the others are saying, but He did not answer that question. At the time, Barabbas (which means false fathers), who is a convicted killer is there in the prison, and because the Negro people of Israel usually practice a little more mercy on The Passover by releasing a convict, Pilate asks them who would they like to release. Meanwhile, his wife is whispering to him saying, he should be careful about Jesus, because she had a dream about Him that had been bothering her all day. Then Pilate asks the Negro people again, who would they like to release, and they said, we want Barabbas, and Pilate tell his Roman soldiers to take Jesus to the Praetorium, which is the place where the Roman soldiers gather, and they take Him there, and strips Him naked in front of the entire garrison. Then they place a scarlet robe on Him, and twist a crown of thorn, and pushed it down on His head, till the blood gushes down his face, and they bow down to Him to mock Him, because He said, he is "The King of The Jews." Then they spit in His face, and take the staff from Him, and hit Him in His head with it, and they take off the robe, and gives Him back His clothes, and takes Him out to crucify Him. And He is so badly beaten by the Roman soldiers that He could barely walk, moreover carry the cross, and they find a man name Simon (from Cyrene), and persuades him to carry the cross to Golgotha (Calvary) to "The Place of The Scull". Which is a killing ground outside of Jerusalem, where the Romans crucifies prisoners on a cross.

When they get to "The Place of The Scull", the roman soldiers offer Jesus some wine, and He takes it. But when He taste it, He realize they had mixed a bitter substance in it, and He does not drink it, even though He is thirsty. Then the soldiers nail Him on the cross, and place Him between two robbers who are also being crucified, and from the cross, He looks down at the soldiers casting lot to see who would get His clothing (psalms 22;18), and when they were done, they sat down to see if He would deliver Himself from the cross. Then they make a sign that says, "THIS IS JESUS THE KING OF THE JEWS", and they nail it on the cross above His head, and many people are there to see Him die, and they wag their fingers at Him, and tell Him to save Himself if He could destroy, and rebuild the temple in three days like He said, and they tell Him if He is the Son of GOD, He should come down from the cross, and they would believe Him. Even the two robbers that were being crucified said bad things to Him.

From 12 noon to 3 P.M., the entire land became dark, and at 3 P.M., Jesus cries out, and said, "Eli Eli Lama Sabachthani? (My GOD, My GOD, why have YOU forsaken Me?)", and when some of them heard it, they thought He said, Elijah, and immediately one of the white soldiers run to Him with a sponge filled with sour wine and place it on a rod and gives it to Him to quench His thirst. But others do not care, and they tell the soldier to let Jesus die of thirst while they look to wait for Elijah, because they thought when He said, Eli, He was saying, Elijah is coming. Then Jesus cry out again, and die, and GOD is no longer with Him, and immediately the veil of the temple building in Jerusalem tear from top to bottom, and there is a great earthquake, and the Roman soldiers see the earthquake, and become afraid, and start to believe that Jesus is the Son of GOD. Mary Magdalene, Mary (the mother of Jesus), the mother of James and Joseph, and the mother of James and John (the sons of Zebedee) are also there, along with many other women, who are believers watching from afar.

In the evening, a rich man named, Joseph (from Arimathea), who is a believer, went to Pilate and asks if he could take Jesus' body, and Pilate gives him the body. And Nicodemus must had learned what it means to be born again, because he is with Joseph (from Arimathea), and they are believers, and they take Jesus' body and wraps it in clean linen cloth, and lay it in a new tomb, which Joseph hewn out of a rock. Then they rolled a large stone against the opening of the tomb, and leaves, and Mary (the mother of Jesus) and Mary Magdalene were also there, and they saw when the body was wrapped, and the stone rolled against the opening.

When the chief priest of the people of Israel remember that Jesus said, He would resurrect on the third day, he appoints Roman soldiers to guard the tomb for the three days, so no one could take the body, and say Jesus resurrected. Then people start to see righteous people they knew were dead walking around the region. Then after the Sabbath rest (Saturday), before the sun came up on Sunday morning, Mary (the mother of Jesus), and Mary Magdalene goes back to the tomb, and when they get there, there is a great earthquake, and an angel descends from heaven, and roll the stone away from the tomb, and sit on it, and the Roman guards that were guarding the tomb, become lifeless. Then the women leave from there, and tell Peter and the disciple who Jesus loved, and the two men go back with the women to the tomb to see for themselves, and they are so anxious to see what happened, they run, but the disciple that Jesus loves, outruns Peter and the women, and waits until they get there before he enters. Then when they get there, they enter together, and they see the linen folded, but Jesus' body is not there, and the men leave, but the women stay, and Mary Magdalene begin to cry for her Lord, and two angels appear, and asks her, why she is crying, and she said, they took her Lord, and she does know where they buried Him, and while she is saying that, she sees a young man in the distant, and the young man also asks her, why she is crying, and who is she looking for, and because she think the young man is the gardener, she tell him, if he carried the body away, tell her, so she could take it with her. Then one of the angels tell her not to be afraid, because he knows she is looking for Jesus, but Jesus is not there, because He resurrected, and went to Galilee to meet the apostles as planned. Then the angels take the women to the tomb, and show them that it is empty, and then tell them to go tell the apostles to remember to meet Jesus in Galilee. So, the women leave from there with joy, and as they run through the garden, they see the young man again, and He tell them to rejoice. Instantly, things become clear to the women, and they realize that the young man is Jesus, and not the gardener, and they cry, "Rabboni" (Teacher) and hold Him around His ankle, kneeling at His feet, worshipping Him. Then He remind them to tell the apostles to meet Him in Galilee, and they leave, and then tell the apostles, except for Judas, because he had already committed suicide by hanging himself when he realized that he betrayed an innocent man for 30 measly pieces of silver.

Yet even though the apostles heard that Jesus is alive, and He spoke to the women, they still could not believe it, though Jesus told them what would happen before it happened. Later that same Sunday morning, after the sun rose, Joseph (of Arimathea) return to the tomb with some women who brought spices to put on Jesus' body, but when they reach the tomb, the stone was already rolled away, and they notice that the body is not there, which perplexed them. Then they go inside the tomb, and two angels appear there with them, and the angels tell them not to be alarmed, because they know they are looking for Jesus, but they want to know why they are looking among the dead when Jesus already rose, as if they do not remember Him saying He would resurrect from the grave. After hearing that, Joseph and the women leave from there to tell others that Jesus resurrected. Later that same Sunday, Peter goes back to look at the empty tomb again, but he still could not believe it. By then, the Roman guards that were guarding the tomb awoke from their fainted state, and went into the city and told the chief priest what they saw happened, and the chief priest went to their Negro elders to talk, and they decided to pay the white Roman soldiers to twist up their version of the story and say the apostles of Jesus came during the night and stole His body while they slept. From then, the Roman guards agree to tell that lie. Even up to this day, they are telling that same story, and many people are being deceived by it.

Then one day, while two believers are walking together and talking about what happened to Jesus, Jesus appear and talks with them as they walk, but they do not recognize it is Him. Yet as believers, they invite Him to stay with them for the night, and He goes with them, and while they are eating supper, He makes things clear, and they recognize Him. Then He leaves and goes to Simon, the leper's house, where all the apostles are gathered and are talking about seeing Him after He resurrect, and He appear amid them, and sits at the table, and they worship Him. But some of them still doubted it is Him, and He rebuke their unbelief and hardness of heart, because they did not believe anyone's report when they said He resurrected. Then He asks why they are worried and doubting, and He show them the wounds in His hands and feet, and tell them to touch Him, because He is still flesh and has not turned into spirit yet. So, they touch Him, and are filled with joy, but they still do not believe He came back in the flesh, and so He asks them for some food, and when they give it to Him, He eats it right in front of them.

After that, He encourage them to go throughout the world and preach "The Gospel" to everyone, so that whoever believed and are baptized would be saved, because those who do not believe would be condemned. And He tell them that after believing, and being baptized, the believer would show signs of it by being able to cast out demons, and speak in tongues, and they would be able to pick up serpents, and if they drink anything deadly, it would not hurt them, and they would be able to lay hands on the sick, and the sick would recover. Therefore, they should be strong and fight against demons and evil spirits, because demons have no power over the believer, as long as the believer abides in Him (the vine). And they should teach the truth to others, so they would be willing to be baptized, because GOD, THE HOLY SPIRIT, would give them the understanding of all truth. And since all authority had been given to Him in heaven, and in earth, He wants them to tell the truth to everyone in the world, so they could know Him, and THE FATHER (GOD), because when they call on (GOD) THE HOLY SPIRIT, HE would teach them how to live like Him (Jesus), and when they are willing to be like Him, He would be with them always, even to the end of time. Then He leads them out to Bethany, and lifts His hands, and bless them, and while He is blessing them, He turns into spirit form, then floats up into the air to heaven, right before their eyes, and they stare into the heavens at Him as He is taken, and as He rise to heaven from their view, two godly men, dressed in white apparels tell them to stop staring into the heavens, because Jesus would come back to earth the same way He went to heaven. Then they worship Him for a while, and then they go back to the temple with great joy to continue with their praise and worship.

After remembering what Jesus said, 120 (Negro) Galileans, including the apostles, go to the place of Pentecost, and they gather with many other believers of many languages, and nations to wait on the promise of THE HOLY SPIRIT of GOD coming back to the earth. Suddenly, there is a sound of a rushing mighty wind, that comes from heaven that fills the house where they are, and there is a flame of fire that looks like a split (cloven) tongue, that sat on all of them, and they are filled with THE HOLY SPIRIT, and start to speak in "**Tongues**". Which means that no matter what language they are speaking in, every believer there could understand what is being said. As if only one universal language is being spoken. Then the unbelievers in the nearby regions heard the loud noise of them speaking in "Tongues", and they go to see what was going on, and because they are unbelievers, they could not understand what's being said, and they start to say the believers are drunk. Right away, Peter and the other apostles speak out, and said, it is too early, and they are not drunk, and it is only what Joel prophesied that is being fulfilled, because Joel said, in "The Last Days, GOD would pour out HIS HOLY SPIRIT on all types of people, and their sons and daughters would prophesy, the young men would see visions, and the old men would have dreams that gives them understanding, GOD would show wonders in the heaven, and on the earth, because even after seeing those things up until then, the righteous Negro people would turn back to being sinners after Jesus, and the resurrected righteous ones get rid of the white officials and their wicked Roman government, so prophesy would continue to be fulfilled. And Judgment Day would come, and at The Great White Throne people would be judged for rejecting Jesus (the cornerstone), but those that called on THE HOLY SPIRIT of GOD would have received HIM and would be saved." Then Peter quotes what David said about Jesus, many, many years before Jesus was born, which said, "I saw GOD always before My face, and GOD is instructing Me in everything, so I would not worry. So, I am happy, and I am always glad to say the right thing with a lot of hope, because even though I know I would die, and go to hell, I know I am going to resurrect before my flesh rot, because I have understanding, and I know GOD would make me happy in the end." Then he tells them that David was not talking about himself in the scripture, because he is dead, and his body is still in the grave, and David was a prophet that was telling people about the promise GOD made to Jesus, and even David himself, said, THE LORD GOD said to Jesus, "Sit at MY right hand, until I make You, both Lord and Christ."

When they heard what he said, they were cut to heart, and they asks him what should they do, and he said, "Repent, and be baptized, if you believe that Jesus died for your sins, and you would receive THE HOLY SPIRIT, because the promises are to you, and your children, and for people all over the world who are called by GOD, because everyone needs to be saved from this perverse generation." Then some of them believe, and they get baptized, and on that day, there were 3,000 new believers, and they continue to live their lives by the teaching of Jesus' doctrine, and celebrates "The Feast of The Unleavened Bread", which is "The Passover", and they fast, and pray often, and the apostles does many miracles around them to increase their faith, and they respect GOD more each day, and worship on a daily basis in the temple, and have supper at each other houses.

Jesus did come, and things happened, and are happening just like GOD said. Prophecies after prophecies had been fulfilled. We are in The End Times near the last seven plagues of the end of the wrath of GOD, which would get worst, and worst until it is done. Continue in your studies and find out where we are in prophecy and what will happen next.

In "Revelation, Past, Present, and Future", see how these prophecies were fulfilled in the past, are being fulfilled in our time now, and how they would be fulfilled in the future.